Fragile
SANCTUARY

CATHERINE
COWLES

Editor: Margo Lipschultz
Copy Editor: Chelle Olson
Proofreading: Julie Deaton and Jaime Ryter
Paperback Formatting: Stacey Blake, Champagne Book Design
Cover Design: Hang Le
Couple Cover Photography: Madison Maltby

For all those walking the path of grief.
It's a winding road that changes but never ends. Just remember,
you're not alone. You carry them with you wherever you go. And
you'll see the world in all its colors because you loved so deeply.

Fragile
SANCTUARY

Prologue

Rhodes
PAST, AGE THIRTEEN

"WHAT WAS IT LIKE?" FALLON WHISPERED AS THE SUV bounced along the gravel road. There was a reverence in her voice, as if she were talking about God or some great work of art on a museum wall.

But we definitely weren't.

I couldn't seem to get that wide, cheesy smile off my face as Fallon's mom drove us through the night, casting the occasional look back through the rearview mirror the way all moms seemed to do. My stomach swirled like I was on one of those carnival rides that spun round and round, pressing you against the wall. Then my grin got wider.

"You know when you're on a rollercoaster and your stomach dips?"

Fallon nodded, her lightly curled hair swishing into her face as her eyes shone.

"It was like that." I collapsed against the far back SUV seat with a sigh.

Fallon tucked her knees up to her chest, resting her chin on them. "I knew Felix liked you. I *knew* it." She kept her voice low, whether it was to keep her mom from hearing or just her typical soft-spokenness, I didn't know.

I couldn't help the giggle that slipped past my lips as my stomach did another of those swirls. I hoped he liked me. But what I *really* wanted was for him to ask me out. Maybe we'd go to the movies. Or walk downtown holding hands.

I could still feel the press of his lips against mine for the count of one, two, three in the dark of the closet in Owen's basement. We'd had seven minutes in that closet. Mostly, we'd talked. About Felix's spring-break trip to the coast and mine to New York. But then he'd gotten quiet, leaned in, and—

"Did he use his tongue?" Fallon whispered in the dark of the SUV.

"No," I squealed, jerking upright.

Our eyes met, and we both burst out laughing.

Mrs. Colson's gaze flicked briefly from the road to the rearview mirror. "What's gotten into you two?"

Her question only made us laugh harder. I collapsed against Fallon as we giggled, not even sure what we were laughing about. Fallon and I spoke in a language that was all ours. Even our laughter had a sound that was ours alone. With how close our families were, she was more sister than best friend at this point.

The fact that my family didn't have any relatives in Sparrow Falls only made the Colsons that much more important. We'd bonded, creating a ragtag group that was our chosen family, spending Thanksgivings and Christmases together.

When my parents moved us from New York to Sparrow Falls six years ago, my little sister and I had not been pleased. We had lives in the city. Friends and school. The last thing we'd wanted to do was move to a town of three thousand people in Middle-of-Nowhere, Oregon.

But I'd slowly fallen in love with it. And Fallon was a huge part of that. With her easy, wide smile despite her shyness, and how she welcomed everyone—even the new kid from New York, who everyone looked at a bit funny—we'd fallen into an easy friendship. And she was the best part of Sparrow Falls.

But Felix Hernandez might give her a run for her money with his dark brown hair, tanned skin, and soulful amber eyes. Just thinking about him made my skin flush hot, like I'd just stepped out into a blistering summer day.

Fallon let out a longing sigh. "With my brothers, I'll probably never get a first kiss."

I sent her a sympathetic smile but didn't argue. Fallon had three older brothers. One by blood, Copeland. One adoptive, Shepard. And one foster, Trace. Her mom and grandma, Lolli, were always taking in kids who needed homes. Most came and went, some staying for as little as just a few days. But Cope, Shep, and Trace were permanent, leaving Fallon with lots of overprotectiveness in her life.

"Is there someone you want to kiss?" I asked. Fallon kept those kinds of feelings to herself most of the time. And her shyness kept her from talking to many of the boys in our class.

Even in the dark, I saw her cheeks flame. "I guess not. Most of the guys in our year are jerks."

A laugh bubbled out of me. "You've got a point." I might have snagged the only decent one.

Mrs. Colson pulled to a stop, putting the SUV in park and turning to face us. "First stop for the giggle brigade." Her gaze flicked to me, warmth spreading across her face. "I'm glad you two had fun."

Fallon's mom had become like a second mother to me over the past few years, and I swore she knew *something* had happened at that party. *Mom radar.* I felt my cheeks heating and fought not to duck my head.

Fallon bit her bottom lip to stave off another burst of giggles and leaned closer. "Call me tomorrow. We can go to the river, and you can tell me *everything.*"

"Right after breakfast." My dad had a thing about Sunday

breakfasts. He would make a massive spread with pancakes or waffles, even crepes if he was feeling fancy. There were no phones or other interruptions allowed. Family time.

It was one of the reasons he'd moved us to Sparrow Falls. Even though he had a big job as a financial planner to lots of hotshot businesspeople, he hadn't wanted us to get sucked into that world. So, he'd moved us here. Finally, I wasn't mad about it.

Fallon threw her arms around me in a huge hug, grabbing me tightly. "I don't know how you're going to sleep."

Another laugh bubbled out of me. "I probably won't."

Unfastening my seat belt, I clambered out of the SUV. "Thanks for driving me home, Mrs. Colson."

"Anytime, Rhodes," she said as the front door to my house opened.

"Thanks, Nora," my mom called from the doorway.

Mrs. Colson gave Mom a wave and a smile. With as much time as Fallon and I spent together, they were used to this back-and-forth trade-off of kids. "Want to hit up yoga tomorrow afternoon?"

"Only if we can make a stop at the bakery afterward," Mom shot back.

Mrs. Colson laughed. "You always have the best ideas."

I jumped down, my sandal-clad feet hitting the gravel. The full moon illuminated the house in a silvery hue. My mom had fallen in love with the ancient Victorian on a trip out here with my dad. He'd, of course, found a way to make it hers.

I'd always been a little self-conscious of the structure with its separate guesthouse that sat on a good twenty acres, the nearest neighbor barely visible. It was different than most of the other homes in Sparrow Falls. The downtown area was full of adorable Craftsman-style creations. Outside the town limits, you found sprawling ranch homes.

But as I practically skipped up the walkway, I had to admit the house was beautiful. It looked like something out of a fairy tale with towers and steeples. But even with all its intricate beauty, it never felt cold. Part of that was the sprawling gardens my mom worked tirelessly at maintaining. But more than that, it was the love inside the home's walls.

The moment I was within arm's reach, my mom pulled me into her embrace. She squeezed me hard, rocking me back and forth.

"*Mom*," I protested, but it was muffled against her chest.

"Let me have this moment," she argued. "My baby went to her *first* boy-girl party. Before I know it, you'll be driving, drinking, and moving out of the house."

I groaned. "I'm thirteen, not thirty."

Mom sniffed exaggeratedly as she released me but slipped her arm around my shoulders. "I'm going to blink, and you'll be there."

I just shook my head. "We've still got some time. Breathe."

My mom laughed. "I'll try. Come on. I made cocoa."

It didn't matter that the days were slipping into the seventies and eighties; I'd take my mom's hot cocoa anytime. It was the kind she made from actual cocoa powder, mixing in sugar and other secret ingredients. Plus, as hot as the days could get in the high desert of Central Oregon, the nights got cold.

"Marshmallows?" I asked hopefully.

She grinned down at me. "Do I look like an idiot?"

"Definitely not," I said with an echoing smile.

My mom kept her arm around me as we walked through the entryway and down the hall toward the kitchen. Intricate woodwork bracketed us on both sides, but it all acted as a sort of frame for the whimsical wallpaper. This hallway was home to a magical fairy scene, complete with a sparkly sheen to the fairies' wings.

When my dad had seen Mom's choice, he'd simply shaken his head and grinned. "My girl has to make it magic."

As we reached the kitchen, the faint scent of chocolate teased my nose, and Mom finally released me. I slid onto a stool at the wide kitchen island and wrapped my hands around the *Alice in Wonderland*-esque mug with its misshapen body and curlicue handle.

I closed my eyes and took a testing sip. The perfect balance of chocolate and sugar hit my tongue. "The best," I mumbled.

When I opened my eyes, it was to find my mom studying me.

Her gaze roamed over my face in slow sweeps as if she were excavating the surface layer by layer to discover what hid behind it. I had the sudden urge to bolt for my room.

Then she began blinking rapidly as her eyes shone. Panic skidded through me. "Mom?"

She waved her hand in front of her face. "It's nothing. I'm just emotional. My little girl's growing up."

The panic fled as my lips curved. "It was one party."

"Your *first*." Her hands wrapped around her matching mug. "Were there any other firsts tonight?"

Heat hit my cheeks fast and hard as my gaze dropped to my hot cocoa.

Mom's hand covered mine. "You know you can always talk to me. I've been there. First parties, first crushes, first kisses…"

I bit my bottom lip, and then it all came out in a rush. "Felix kissed me. I like him. Like *really* like him. He's nice and cute, and every time I'm close to him, I feel like I'm on one of those Tilt-A-Whirl things. But he didn't say anything when we left. What if he doesn't like me back? What if I'm a bad kisser? What if—?"

My mom's light laugh cut into my panic-induced spiral. "Rho," she said softly.

My gaze lifted to hers.

Those hazel eyes, the same ones she'd given me, stared back at me. "He'd be a *fool* not to like you."

My shoulders slumped. "You're my mom. You're biased."

"You're right. I am. But I've seen him looking at you when I pick you up from school. He likes you back."

Hope flared to life somewhere deep. "Really?"

She grinned. "Really. Although I'm not sure how I feel about that. Thirteen is young for a boyfriend."

"So many girls in my class have them," I protested.

My mom sighed, squeezing my hand. "If he asks you, group dates only. No one-on-ones."

"Mooooom, come on."

She gave me a look that said arguing was futile.

I sighed. "Fine. He's gotta ask me first anyway."

Mom released my hand. "He will. Just give him time."

I'd have given anything for just a little bit of her confidence. But I was still a jumble of nerves and countless other emotions I couldn't identify. So, I drank my hot chocolate as Mom asked me about the party. Thankfully, she stayed away from the Felix subject.

"What about Fallon? Anyone she has her eye on?" Mom asked.

I shook my head. As fun and free as Fallon could be with me, she shut down completely when we were in a group. She pulled everything that was so wonderful and special about her away and put it behind the shell she'd constructed to keep everyone out. "Not really."

My mom tapped her fingers against the island. "Just make sure you include her in those group dates, even if she doesn't have anyone she wants to go with."

I rolled my eyes at her. "Like I go anywhere without Fallon."

Mom laughed as she took our mugs and put them in the sink. "How could I forget?"

As I slid off the stool, she wrapped me in another hug. "Love you to infinity."

"Love you to infinity times infinity."

Mom smiled against my dark brown hair. "Infinity squared."

I squeezed her harder. "Infinity to infinity power."

She released me with a chuckle. "I guess you have me beat. This time."

I grinned as we headed up the stairs, my mom flipping off lights as we went.

"Are Dad and Emilia already asleep?" I asked as we moved toward the second floor.

"I think Emilia's still up, but you know Dad's been asleep for hours."

Because the majority of Dad's clients were on the East Coast, he still kept those hours. He was up and working before the sun rose, but it also meant he was there to greet us when Emilia and I got home from school.

Mom tapped my nose. "He left a new book on your bed, though."

I grinned. While Mom's and my bond was planting flower gardens every year, for Dad and me, it had always been books. He was forever finding new adventures for us to go on together between the pages of a good book. We'd just finished *A Wrinkle in Time*, and I knew he'd been hunting for our next fictional journey. I couldn't wait to see what he'd come up with.

Mom stopped to kiss my forehead as we reached my room. "Any requests for breakfast? I can put in a word with the chef."

I bit my bottom lip. "Crepes?"

"Going for the big guns."

"They're my *favorite*."

She gave me one last squeeze. "I'll see what I can do. Sweet dreams."

"You, too."

As I moved into my room, a wave of tiredness hit me like a truck. I winced at the clothes strewn everywhere. I'd been frantic in my search for the perfect outfit earlier and had left destruction in my wake. I'd clean it up tomorrow. If I didn't, my clothes had a way of disappearing—my mom's punishment for me not taking care of them.

I made quick work of brushing my teeth in my adjoined bathroom and slid on my sunflower pajamas. As I came out of the washroom, I pulled up short to find Emilia sitting on my bed, holding up one of the tops I'd been considering for the night.

"Can I borrow this?" she asked hopefully.

My little sister was just over a year younger but forever trying to take my things and hang with my friends. I frowned. "For what?"

She shrugged. "I dunno. Maybe to go to The Pop?"

The Soda Pop was a fifties-era diner that was a favorite of people of all ages thanks to its incredible burgers and delicious milkshakes, but most locals simply called it *The Pop*.

"It's too fancy for The Pop," I said, crawling under the covers.

Emilia's mouth thinned. "Shouldn't *I* decide what's too fancy?"

Alarm bells flashed in my head. Emilia was the most stubborn twelve-year-old I'd ever met, and I was way too exhausted to get into it with her tonight. "Take it," I said, reaching for my lamp and switching it off.

The moonlight spilling in from the giant windows leading to my balcony still illuminated the space. And I saw that Emilia had zero plans of moving.

I groaned. "What is it, Em? I'm tired."

She was quiet for a moment. "You have a boyfriend?"

I jerked upright in bed. "Were you spying on me and Mom?"

Emilia's jaw set in that defiant bent I recognized far too well. "I was thirsty. I needed a glass of water."

"Then you should've come into the kitchen and gotten one like a normal person, not hovered in the hallway like a nosy sneak."

She leapt from the bed. "I'm not nosy! You and Mom weren't being quiet."

"We didn't know you were there."

Hurt flashed across Emilia's face. "Whatever. I don't want to know about your stupid boyfriend anyway."

She dropped the shirt onto the floor and stalked out of my bedroom, letting the door slam behind her.

I groaned as I flopped back on my pillows. Freaking little sisters. Guilt flickered in my belly, tiny pinpricks against my flesh. I should've gone after her. But I was so dang tired. I'd make it right in the morning. I'd bring her the shirt and her favorite lip gloss of mine, and all would be right with the world. But right now, I needed sleep.

∽

Something teased my nose, spreading through my airways and tickling the back of my throat. A cough had my eyes fluttering. I blinked against the dark room. The moon wasn't quite as bright, having disappeared behind a wall of clouds. But even with less light, I knew something was wrong.

That was when I heard it. The wail of an alarm. I frowned as another cough racked me. The source of the smell hit me fast and hard.

Smoke.

I jerked upright, trying to swing my legs out of bed, but they got tangled in the sheets. My upper body kept right on going, my palms hitting hard on the rug beside my bed. The fibers dug into my skin as I pulled myself out of the knot of linens and struggled to my feet.

Another coughing wave hit me, and I dropped low again, images of the firefighter who'd come to visit my fifth-grade class filling my mind. *Drop low. Cover your mouth if you can.*

I grabbed a fallen piece of clothing—the same shirt Emilia had dropped earlier. *Emilia.* I pressed the gauzy fabric over my nose and mouth and crawled toward the door.

Emilia's room was down the hall, closer to my parents'. She'd been scared when we first moved into the house six years ago. It was so different from our Manhattan apartment. She'd had nightmares and disrupted sleep for the first month and had opted for the room next to my parents' instead of the one next to mine as they'd originally planned.

Reaching the door, I slowed as another command flashed in my head. *Feel the doorknob.* I lifted a hand, gently tapping the brass fixture. Heat bloomed in my palm the moment I touched it.

A fresh wave of panic ripped through me as tears stung my eyes. I didn't know what to do. This was the only way out of my room. And it wasn't like I had a phone. Both my parents were staunchly opposed to me having my own line or, God forbid, a cell phone. And now, I was trapped.

I bit down hard on the inside of my cheek. The metallic taste of blood filled my mouth, but I barely noticed. More smoke billowed in from under the door. I was running out of time.

"Mom!" I screamed. "Dad!" But there was no answer.

Maybe they'd gotten out. Maybe things were just blocked between me and them. But I had to open my door to see.

I worried the raw spot on the inside of my cheek, the pain keeping me in the here and now. I wrapped the shirt around my hand and twisted the doorknob. The moment the door opened, a wall of flame burst forward.

I scrambled back with a strangled scream that sent me into a coughing jag. The flames licked forward in a dance that would've been beautiful if it weren't so terrifying. Smoke billowed into my room like a monster from long-ago nightmares.

Fear spiked and had me tumbling farther into my room until my back hit the wall. My lungs seized in a vicious squeeze. Out. I had to get out.

My hands fumbled, feeling across the wall. The intricate woodwork gave way to windows. I stumbled and tumbled until I hit the doorknob for the French doors that led to my balcony.

It took three tries to get the door to do what I wanted. As it finally flew open, a gust of fresh air hit me in the face. It only made me cough harder. I pulled myself onto the ledge, the wood planks skinning my knees through my thin pajamas.

My hands curled around the wooden rods holding the railing as fire blazed brighter behind me. So much heat. It made my skin feel like it was crackling.

I scanned my surroundings, looking for a way out, for help. There was nothing. I had to pray a neighbor had seen the blaze in the distance and called for help, but there was no guarantee. It was the middle of the night.

Glancing at the ground, I tried to judge the distance of the drop. I didn't think the fall would kill me, but I'd definitely get some broken bones. Still, that was better than burning alive.

I looked to my right and caught sight of a drainpipe. It looked antique, just like the rest of the house. Struggling to my feet, I made my way over to it and pressed a hand to the surface. It was warm but not hot. Maybe I could use it to slide down the side of the house.

A deafening boom sounded from inside, nearly sending me flying over the side of the railing.

Now. I had to move now.

I threw one leg over the railing, not letting myself look down, then the other. I scooted over to the drainpipe and grasped it as hard as I could. It was affixed to the house with brackets that gave me some footholds.

Squeezing my eyes closed for a moment, I shifted completely

to the pipe. The metal dug into my bare feet and pain flared, but I ignored it.

Holding as tightly as possible with my hands, I let myself down a bit until my toes felt another metal bracket. Cracks and snarls sounded from inside the house as if the fire were a living, breathing thing. And maybe it was.

The pipe got hotter as I tried to shimmy down it, and fear bloomed in my belly. I was closer to the ground but not close enough to jump. Tears streamed down my face. I wanted my dad. He always knew what to do. We'd talk a problem round and round until I found the solution right along with him. But he wasn't here. And I didn't want to think about what that meant.

The fire seemed to go silent for a moment—a terrifying quiet I should've recognized as a precursor to the worst. There was almost a faint whistling sound and then nothing but flames.

Agony wrapped around me in that blanket of fire. If I hadn't been so consumed by the pain, I would've realized I was falling. And then, thankfully, there was nothing but the blessed dark.

Chapter One

MY SUV BUMPED ALONG THE GRAVEL ROAD, JARRING MY SPINE as I hit an especially painful divot. I added regrading the driveway to my mental list. What was one more thing when the list was already at least two hundred tasks long?

I forced myself to loosen my grip on the steering wheel, my knuckles starting to ache from the force of my hold. As I shifted my hands, I glimpsed the damp patches my palms had left behind. The little smears of wetness had anger flaring to life somewhere deep.

I was grateful for the emotion. It was a heck of a lot better than the fear and anxiety that had been swirling around me for weeks as I packed up my cottage in town. I wouldn't fail at this. Not again.

Taking a deep breath, I lowered my speed to better navigate the potholes. If I focused on the road and nothing else, maybe the panic couldn't get me. At least, not this time.

I made the trek into a game. How steady could I keep my vehicle on this beat-to-smithereens road? I did a pretty damn good job, but the road came to an end eventually, opening to a makeshift parking area of sorts.

I slowed to a stop but still didn't look up. Instead, I focused on my gratitude. The incredible chocolate chip scone I'd had for breakfast. How the sunrise had painted the mountains in a rainbow of colors. The text I'd gotten from Fallon telling me I had this. The fact that I was breathing.

I switched my focus to those breaths. In for three, out for three. The counting kept them even, a math equation saving me from a vision-blackening panic attack.

In. Two. Three.

I lifted my focus a few inches.

Out. Two. Three.

My gaze caught on a massive flower bed. It was once a riot of color, full of penstemons, iris, and yarrow. Now, it was all just…dead.

Like my mom. My dad. Emilia. And me, in a way. The *me* I'd been then had died right along with them, thanks to old wiring in an even older house. A home that had been so full of life and love once but had been left half-burned for the past fourteen years.

Now, finally, I was ready to change that. To bring it back to life. And maybe, just maybe, I'd find some of the pieces of me that had died that night along the way.

I opened my SUV door and slid out. My boot-clad feet hit the gravel, and I forced my gaze up, up, up. There it was.

My mouth and throat went bone-dry. I tried to swallow against it, but everything just seemed to stick. My eyes burned, and I started counting.

In. Two. Three.

Out. Two. Three.

I'd already made it longer than last time. Thirty seconds into my last attempt, a panic attack had grabbed hold—one so vicious I'd needed days to recover.

But that was a year ago. A lot had changed in a year. I was braver. Stronger.

I'd already been through hell. I could reclaim the place that had once held my happiest memories. *No.* A place that *still* held those memories. I just needed to excavate them from the rubble.

I kept up with my counting in the background, the steady one, two, three keeping my panic at bay, and really took in the structure in front of me. The historic Victorian looked completely normal on one side, as if nothing out of the ordinary had happened. But on the other, there was only wreckage and ruin.

The fire had sparked in the southeast corner of the house, somewhere between my parents' and Emilia's rooms. They hadn't stood a chance. The only mercy was that the smoke had gotten to them long before the fire did.

My hand slipped beneath my worn tee, fingers wandering over the puckered skin on my side. It was the only evidence the nightmare had been real. A mark of everything I'd been through.

The fire. The fall. The month in the hospital, where my only real comfort was Fallon. It was a miracle that one of our neighbors had gotten up to let their new puppy out to pee in the middle of the night and saw the blaze in the distance. They'd reached me before the EMTs had, but Fire and Rescue had been quick to follow, putting out the blaze and saving the remaining two-thirds of the house.

I didn't remember any of that. I'd been comatose and numb to it all. But that numbness hadn't lasted long. Even with the powerful drugs the ICU doctors gave me, I lived in agony for weeks. And the physical aspects of that were only the tip of the iceberg.

My aunt had come immediately, of course, but when she found out she wouldn't have access to the trust my parents had left behind, she suddenly didn't have the energy and resources to take care of a thirteen-year-old. And there was no one else. So, it was in that sterile hospital room that a social worker told me I'd become a ward of the state.

Tears hadn't found me then, the mental numbness returning. I let the physical pain grab hold as I endured torturous hours of rehab and therapy. I held tightly to that so the pain in my heart didn't swallow me whole.

I'd needed that numbness when I didn't know where I'd end

up. I'd needed it when I heard whispers about my burned flesh and dead family.

And just when I thought I would break, a miracle came.

In the form of the five-foot-two spitfire package of Nora Colson. Fallon's mom. A woman who'd lost her husband and son years before and opened her home to children in need. I'd heard my mom say Nora took the tough cases that nobody wanted because the kids were too much work, and foster parents and social workers alike were already stretched too thin. But living with them, I saw it firsthand.

She'd demanded that I be placed with her, and the state listened. Because as tiny as Nora was, she had a fire that made others pay attention to whatever she had to say. So, I went to live with her, Fallon, and the rest of their patchwork family. And it made me one of the lucky ones. The luckiest.

The sound of gravel crunching had me turning around, away from the pull of the house that had once been a home. A familiar massive SUV barreled down the gravel road, not bothering to avoid the potholes.

I couldn't help the grin that pulled at my lips. One of my brothers would have to take her vehicle into the shop for sure. My money was on Shep or Trace. Shepard always took ensuring everybody's well-being on his shoulders. He was the ultimate caretaker. But Trace made sure everyone was safe and had since the state placed me with Nora. It made sense he'd ended up sheriff of the entire county.

The door to the SUV slammed, and Nora hurried toward me, light brown hair peppered with gray flying behind her. "I told you to wait for me, but when I got to your cottage, you were already gone."

A hint of guilt swept through me at the true worry carving lines into her face. I grabbed her hand, squeezing it in reassurance. "I needed to stand on my own two feet."

Nora's green eyes swept over my face. The pass felt achingly familiar, something she'd done countless times. My mother had made it an art, too.

"There's no rush," Nora said carefully.

I winced. "Well, a new tenant is moving into the cottage on

Monday, and Shep is set to start restoration work tomorrow, so I think the ball is rolling."

"You can move back in with me and Lolli," Nora said quickly. "We've got plenty of room."

My lips twitched. Nora and her mother certainly did have space. The house I'd spent my teen years in was so large you needed a map to get around it. But it fit the land it had been built on—thousands of acres spread out as far as the eye could see.

"I think I'm a little old to move back home," I chided.

She pulled me into a hug. "Never too old for that. Not ever."

The ache intensified, a mixture of happy and sad, pleasure and pain. "Love you," I whispered.

"More than there are stars in the sky," Nora whispered back.

"Enough with the mushy stuff," a female voice cut in, one that sounded like it smoked eight packs a day and followed them with a whiskey chaser. "I need you to help me hang my gift in the guesthouse."

Nora released me, and we both turned to face the older woman standing in my drive. Lolli was dressed in a flowy maxi dress with more necklaces and bracelets than I could count, her gray hair tied up in a wild bun. She held something that sparkled in the sunlight—a canvas covered with hundreds of glittering stones.

"Mom," Nora began.

"I'm thinking in the hallway as you come in," Lolli interjected, then drummed her fingers on her lips. "No. Over your bed. What do you think, Rho?"

I stared hard at the result of Lolli's newest hobby, diamond art. At first glance, it looked like some sort of flower you might find in the Amazon rainforest. But I knew better. I squinted and studied it harder.

Nora gasped to my right. "Mom! Tell me that isn't a penis."

I choked on a strangled laugh as the dick and balls came into focus. Lolli wasn't happy with simple diamond art. She needed inappropriate gemstone creations.

Lolli arched a brow. "There's no reason to be embarrassed about the human body. Our forms are what inspire the very best art."

I rolled my lips over my teeth, trying to keep the worst of my laughter in.

"That may be true, but Rho can't hang this in her *home*. Not where people will see," Nora hissed.

Lolli straightened her shoulders and jutted her chin. "Would you tell that to The Met? The Louvre?"

Nora's eyes narrowed on her. "I hate to break it to you, Mom, but you are not the Michelangelo of diamond art."

I moved then, knowing we were about to descend into an argument we'd never get out of. Crossing to Lolli, I took the canvas from her hands. "I love my dick flower. I'll hang it with pride."

Nora let out a squeak, but Lolli just beamed. "Have I ever told you that you're my favorite?"

I snorted. Lolli's favorite changed daily, and it was a constant source of competition between our hodgepodge of found siblings. "You said it was Cope today. He sent you front-row tickets to his next game."

Lolli drummed her fingers on her lips again. "True. I guess he does win. There's just something about watching those brawny beefcakes smashing each other into the boards."

Nora threw up her hands. "I give up."

A laugh bubbled out of me, and, God, it felt good. The tiny expulsion of air released all the pent-up anxiety that had been stewing for weeks. I could do this. Because with as much as I'd been through, it only made me appreciate the good things in life. And there was so much good.

I wrapped an arm around Nora. "It's better to just let Lolli have her way."

"Damned straight," Lolli said with a nod, making her vast array of necklaces jangle.

Nora simply shook her head and looked toward the small guesthouse to the right of the dilapidated main building. "The movers are already gone?"

I nodded. "Shep let them in this morning when he was here accepting a shipment of lumber. He said it only took them an hour."

This time, Nora focused her disapproval on me. "You need to settle. Nest."

I fought the urge to shift, or better yet, bolt. Nora was always on me to make my cottage more of a home. But it had seemed like a waste. It was a rental. Temporary. Why spend all that time and money to fix it up?

Not that money was an issue. My parents had left every single penny of their estate in a trust fund for Emilia and me. Since she was gone, too, all that had fallen to me. But this was the first time I'd touched it. Just thinking about it made me a little nauseous. Using the funds somehow felt like getting pleasure from my family's deaths.

"Rho," Nora whispered.

Her face came into focus in front of me, the gentle lines around her eyes and mouth that spoke of easy, frequent smiles. The green irises that held such gentleness. "The only thing they would want is for you to be happy."

My throat burned as it worked to hold back a sob. "I know. But sometimes being happy feels like the worst betrayal of all."

Nora pulled me into a tight hug, my ridiculous diamond art gift smooshed between us. "Never. Your happiness honors them. Because they taught you how to find the joy in every single day."

I took a deep breath and slowly let out the air. As Nora released me, I tipped my face up to the sun. I let the rays beat down on me and remembered dancing through the sprinkler with Emilia on a day just like this one. I remembered plunging my hands into the dirt with my mom to put in new blooms. Remembered my dad chasing Em and me with a water gun. There was so much good here. So many memories to be grateful for.

A callused hand cupped my cheek, and I found Nora's green eyes again. They shone with pride and a hint of some deeper emotion. "There she is."

I took Nora's hand and squeezed. "Come on. Let's go hang my dick flower."

Chapter Two

Anson

I DUMPED A FEW BOTTLES OF BLEACH AND A DOZEN N95 MASKS on the hardware store counter. The clatter had the young clerk looking up, her blond hair swishing with the movement. Her gaze went from me to the items and back again. She grinned as she smacked her gum. "Cleanin' up after a dead body?"

I didn't laugh. Didn't respond at all. A few years ago, I would've bantered with her, charmed her. Not now. It all felt like a waste of time and energy. Neither of which I had.

The clerk's cheeks flushed, and she ducked her head, hitting keys on her register.

I was an asshole.

But an asshole was better than the alternative. Better than caring. About anything or anyone. Caring was a recipe for nothing but agony.

"That'll be fifty-two seventy-five," she said, her words barely a whisper.

"It's on the Colson Construction account." I shoved the items into a plastic bag. It was the least I could do. As much as I tried to focus on the task at hand, I didn't miss the slight widening of the clerk's eyes. Surprise and curiosity.

People knew Colson Construction. The company had a stellar reputation for good work and fair prices. But people knew the owner better. Shepard Colson had an even better reputation than the company did. He was one of those town golden boys.

Given how my brain was trained because of my past life, I couldn't help but analyze the *why*. Why was Shep so determined to be everything to everyone? To always ride in on his white horse to save the day. I'd put a hell of a lot of money on the idea that it was tied to his abandonment.

Knowing you were left outside a fire station when you were barely a month old could mess with someone's head. Make them feel like they needed to prove their worth. Shep had done all that and more.

I grabbed the bags from the counter, shoving the need to analyze and dig deeper from my mind. My profiling days were long gone. They had to be. It was the only way I had any prayer of holding on to my sanity.

"Thanks," I muttered, heading for the door.

Just as I reached the parking lot, my phone started buzzing. I shifted, sliding the device out of my pocket and glancing at the screen. Only about five people had the number these days, so the possibilities were limited. Still, relief slid through me at the sight of Shep's name.

"Yeah."

Shep's easy chuckle filled the line. "You know that isn't actually a greeting, right?"

"What do you want, asshole?" I grumbled.

The last thing I should be doing was giving Shep shit. He'd saved my ass. Had given me somewhere to land when everything went up in fiery flames. A job. A purpose that had kept me from descending into a bottle or worse.

I'd worked a few construction jobs in college, so I knew the basics. But working with my hands, building something up instead of tearing it apart was so different from my time with the bureau. I'd needed that. And I had my college friend to thank for it all.

"Why so grumpy?" Shep chided. "Need a snack?"

I grunted. "I had to run your errands."

Shep snorted in response. "Sorry I made you people, but I had to meet a client for a job update and sure as hell knew you didn't want to do that."

Beeping the locks on my truck, I opened the back door to the cab and shoved the bags inside. "What do you need?"

It could've been nothing. Shep liked to check on his people and make sure they were okay. But not typically in the middle of a workday. He'd save that for stopping by for a beer to nose around in our business.

"Can you meet me at Rho's Victorian? I want to go over our restoration plan before we're a go tomorrow."

"Sure. Now?"

"If it works for you."

I glanced at my watch. The day was only half over, and I'd been itching to get into the space ever since Shep had told me about it. As I worked with Shep and his team, I found I had a gift for buildings with fire damage. I'd taken that gift and expanded on it with some training and digging into research. Now, I took point on those restoration projects.

It was fitting. My idea of messed-up atonement. Only it wouldn't come close to paying the price I owed.

"I'll head that way now," I said, climbing behind the wheel.

"I'm still a ways out, but feel free to poke around. Don't think anyone's there. Rho was finishing up at her old place."

I'd never laid eyes on Shep's sister. Not for his lack of trying. He was always trying to bring me into his family's fold. And they were that to him. Family. It didn't matter that not all of them shared blood or that some had only joined the brood midway through life. They were his, and that bond was everything to him.

But just the thought of those kinds of familial ties had my ribs tightening around my lungs. My breaths got shallower. Each inhale brought a stab of pain.

I shoved it all down and locked it away in a place I never went. Because if I ventured there, the darkness would swallow me whole.

"Anson?" Shep's voice cut into my spiraling thoughts.

"Sorry, what?"

He was quiet for a moment, and the brief pause told me he was worried. "I asked if you wanted to come to dinner after. Mom's making lasagna."

When was the last time I'd had a home-cooked meal? I couldn't even remember. God knew I didn't have a prayer of cooking one. "I'm good."

"Are you?" Shep probed.

Aw, hell. "I'm fine. Just don't want to do dinner."

Two years working for Shep, and I'd managed to get by with only one brief meeting with his mom and grandma and a handful of quick words with his eldest brother, Trace. The sheriff always gave me an assessing stare that had my Spidey senses tingling, as if he knew there was more to my story.

But Shep had kept his word. He hadn't told a soul about my past or my previous occupation. To anyone who asked, I was simply a friend from college who needed a job. A loner asshole who didn't especially like anyone, so there was no need to take my lack of conversation personally. It worked. Even if it was lonely as hell at times.

"One of these days, Lolli is just gonna hog-tie you to get you there," Shep muttered.

My mouth twitched at the mention of Shep's grandmother. In just the few seconds I'd been around her, I already knew I was a fan. "I don't really wanna get sucked into modeling for one of her *art* pieces."

Shep made a gagging noise. "Please don't remind me. She tried to offload one that was some sort of shirtless elf prince and his fairy love."

I didn't laugh, but I wanted to. "It's hanging in your house right now, isn't it?"

"It's in my office," he grumbled. "Behind the door so I don't have to see it."

I grinned as I turned onto Cascade Avenue, the main drag through town. "You're a good grandson."

"Yeah, yeah," Shep muttered. "I'll see you in a few."

"Sounds good." I hung up without another word. My lack of hellos and goodbyes annoyed the crap out of Shep, but he'd grown used to it over the past couple of years.

I slowed to a stop at one of the three stoplights in town. Shep had told me the town had descended into a riot when they were put in. Half the residents thought they were necessary for safety, and the other half was certain it would ruin everything about Sparrow Falls.

I wasn't sure you could ruin a place like this. There was a simplicity to it that hung in the air. A peace. It was the first place I'd felt like I could breathe since losing Greta.

Just thinking her name lit a burn in my throat and down into my gut, an image of my sister flashing to life in my mind. They were rarely of her grown. Almost always something of us as kids. Racing around the yard as our parents called us in for dinner or climbing up into our treehouse to try to escape bedtime in the summer.

A horn honked behind me, shaking me from the agonizing thoughts. I never used to think happiness could be painful. But now I knew the truth. Happiness was the greatest torture of all because it could all be taken away—and it was so much worse than if you'd never experienced it at all.

I shifted my foot from the brake to the accelerator as a gray-haired woman in the sedan behind me glared at me through her windshield. I couldn't help but build her profile in three quick snapshots. Car old and sputtering but impeccably clean. A bumper sticker that read *Jesus Saves*. A car seat in the back.

She was proud, a tinge of righteousness sneaking in there. She followed the rules but also did the right thing, the caring thing. She was a caregiver to a small child, and she did what she could to make her life the best it could be. But she thought others needed to live life the same way she did and wasn't happy when they didn't. Hence the honking.

I forced my gaze away from her and to the shops along the street as I drove. Most of them were made of aged brick, giving the downtown character, something I hadn't experienced in my development in the DC suburbs. Every structure here held a story, and something about that fact resonated.

I passed the diner, a bakery, and the bookstore. There were tourist shops, cafés, and a coffee place on the other side. Galleries here and there. But I could count on one hand the number of times I'd entered any of them, other than the small grocery store.

The more you ventured into town, the more you made yourself a part of the fabric of the place, and the more people felt they had a right to talk to you. To ask questions. That was not on my list of desired outcomes.

It took less than ten minutes to reach the turnoff for the Victorian. As I made a right onto the gravel road, I couldn't help but be struck by the sheer beauty and power of the image that greeted me.

A range of four mountains was to the east, their craggy peaks covered in snow. To the west was a series of rock cliffs that made you want to stop dead in your tracks in hopes of taking them in for just a moment longer. The gray-blue of the mountains was the perfect juxtaposition to the golden hue of the cliffs. Shep's sister had sure landed herself one hell of a view, even if she had bought a half-burned-out house.

As the structure came into view, I slowed, letting out a low whistle. The gorgeous Victorian was completely decimated on one side. The walls were caved in, and charred beams poked at the tarp-covered roof. Most people would consider it a gut job—tear the whole thing down and start new.

But Shep had made it clear that wasn't an option. His sister wanted the house restored, not rebuilt from scratch. It'd cost her at least a third more to do things that way.

My sixth sense began to prickle on the back of my scalp as I wondered why.

Chapter Three

Rhodes

I STEPPED BACK, LEANING AGAINST THE SMALL KITCHEN ISLAND in the guesthouse that had thankfully escaped any fire damage, to admire my artwork hanging over the fireplace in the living space. Then I burst out laughing. The dick flower was up in all its glory.

But it was so much more than inappropriate art. Lolli had known exactly what she was doing when she brought it for me today of all days. She knew I'd need to laugh and be reminded of the family that surrounded me.

Over the years, I'd had to find a way to hold both—the family I'd lost and the one I'd found—and be grateful for the time I had with them. Today, Lolli topped that gratitude list.

As if to punctuate that, my phone dinged. I swiped it up, seeing a group chat name and icon pop up. The name constantly changed, usually a result of Cope and Kyler trying to one-up each other or piss off our law-and-order eldest brother. Cope and Kyler had been getting into mischief since Kye came to live with us when he was sixteen.

Today, the group chat's name was *Don't Tell Mom*. That made me snicker as I slid my thumb across the screen.

Cope: *How are the new digs? Ready for a rager?*

My fingers flew across the screen.

Me: *Like the time you guzzled peach schnapps and smelled like cobbler and rubbing alcohol for five days straight?*

Cope: *Don't say peach. I'm still traumatized.*

Kye: *I'm the one who's traumatized. You puked in my closet. When a girl came in asking for a peach inked on her ass, I started gagging.*

A new message flashed on the screen. *Arden has changed the group name to Nonstop Notifications.*

Cope: *Harsh, A.*

Our youngest sister, who had come to live with us when she was twelve, liked her solitude and didn't appreciate being interrupted. Especially when she was working on a new art piece—and she almost always was.

Me: *Put the chat on do not disturb. That's what I do when Cope's getting all needy. Like his millions of adoring fans aren't enough.*

Arden: *Smart. Should've done that years ago.*

Cope: *Can you divorce your siblings? What are the legal ramifications of that?*

Me: *It means you won't get any peanut butter poke cake the next time you're home.*

Cope: *Cruel and unusual punishment, Rho.*

I chuckled to myself, knowing I'd won that battle, and shoved my phone into my back pocket. I let my gaze roam over the rest of the small space. It was still mostly a disaster. Even though I didn't have a ton of belongings, I still had *stuff*. And that stuff was currently in a mishmash of half-open boxes scattered around my living room.

I'd pulled out the important things. My coffeemaker. A skillet, a saucepan, a few plates, and some cutlery. A girl had to eat, after all. And no one wanted to see me uncaffeinated tomorrow morning.

But the most important of all had been a handful of worn books. Novels that contained shared journeys I'd taken with my dad. *The Perks of Being a Wallflower*, *The Hunger Games*, *The Outsiders*, and, of course, *A Wrinkle in Time*. They pulled me toward them as if they had their own gravitational force, and I let my fingers ghost over the titles' cracked spines and yellowed pages.

The library had sustained some fire and water damage, but mostly smoke and soot stained the covers and the edges of the paper within. Over time, given how much I reread them all, most of that had worn away.

Only the last section of each book remained dusted with black flecks from the fire. Because as frequently as I revisited each one, I couldn't seem to force myself to make it to the end. Of any of them. Something about the endings was too painful, too final, even if they were happy.

I let my hand fall, glancing around at the rest of the room. So many boxes. But they could wait.

Because I was itching to get a better look at the ol' girl. After getting past the first tidal wave of memory, I realized I'd missed her—her intricate trim and steepled roof. I'd missed how it felt like home more than any other physical place, even Colson Ranch.

Moving away from the bookcase, I headed out the front door. The first glimpse of charred siding had me sucking in a breath, but I pushed on, stalking toward the house. The burned half was on the side closest to my guest house, so I'd have to get used to seeing it.

The few years I'd been forced into therapy, my shrink at the time kept saying over and over that I needed to face what had happened. Until Nora got outright furious one day and screamed at the man that I'd face it when I was ready and told him to stop being such a pushy bastard. That had been my last session with him. But her outburst had made me feel more loved than I could express.

And Nora was right. I needed to do this at my own pace. It might've taken me fourteen years, but I was here now. Ready.

My worn boots kicked up gravel and dust as I walked. Instead of looking at the house, I focused on the dried-up garden beds surrounding it. My mind instantly began drawing up plans, and I pictured them coming to life with poppies and lupine. I wanted an explosion of color everywhere I could root it.

Rounding the back of the house, I caught sight of the kitchen. Through the windows, I saw a bit of smoke damage but not much else. The same four stools stood sentry at the oversized island—the ones Mom and I had sat on the night it all happened. They were where I'd told her about that first kiss.

God, that felt like a lifetime ago. A fumbling press of lips in the dark of a closet in Owen Mead's basement. I saw Felix around town now and then. He had that same sweetness to him that he did all those years ago. But it wasn't something I'd ever truly know.

He'd tried back then. To be my friend, and to be *more*. He'd visited me in the hospital. Had gone to the memorial Fallon, Nora, and Lolli had arranged so I'd have a chance to say goodbye. But I'd never truly let him in. Eventually, he quit trying. But now, he stopped to say hello whenever he saw me and always gave me that warm, easy smile.

Taking a deep breath, I moved toward the house. I swore I could still smell the smoke in the air. Just a hint. It wasn't something I'd ever miss.

I reached for the handle of one of the back French doors and simply let my hand rest there for a moment. A company my aunt had hired had tried their best to board up the place and cover the roof with a heavy-duty tarp. But when she realized any costs for repairs would be coming out of her pocket, she'd ceased helping altogether. The local sheriff's department had been forced to oust the occasional person who tried to use it as a crash pad, but mostly, it had lain vacant all these years.

On a single exhale, I pressed on the knob's lever. The movement was a bit jerky, the mechanism not used to it, but it was unlocked. I'd given Shep the keys so he didn't have to wait around for me.

Slowly, I opened the door. This time, there was no denying the scent of smoke in the air. How it was possible after all these years, I didn't know. Maybe it was baked into the walls.

Shep had assured me he had a guy who was a magician when it came to fire damage. Swore up and down, they'd bring the place back and help me come home again. But as I stepped deeper into the space, I wasn't sure how that was possible.

Soot stained the walls to my right, making dark, inky swirls on the wallpaper that had once brought my mom so much joy. Those smoky patterns seemed to hypnotize me, pulling me deeper into the house and toward the worst of the destruction.

I ambled down the hallway, taking in every inch of damage and wondering about the small pieces that had magically seemed to escape the same way I had. Some tiny miracle that held no rhyme or reason as far as I could see.

When I reached the entryway, I turned to my left and felt as if a prizefighter had leveled a punch just below my rib cage. The library. My dad's favorite place to hole up with a crime novel on the weekends. You could see exactly where the firefighters had stopped the blaze. The room was how I pictured my heart at times, half destroyed and half still beating.

Pressure built behind my eyes, and my throat worked to pull the tears back in as I took in the burned parts. All the thrillers that had been so well-loved were now nothing but ash. I bit the inside of my cheek. I'd give my dad back his library. And I believed he'd somehow see it as I stocked the shelves with John Grisham, Stieg Larsson, Truman Capote, and Patricia Highsmith. Along with novels we'd read together, saving whatever I could along the way.

Turning, I looked up the stairs. The landing above was half burned away, but the stairs, while soot-stained, looked steady enough. I stepped onto the first one, testing its strength. It held easily.

I climbed a few more with a desperate urge to see more. A breeze picked up, sending an eerie howl through the house. I knew it was because of the burned-out walls and smashed windows, yet a chill skittered down my spine.

But none of that stopped me from climbing. I told myself only two more steps, just to get a peek into the room that had held all my childhood dreams. Maybe I wanted to look into the girl herself. The one who'd thought a single kiss would change her life. And maybe it had, in a way.

"What the hell are you doing in here?" a deep voice snarled.

There'd been nothing but me and the eerie howl for the past ten minutes—nothing but me and the ghosts. So much silence that I wasn't ready for anything else. I whirled around, my foot catching on the broken step above me just as a man's dark blond head came into focus.

I had a moment to see panic streak across his blue-gray eyes and his tanned skin pale as my arms windmilled. And then I was falling.

Chapter Four

Anson

I'D SEEN THE WOMAN NOSING AROUND THE OUTSIDE OF THE house, peeking in through the back French doors, and then finally getting up the nerve to come inside. I'd called Shep, but he hadn't picked up his damned phone, and I really hadn't wanted to call the cops for a Nosy Nelly. I was sure the woman was just curious.

But sneaking around a construction site was a surefire way to get hurt or worse, which was exactly what was about to happen. The woman's eyes widened at my barked question, revealing stunning hazel irises. Her shock seemed to make them spark, the gold in the green a living, breathing thing. But then her foot got caught on a broken step.

That shock turned to fear as she windmilled her arms. I let out a stream of curses, trying to predict which way she might tumble. She was only about ten steps up, but if she hit wrong, it could be really damn bad.

The woman's mahogany hair flew around her face as she tried to regain her balance. It was futile. She crashed into the railing, already weak from fire and smoke damage, and went straight through it.

I moved on instinct, charging forward to catch her. She landed with an oomph against me. She was petite, but the force of the impact knocked the air right out of my lungs.

Or maybe it was the fire in those hazel eyes that stole my oxygen—hazel eyes locked on me in fury.

The woman shoved at my chest, squirming out of my arms. "What the hell do you think you're doing?"

Her ire raised my brows a fraction, my practiced mask slipping just the tiniest bit. "What am *I* doing? You're the one sneaking around a construction site. This is private property. I could've called the cops on your ass. Or worse, you could've broken your neck."

She let out a huff of breath that made wisps of hair dance around her face. "I know it's private property, you overgrown oaf."

A muscle along my jaw ticked in a staccato punch as I tried to rein in my annoyance. "Then why the hell are you on it?"

"Because I own it," she said with a haughty glare.

Well, shit.

I took in the woman with new eyes, my gaze raking over her in a fresh sort of assessment. Her deep brown hair was just a bit wild like it needed to go its own way no matter what anyone had to say about it. Her skin was a deep bronzy-gold and looked smoother than anything I'd touched in years. While petite, she had curves for days. Dips and valleys that had images of my best friend's little sister swirling in my brain—thoughts I had no right to.

Shit *was an understatement.*

"Nothing to say now?" Rhodes demanded.

My gaze flew back to her face, taking in the defiance in her eyes. I respected the hell out of it, but I wasn't about to let her win this battle. "Still shouldn't be in here. Might be your property, but exploring it when it's condemned is reckless and stupid."

Rhodes' jaw went slack. "Did you just call me stupid? And who the hell *are* you?"

"Didn't call *you* stupid. Called your actions stupid. Reckless. Take your pick." Neither was something I needed in my life, that was for damn sure.

A throat cleared, and we both whirled. Shep stood there, ball-cap still on but amusement clear as day on his golden-boy face. "I see you two met."

"Met?" Rhodes parroted.

Shep's grin only widened. "Rho, meet my friend and your fire-restoration expert, Anson. Anson, meet my sister, Rho."

Rhodes whirled back to me. "You're Anson? College best friend? The one Shep got arrested with for streaking the quad? That Anson?"

I sent Shep a withering look. He just loved telling that story. "You can't actually get arrested by campus security."

She rolled her eyes. "Fine. *Detained* for streaking the quad."

I shrugged. "The right words matter." God, did I ever know that.

Rhodes turned to her brother. "Your bestie almost killed me."

"You almost got yourself killed," I shot back, turning an annoyed glare on Shep. "She was walking up those damn stairs that could give at any second. I tried to warn her."

"They're *my* stairs," Rhodes huffed. "And I wouldn't have tripped if you hadn't snuck up on me."

"I wasn't exactly quiet, and your gate was wide open." It was basically a welcome to anyone who wanted to stop on by and have a go at the place or her. Reckless. That's exactly what she was.

All amusement fled Shep's face as he pinned Rhodes with the same stare a pissed-off parent might give. "I told you that you can't be in here. It's not safe."

Rhodes' cheeks pinked. "I just wanted to get a little look." She paused for a moment, and there was something in that silence, a charged energy I couldn't quite pin down. "I needed to."

The hard edge to Shep's expression faded away. He wrapped an arm around her shoulders and dropped a kiss on the top of her head. "Okay. But no more. Promise me. You could get seriously hurt."

"I promise," she grumbled.

He released her and gave her a gentle shove toward the kitchen and the open French doors. "Go on. I'm gonna do a quick once-over with Anson, and then I'll come talk to you about our plan of attack."

Rhodes cast me a quick look. It wasn't as heated as earlier, but it certainly wasn't happy. Still, she did as Shep asked without protest.

When she finally disappeared from sight, Shep let out a low whistle. "Jesus, Anson. I've never seen anyone piss her off that quick."

I forced my gaze away from the now-empty spot Rhodes had filled and looked back at her brother. *Her brother*, I reminded myself. "I thought someone had broken in. You could've gotten sued if someone got hurt."

"So, call the cops," he argued. "They're the ones who deal with break-ins."

My jaw worked back and forth. "You know my feelings on cops."

Shep shook his head. "This is a small-town county sheriff's department, not the FBI. It's my brother, for fuck's sake."

I shrugged. It didn't matter if it was Mother Teresa; I didn't want anything to do with law enforcement anymore. "Thought I could handle it myself."

"Well, do me a favor next time."

I simply waited for Shep's request.

He didn't disappoint. "Don't."

I didn't bother agreeing because it'd be a lie. "You wanna take a look around the place or not?"

Shep groaned, casting a look over his shoulder. "Actually, let me talk to Rho first. Make sure she's all right."

Something about that made my sixth sense prickle. Not that Shep wasn't someone who checked in, he was, but something else was going on. I bit back the urge to ask questions. I didn't need to know. Didn't want to. The less information I had, the better.

"Need to make sure she's shutting that gate and locking her doors. She's not living in town anymore. She needs to be careful." I pinned Shep with a stare to punctuate my point.

He jerked his head in a nod. "I will."

"Good," I muttered, heading into an area on the lower level with the worst fire damage and trying not to worry about whether Rhodes would take the appropriate precautions. Because I knew what could happen to people, especially women, if they didn't.

Chapter Five

Rhodes

I TOOK IN LUNGSFUL OF FRESH AIR AS I WALKED FROM THE MAIN house to the guest cottage. The scent of ponderosa pines filled my nose instead of stale air laced with smoke. Each inhale washed away the tendrils of panic and haunting memories still swirling.

What they didn't erase was my annoyance. I could still see Anson's smug expression. There was no hint of a smile. The opposite, in fact. He seemed pissed the hell off that he had to deal with me at all.

I'd heard Shep talking about his best friend from college countless times, but the stories he'd shared from their days at the University of Oregon didn't match the man I'd met today.

The Anson that Shep had described was easygoing and almost mischievous. The person I'd met today was cold with a harshness that didn't compute. Even if he *had* saved my ass, quite literally.

I winced at my reaction. Biting someone's head off wasn't me— not even when they deserved it. But Anson had caught me at my most vulnerable, and that wasn't something I liked anyone seeing. Ever.

My phone buzzed in my back pocket, and I tugged it free,

grateful for the distraction. That gratitude fled the moment I saw my ex's name on the screen. No, *ex* wasn't right. But what did you call someone you'd gone on all of four dates with, who now wouldn't leave you alone?

Davis: *How about dinner tonight?*

I scowled at the phone. There would be no dinner tonight, tomorrow night, or next year. I blamed the stroke I'd clearly had when saying yes to more than one date. Either that or the memory of who Davis had been in high school. That guy had been funny and into hiking and rock climbing back then. A bit of a player, but not a jackass about it. The guy he was now was a pompous douche canoe.

The sound of boots crunching gravel had me turning around and sliding the phone back into my pocket. Shep strode toward me with a single-minded purpose. Even with his ballcap hiding his eyes, I saw the concern there. My stomach twisted. I hated being the source of Shep's worry. He took far too much on his shoulders already.

He pulled me into a hug before I could get a word out. "You okay?"

I let out a long breath. "I'm good."

Shep released me, but his gaze roamed over my face, studying me as if checking for lies.

"Swear. Other than your grumpy bestie scaring the bejesus out of me."

Shep winced but then pinned me with a stare. "You shouldn't have been messing around in there. I warned you it wasn't safe."

A prickle of guilt spread through me. More of that worry on my conscience. "I know. I just—I needed to get a look when no one was around." I swiped my hands over my jeans. What I really meant was that I needed to go inside when no one could see. Just in case I broke.

The tension wrapping around his shoulders eased. "Rho."

"I didn't lose it. I'm fine."

Shep ducked down a fraction, forcing me to meet his amber gaze. "It would be okay if you needed to let a little of what you're feeling out. To share it with the people who care about you so they can lessen the load."

I worried that spot on the inside of my cheek. "I do. I've talked about it with Nora. And Fallon."

"The bare minimum," Shep challenged.

"And you're any better? I don't see you laying down all your trauma for people to pick over."

A mask slipped over Shep's face, and I instantly felt like the lowest of the low. His features shifted into something completely unreadable. "I'm not hiding anything. I don't have the weight you, Arden, Trace, and Kye do."

He wasn't wrong that the four of us had our share of baggage and scars, both emotional and physical. Shep had his own; he just didn't want to face them. But at the end of the day, we were all lucky to land where we did. The Colsons gave all those they'd taken in long term a sense of safety and stability we desperately needed.

I toed at a piece of gravel with my boot. "It's not a competition."

Shep sighed. "Of course, not. I just want you to know that you can talk to me if you need to."

My ribs tightened around my lungs. God, Shep had the best heart. "I know that."

"Good." Shep swiped off his hat, flipping it around so he could get a better view of the house. "It's going to take us a while to move through the damage. But as soon as sections are secured, you can come in and remove any items you want. Or I can do it for you."

My tongue felt thick and heavy in my mouth, making it hard to swallow, and harder to breathe. I had almost nothing of my family's: a few photos, favorite books from the library, a quilt of my mom's that had been in the living room that Nora had insisted on taking for me. But when the fire department offered to go back in for more, I'd said no.

I hadn't been ready. It was as if seeing their things, all our belongings, would've made it too real.

But now, I wanted those items. Wanted to remember. Honor.

"Thank you," I whispered.

Movement caught my eye, and I watched as Anson's massive frame ambled out of the house, moving toward his truck. The sun caught his dark blond hair, illuminating the lighter strands. The color didn't suit his storm-cloud personality, but it did match his blue-gray eyes. They reminded me of an ocean turned upside down by a hurricane.

"You gonna be okay with him?" Shep asked, breaking into my thoughts.

I shifted my gaze back to him. "What's his deal? He's not exactly what I pictured when you told me about the guy who convinced you to take your couch sledding during a blizzard."

Something passed over Shep's expression. It was quick, but I'd caught hold of it long enough for it to pique my curiosity. Shep's focus slid away from me, but it didn't go to Anson. He focused somewhere out on the horizon between Castle Rock and the mountains. "He's been through some stuff. Changed him. You know what that's like."

God, did I ever. There was no way losing my family the way I had *wouldn't* have changed me. I was a different person than I was back then. Not just because I'd grown up but because I knew what life could throw at you. I knew you had to be grateful for every moment because you weren't guaranteed a certain number of them.

I studied Shep's profile. Lines bracketed his mouth, carving in and revealing his worry. The image made my stomach twist. "What happened?"

Shep shook his head as he turned back to me. "Not my story to tell. But I wouldn't hate it if you cut him some slack."

Annoyance flickered. Shep was an open book. He told me everything. Told everyone he considered family everything. But he was holding something back for Anson. That told me whatever it was, it wasn't something small.

A million and one questions swirled around in my mind. Because as much as I didn't like people poking around in my past, I was nosy.

"He's been through a lot," Shep said softly.

The almost pleading tone to Shep's words had the tiny hairs on my arms standing on end. "I'm sorry. As long as he doesn't play ninja again and scare the crap out of me, I'll be nice."

Shep's lips twitched. "I'll have a word with him about making noise when he walks."

My fingers drummed the outside of my thigh. "Maybe I could get him a bell. You know, the ones they put on cats' collars so they can't surprise birds."

Shep choked on a strangled laugh. "I'm sure Anson would just love that."

I bit my lip to keep from outright grinning at the image of the broody bastard wearing a kitty collar—something in a glittery pink.

A horn let out two quick, light bursts as a sedan sped down the drive. I didn't miss Anson's scowl at the intrusion of noise and dust. It only had me fighting my smile harder.

The blue car stopped a few feet from us, and my best friend got out of it in two seconds flat. Fallon made a beeline for me, and even though she was tinier than I was and certainly willowier, she nearly took me out with the force of her hug. Honestly, it was more like a tackle.

"I'm so sorry I'm late. My home visit went longer than expected. Are you okay? How was it? Do you need anything? You know you can come stay with me if you want. I've got that extra room. We can move a bed in there and—"

"I'm good," I said, cutting her off. "Swear."

Fallon released me, her eyes surveying like Shep's.

I threw up my hands. "I'm not going to crumble. I'm good. If I'm not, I'll come stay with you while reno is happening."

Shep, taking pity on me, pinched Fallon's side. "What am I, chopped liver?"

Fallon rolled her eyes. "I saw you this morning at the bakery."

"I still deserve a hello," he argued, looping his arm around her neck and giving her a noogie.

Fallon squealed, smacking at him. "Get off, you Neanderthal!"

"What? You don't like the new 'do?" Shep asked, laughter in his voice.

Fallon glared at him as she patted down her hair. "The last time you did that, it took me an hour to get the tangles out."

As annoyed as Fallon was with Shepard at the current moment, it only made warmth spread through my chest. I loved their closeness and teasing care.

A series of tones sounded, and Shep pulled out his phone, scanning the screen. "Aw, crap. I gotta run. Issue on our other jobsite. See you guys for dinner?"

Nora's dinners were legendary and frequent. She had an open-door policy where everyone was welcome, and the food seemed to never end.

"Yup," I said.

Fallon scowled at our brother. "If I can untangle my hair in time."

Shep sent her a mock salute. "I believe in you."

Fallon stuck her tongue out at him.

He just laughed as he jogged toward his truck.

Fallon didn't even wait for him to get behind the wheel. She simply grabbed my arm and tugged me toward the porch steps, pulling me down. "Tell me how you're really doing."

The late-afternoon sun cast a golden hue around the property, encircling us like a warm blanket. "I really am okay. Wasn't sure I would be when I first pulled up, but Lolli brought me a dick flower, and that helped."

Fallon's brows just about hit her hairline. "Did you say a...dick flower?"

A chuckle left my lips. "Her newest diamond art creation. It's now hanging over my mantel."

Fallon dropped her head into her hands. "You aren't seriously putting a—" She drastically lowered her voice as she stole a quick glance at me. "—penis over your fireplace?"

I grinned widely at her. "As Lolli says, it's just the human body."

"I can never look in that direction. You know that, right?"

A laugh bubbled out of me as I pictured Fallon walking into my new home, laying eyes on the artwork, and promptly turning the shade of a tomato. "I bet she'd make one for you, too."

The blood drained from Fallon's face. "Please, don't suggest it.

Lolli will make one, and then I'll be forced to find a spot for it, and I'll die every time I look at it."

"Shep has his behind his office door."

Fallon dropped her head back to her hands, groaning.

I pulled my gaze away from her and toward the flicker of movement I saw out of the corner of my eye. At least, I told myself it was a flicker of movement that had me seeking him out. Anson had the tailgate of his truck down and was bent over some large pieces of paper. Blueprints, maybe? He had a pencil balanced between his lips as he studied them.

"New guy on the crew?" Fallon asked.

I quickly tore my gaze away from him, clearing my throat. "That's Anson."

Fallon's eyes went wide. "Bestie from college, who's basically been a ghost since he moved here? That Anson?"

"The one and only."

Nora and Lolli had tried to get him to come to dinner or other family get-togethers more times than I could count. But Shep always came back with the same answer: No. There were excuses at first, but eventually, Shep just shook his head when Nora or Lolli asked if Anson was coming.

Fallon nibbled on the corner of her lip. "He's certainly not hard to look at."

"Nope," I said, popping the P. "But his personality ruins it."

Fallon choked on a laugh. "Tell me how you really feel."

I leaned back against the porch steps, letting the sun heat my skin. "He's just not the warm-and-fuzzy type."

She studied me for a moment. "You'll fix that in a matter of days."

I arched a brow in her direction.

"Please. I've seen you turn the most cantankerous rancher into a puddle of sweetness at the nursery. This is nothing."

"Cantankerous, huh? Pulling out the big guns."

Fallon grinned at me. "I just speak the truth. You have a way of making people see the brighter side. I'm sure Anson will be no different."

She wasn't wrong. I'd never seen the point in letting the hard things you were going through weigh you or others down. Not even a bad day, for that matter. If a customer at the nursery was in an especially foul mood, I just made it a game. How could I get them smiling before they left?

I pushed to my feet, brushing off my jeans. "You're right."

Fallon scrambled up after me. "I'm always right, but why am I slightly terrified of the gleam in your eyes right now?"

"I'm just going to invite the man to dinner," I said simply.

She swallowed hard as she glanced from him to me and back again. "He seems like he's pretty busy right now."

"It'll take two minutes."

"I'm just going to wait here because I'm having secondhand anxiety."

I snorted. "Go check out the dick flower. Maybe that'll help."

"You're the worst," Fallon grumbled.

"You love me," I called, striding across the drive.

"I'm taking out an ad for a new best friend and sister," she yelled back.

"You'd never," I shot over my shoulder.

Fallon simply let out a huff and sank back to the steps, but I didn't miss the way she twisted her fingers into an intricate series of knots. She was an empath through and through. She felt everything those around her did, maybe to an even greater degree. I had no idea how she maintained a job with Child Protective Services with everything she saw there. But I knew that every child who crossed her path was better for it.

As I made my way down the gravel drive, I really let myself take Anson in. He was bent over the tailgate, studying his papers, the pencil now behind his ear. The angle of his body showed the true width of his shoulders as his tee pulled taut across them. The thin cotton revealed ridges of muscle at his sides, too.

Good God, that kind of thing should be illegal. It was like his six-pack had another six-pack on either side of it. That was just ridiculous.

I swallowed the flicker of annoyance at his too-muscled self and forced a wide smile to my lips as I approached.

Anson didn't look up.

I had a sneaking suspicion he knew I was there, though. I cleared my throat.

He still didn't look up. "Need something, Reckless?"

Heat flared in my cheeks. "I'm sorry we got off on the wrong foot."

Anson straightened slowly. Something about the movement reminded me of a panther rising from a nap and preparing to hunt. His stormy gaze swept over me in a quick assessment. "You mean the foot you tripped over and almost broke your neck because of."

The heat in my cheeks spread down my neck as I struggled to keep my breathing even. "You're right. I shouldn't have been in there. I'm not going inside again until Shep clears it."

Anson merely grunted.

"Look, we'll be running into each other a lot over the next few months. Maybe we can start over." I extended my hand. "I'm Rhodes, but everyone calls me Rho."

He stared at my hand like it was a snake poised to strike. "We don't have to play nice. I'm here to do a job. You stay out of places you shouldn't be, and I'll be out of your hair."

My jaw slackened a bit at his rudeness. But before I could say anything, Anson turned back to the blueprints.

My hand slowly retreated to my side as I gaped at him. "So much for being friendly," I muttered as I turned to stalk back to my new home.

It was going to be a long few months.

Chapter Six

Rhodes

THE SOUND OF MUSIC, LAUGHTER, AND VOICES REACHED MY ears before my foot hit the top step. The familiar feelings of warmth and heartache slid through me—gratitude for the family I found myself a part of, mixed with a dash of longing for the family I'd lost. But somewhere along the way, I realized that losing so much had made me appreciate what I'd found even more.

I reached for the doorknob to the massive white farmhouse and twisted. It was unlocked, like always. And that state had Trace and Shep lecturing Nora and Lolli to no end. They never listened.

"Sounds like a party in here," I called.

"Auntie Rho!" a tiny voice squealed. She was more a blur of motion than a six-year-old little girl and hit me with a force that had me stumbling back a step.

"Careful, Keels," Trace called from the kitchen.

The little girl beamed up at me. "Missed you."

I brushed the dark strands of hair away from a face that looked so much like her father's. The green eyes, the smile, though her grin held a tiny gap between the two front teeth. "Missed you, too. What trouble have you been causing?"

Her smile only widened. "I'd never."

Trace snorted. "She hid water balloons in the barn and doused me."

Keely let out a giggle that was all carefree innocence. "He told me I couldn't get him. But he was wrong."

I wrapped an arm around her slender shoulders, guiding her toward the kitchen island where Fallon was perched next to Lolli, sipping wine. "Never give a girl a challenge," I chastised Trace.

He smirked at me. "Lesson learned." His gaze did a quick roam. It was a check similar to Shep's earlier, but I knew Trace took in more during his quick glance. Maybe it was his years in law enforcement, or perhaps it was how he'd grown up before his placement with the Colsons, but Trace saw more than the average person and could pin it down faster, too. "Everything went okay?"

I nodded. "All's good."

Keely tipped her head back to look up at me. "You're moved?"

"Yup. Just need to unpack."

She bounced up and down on her tiptoes. "I wanna come see it. Dad said there's lots of land. That you could have horses like Auntie Arden does. Are you gonna? Are you?"

I tugged on one of Keely's pigtails. "You're horse-crazy."

"You're telling me," Trace grumbled.

His daughter had been begging for a horse for years, but she had to settle for riding the ones on the ranch or those at Arden's place.

"I'm ready, Daddy. I swear. I'm responstable enough."

Trace's lips quirked as if fighting a laugh that wanted to surface. "We don't have space for a horse right now."

Nora's fingers tightened on the whisk, and I knew she was fighting the urge to offer up her barn. Keely would be spoiled silly if Nora had her way. But it was important to Trace that his daughter grow up with rules and responsibilities. He was gentle with them, wanting his little girl to have the experience of being a carefree child that he'd missed out on, but they were still there.

Keely grinned up at him. "We could totally fit a pony in our backyard."

He rounded the island and grabbed his daughter, hoisting her into the air as he tickled her side. "Oh, really? You might have to give up your swing set, then."

She let out a peal of laughter. "Daddy!"

"Sorry I'm late," Shep called as the door slammed behind him.

"Uncle Shep!" Keely yelled. "Save me from the tickle monster."

Shep beamed, hauling her into his arms. "I've got you, Warrior Princess. Should we vanquish him together?"

Keely giggled, bobbing her head up and down in a nod.

Shep grabbed a towel from the counter and snapped it at Trace.

Trace jumped back a few steps and snagged a grape from the charcuterie board Nora had put out, pelting it at Shep, who batted it away easily.

"You'll never win. The Warrior Princess is safe from your clutches," Shep said with an exaggerated evil laugh.

Keely shrieked happily as Shep carried her around the living room at a gallop.

He's made for this, I thought as I watched the two of them. He was the kind of man created for family. Yet, he hadn't found it. There were plenty of interested women in Sparrow Falls. As much as he was a brother to me, I could tell in a clinical sort of way that he was good-looking. Add to that the fact that his construction business had grown and multiplied over the years, and more than a few women were looking his way.

But Shep chose his romantic partners carefully. He moved slowly getting into things, and quickly getting out of them. The first hint of someone not being what he was looking for and he was gone. The problem? Perfection was a figment of the imagination. If he really wanted marriage and a family, he'd have to settle for someone human like the rest of us.

Nora pinned Trace with a stare. "Pick up that grape, young man."

He sent her a sheepish smile. "You're not going to lecture Shep for the towel stunt? He could've taken my eye out."

Nora just shook her head. "I swear you two will be thirteen until the day you breathe your last breath."

But I knew Nora took that as a point of pride when it came to Trace. He'd been older than his years when he came to live with her and Lolli, taking on way too much responsibility for his twelve-year-old self. So, seeing him find that sense of carefree fun, even now, would always make her happy.

"Where's Arden?" Lolli asked, setting down her wine. "I want an update on her latest piece."

Shep set Keely down, barely out of breath. "Still working on said piece. I couldn't convince her to break away."

Nora frowned. "She needs to eat."

"I told her I'd drop a plate by later."

Nora shook her head. "That's not good enough. She needs to take a break and spend time with her family."

Lolli patted Nora's hand. "Don't be such a worrywart. You know how we artists can get when we're in the throes of a new project. She's making magic."

Shep's lips twitched. "Looked mostly like a hunk of metal to me."

Lolli made a *pssh* sound. "You just don't have vision."

"Vision like you and your dick flower?" a deep voice asked from the entryway.

We all turned to see Kyler striding into the space, his scuffed-up motorcycle boots eating up the distance. If you didn't know him the way we did, you'd likely cross the street if you saw him coming. He looked like part mountain man and part tattoo god, with ink wrapping around his arms and beginning to trail up his neck.

"What's a dick flower?" Keely asked, her voice sounding extra angelic.

Trace glared at Kyler. "Thanks for that."

Kye winced. "I didn't see her there. She's tiny, man."

Lolli patted Trace's arm. "Now, now. There's nothing wrong with the human body." She turned to Keely. "He's talking about the picture I made for Rho's new house."

Keely brightened at that. "Can I have a dick flower, too?"

"No!" Trace and Nora said at the same time.

The rest of us dissolved into laughter.

"Will someone help me set the table?" Nora asked, exasperation lacing her tone.

"I will," I offered, moving to open the silverware drawer.

She wrapped an arm around me, pulling me in and kissing the top of my head. "You settling in?"

We were an affectionate bunch, easy with our hugs. The only one who steered clear was Kyler. Maybe because he'd ended up with us later in life at sixteen and had been through so much. He seemed to keep everyone at arm's length.

Kyler crossed to the island, grabbing a grape and popping it into his mouth. Then he glanced down at Fallon. "How was the home visit?"

The faintest blush lit the apples of her cheeks, but her mouth thinned. "It went all right."

Kyler's forearm bunched and flexed like a cobra ready to strike. "Just all right?"

Fallon shrugged. "The dad was kind of a jerk."

Kye's jaw worked back and forth. "How so?"

Her eyes flashed in challenge. "Nothing I couldn't handle."

"Fallon—"

"It was fine," she said, cutting him off.

She was the one person Kyler had let in after coming to live with Nora and Lolli. Maybe it was the gentleness that radiated through Fallon or that she was someone he could protect, but the two had become attached at the hip. Even now, I couldn't understand half of what they said to each other. It was as if they had their own unique language.

"What'd you work on today?" Lolli asked Kye, saving us from any battles of wills before dinner.

"Pretty decent chest piece and a tribal on a calf." He rolled his eyes at the second one. "Lots of idiots turning eighteen this spring."

Lolli chuckled. "I got a tattoo when I turned eighteen."

Kyler's brows rose at that tidbit of information.

"*Wild child*, right across my—"

"Okay," Trace cut in as he picked up Keely. "I think that's enough corruption for one night."

Keely looked up at her dad. "What's corrupston?"

"It means your uncle and supergran are bad influences."

Keely just giggled. "No, they're not. They're the besterest."

"Listen to the child," Lolli said, grabbing her wine. "She could teach you to live a little."

"Don't start, Lolls."

She just sent Trace a pointed look. "It wouldn't hurt for you to go out on the town. Have a beer. Do some…dancing."

Keely patted her dad's chest. "You should, Daddy. Dancing is the best!"

Shep choked on a laugh. "Your dad hasn't been dancing in a long time. Maybe that's why he's so grumpy."

She frowned at him. "Are you missing dancing? I'd be grumpy if I couldn't dance."

Trace covered his daughter's ears. "I hate you all."

"It's not nice to hate, Daddy," Keely yelled too loudly.

Nora shook her head as she carried a massive baking dish of lasagna to the table. "Fallon, will you get the salad?" She glanced at Shep, a hopeful glint in her eyes. "Is Anson able to make it?"

A little of the levity left his expression. "Not this time."

Nora's shoulders slumped, and my annoyance at the broody bastard flared. The idea of anyone being on their own, without *people*, would hurt her heart. But Anson wouldn't care about that. He'd just be off in his sulky corner.

Lolli made a tsking sound as she carried her glass and the open bottle of red to the table. "Gotta get past that boy's defenses. He's too pretty to be wasting away all alone."

I couldn't help the scoffing sound that slipped past my lips.

Lolli sent me a pointed look. "Don't tell me you haven't noticed those muscles and piercing eyes."

"Doesn't make his personality any more charming," I grumbled.

"Their personality doesn't matter if their mouth is busy doing *other* things," she said with a devious grin.

Keely's face scrunched. "What would their mouth be doing? It's rude to talk with your mouth full. Dad says."

Trace pinched the bridge of his nose. "For the love of all that's holy, will you all please rein it in before my girl gets expelled from the first grade?"

A chuckle slipped past Kye's lips, then Fallon giggled. It only took a matter of seconds before laughter engulfed everyone. But I couldn't help but remember the flicker of coldness in Anson's gaze. Something that didn't seem as if it had always been there. A coldness that something awful must have put there.

Chapter Seven

Anson

I LEANED BACK IN THE ADIRONDACK CHAIR, KICKING MY FEET onto the porch railing. The sun hovered just below the horizon, only a sliver of it still peeking out. It cast an orangey hue on the land around us.

I could give Sparrow Falls that. Her sunsets were beautiful. And the small cabin I rented halfway up one of the area's many mountains gave me a damn good vantage point.

But it didn't carry the peace it usually did today. A twitchiness had descended over me, even with a full day of work. Typically, I could count on my new career path to exhaust me so thoroughly that I slept like the dead.

I needed that. And on days when I wasn't working, I ran. Years ago, I'd logged hours at the gym to stay in shape. Now, I raced through mountain trails in an attempt to escape my demons.

My fingers itched to pull out my phone, text Shep, and make sure Rhodes had locked her damn gate. I didn't even want to think about her doors.

A muscle in my cheek fluttered, and I forced my hand to grab a glass bottle damp with condensation instead. I lifted it to my mouth, taking a deep pull. It didn't have the kick I needed, but it would have to do.

My gaze resettled on the book in my lap. The black-and-white squares stared back at me. Half were already filled in, but the puzzle didn't have the same sort of pull it usually did. And that only made the tic in my cheek intensify.

It was the only sort of word game I could handle these days and the only way I could let my brain have the outlet it needed without ramifications. The letters danced and spun in front of my vision. I could look at the prompt for a clue, but once I got things about half-way filled in, I liked to move without them. It was more of a challenge that way.

My brain flipped through the letters in the alphabet like a running in board in a train station. It came up with possibility after possibility until one hit that actually worked. I scrawled the letters onto the page.

The sound of tires on gravel had me putting the puzzle and pen on the worn side table. I reached underneath to where I stored my Glock, my hand hovering over it until I saw the familiar silver of Shep's truck.

The vise around my torso eased a fraction, but I didn't move. Shep pulled to a stop in front of my cabin and climbed out of his rig, holding some sort of dish. "Brought you leftovers."

I stared at him as he headed up the porch steps. "I do know how to feed myself."

Shep shoved the plate at me. "You eat one more of those frozen meals, and you're going to get heart disease and croak on the job."

He lowered himself into the chair next to me without waiting for an invitation. I needed to use that chair for kindling.

I unwrapped a corner of the plate, and the scents of garlic, tomatoes, sausage, and cheese hit me. I tugged the foil off. Shep's mom was always thorough. Next to the slice of lasagna and salad was a plastic fork. And beneath the paper plate was a napkin. I didn't pretend to be uninterested; I simply dug in.

Shep kicked his feet up onto the railing. "If you'd come to dinner, you would've gotten garlic bread and brownie sundaes, too."

I just grunted. Brownie sundaes weren't worth dealing with the football team that was Shep's family. I'd take leftovers over people any day.

Shep glanced down at my crossword puzzle and shook his head. "I'll never understand how you do those damned things in pen."

I took a pull of ginger beer, swallowing it down. "Pencils are for amateurs."

He just rolled his eyes. "Sometimes, I forget what a pompous prick you can be."

Shep wasn't wrong. But it used to be so much worse. I was so sure I had the answers to everything. And I'd been so fucking wrong— in the worst way. A way that had me losing the person who meant the most to me.

I shoved down the thoughts and memories, burying them under pounds of denial and self-flagellation. "You talk to Rhodes about locking her gate and doors?"

Shep's brows rose as he turned to face me. "She knows how to take care of herself."

Annoyance pricked like those tiny stickers that got stuck in my shoes on trail runs. "Clearly, she doesn't since the last time I saw her, she almost broke her neck doing something stupid."

His jaw worked back and forth. "She knows it was a mistake."

"Good." But that wasn't enough. Images of her living on that massive piece of property, alone, swirled in my head. "That house is way out, though. She needs to take different precautions than when she lived in town. Those properties can be targets because there aren't neighbors to hear. And word'll get around that a single woman is living out there alone."

Shep was silent for a good long moment, but I felt his gaze boring into me. "You doing okay?"

Fuck.

I did not need this. Not tonight. For whatever reason, my demons were already stirred up. They didn't need Shep's help.

"Fine," I clipped.

"You have to talk about it sometime," Shep said carefully. "You don't, and it'll eat you alive."

"Shep," I growled.

"It's been over two years, and you won't even say her name."

The lasagna I'd eaten felt like a brick in my gut. "Now's not the time."

"Then when is?" Shep pushed. "Tell me, and I'll make a goddamn appointment. Because I don't want to keep watching my best fucking friend fade away."

I snapped my mouth closed. *Hell.* An ugly stew of guilt and rage swept through me like vicious waves on a stormy sea. My throat worked as I struggled to swallow. "I can't go there. It'll kill me."

Quiet swirled around us, only broken by the occasional rustle of leaves. Finally, Shep spoke words I knew he'd picked carefully. "I'm scared that if you don't talk about it, it really will kill you one day."

I didn't say anything in response. Because I knew the truth. If I opened the door to that place where I'd locked it all away, it would be the thing to truly end me.

I took a swig of my ginger beer, hoping like hell it'd settle my stomach. "Worked up a plan for the Victorian."

Shep stared at me for a long moment and then sighed. "Walk me through it."

The slightest fraction of pressure left my chest. "We start in the library and fan east. We need to stabilize from the bottom up." Shep already knew this. We'd worked enough fire-restoration projects for him to know more than the basics, but I was desperate to talk about anything but the subject he'd tried to broach.

"Sounds good. We'll have our full crew tomorrow. What do you want 'em on?"

My breaths weren't quite as painful, and it no longer felt like each inhale was wrapped in barbed wire. "Let's clean out the downstairs.

I've got fresh N95 masks for everyone. Dumpster's supposed to get there between noon and one."

Shep nodded, his gaze locked on the horizon. "I'll make sure everyone's there at one."

"Thanks," I said. But it was so much more than just gratitude for getting our crew there. It was for all the things I couldn't say and couldn't touch. I just hoped like hell he knew it.

~⁀୨

Branches slapped my arms and face. The hits stung, tearing at my skin. I felt wetness on my cheek. Blood.

But it didn't matter. I pushed my body harder, my muscles straining and lungs burning. My feet slapped against the dirt path. The occasional rock or root stabbed my shoes, footwear that wasn't cut out for trails and meant for an office.

I skidded to a stop as I broke into a clearing. A massive oak tree stood in the center of the space. The trunk was wide and gnarled, and curved branches sprouted from it, moving every which way. But I could barely take any of that in.

My breaths came in quick pants, but I only knew that because I felt the rise and fall of my chest. I couldn't hear anything over the blood roaring in my ears.

A woman's body was slumped against the tree. Her head lolled to one side, blond hair covering her face. But I saw the telltale rope peeking out from under that fall of hair.

My stomach roiled, but I forced my feet to move—feet clad in those ridiculously expensive loafers I got for a damn book signing. Each step wound a cord around my throat as if I could feel what the woman had. But it wasn't even close.

Her feet were bare but not dirt-covered. He'd killed her elsewhere and brought her here. All so he could play his goddamn game with me.

Ragged breaths tore from my throat as I bent. I needed gloves, my team…but I didn't wait. Couldn't. I had to know.

I was going to hell for praying it was someone else. Anyone but my sister. *And what did that say about me? That I was no better than* him. *A monster. Because whoever this was, she was someone's daughter, sister, friend. Maybe even someone's wife and mother.*

I reached down, my hand trembling like a rookie seeing his first stiff. I swept back the pale blond locks.

And my whole world shattered.

I jerked upright, the sheet clinging to my damp chest as my lungs heaved. A breeze picked up through my open window, bringing in cold mountain air. But it didn't do a damn thing for the fire racing through my veins.

The image was still fresh. Too real. Because it had been.

Greta's face leached of all color. Her blood spilled all around her.

I shoved the blankets back and stalked out of bed. I needed to breathe. My feet pounded the rough-wood floors of the cabin as I crossed the loft and hit the stairs one by one. Unlocking the front door, I hauled it open.

Normally, I didn't venture outside without a weapon. It was stupider than shit when there was a serial killer out there who thought messing with my life was fun and games. Someone who'd never been caught.

But tonight, I didn't give a damn. I almost wished he *was* out there. Wished he'd take me, too. At least, it would mean the end of this torture spiral.

That was what he wanted. Not to end my life but to see me suffer. But you could never tell when a psychopath would grow tired of waiting and need more. Need to see the life drain from your eyes or the blood spill from your body.

An owl hooted as the cold night air hit me full blast. Even though we were into April, the nights in the mountains could still hit freezing. I welcomed it. Maybe the cold could beat back the memories.

I stared out at the landscape in front of me, the forests dipping into fields and ranch lands. I didn't feel any of the peace it sometimes gave me.

This was why I didn't talk about the past. Because when it got a foothold, it could drag me down and swallow me whole.

Chapter Eight

Rhodes

A CACOPHONY OF BIRDSONG FILLED THE AIR AS I OPENED MY SUV door. Grinning, I slid out and shut the door behind me. I loved working first shift at the nursery. Thanks to all the plants around us, we could've doubled as a bird sanctuary.

Three swooped through the air, landing on a display of shrubs near the front. They chattered back and forth in their bird-speak as the early sun streamed over the horizon. A chill still clung to the air, but I had my thick Bloom & Berry Nursery sweatshirt to keep me warm. The same one I'd had since junior year of high school. It was just the right amount of worn while somehow managing to hold on to a bit of its cozy softness.

Another bird let out an especially shrill call, and I winced. "A little early for that, don't you think?"

It seemed to stare at me in judgment.

I chuckled and pushed off my SUV, heading for the main greenhouse. We had several on the property. Bloom wasn't a small operation. Duncan's family had been running it for generations, and it had grown a bit each year. Now, it was a sight to behold, complete with a small café where customers could grab breakfast, lunch, or coffee.

Testing the doorknob to the greenhouse, I opened the door, not at all surprised that Duncan had beaten me in, even with me being fifteen minutes early to my shift.

"You in here, Dunc?" I called.

A figure straightened midway down the second row. A handful of years older than me, Duncan was brawny with tanned skin that spoke of a life spent in the sunshine. "Morning."

"How are the babies?" I asked, inclining my head toward the seedlings in front of him.

He grinned. "Holding steady." That curve of his mouth slipped a bit as he scanned my face. He cleared his throat. "How'd yesterday go?"

I rolled my lips over my teeth to keep any annoyance from slipping out. The problem with living in a small town was that everyone knew your past. Knew your business. Even if the concern came from a good place, it sometimes felt stifling.

"Good," I finally said, then smiled. "Lolli made me a dick flower for my new place, so how could it be anything else?"

Duncan's brows nearly hit his hairline, and he started coughing. "Did you say dick flower?"

I pulled out my phone and tapped the screen a few times until I navigated to my photos. Turning it around, I showed Duncan. His cheeks turned pink, and he started shaking his head.

I couldn't help it, I burst out laughing. "We could offer her a show here. She'd love it."

Duncan scrubbed a hand over his bearded cheek. "I really don't need to get arrested for corrupting minors."

"Keely asked for her own dick flower last night at dinner. Trace was not pleased."

Duncan chuckled. "I don't imagine so. Speaking of brothers, we need to pull a few more things for Shep's order."

"Sure. You got the list?" I locked my phone and shoved it back into my pocket. Shep was finishing up a stunning new build in the foothills, and being a perfectionist meant he had to handle the land-scaping, too.

Duncan tugged a scrap of paper from his back pocket and handed it to me. "Got most of it pulled and in the loading area last night, but I didn't want to chance some of the flowers. Think you can handle the rest?"

I scanned the list, my lips twitching. It'd taken me years to deci-pher Duncan's scrawl. A good seventy-five percent of the items were scratched out already. The only ones left were things the deer might decide to make a snack of. "Got it. I'll start watering after. We should move the peonies up to the front, too. Some of them are starting to bloom."

Duncan pinned me with a stare. "When are you going to take the manager position?"

I winced. "A quarter to never?"

He shook his head. "You know almost as much about every plant on this property as I do. You've got great instincts and people skills, and the pay is practically double."

I didn't care about the pay. I lived simply and didn't have es-pecially extravagant tastes. And now that I was living in a place that was already bought and paid for, I needed even less. "I don't need the headache, Dunc."

He muttered something I couldn't quite make out.

A hint of guilt churned in my stomach. A manager position meant the kind of stress I didn't need, like people counting on me for more than just working a set number of hours a week. Even though I'd worked at Bloom since high school, I didn't feel the pull for more. I liked my life exactly how it was. I had a paycheck that covered the necessities and time to enjoy things outside of work. I didn't take any of those moments for granted because I knew none of them were guaranteed. So, I lived each one to the fullest and enjoyed the sim-ple beauty in all of them.

"Tell me if you change your mind," he grumbled.

"I will. Promise." But I didn't wait for anything else. I made a beeline for the greenhouse door and headed out into the early morning sunshine. I sucked in a lungful of cool air. It soothed my anxious edges.

Squinting down at the list, I made a quick plan. I grabbed a cart from the row near the gravel parking lot and got to work. It only took about twenty minutes to get everything pulled, and I made it to the loading area just as a truck headed my way. Only it wasn't Shep's familiar silver one towing a trailer. It was a black one that fit the personality of the man behind the wheel.

I steeled myself, pulling my armor into place and trying to remember what Shep had told me. Anson had been through something. And that something had left him a shell of the person he'd once been. It had wrapped him in coldness. Maybe that frostiness was his armor—a way to keep people at arm's length.

The truck swung around so Anson could reverse into the makeshift spot. I tried to focus on the beeping alerts, not the prickle of awareness skating over my skin. The moment the rig was in park, I stepped forward and unlatched the trailer.

Footsteps sounded on the gravel. "Shouldn't have done that."

My gaze flicked to the side as I opened the back door. Anson wore a ballcap that shielded his eyes from the light, but the sun still picked up on the lighter strands of blond in his thick, wild scruff. "Do what?"

"Moved behind the trailer before you knew I was done backing up."

I rolled my eyes. "I could see you weren't in reverse."

Those blue-gray eyes swept over my face, assessing. "Easy to change that."

"Good morning to you, too, Anson. How'd you sleep?" I said with an exaggerated smile bordering on the look of a deranged clown.

Something passed over those stormy eyes, but it was gone so quickly, I second-guessed myself. He turned to the array of plants. "These all ours?"

I nodded. "Shouldn't take us too long to load things up."

Anson jerked his head in a nod and moved toward the heaviest items. He bent and lifted an Aspen sapling with ease. His tee stretched tight across his muscled chest as his biceps flexed.

I quickly averted my gaze and moved to some of the shrubs. We worked silently, but it was only a matter of minutes before the quiet made my skin crawl.

"So, you think you guys will finish the place today?" I asked, desperate for noise to break up the silence. If Anson didn't start talking, I was going to start singing, and I couldn't imagine he wanted that.

"Likely."

That was it. One word and on to the next shrub.

Instead of annoying me this time, it made a small snicker leave my lips.

Anson's smooth gait hitched before he reached the trailer. "What?"

I grinned at him. "You're a real Chatty Cathy."

He scowled at me and headed into the trailer.

"So," I tried again, "how do you like Sparrow Falls?"

I could make a game out of this. See what buttons I needed to push to get Anson talking.

"Fine," he clipped, moving for a lilac.

I bit my lip to keep from laughing. "You ever give more than one-word answers?"

"No."

A laugh did bubble out of me then. Couldn't be helped. "Fair enough. Let's play a one-word game, then. Lakes or oceans?"

Anson stopped in his tracks and turned slowly toward me. "What are you playing at?"

I shrugged. "You're my brother's best friend. You're going to be working on my house for the foreseeable future. Don't you think it might be nice to get to know each other a little bit? Maybe even be friendly?"

That was the wrong word.

The blue bled out of Anson's eyes, leaving them pure gray. "I don't do friends. I don't do silly little girls playing games. Just let me do my job and stay out of my way."

A slap would've stung less. But I didn't let it show. "I might be silly, but silly's a heck of a lot better than being an asshole."

And with that, I headed to water the plants in the north greenhouse. Anson could load the damn trailer himself.

∾

"Thank you for taking him," Nancy said as she handed me a leash. "I didn't want to call you for another week, at least. Hoped to give you a chance to get settled in your new place. But desperate times call for desperate measures."

I took hold of the thick green leash as the dog looked up at me with sad eyes. It was anyone's guess what mishmash of breeds he was. He had a stocky body with short, stubby legs, and his head looked two sizes too big for the rest of him. His black fur was dull, but I knew that would change with a month of good meals.

"It's not a problem. Kitten season is always hectic." I crouched down to get on the pup's level but didn't offer my hand yet. I wanted him to get used to my scent first.

Nancy swiped the tendrils of frizzy hair out of her face. "You're telling me. I've got two litters right now."

I looked up at her, taking in the dark circles under her eyes. "Are you getting any sleep at all?"

"Ken and I are taking shifts, so I'm cobbling together five or six."

"Angel points," I said with a smile. "But you deserve a trip to the spa, too."

Nancy's big, bawdy laugh swirled in the air around us. "I'm not against it once we're deep into summer, maybe fall."

But she wouldn't ever go. She'd feel like a trip away meant letting down the animals that needed her. Wags & Whiskers Animal Rescue was her pride and joy, her purpose. And she didn't trust anyone to run it in her absence.

My gaze shifted back to the black dog. His ears twitched.

"What do I need to know about him?"

Nancy sighed. "He got dumped down by Castle Rock. He does okay around women, but he's not the biggest fan of men."

An ache settled deep in my bones. That could only mean that some man hadn't treated him well. Bastard.

"He have a name?" I asked.

"Thought you could do the honors there as you get to know him."

The dog shifted a bit, easing toward me.

"Hey, buddy," I crooned.

At the soft tone, he scooted even closer.

I pulled the packet of treats I kept in the car from my back pocket. "How do you feel about liver? I think it's nasty, but it smells extra strong, which usually means pups love it."

The moment I broke the seal on the bag, the dog started sniffing wildly. I chuckled and plucked a treat from the pack. Holding out my palm, I waited.

He stretched out his neck as far as possible and quickly snatched the treat.

"That's a good boy," I encouraged and pulled out another treat.

This time, he edged a bit closer to me to get the treat easier. After treat four, I slowly lifted my hand to scratch under his chin. He melted into me, his back leg thumping.

"That's your spot, huh?"

The dog's booty started wagging back and forth.

"You've got a way with them," Nancy said with a smile. "You always have."

A phantom pain drifted through me. It wasn't acute in any way; it was an echo of agony. A month after I'd come to live with the Colsons, Lolli dragged me with her to pick up a cat someone had found scrounging in a dumpster in the back of The Pop.

The cat had patchy, coarse fur and fleas. We'd had to bathe her twice, which she really hadn't loved, and she'd given us the scratches to prove it. I hadn't wanted any part of the project. I'd still felt like I was drowning in grief, but taking care of the fiery, mangy cat and helping her find her way toward healing and trusting again had healed something in me, too.

I'd been fostering animals ever since. There was no greater sense of pride than when I gave one of them over to their forever families, knowing they'd finally get the life they deserved.

"Well, this one is just a love," I cooed as the dog pressed his whole body against my side. "You wanna come home with me?"

The pup looked up at me with those huge eyes. So much uncertainty swirled in their depths, but he easily followed me to the SUV when I pushed to my feet. I opened the back door, and he hopped right in. I gave him an ear scratch as a reward.

When I closed the door, Nancy pulled me into a hug. "Thank you."

"Anytime," I said, squeezing her back. "I'll keep you updated on his progress and take plenty of pics for the website."

We liked to post the animals as soon as we got them so we could begin getting the word out. When we were getting closer to a critter being ready for their forever home, we'd start accepting applications. But I had a feeling this guy would need a few weeks with me, at least.

I released Nancy and climbed behind the wheel. The dog's head popped up over the edge of the sort of hammock I had to keep dogs in the back seat. I chuckled and offered him one more treat. "How do you feel about car rides?"

His tongue lolled out of his mouth, and he panted happily.

"I'm taking that as a good sign." I put the car in drive and headed away from Nancy's home on the edge of town. As we drove, I cracked the back window just enough for my new pup to poke his head out if he wanted.

It took two point five seconds. Those oversized ears that had been standing at attention now blew in the breeze. I couldn't help the laugh that burst out of me. Ah, the simple joy of the wind in your ears.

"Car rides, check." One less thing I'd have to master with him.

It only took a few minutes to reach the turnoff to home. *Home.* It felt like such a foreign word. Even though I'd felt nothing but welcome with the Colsons, it was never completely home. And since then, I'd been afraid to reach for it.

The dog pulled his head back in, shifting positions so he could see out the front window.

"We're both going to do some hard things, but we'll face them together."

I kept one hand on the wheel and used the other to scratch under my foster pup's chin. The thumping of his foot against the seat was the only answering sound.

As I headed down the drive, I caught sight of several vehicles by the main house. The majority were trucks of various makes and models, and I recognized almost all of them. But my stomach still flipped a little. Work was officially starting.

It was a good thing. A necessary thing. And most of all, it was time.

I parked outside my guest cottage and hopped out. Opening the back door, I grabbed for the leash. The dog jumped out, his nose in the air, sniffing like crazy. And then, out of nowhere, he let out a series of barks and growls that sounded more like the hounds of hell than a canine.

I turned to see the source of his rage and caught sight of familiar dark blond scruff peeking out from under the shadows of a ballcap. Anson's footsteps halted as he took in the dog next to me. "Didn't know you had a dog."

"I don't," I clipped, not forgetting our earlier interaction.

Anson simply arched a brow. Of course, he could ask a question without uttering a word.

"I foster for a local organization. He's not a fan of men."

To my surprise, Anson lowered himself to the gravel, hunching his shoulders to make himself as small as possible. "Got any treats?"

I snagged the bag from my pocket and tossed it to him without saying a word. The motion of Anson catching the bag made my new pup's snarls intensify, but Anson simply ignored them. He opened the bag and palmed a few of the liver treats.

The dog kept up his low growls but sniffed the air.

Anson tossed a treat at the dog's feet. He stopped growling just long enough to gobble it down.

"Give the leash some slack," Anson said, keeping his eyes downcast.

I glanced between the dog and the broody bastard. "You sure about that?" Anson might be on my shit list, but I didn't want him mauled by my newest foster.

"Give him some slack, Reckless," he echoed.

I scowled at the nickname but gave the dog another couple feet of leash. It would let him have some freedom but not enough that he could take a chunk out of Anson's face.

Just as I gave the slack, Anson tossed treats. One. Two. Three. The dog couldn't eat the snacks and charge Anson. He went for the treats.

"Good boy," Anson said, his voice low as he tossed two more treats.

The dog's growls subsided, and Anson made a clicking noise with his tongue, tossing two more treats. "You got a clicker?"

My brows furrowed. "Like for the garage?"

"No," Anson said, still not looking up. "Training tool. The sound marks good behavior. You can click faster than you can get them a treat. The click lets them know they did something good, and a reward is coming."

I did basic training with all the dogs that came into my care, but it was more about getting them used to certain stimuli and making sure they were potty-trained.

Anson showed the dog the treat and then lifted it into the air. My new pup plunked his butt right on the ground. Anson clicked and tossed the treat.

Without making a sound, Anson lined up treats that led closer to him. The dog took the first two easily but then started to get a bit apprehensive. He would dart forward and then back. But Anson simply stayed still, letting him do what he needed.

Slowly, the dog nosed closer. He took one treat, then another. Finally, Anson held out his palm with two treats on it. The dog kept looking between the treats and Anson. In a blur of motion, the dog took a treat and dashed back.

Anson made the clicking noise and tossed another treat a few feet away from him. The dog took it and then hurried back to my side. Anson rose, taking his time to make sure there were no sudden movements.

I stared at him as if he were an entirely different human than anyone I'd met before. "What was that?"

Anson just stared at me, not answering.

"You've been nothing but a grumpy asshole since I met you. But with him…"

"Don't do people. Love dogs." And with that, he stalked back to the main site and his crew.

I looked down at my new friend. "What the hell was that?"

The dog just stared up at me, tongue lolling.

I shook my head. "Come on, let's get you inside. I really hope you don't puke after all those treats."

I showed my pup around the tiny guest cottage, letting him sniff to his heart's content. Then as he settled on a dog bed by the fireplace, I got to work hauling in his food and other essentials. I kept a lot of things on hand, but each animal had a different type of food, meds, and other paraphernalia.

By the time I got everything inside, the pup was snoring so loudly it was a wonder the walls didn't shake. Since he was fast asleep, I headed back outside and hit my key fob to open the SUV's back hatch.

As it swung up, various brightly colored blooms met my gaze. As much as I never decorated the inside of my home to Nora's satisfaction, my garden, porch, and deck were the places I always made mine. Sinking my hands into soil and creating a cacophony of color and texture made me feel closer to my mom, even though she was gone.

Having the garden spaces around the guest cottage lie fallow, and the small porches empty, made me twitchy. So, there was only one solution. Fill them.

I hauled out bags of soil, carrying them toward the array of pots in various shapes, sizes, and colors. Then I got to work on the flats of flowers and the larger statement blooms. By the time everything was out of my SUV and by the side of the house, my hair was sticking to the back of my neck. Spring was definitely here.

Bending over, I pulled all the strands into a chaotic bun, tying it off with a hair band. I had to buy specialty ones because the regular kind simply snapped with the force of my tendrils.

As I straightened, I saw a shiny silver sedan driving too fast toward me. The BMW emblem shone on the hood, and a familiar license plate stood out on the front grille.

Everything in me strung tight. "Oh, crap."

THE FLASH OF METALLIC SILVER IN THE BRIGHT AFTERNOON sun caught my eye as I turned to watch the BMW drive way too fast toward the guest cottage. Toward Rhodes. Something about that made my gut churn.

Who was I kidding? Everything about her twisted my insides. Too beautiful. Too bright. Too kind. She even took in damn dogs.

"Prick," Saul muttered next to me as he scribbled something on his clipboard and then offered it to me.

I signed the bottom line without bothering to read the fine print. Saul handled our dumpsters for every project. He'd never screw us. "You know the flash?" I asked.

Saul grunted. "Grew up here. Always had a bit of a cocky shit in him, but then he went down to Silicon Valley. Made some millions. Came back thinking he was God's gift. Prick."

I watched as the tall, lean man climbed out of the sedan. I couldn't help but profile him in swift strokes. His brown hair was styled in a way that told me he didn't want a thing out of place. Same with his perfectly pressed slacks and button-down. He needed control. To force everything around him into submission.

The luxury car brand, Gucci loafers, and gold watch I had a feeling was a Rolex told me his image was everything, too. He wanted the best of the best, and nothing else would suffice.

I had a feeling Saul was right. Total prick.

As the douchebag prowled toward Rhodes, a prickle of unease skated over my skin—something about his single-minded focus on her, and the way Rhodes held herself. She was usually relaxed, muscles loose and easy. There was none of that now. Her shoulders were up, revealing the tension wound through them. Her jaw was set, telling me her teeth were clenched. She didn't want him here.

"They know each other?" I asked, handing the clipboard back to Saul.

His brows rose a fraction in surprise. I'd never asked him a question other than what time drop-off would be. "Everyone in this town knows each other if they've been around long enough. Everyone except loners who hide up in their cabins and don't talk to a soul."

I didn't respond to the jibe, simply kept staring at him.

Saul chuckled. "From what I hear, they dated for a bit. Rho broke it off a few weeks ago. Davis wasn't overly pleased."

My gaze shifted back to the two of them. The douchebag wasn't what I thought Rhodes would go for. I would've pegged her as either going for some Pollyanna do-gooder, the Peace Corps type, or someone broken she thought she could fix. Not a guy who cared first and foremost about his image. But maybe I was slipping by not being in the field.

The douchebag smiled at Rhodes, all too-white teeth and a smarmy attempt at charm. She grimaced in response. He moved closer, invading her space. Rhodes tried to move back, but there was nowhere for her to go.

Hell.

I was moving before I registered the thought. I stalked toward them, my boots sending gravel flying. It wasn't long before I could hear snippets of their conversation.

"Let me have my interior designer consult on the project. I'll handle the cost. You want to make sure you're making the appropriate design choices with a house of this magnitude," douchebag said.

Rhodes scowled at him. "I don't need an interior designer. Shep's helping me with everything."

Douchebag scoffed. "Shep runs a good company, I'll give him that, but he doesn't have the elevated tastes required—"

"Rhodes," I interjected. "Need your take on something."

Davis whirled at the sound of my voice. "Who's this?"

A little of the tension bled out of Rhodes' shoulders as she edged toward me. "Anson works with Shep. He's handling the fire-restoration piece of things."

Davis's eyes narrowed. "Shouldn't you be advising her to start from scratch? It's ridiculous to try to repair a structure that's been so badly damaged."

A muscle in Rhodes' cheek ticked, but she stayed quiet.

"It's a historic home. Can't put a price on that," I said coolly. "Some people are just blind to the beauty beneath the damage."

Rhodes' gaze jerked to me, her eyes widening a fraction, lips parting.

Davis scoffed. "Waste of time and money."

I ignored him and turned to Rhodes. "You got a minute?"

"Sure," she said quickly, wiping dirt from her hands on her shorts that revealed tanned legs with sinewy muscle. Legs I did *not* need to be staring at.

"We're talking," Davis clipped.

Rhodes turned to him. "No, you were monologuing."

He snapped his mouth closed, the look in his eyes going hot with anger.

She sighed. "I appreciate the offer of help, but I don't need it. Enjoy the rest of your day."

Davis's jaw worked back and forth. "You're in over your head." Then he turned and climbed back into his BMW, tires spitting gravel as he swung in a tight circle and took off.

Rhodes' shoulders slumped as he disappeared in a cloud of dust. "Sorry about that," she mumbled.

"Not yours to be sorry about."

Her head lifted, those green-gold eyes locking with mine. "What did you need?"

"Nothing. Could just tell you were uncomfortable. Wanted to give you an out."

Rhodes kept staring at me, confusion swirling through her expression. "You're never predictable, are you, Anson?"

She said my name with a softness that had my entire body standing at attention. Everything in me wanted to lean closer, yet at the same time, my brain was screaming at me to cut this off, lash out, and push her away.

"Just don't like seeing women intimidated. That's all." I turned to stalk away before she could say another word, or her voice could curl around my name like a physical caress.

I had to keep my distance from Rhodes. She had a way of breaking through the numbness I'd made my home for the past two years. And that was just as dangerous as she was.

"You kick the douche to the curb?" a voice called from the makeshift table we'd set up in front of the house.

I glanced at the crew member who'd asked the question. Silas was a hard worker with a single-minded focus that came in handy on every job we came across. And he was a good guy, other than moving from woman to woman with a speed that made my head spin.

"Think he kicked himself to the curb," I muttered.

Another of our crew ambled over, water bottle in hand. Owen didn't have quite the work ethic Silas did. His breaks were legendary, and he had a reputation for punching first and asking questions later. "He'll be back. Money like that don't like hearing no."

"He might want to get used to it," I gritted out.

"Shep won't stand for it," Silas said. "He'll make sure the message gets across. Or he'll put Trace on it."

As if saying his name had conjured him, Shep's silver truck

bumped along the uneven drive. We needed to get the thing regraded before one of us broke an axle.

Shep pulled in between various other vehicles and quickly hopped out, glancing toward the guest cottage as he walked toward us. "A silver BMW come by here?"

Carlos, another crew member, grinned as he walked over. "Moneybags came and went."

Concern spread across Shep's expression as he cursed.

"Don't worry," Silas assured him. "Anson sent him packing."

Shep's focus sliced to me in silent question.

I shifted my weight. "It was nothing. Just made sure she was okay, and he took off."

"Took off looking like he was about to have the shits or sucked on a lemon," Silas shot back.

Shep inclined his head to the side. "Walk with me. I need to run something by Rho."

The last thing I wanted was to walk any closer to Rhodes. To her brightness, her color. It only made me realize just how gray my world had become.

Still, I followed Shep just out of earshot of the guys. He dipped his head and lowered his voice. "I need to be worried?"

I mulled the question over. There were so many threads to it. I didn't want to tug on any of them. But I owed Shep. Everything, really. "How long did they date?"

"About a month. Not serious. A date or two a week."

I gnawed on that. So, a max of eight dates. Chances were, they'd slept together. That could be a trigger for someone with control issues or obsessive tendencies. I knew for sure Davis was the former, but hoped he wasn't the latter. "How long ago did Rhodes end things?"

Shep scrubbed a hand over his jaw. "It was just before Lolli's birthday, so about three and a half weeks."

That pinged my radar. Davis still coming around almost a month after the breakup of a relationship that hadn't gotten all that serious? Not a good sign.

"Probably a good idea to keep an eye out," I said carefully. "But she's got a lot of people around her right now. He's going to know there's the potential of him making a fool of himself with an audience like he did today. A guy like him? He's not going to like that much."

Shep grunted. "He's all about image. I think that's half of why he's still after Rho. She ended things, not him."

That thought eased a little of the tension thrumming through me. Ego was a much better option than obsession. Ego wounds could heal. Obsession, not so much. And sometimes, you didn't know what you were dealing with until it was too late.

Chapter Ten

Rhodes

EASING ONTO THE STOOL BEHIND THE REGISTER, I LAID THE egg sandwich on the counter. Dog looked up at me with pleading eyes. I'd had him for a week, and he still didn't have a name. Nothing quite seemed to fit, and he deserved the right one.

I'd been working on his training, though. I'd found one of those clickers Anson had mentioned at our local feed and pet store. Looking up the training methodology, I'd found loads of stuff. And even better, it worked.

Every now and then, I caught Anson watching our training sessions from afar. But he never came over. Never said a word to me. And if I ventured over into crew territory, he conveniently disappeared.

Seemed he'd been honest when he said he did dogs but not people.

I leaned down to scratch Dog's head. He had quite the setup at Bloom. A dog bed behind the counter with a bowl of water, a handful of toys, and a cozy blanket. I was damn lucky I had a boss who let me bring my fosters to work.

Unwrapping the sandwich, I took a huge bite of the flaky biscuit, egg, and sharp cheddar and nearly moaned. Thank the food gods for our onsite café. I'd started earlier today because we'd received a delivery of new shrubs just as we closed last night.

My phone dinged, and I glanced down at the screen. Our sibling group chat had another new name. *The 7 Deadly Sibs.*

I snorted as I picked up the device.

Cope: *Who sent the basket of peaches to the practice arena?*

I bit my lip to keep from laughing.

Me: *Want me to send you Nora's cobbler recipe?*

Fallon: *I've got a jam recipe you could use.*

Cope: *You're all assholes. I almost puked on the receptionist when she gave it to me.*

Kye: *Nothing like a little puke to charm the ladies. Didn't you see the card?*

Cope: *You little shit. Payback is coming.*

A second later, a photo appeared in the text chain. The stationery had the fruit embossed on the top. *For our Little Peach. Don't bruise too easy in tonight's game.*

I choked on my laugh as I set the phone back down. There was nothing like a little sibling shit-talking to make sure your ego stayed in check. And with all the attention Cope got, that wasn't a bad thing.

I shook my head and arched my back, feeling a twinge in the muscles there. I might've overdone it just a bit. But it was nothing two ibuprofen and a long, hot bath wouldn't cure.

A flicker of movement caught my attention as a familiar figure moved quietly through the rows of plants and toward the counter. Everything about the woman screamed *Don't look at me!* Her clothes were all in neutrals—jeans and a beige T-shirt. Her hair, while thick and shiny, was usually pulled back into a braid to hide its luster. She moved quickly but silently as if practiced in making no sound at all.

I sent her a wide grin. "Morning, Thea."

Her answering smile was more hesitant, a bit unsteady. Or maybe she was just rusty. "Morning."

"What are you after today?" I asked.

She worried the corner of her lip and glanced over her shoulder. "I wondered if you had any peonies that might be hitting the sale aisle soon."

An ache took root somewhere deep. Thea was a plant lover like me, but Bloom's offerings were on the pricier side. Because we stocked quality. Duncan's markup was fair. Just enough to guarantee a healthy bottom line but not enough to price gouge customers. But if you were watching your wallet, making constant purchases from our store would be hard.

I didn't know much about Thea. She kept any chatting purely surface-level and centered on the plants. I sensed that I'd only send her running if I pushed too hard. But I knew she worked at our local bakery, The Mix Up, she lived somewhere outside of town, and she loved all plants, from the ones you ate to those that simply brightened your day.

Drumming my fingers on the counter, I nodded. "I think we've got a few that are about to tip over into sale territory. Let's go take a look."

It was a lie. Peonies were one of the few things that never landed in our sale rows unless they were on death's door, but I'd just cover the difference. I slid off my stool, giving Dog a quick pat on the head. "Be good."

His tongue lolled to one side.

Thea peered over the counter, and her face lit up. "New one?"

I nodded. "Still working on a name."

Longing swept into her expression. "The right one will find him."

"That's what I keep saying, but my gran is giving me crap for not having something to call him."

A soft smile tipped her lips. "As long as he's loved, that's what matters."

"So true." I glanced over at Thea. "What are you working on?" It was the one thing I could ask that wouldn't get Thea's back up.

Her smile widened. "The beds under my bedroom window. Thought it might be nice to look out and see a sea of peonies."

"Sounds like heaven to me. Any colors in particular?"

"I'll settle for whatever you have, but I was thinking that peachy pink if it's available."

"Let's see." I scanned the rows of blossoms until I settled on a section of that color just shy of full bloom. "Perfect! Duncan will be moving these over today or tomorrow. I can give you the sale discount now."

Thea's teeth tugged on the corner of her lip as she studied the flowers. "Are you sure? They still look pretty prime to me."

"Not compared to the others," I said, gesturing to the rest of the row. Most of them only had a flower or two blooming; the rest were still buds.

Thea was quiet for a moment before finally shaking her head. "It's okay. I'll just wait until they're actually on sale."

I almost let my curse slip free instead of just letting it loose in my head. "Really—"

She cut me off with another shake. "It's really kind of you, but I don't want you to break the rules for me."

I bit the inside of my cheek to keep from arguing with her. Beautiful flowers were such a simple pleasure. The kind of thing everyone deserved. And it bothered me that Thea wouldn't have them. I studied her for a moment. "Are you full time at the bakery?"

Confusion swept across her face. "No, still part time, but I get decent hours, and Sutton's hoping to expand soon."

I didn't know much about the new bakery owner other than she had a huge smile for everyone and the most adorable son I'd ever seen. But from all the changes I'd seen her implement, it was clear she had a sharp business mind and good instincts.

My fingers tapped against the side of my thigh. "Would you ever want to work part time here, too? I know it doesn't give you the kind of benefits you would get from being full time somewhere, but we always bring on a few extra hands for the summer. And you'd get the employee discount on everything we have here."

Thea's lips parted on a silent inhale. "You guys are really hiring?"

"Check the local paper. I think Duncan's ad runs on Wednesday. But I can give you an application now."

She rolled to the balls of her feet, almost bouncing. It was the most excitement I'd seen from Thea since I'd met her nearly two years ago. "Do you know what the pay is?"

I nodded with a smile. "Starts at twenty an hour plus overtime. And the discount is forty percent."

This time, Thea's jaw went slack. "Forty percent off *everything*?"

I grinned. "Pretty sweet, huh? Duncan likes his staff to be knowledgeable about what they're selling. The discount is his way of encouraging that."

Thea's eyes went a little glassy. "I'd work for free for that discount."

I chuckled. "Well, you don't have to. Come on. I'll get you the application."

She followed me into the greenhouse and toward the counter. As we got closer, my steps faltered. Something about the counter was different.

"You didn't," I muttered.

"What's wrong?" Thea asked, concerned.

I instantly hurried around the counter to find my egg sandwich wrapper on the ground and a pup licking his lips. "Dog!"

He instantly laid his head down between his paws.

"Don't look all ashamed and make me feel bad for you. You ate my breakfast."

A soft giggle sounded behind me as Thea surveyed the scene. "Maybe you should name him Biscuit. He's obviously got a taste for them."

Dog's head lifted at that, ears twitching.

I couldn't help my laugh. "I think he likes it. You want to be called Biscuit?"

He barked in answer.

"Either that or he wants another one," Thea said.

I shook my head. "He's probably going to be sick as it is."

She winced. "Not a fun cleanup."

"No kidding." I pulled open the filing cabinet drawer and found the folder for our applications. Grabbing one and a pen, I handed them to Thea. It was only a single sheet with some basic information and a section for experience and why you wanted to work at Bloom, but Thea scrutinized it as if it were the SATs.

She swallowed hard as she rolled the pen between her fingers. "Do you think...I mean, would it be possible for Duncan to pay me in cash?"

I studied Thea for a long moment. It wasn't that we never got the request, but it was usually because someone didn't have a green card. As long as the person was a hard worker, Duncan found his way around those cases, paying them out of the till each week. But I didn't think that was the case for Thea. So, why did she need things done that way? She didn't seem the type to try for tax evasion.

"Duncan's usually pretty good about working with those kinds of requests," I said finally.

Thea's grip on the pen loosened a fraction, and she began scrawling her information across the page. "Great. Thank you."

In less than five minutes, she was done and handing it back. I quickly scanned the sheet. Her phone number, email, and address were blank. Between that and the cash request, my stomach started to twist.

"We just need a phone number or email so we can contact you about an interview," I said softly.

Thea licked her lips. "I don't have either. Not really a tech person. But I can check in tomorrow or the next day and see if Duncan's interested."

No phone or email. I didn't know anyone without both. Even Lolli, who was always going on and on about the evils of technology, had a cell phone and email—even if she only used that email for ordering diamond art supplies and weed.

"Sure," I told Thea. "That's not a problem at all."

"Thanks, Rho." Her cheeks flushed. "You're a really good person."

I opened my mouth to say something, anything, but Thea was

already turning to leave. I watched her thread her way through rows of plants until she slipped out the door. But even after she disappeared, I couldn't stop wondering what the heck she was hiding from.

☙

As I slowed to a stop at the last traffic light in town, I rolled my shoulders, trying to relieve some of the tension there. Duncan and I had spent hours rotating displays this afternoon. Between that and doing heavy lifting first thing, my body was paying for it. I really needed that hot bath and some ibuprofen.

The light changed from red to green, and I eased off the brake. I stole a quick glance at the newly painted sign for The Mix Up and wished like hell they were still open. I would've done bad things for their spinach and artichoke grilled cheese right about now.

Biscuit stuck his head over the hammock, resting it on my shoulder. Everything inside me twisted at the simple action. He was coming out of his shell more and more.

I scratched the side of his jaw as I guided my SUV toward home. "We'll just have to settle for my grilled cheese creation and kibble for you."

I swore I could see Biscuit glaring at me in the rearview mirror.

"Don't give me that look. You already had one sandwich today. We're lucky you didn't have the Hershey squirts all over the nursery. Dunc never would've let you back in after that."

Biscuit let out a huff of air, and I couldn't help but laugh.

In a matter of minutes, I was turning onto my drive. *My* drive. To *my* house. It was all still a little surreal. That familiar twitchiness came over me—the feeling of my skin being too tight for my body, making it itchy.

I forced myself to take a deep breath.

In. Two. Three.

I took in the stunning view as I inhaled. The rock formations. The mountains. The place my family had loved.

Out. Two. Three.

I tried to release the edge of panic as I exhaled. Some part of me worried that if I ever truly put down roots again, something awful would happen to take it all away. But I couldn't let that ugly fear win. It would mean the fire had won. And I wasn't about to let that happen.

I slowed my SUV as I reached the makeshift parking area in front of the Victorian. Owen was chugging a bottle of water, and Silas and Carlos were shoving gear into the backs of their trucks. I rolled down my window, sending them a grin. "Working hard or hardly workin'?"

Silas shot me a wide smile. "Just calling off for the day. You want to hit the bar with me?"

A chuckle slipped free as I shook my head. "Hitting the bar with you means dealing with death glares from your *many* adoring fans."

Silas mimed a dagger to the heart. "Killing me. You know I'd send 'em all packing for you, dream girl."

Carlos snorted, smacking him on the back of the head. "You want Shep to tan your hide?"

Silas just laughed. "Gotta shoot your shot."

Owen sent Silas a glare. "Or you could try something new and leave her the fuck alone."

Oh, hell. I didn't know what it was that made Owen think he needed to play the protective brother role when I had four of them already. Maybe it was because we'd been classmates since I moved to Sparrow Falls, and he'd worked for Shep since getting out of high school.

Only it was hardly necessary when it came to Silas's antics. We'd been running this back-and-forth forever. But it seemed to get on Owen's nerves more and more lately.

It wasn't like any of this was new. Silas had been a player since puberty, moving from one girl to the next in rapid-fire succession. He wasn't the type that promised more, but still somehow managed to leave a trail of broken hearts in his wake.

Owen had his share of romantic partners, but not nearly as many. He struggled to commit to *anything*. He came and went from Shep's crew with a frequency that made me dizzy. And his temper was one of legend.

Carlos was the only one of the three of them to settle down. He had a wife and an adorable baby girl named Gabby now. Maybe he'd rub off on the other two someday. And from the look he flashed them both right now, he'd be giving them an earful later.

"Chill, dude," Silas said, frowning at Owen.

Owen laughed, but the sound didn't quite ring true. "Just givin' you shit."

Silas didn't join him in laughing.

Carlos broke the awkward silence by moving toward my truck and tapping the open window. "Good day in the plant biz?" Before I could answer, Biscuit let out a low growl, and Carlos stepped back. "You sure that one's safe to have at your place?"

I scratched under Biscuit's chin, easing his snarls. "Just not partial to people of the male variety."

Carlos snorted. "My wife would say he's smart."

"You said it, not me. Have a good night, guys," I said with a wave as I eased off the brake. I kept the window down as I headed for the guest cottage. Shep's truck was gone, and the only other one by the Victorian was a familiar black one. I couldn't help but stare at it a little too long.

Anson had felt like a ghost this week. I rarely saw him, but I felt his presence. It was as if the air moved differently when he was around.

I tore my gaze away from the truck and focused on the drive that curved around the main house and toward the cottage. Pulling to a stop in front of my temporary home, I cut the engine. Biscuit let out a deep woof.

I reached back and scratched under his chin. "You happy to be home? You had to do a lot of peopling today."

And Biscuit had done remarkably well until just now. He'd let out a low growl or two at men who'd come to check out, but having the counter between him and them had allowed Biscuit to feel safe while getting used to the gender.

Hopping out of my SUV, I moved to the back door. I opened it and quickly hooked on Biscuit's leash. When he jumped down, I shut the door behind him and led him toward the cottage.

My muscles ached as I walked. Maybe I needed a bath before food. My stomach rumbled in protest. Apparently, that was a no.

I trudged up the steps to the front porch, slowing as I spotted something lying on my welcome mat. I squinted as I crouched down.

The moment I caught sight of the image, it was as if all the air had been knocked out of me. The photograph was charred around the edges, the image itself a bit warped from the heat. But I could still make out what it was.

My family. Happy. Carefree as we sat having a picnic at the creek not far from here. My eyes were shining in the photo, my mouth open in a half laugh, half yell as my dad tickled my side. Mom's arms were around Emilia, squeezing her tightly and making her grin.

I hadn't wanted to take the photo. It was why Dad was tickling me, trying to get me to smile. Why had I been such a brat that day? Why hadn't I appreciated what was right in front of me? Why hadn't I soaked up every minute I had with them?

My breaths came faster and faster, each one tripping over the previous in an effort to get out. My lungs burned like they had that night as I breathed pure smoke. The sensation, so embedded in my brain, only spurred the panic on.

Biscuit let out a whine as I struggled to get even a shred of oxygen into my system. Black dots danced in front of my vision, and I knew I was going down.

Chapter Eleven

Anson

I WATCHED HER FROM THE MOMENT HER VEHICLE HIT THE DRIVE. It was like I had some damn radar for Rhodes. One I couldn't turn off, no matter how hard I tried.

So, I watched through the soot-stained window like some sort of creeper as she stopped to talk to Owen, Silas, and Carlos. I watched as Silas tried his most charming smiles on her, but none of it worked. Rhodes brushed him off in a way that told me she'd done it countless times before. And while Silas took it in stride, Owen looked pissed the hell off as they all headed for their trucks.

But I didn't stop watching her.

My gaze tracked Rhodes as she parked in front of her guest cottage. As she climbed out of her SUV and helped the dog out of the back seat. Even the damn dog looked up at her adoringly.

There wasn't a person who crossed Rhodes' path that *didn't* seem transfixed by her. It only annoyed me more that I'd become one of the horde.

My back teeth ground together, but I didn't look away.

Rhodes slowed as she reached her front door, not pulling out keys or anything else. She just stared down.

I lifted my hand, scrubbing at the glass with my palm. The soot barely shifted.

Rhodes bent down and picked something up. A prickle of unease, that sixth sense I had, skated over me. I was moving toward the side door of the house before I even had reason to.

The moment I stepped outside, I ripped off the N95 mask I'd been wearing to protect my lungs from any toxins the fire had left behind, keeping my eyes locked on Rhodes. Her shoulders rose and fell in rapid succession, but the movements were shallow.

Shoulder breathing instead of from her diaphragm. Her skin was pale, and she wobbled just a bit.

Fuck.

I picked up speed. Whatever was going on, it wasn't good.

I reached the front porch just as Rhodes' knees buckled. I dove forward, catching her before she hit the wooden planks.

But it was as if Rhodes didn't even register the action. Her breaths rushed in and out so fast I knew she wasn't getting the oxygen she needed. If she didn't slow her breathing, she would end up passing out.

Slowly, I lowered us both to the porch, leaning against the railing as I held Rhodes against me. The dog's gaze went back and forth between us. I expected him to snarl or even lunge; instead, he let out a keening sound. He knew something was wrong.

"Rhodes," I said, my voice gruff. It held a command that I hoped would break through her panic.

Her head turned so she looked in my direction, but her eyes were glassy and unfocused. I knew she wasn't really seeing me.

I cupped the side of her face. Her skin felt incredibly soft, so in opposition to my torn and callused palms. "Look at me," I ordered.

Rhodes blinked, her eyes still unfocused, but I could tell she was trying to come out of it. Attempting to fight.

"You need to slow your breathing," I told her.

Nothing about Rhodes' breathing changed. If anything, it worsened.

I let out a stream of curses. If she didn't slow down, she'd end up unconscious for sure. I threaded my fingers through her hair, pulling it tight. Another sensation for her to focus on, something other than panic.

Rhodes blinked again, her eyes flicking back and forth as she registered the tug on her hair.

"That's it," I encouraged. "You feel that? That means you're here. Feel the wood beneath you. Feel me."

Rhodes shifted as if feeling the things around her for the first time.

I kept up the tiny pulls and releases on her hair. "You've got this. I want you to follow me. Breathe in for four."

I squeezed her arm in a one, two, three, four beat.

"Now, hold it in for a count of seven."

I counted off seven in the same way.

"Now, out for eight. Nice and slow. Don't let the air out all at once."

My hand counted off for her again.

Rhodes couldn't last the full eight, but her breathing became slower overall. I started us back at the beginning and walked her through it four more times before her eyes truly focused on me.

She blinked a few times, finally taking me in. "Anson?"

Rhodes was confused and didn't seem to know how she'd gotten where she was or what had happened.

I tugged my fingers from her hair, instantly missing the feel of the silky strands. "Gotta stop meeting like this, Reckless."

"I—What happened?" she asked as the dog licked her hand.

"You tell me. Saw you through the window. You picked something up and then started having a panic attack."

Rhodes looked up at me. "How'd you know it was a panic attack?"

The truth nearly slipped from my lips, but I caught it just in time, grunting instead. "Know the signs."

She frowned at me, something telling her that wasn't the whole truth.

"What'd you pick up?" I pressed, steering her away from me but also toward the information I needed.

Rhodes' head jerked at that, and she pushed off me, scanning our surroundings. Her gaze stopped on something a few feet from us. She leaned over and snatched it up. "I wasn't sure if I'd imagined it."

I looked down at the piece of paper. No, the photograph. The corners were curled, and the image was warped. Black soot smeared it in places. But you could still make out the people in the picture.

Something about the woman was familiar. Her dark, wild hair and tanned skin. But I stopped dead on the eyes. They were so similar to the ones that had haunted my thoughts for the past week—that mossy green with flames of golden fire throughout.

That had me quickly scanning the rest of the photo and landing on a girl. She couldn't be more than twelve in the shot, but the wildness and recklessness were still there. A living, breathing thing that made Rhodes more real than anyone I'd ever met.

"It's my family," she whispered.

My gut churned. I knew Rhodes had been a foster placement with the Colsons, but that was it. There weren't typically *good* reasons for ending up in foster care, but I hadn't let myself wonder why she'd been put there. Because I hadn't wanted to think about Rhodes at all.

Every thought that worked its way into my brain held a price I couldn't pay. So, I'd done everything I could to keep her out. I couldn't let myself care. Not in any way.

I'd turned away from her. Hadn't wanted to see her pain. And what an asshole that made me.

But now, I couldn't ignore it. Not as Rhodes stared down at the distorted picture, agony in her hazel eyes.

"What happened to them?" The question was out of my mouth before I could stop it. Now that I truly saw her, a desperate need to know more coursed through me. A need to understand all the pieces that came together to create the woman before me.

Those captivating hazel eyes flashed in surprise. "Shep didn't tell you?"

Another prickle of unease skated over me. "No."

Rhodes' throat worked as she struggled to swallow, her gaze shifting to the Victorian. "This was my house." She traced the structure with her eyes as if filling in the burned parts from memory. "Until it wasn't." She bit down on her lip, and I struggled to keep from pulling the flesh out of her teeth's clutches. "They didn't make it out of the fire."

Fuck.

No, I needed a word a hell of a lot stronger than *fuck*. But I wasn't sure the English language had one.

Everything shifted, like one of those tricky images within a picture. You thought you'd figured it out, but then your vision changed, and everything came into crystal-clear focus.

The request to rehab instead of gut the place and start fresh. Rhodes' need to go into the house while no one was around. The way Shep tiptoed around her and constantly checked in. Rhodes was facing her demons here.

My gut twisted. "Where were you when the fire happened?"

I didn't offer her platitudes or I'm sorries. Because none of that did any good. It didn't comfort. It didn't ease. Nothing could. Not in the face of that kind of loss.

Rhodes didn't turn away from the house. "In my bedroom."

A fresh slew of curses slid through my brain. "You got out."

I wasn't sure why I said it; she obviously had if she was sitting here today. But the words somehow reassured me it was true.

Rhodes nodded shallowly. "Tried to climb down the drainpipe outside my balcony. It worked until the fire exploded a window and me with it."

Everything in me stilled. Everything except my eyes. They tracked over her, searching for any signs of the injury. It was then that I saw it. The slightest bit of scarring peeking out from the shorts that stopped at mid-thigh. Shorts that had been taunting me this past week. I'd been so caught up in trying to ignore the toned legs that I'd missed something I never would've at any other time.

The proof of her agony had been everywhere, and I hadn't seen it because I'd been so caught up in my bullshit. The skin was no longer red. It was a kaleidoscope of tan and pale. It looked as if her skin had been painted in staccato brush strokes.

"I don't try to hide them," Rhodes said coolly.

My gaze jumped from her leg to her face. My eyes locked with those haunting hazel ones, something I'd been trying to avoid. But I didn't look away. "Good."

My voice was rough, even to my ears. It sounded like I'd just chain-smoked half a pack and chased it with whiskey.

Rhodes' eyes flared in surprise.

"You shouldn't hide a damned thing, Reckless. Especially not something that proves how strong you are."

She stared at me for a long moment. Something passed between us. Some sort of understanding without words. Finally, Rhodes shoved to her feet. I followed, reaching out to steady her as she wobbled.

"I'm good," she promised.

I didn't call her a liar, even though she was. I glanced down at the photo. "Who left it for you?"

Rhodes frowned. "What do you mean?"

My jaw worked back and forth. "You didn't leave it for yourself, I'm assuming. So, someone else had to."

She glanced back to the house. "Probably one of the crew. Most of them grew up around here and know the story. They probably figured I'd want it but didn't want to give it to me directly. It's not like most of them are great with the feelings stuff. Tears terrify them."

Rhodes was trying to joke about it, but something didn't sit right with me. The area of the house we were currently working on was completely burned out. There were no photos that weren't entirely ash. So, someone must have nosed around before we started the work. I hadn't seen a single soul over at the guest cottage after we started at nine. But things were busy enough that I could've missed it.

Rhodes' eyes narrowed on me. "What?"

"Nothing," I clipped. "You need to go inside and eat. Think you can stay upright long enough to do that?"

Instead of being annoyed with me, Rhodes just smiled. It was far too wide for the situation.

"What are you doing?"

"You like me."

My whole body stiffened. "I do not."

Rhodes' smile only widened more, making the gold in her eyes spark and swirl. "Do, too."

"What are you, five?" I snapped.

She laughed, and the sound hit me somewhere in the vicinity of my chest, digging in and spreading through me. That pins-and-needles sensation you got when a numb limb finally regained feeling. I fucking hated it.

"Anson." Her tongue wrapped around my name in a languid stroke. "If you hated me, you would've left me alone in my panic attack. You would've ignored the fact that I was hurting. But you didn't. You helped. You're not the bad guy you want people to think you are."

The pins-and-needles feeling intensified until it was just shy of pain. "You don't know me," I croaked.

Something passed over Rhodes' expression. "No, I don't. But I'd like to. Because I think you could use a friend."

Friend.

The urge to scoff was so strong. *Friends* wasn't something I could be with Rhodes. For many reasons. A *friend* didn't think about shoving the other against a wall and driving into them so hard they couldn't breathe. A *friend* didn't imagine wrapping the other's hair around his fist as he fucked her mouth. A *friend* didn't picture what the other would look like sprawled across his sheets while he ate her until she screamed.

"Anson?" Rhodes said, breaking into my spiraling thoughts.

"Go inside, Reckless." That rasp was back, but this time, it wasn't pain lacing my tone. It was need.

Her brows pulled together. "Are you—?"

"Inside." My command wasn't harsh. I couldn't find it in me to push her away in that manner anymore. Not when I knew the truth about what she'd been through.

As if Rhodes saw that I was at my breaking point, she nodded slowly and tugged the dog toward the door. But as she slipped her key inside the lock, she turned. "Thank you, Anson."

Hearing her say my name was the most beautiful kind of torture. I didn't reply. Didn't trust what might come out of my mouth.

Finally, Rhodes turned back and opened the door, slipping inside with her faithful companion. I stood there for a moment, unable to move. A deep woof from inside finally spurred me into motion. The last thing I needed was to still be standing here if Rhodes came back outside.

I stalked off the porch and headed down the driveway. I pulled my keys out of one pocket and my phone out of the other. While I beeped the locks on my truck, I tapped a few icons on the screen of my phone. I hit my favorites list. It was embarrassingly short. Shep topped it, being the person I talked to the most. Followed by my friend, Lawson, who had refused to let me disappear from his life. He'd blackmailed me into bi-monthly check-ins, telling me if I didn't answer, he'd come to Sparrow Falls for proof of life. And lastly, a contact at the bureau. I hadn't used that one in over a year.

I hit Shep's name. He picked up on the second ring. "What's wrong?"

"Jesus," I muttered.

"You don't call unless something's wrong," Shep defended. "Unless you've suddenly developed a taste for pleasant chitchat."

"Fuck off," I muttered.

"You called *me*," he shot back.

Fair enough. I worked my jaw back and forth. "Why didn't you tell me the house belonged to Rhodes' family?"

Shep was quiet for a moment. "I didn't hide it. I just figured it wasn't something you'd want to hear about."

He wasn't wrong. I hadn't exactly been champing at the bit to hear others' sob stories. I'd been too caught up in mine. Couldn't handle feeling any more pain. God, it was time to pull my head out of my ass. "Well, it might've kept me from stepping in it if I'd known."

"What'd you do?" Shep demanded.

"I didn't *do* anything. But someone left a picture of Rhodes and her family on the guest cottage's front porch. She had a panic attack."

"Hell," Shep muttered. "Where is she now? Is she okay? I'm on my way."

"Take a breath," I ordered.

"You just told me my sister had a panic attack," he growled.

"She's okay," I assured him. Even if that wasn't the case, at least not entirely, I knew Rhodes would get there. She was too tough not to. "Walked her through a breathing exercise, and she was able to get through it." I left out the part about me catching her. Holding her. Even though the memory was burned in my brain.

The sound of an engine starting up came over the line. "Thanks, man. I know—"

"She matters to you. I wasn't going to walk away." But that wasn't entirely true. I hadn't run across the gravel drive because of some sense of duty to Shep. I'd charged over because I couldn't stand the thought of Rhodes in pain or danger. And that meant I was screwed.

I hurried to change the line of conversation. "You need to have a word with the crew. No more surprise gifts."

"I will," Shep clipped. "I'm sure they thought they were doing the right thing, but…hell, she wasn't ready for that."

Endless questions filled my mind. My profiler brain wanted to put all the pieces of the story together, but I had no right to a lot of those pieces. I stuck with the ones that were fair game. "It was electrical, right?"

"Yeah," Shep said, his blinker sounding in the background. "Someone on the fire crew found frayed wiring while doing cleanup. An antique lamp that never should've been plugged in."

My jaw clenched, the muscles along it popping. A damn lamp. A piece of decoration someone had bought because they thought it added character. Something they never would've done if they'd known what it was capable of.

I cleared my throat. "She said she was hurt in the fire."

Shep went quiet again. I couldn't tell if it was because of surprise or him taking time to choose his next words carefully. "She was in the hospital for a month. Skin grafts, rehab, the works. Toughest person I know, fighting through that kind of pain."

An invisible fist shoved against my chest. Twisted. "How old was she?"

"Just turned thirteen."

So damn young. Way too young to endure that kind of loss and trauma. But I knew better than most that the Universe didn't pull any punches when it came to pain. It could lash out when you least expected it. And take out the most undeserving in its wrath.

Chapter Twelve

Rhodes

A WARM, FURRY BODY PRESSED AGAINST MY LEG AS I SAT perched on a stool at the Bloom counter. I looked down into pleading eyes. "Biscuit," I warned. "Egg sandwiches are for people."

He let out a short but piercing bark.

My eyes narrowed on him. "That is not how to get what you want."

Biscuit plunked his butt on the floor, his tongue lolling out of his mouth.

"That's better." I broke off a piece of bacon sticking out of my breakfast creation. "Down."

Biscuit immediately dropped his belly to the concrete.

I let go of the piece of bacon, and the dog caught it easily.

"You're going to give that dog bad manners," a deep voice warned.

At the sound, Biscuit was instantly up, snarling and barking. He put his paws on the counter, trying to see over it to the other side.

Trace simply arched an eyebrow, his sheriff's star shining as he shifted to get a better look. "At least you've got an early warning system now. Thinking about keeping this one?"

"I foster them. The whole point is to get them ready for their forever families."

Trace leaned against the counter, his gaze still on Biscuit, who had finally stopped growling but was sticking close. "You don't want to be a forever family?"

Twitchiness swept through me, but I did my best not to show it. Trace saw too much as it was. "I like helping them on their path. If I had a pet at home, they might not get along with my fosters. It could create all sorts of problems."

Trace made a humming noise in the back of his throat.

"So," I said, searching for something—anything—that would deflect Trace's analytical focus on me. "You talk to Arden lately?"

I was the worst sister ever. Throwing Arden under the bus was lower than low. But everyone was always a little worried about her. Maybe because she was the youngest, maybe because of what she'd been through.

Trace stiffened. "Something wrong? Someone bothering her—?"

I shook my head quickly. "No, no. Nothing like that." *Shit.* I should've known our most protective sibling would freak. "I just haven't seen her in a while. I need to go over there. Maybe I'll bring her a plant."

Trace relaxed, the tension bleeding out of his muscles. "You know you're not going to see her unless you go over there."

That was a bit of an exaggeration, but it was true that Arden rarely left the guesthouse on Cope's massive property. She served as a sort of caretaker for the place while he was up in Seattle playing hockey, but it was a mostly made-up position. A way to give her someplace safe and quiet to make her art.

But she did venture out for family dinners or to go into town for supplies. Just not much else.

"I've been falling down on the whole sister gig," I muttered.

Trace reached over, squeezing my shoulder. "Never. But you are falling down on letting us know what's going on."

It was my turn to stiffen.

Trace pinned me with that all-too-knowing stare. "You had a panic attack."

I blew out a breath. Who knew that Anson, a man who could barely string two sentences together, had such a big mouth? But I knew it wasn't actually him. He'd told Shep, and Shep would share it with anyone he thought *needed* to be in the loop.

"As you can see, I'm just fine. It was a surprise, that's all. But I have to get used to seeing photos and mementos. It won't be long before I can get into the house to go through things."

Concern swept over Trace's face. "You don't have to do this, Rho."

I met his gaze, forcing myself not to look away. "I know that. But I want to. I miss them."

Being brought into the Colsons' fold had been a beautiful thing. Some foster kids didn't like the idea of being a part of a new family, but I'd welcomed being surrounded by their care and love. While I didn't call Nora *Mom,* she knew she would always be that to me in all the ways that mattered. I'd slipped easily into thinking of Cope, Shep, Trace, and Arden as siblings. Even Kye, who'd come to live with us later. And I'd always thought of Fallon as a sister.

But that didn't mean I missed my family any less. Their absence was an ache I felt each and every day. We'd shared things that I'd never have with anyone else.

Sympathy swept across Trace's face. "Of course, you do. But they wouldn't want you to put yourself through something that could affect your mental health."

I gripped the edge of the counter, letting it press into my palms. "I want to remember them." I'd boxed them away for so long because I couldn't deal with the reality of them being gone. I was ready now. I didn't want to pretend like they never existed anymore.

I felt more than a small amount of guilt about that. But I knew none of them would want that. They'd want me to go at my own pace.

When I felt overwhelmed growing up, my dad would bend down to meet my eyes and say, *"You can only do what you can do."*

Trace sighed. "Okay. But I don't want you doing it alone. And I don't want people leaving damn photos on your porch. It's like a sneak attack. Shep's having a word with the crew."

I groaned. "He doesn't need to have a *word*. I'm a grown-up. I can deal."

"Maybe so, but you've also got family who cares about you. You're not alone in this."

Knowing that was the most beautiful pain. Knowing that I'd been given this amazing ragtag group of humans because I'd lost my family. I took in a lungful of air, letting the scents of flowers in the greenhouse fill my senses. It grounded me and reminded me to be grateful for the here and now.

"Thanks, T," I said softly.

"Anytime." He pinned me with another of those Trace stares. "You tell me if any more shit gets dropped on your doorstep."

"Yeah, yeah," I grumbled.

"I'm serious, Rho. I don't like someone nosing around."

A shiver raced across my skin at the thought, but I shoved the sensation away. "It's just someone on the crew trying to be helpful."

Trace grunted. "Either way, I want to know."

"Okay," I promised. "I'll tell you."

"Thank you." Trace tapped the counter twice. "I'll check on you later. Keep that dog close."

I rolled my eyes but waved to him. Bending down, I scratched Biscuit between the ears. "He's kind of overbearing, huh?"

Footsteps sounded, and I looked up to see Duncan approaching.

"Saw Trace stop by in uniform. Everything okay?" he asked, little lines appearing between his brows.

"Totally fine. Just checking in big-brother-style."

Duncan didn't seem convinced. "He doesn't usually do that when he's on duty. Are you sure everything's okay?"

I fought the urge to scream. "They're all just being a little extra attentive now that I'm back at the Victorian." I couldn't bring myself to say *home*. Not yet.

"Rho." Duncan's entire face morphed into sympathy. He reached across the counter and took my hand in his. The action was so startling I had to fight the urge to jerk back. Duncan and I were friendly but not touchy-feely. We hugged once in a blue moon, but that was it. He squeezed my hand. "Maybe it's too much. Maybe you should stay in the cottage in town."

I tugged my hand out of his grasp, shoving it beneath the counter. "There's already another tenant there."

"There are plenty of other places to stay. You know you're always welcome in my guesthouse. For as long as you want."

Duncan's offer was more than kind, but it annoyed me somehow. "I'm good where I am. It's where I want to be."

He opened his mouth but then closed it again, sighing. "All right. But my offer doesn't have a time limit."

"Thank you," I said, my voice stiff.

Duncan shifted his weight from foot to foot. "Your friend came by while you were on break."

I frowned. "My friend?"

"Thea."

I brightened at that news. "Did you interview her? What'd you think? She's super nice and knowledgeable about plants."

Duncan chuckled. "I offered her the job, and she took it."

"That's amazing! Thank you so much. I know she'll be an asset to the team."

Duncan scrubbed a hand over his cheek. "She knows more than a lot of people we currently have on staff." He paused for a moment. "You know what the request to be paid in cash is all about?"

I shook my head. "No clue."

"It's weird. She said to go ahead and report it to the IRS, gave me her social and everything, but just asked that I not store anything electronically."

I frowned. "She said something about not being a fan of technology. She doesn't have a phone or email."

Duncan let out a low whistle. "Can't imagine not having my cell."

It was my turn to laugh. "You mean you can't imagine not being able to play Candy Crush on your breaks."

Color hit his cheeks. "Truth. Speaking of, I'm about due for my fix."

"Enjoy," I called as he headed toward the door.

I made quick work of finishing my sandwich, giving in to Biscuit's pleading eyes twice. "I'm hopeless," I muttered as I slid off the stool.

Biscuit just licked his lips in answer.

I headed down each aisle of plants, taking inventory of how everything was doing. I paid close attention to the seedlings, as it was easy for them to go the wrong direction—and fast—but they were thriving. I swore they'd grown an inch since yesterday.

"Hey, Rho," a masculine voice greeted.

I straightened and turned to face the man. Same tanned skin, amber eyes, and kind smile. That smile would always remind me of simpler times when I thought a kiss was the answer to all my hopes and dreams. "Hi, Felix. How are you?"

He smiled wider. "Good. Just picking up a few things for my mom. She's determined to outdo Ms. Cathy next door with her pots this year."

I couldn't help but laugh. "Well, given everything I pulled for her earlier, she shouldn't have any problems. It's all in the loading area, but I can ring you up in here."

"Thanks. That'd be great."

I led the way to the counter. At the sound of approaching people, Biscuit scrambled up. He let out a low growl as he caught sight of Felix.

"Easy, Biscuit. He's a friend."

Felix took in the dog. "New foster?"

I nodded as I went in search of Mrs. Hernandez's invoice. "Not the biggest fan of men, but we're working on it."

"You'll get him fixed up," Felix assured me.

I tugged the piece of paper out of a file folder. "I hope so. That'll be six hundred thirty-six dollars and thirteen cents."

"Jesus," he muttered. "She really went to town."

I bit back my laugh. "I hope you brought your truck."

Felix handed me his credit card. "I have a feeling that's why she asked me to run this *little errand* for her."

"She always was a smart woman."

I could feel Felix's eyes on me as I punched in the amount on the credit card machine without looking up.

He shuffled his feet, his boots scraping against the cement floor. "Heard you're back at your parents' place."

"Small towns," I muttered. "Nothing's secret."

Felix chuckled, the sound warm and easy. "I'm glad for you. I know it has to be a mixed bag, but I think it's good you can finally go home again."

I lifted my gaze to his. "Thank you." I was pretty sure he was the first person to tell me he was happy for me. And, God, I'd needed that more than I realized.

Felix took his credit card back from me. "If you need an extra set of hands for anything, just let me know."

"Will do."

I watched as he headed out of the greenhouse, his words swirling in my head. *It's good you can finally go home again.*

It *was* good. I just had to make it through the hard to get to that good. Panic attacks and all.

Chapter Thirteen

Anson

"**Y**OU SURE THIS DRYWALL HAS TO COME OUT?" OWEN ASKED, his voice raised to carry through his mask.

I jerked my head in a nod. "It's all gotta go."

"Fuck, man," he whined. "It's gonna take us all day tomorrow. There's not even fire damage."

Annoyance ate at me. It was always the same with Owen. He wanted to cut corners or thought he knew more than everyone else. I sure as hell wouldn't want him working on my house without supervision.

I picked up my crowbar and placed it between the seams of drywall. I freed the panel with two hard cranks and tossed it to the side, revealing the framing. It was covered with soot and who knew what other things from the fire. Leaving this sort of thing behind could mean serious health risks to the residents of the home. Not to mention the fact that we needed to make sure there hadn't been actual damage to the frame.

Silas let out a low whistle as he crouched low to examine the framing. "I can't believe the smoke made it all the way to the other side of the house."

"It's just smoke," Owen grumbled.

"Smoke that can mean serious health implications if it's not cleaned properly," I snapped.

"Whatever. It's five. I'm calling it." He headed for a side door without asking if it was okay.

That was part of the problem with Shep's company getting so busy. He wasn't always around, and Owen didn't follow the rules unless Shep forced him to.

Silas pushed to his feet. "Don't worry about him. He has a hangover from hell today, that's all."

I didn't care what the reason was. I cared whether Owen did his job. "I want you on treatment tomorrow. Owen can pull drywall."

Silas's brows lifted. "He's gonna be pissed."

"Don't care," I clipped. "He's proven time and again that I can't trust him."

Silas sighed. "Fair enough. You need anything else before I head out?"

I shook my head. "I'll see you tomorrow."

"You got it, fire man." He headed for the door with a half-hearted wave.

I made one last pass through the downstairs. We'd made good progress over the past week or so, but this job was a true marathon and not one we could rush.

After giving everything a last once-over, I slipped out the back door and locked it behind me, pulling off my mask. Now that people in town knew we were rehabbing the place, we ran the risk of more lookie-loos. Locking up was good, but I wondered if I should talk to Shep about installing some cameras.

Laughter caught on the breeze, light and free. The sound was so pure it almost hurt to listen to it. Yet I couldn't stop myself from searching out the source.

Rhodes sat with her toned legs on either side of a blue pot while her dog danced toward her and then away, something in his mouth.

Her head tipped back again, laughter set free as her wild mahogany hair spilled down her back—strands I wanted to sink my fingers into as I took her mouth and swallowed that laughter whole.

I moved toward her without thought, as if she held me in some sort of trance, that laughter her siren's song.

"Biscuit," she chided, eyes shining.

The dog just kept dancing, and as I approached, I saw he had a trowel in his mouth.

Rhodes dove for him, but he danced out of her grasp yet again. The exchange only made her laugh again.

That damn sound. I'd never get it out of my head.

As she straightened, she caught sight of me. "Anson."

I didn't say anything. Couldn't. Didn't trust whatever words might come out of my mouth.

She was too fucking gorgeous for her own good, all tumbling waves and tanned skin. Curves peeking out of shorts and a tank top. And those hazel eyes. Witch eyes that entranced with their golden flames.

Her brows pulled together. "Everything okay?"

I forced my gaze away from her face, taking in everything around her—the pots, the flowers. I scowled. "Everything's so bright."

Another laugh burst out of Rhodes, but this one was stronger, wilder. It hit me like a freight train, nearly making me stumble back a step.

She grinned up at me, the second blow in a one-two punch. "Says the king of anti-color."

My scowl just deepened. "King of anti-color?"

That grin morphed into a full smile as she gestured behind me. "Black truck with not even so much as a bumper sticker."

Of course, there were no stickers on my vehicle. That kind of thing just gave people insight into who you were.

Rhodes drew a circle in the air between us. "Gray T-shirt." Her hand lowered. "Dark-wash jeans. I guess there is a little blue in there, but barely." Then she pointed to my shoes. "Even your boots are black. What did color ever do to you?"

"Reminds me of what I lost." The words were out of my mouth before I could stop them. I blamed those hazel eyes holding me hostage.

All the amusement fled Rhodes' face in an instant. I braced for an onslaught of questions, but they didn't come. Instead, she kept her gaze on me, not looking away from the pain I was sure was carved into my face. "I'm sorry. For whatever you lost."

So many people were uncomfortable with agony. They couldn't stand to see others in the throes of grief because it reminded them of what was at stake in their lives. That they, too, could lose everything in a flash.

Rhodes kept those hypnotizing eyes on me as she took a deep breath. "I know it's hard to have the reminders around. It's easier to lock them away. But sometimes you need to just take the first step."

Pain pulsed deep in my chest, the memory of my sister still beating there. Greta's vibrancy. Her laugh. She would've loved Rhodes on sight.

Rhodes patted the ground next to her. "Maybe you start with one pot of flowers." She shot me a smirk. "I'll even give you my most boring pot. Least amount of color."

I scanned the pot between her legs. It was deep indigo blue. Not the brightest of the bunch, but its variegated tones were still more than I was used to. Everything in my life was about necessity and nothing more. No extra comforts or luxuries. Maybe that was part of my self-inflicted punishment.

Even knowing all of that, I couldn't find it in me to reject Rhodes' offer, couldn't quash the hope in her eyes. "You want me to help you pot flowers."

She smiled full-out again, that punch of light, life, and beauty. "Yes. For your front porch."

I stiffened. "It's your pot. Your flowers."

"Ever heard of a gift, Anson?"

I glared at her. "I don't need any gifts."

Rhodes rolled her eyes. "It's flowers, not a diamond tennis bracelet. I've got more of these than I know what to do with."

I didn't respond, simply kept staring, caught in the battle between risk and reward.

"Stop being such a grump and sit down. It'll take five minutes."

Something about the exasperation in her tone had me obeying. I lowered myself to the patchy grass, but I made a fatal error.

I was too close.

Close enough to smell the mix of sunscreen with the hint of sweet peas. I knew what those flowers looked like because they'd been one of my mother's favorites. But they weren't anywhere in the bunch surrounding us. That meant it was Rhodes' perfume, or worse, her body lotion. Just thinking about her working that into her legs, her arms, her—I shoved the thoughts from my head as I shifted uncomfortably.

A snort sounded beside me, and I jerked my head up.

Rhodes was full-on grinning. "You look like you're about to be tortured, not plant a few flowers."

"I do not," I grumbled.

She grabbed the cell phone lying next to her in the grass, and the shutter sounded. "A picture is worth a thousand words." She showed me the screen.

I winced. I looked like I'd been sucking on a lemon. *Jesus.* I needed to get a grip. "It's been a long day," I defended.

"Mm-hmm," Rhodes hummed, not sounding at all convinced. "Maybe these poppies will put you in a better mood. They're one of my favorites."

I glanced at the plastic pots next to her, taking in the riot of colors. "They're pink."

Rhodes raised her brows in a challenge. "Not man enough for a little pink on your front porch?"

My back teeth ground together. "Let's just pot them already."

The dog moseyed over and dropped the trowel next to me as if in agreement.

"Good job, Biscuit," Rhodes praised, giving him a treat.

"Biscuit?" I asked.

"He's got a penchant for them."

"Shouldn't be giving him human food."

Rhodes sent the dog a sidelong look. "You hear that, Biscuit? He doesn't think I should give you any bacon."

I swore the damn dog understood every single word. His head swiveled around, and he glared at me with accusing eyes.

"Throw me under the bus, why don't you?"

A soft chuckle escaped Rhodes. She had so many different kinds of laughs, and I was starting to get addicted to finding each new one. Her hazel eyes shone as they connected with mine. "It's only fair that Biscuit knows who he's dealing with."

I shook my head. "Better if you don't give him a taste of the good stuff. He could get used to it."

"A little of the good stuff never hurt anyone."

Not unless you lost it.

As if sensing my shifting mood, Rhodes turned to the flowers. "I already prepped the pot with gravel at the bottom and a good, rich soil. Now, we just have to create space for these babies."

I picked up the small shovel that Biscuit had dropped. "How many holes do you need?"

"Three," she instructed.

I got to work moving the soil around to create homes for the poppies.

Rhodes leaned forward, examining my work. I felt her more than I saw her. The shift in the energy in the air, the scent of sweet peas teasing my nose.

"You're pretty good at that," she said.

"Done it a time or two." Whenever my mom had badgered me into it. Maybe I would've done it more often if I'd known I'd lose her and my dad along with Greta. My mom wasn't six feet under, but she might as well be for all she wanted to do with me.

Rhodes didn't press with questions; she simply placed one of the poppy plants into a hole I'd created. With gentle fingers, she pressed them into the soil, covering their roots with some excess.

"No gardening gloves?" My mom had been religious about wearing them, never wanting the dirt to stain her fingers.

Rhodes shook her head. "I can't feel what I need to with gloves."

I frowned as I watched her place the next two bundles of blooms. "What do you need to feel?"

She shrugged, the action sending some of that wild hair into her face. "The give of the soil. Whether there's resistance or not. If the plant works where I'm placing it." A small smile played on her lips. "Might sound woo-woo, but I swear the soil talks to me. There's an energy to it. I never want to miss what it tells me."

Rhodes lifted her head, brushing the hair out of her face and leaving a smear of dirt behind.

I lifted my hand without conscious thought, my thumb swiping across her cheek. "It is fucking woo-woo. But it's you."

Our gazes locked, and those golden flames swirled in her mossy green depths. Rhodes' breath hitched, making her chest rise as her lips parted.

Fuck. Fuck. Fuck.

I jerked my hand back as if I'd been burned. I didn't think I'd ever gotten to my feet faster, and that included when a suspect unexpectedly started shooting at my team. "I gotta get home."

I expected to find rejection, even hurt in Rhodes' eyes, but there was something entirely different. Understanding. She just smiled easily and inclined her head toward the pot. "Don't forget your poppies. They need full sun. Water them about once a week. You can stick a finger in the soil to see if it's dry."

I didn't waste my time arguing with her. I didn't trust my restraint. I just bent, grabbed the pot, and took off for my truck without so much as a muttered *thank you.* God, I was an asshole. But what else was new?

⁓

I took a pull of my ginger beer and glared at the pink flowers on my porch steps. Having them there made me realize just how devoid of color the rest of the cabin was. It had come furnished but without linens. Apparently, everything I'd bought had been in shades of gray. Even the damn Adirondack chair I was sitting in.

Forcing my gaze away from the accusatory blooms, I returned to my crossword. It wasn't cutting it today. I'd gotten too many too easily. Five-letter word for pirate's woman. Really? Wench wasn't exactly a stretch.

I shifted in the chair, setting down my bottle. Rho's face kept playing in my mind—such light, even though she'd walked through so much darkness. What was it that allowed people to keep that light? Whatever it was, it was clear I didn't have it. But it only made me more curious.

It also made me realize why people called her Rho. Rhodes, as pretty as the name was, was too formal. Too, fancy. Rho felt more salt of the earth. More *her*.

With an annoyed grunt, I dropped my crossword book and pen to the ground and reached for the laptop on the table next to me. I flipped it open and signed into my virtual private network. The bureau had some of the best hackers in the country on their payroll, and I'd picked up a thing or two from them over my years there. I wished like hell I'd heeded their warnings back then, but I took it seriously now.

You left breadcrumbs in your wake every time you ventured onto the internet. Now, I made sure the path I left could never be traced back to me.

Opening a browser, I typed in *fire, historic home, Sparrow Falls, Oregon.* A slew of articles populated the screen, and it didn't take me long to find one that hit.

Stirling Family Killed in Blaze.

My brain kicked into focus, that speed-reading class I'd taken as part of my training coming in handy. People didn't think about the amount of research in profiling. Reading crime scene reports and case files, not to mention shrink records. It wasn't always chasing bad guys in dark alleys. In fact, it rarely was. Because the bad guys were often the people you least expected.

A few sentences stood out in my perusal.

Thirteen-year-old daughter in critical condition.

Fire started by faulty wiring.

Victims killed by smoke inhalation.

There were small mercies in the fact that none of them had been burned alive. Everything about it seemed fairly typical. Accidents happened. But something didn't sit right with me. Why hadn't a smoke detector woken them in time? At least enough time for the parents to get a call out.

That prickle of warning scratched at the back of my skull. I opened a different browser window and typed in a new search. *Fire, Sparrow Falls, Oregon.*

Countless results popped up. I narrowed them to the few years before and after the fire that killed Rho's family. A bunch of the hits were for a wildfire the year after. I added *wildfire* to the negative search terms.

Bingo.

My gaze narrowed on the refreshed results. I clicked on one that caught my eye.

Series of Downtown Dumpster Fires Remains Unsolved

I quickly scanned the article. Half a dozen fires had cropped up over a series of weeks a few months before Rho's fire. They were always at night, and they'd had no luck in catching the perpetrator.

Security cameras weren't as prevalent fourteen years ago, especially in small communities like this one. There was no way shops and restaurants would've been able to afford them.

I navigated back to the search page, skimming over the results again. My gaze halted on another article from the local paper. My gut churned as I clicked on it.

Fire at Middle School, Prank Suspected

Reading the article as quickly as possible, I gleaned a few important facts. It had started in the girls' locker room while various sports teams were practicing. It was quickly contained but looked to have been started by fireworks lit in a trash can set on one of the benches.

The prickle of warning turned into an inferno. Something wasn't right here. What if the fire crew had missed something in Rhodes' house all those years ago? What if it hadn't been an accident? What if someone had set that fire?

Chapter Fourteen

Rhodes

I HOISTED THE BAG OF SOIL OUT OF THE GATOR AND ONTO THE pile for sale. My back, thighs, and arms burned with the strain, but it was a good burn, the kind that reminded you what your body was capable of. And for me, it meant that I was still alive to feel the strain.

I lost myself in the repetition of it all. The back and forth, up and down. But a single face played in my mind as I did. The dark blond hair, the thick scruff. Those haunting blue-gray eyes. And I heard Anson's words over and over in my head. *"Reminds me of what I lost."*

A sharp ache carved itself into my chest. I was familiar with the sensation. It created a hole so deep nothing could ever fill it. You just walked around the world with this gaping wound that left you with a permanent grasping sensation at your very core. Because you were missing something fundamental to who you were.

What was Anson missing?

Some variation of the question had been playing in my mind since yesterday. When I left for work this morning, I'd seen the king of anti-color's black truck, but no sign of the man. Sometimes, I thought he was part ghost. Or maybe he was just an expert at avoiding me.

Because we'd had a…*moment*. And I got the sense that Anson didn't allow himself to have those with anyone. He didn't even really seem to let his guard down around Shep, and my brother was his best friend. It made me sad for Anson because that had to be one lonely existence.

A beep sounded, bringing me out of my Anson-obsessed thoughts. I looked up to see Thea backing up another Gator stacked high with bags of soil.

"This is the last load," she called over the sound.

"Thank the plant gods," I said, raising my hands to the sky.

Thea laughed as she climbed out of the vehicle. "I feel like Duncan might owe us hazard pay for this one."

"He at least owes us a beer," I muttered.

The work at Bloom was always physical, but today had been on another level. A delayed delivery had finally shown up on top of another that had come early, and that was all in addition to the two deliveries we'd been expecting.

I sent Thea a smile. "Have I told you lately how glad I am that you started working here?"

She snorted as she hoisted a bag of soil onto her shoulder. "I definitely don't need any fancy gym membership."

I arched a brow. "Did you have one?"

Thea tossed the bag onto our growing pile. "Definitely not. Although I wouldn't mind sitting in a hot tub after a day like today."

"Same," I said with a groan. "I think I need to talk to my brother about what it would take to put one in at my place."

Thea moved back to the Gator for another bag of soil. "Does he sell them or something?"

I shook my head. "He's a contractor. Runs Colson Construction."

Her eyes widened a fraction. "I've seen some of his builds. They're incredible."

I beamed with pride. Shep had worked hard to grow his business. And while he didn't have an architecture degree, his designs *were* incredible. He often drew up his own plans, complete with an infinite number of high-tech gadgets, and had an architect friend look them over and sign off. It was incredible to see people appreciate everything he did.

"Shep is pretty amazing. He's doing a restoration project for me right now on a historic home, but I'm thinking I might need some updates when it comes to the backyard."

Thea tossed the next bag of soil onto our pile. "If that includes a hot tub, I think you're a genius."

I chuckled. "I promise to invite you over if it happens."

A little of Thea's smile slipped then, as if the idea of coming over wasn't something she was all that comfortable with. She didn't have any close friends, at least as far as I could tell, and that had to be hard.

"Rho," a voice called out.

I turned and fought a groan as I saw Davis heading toward me. He looked so out of place in his slacks and Gucci loafers. I was sure he'd be madly cleaning the dirt off the expensive shoes the moment he got back into his car.

It was so opposite of the boy I'd known in high school. That one had favored hiking boots and Carhartts. Now, all he seemed to care about was computers, money, and status.

Why I'd said yes to that date a couple of months ago was beyond me. I should've seen the changes in him and run as fast as my legs could take me. But Nora had kept asking me those carefully couched questions about whether I was interested in anyone. And suggested I should sign up for one of those online dating services. She didn't mean to be pushy, but she wanted all her *kids* to be happy and taken care of. And I'd felt the weight.

"Hey, Davis," I greeted, trying to keep things cordial. "Looking for some plants?"

He scowled as if flowers were somehow offensive to him. "No, but I need to talk to you. Away from that brute."

Brute? Since when did Davis use words like that? "You mean Anson?"

I had to admit, seeing Anson put Davis in his place had been more than a little amusing.

Davis's eyes narrowed. "Who is he anyway? I've never seen him before. I hope Shepard didn't hire some random off the street. He should let me run a background check."

Annoyance stirred. That was something else Davis had started doing in the last couple of years. Calling everyone by their full name, even if they clearly preferred their nickname. "Anson is *Shep's* best friend from college. So, I hardly think a background check is necessary."

Davis visibly stiffened at the revelation. "Then why haven't I met him before? I asked around about him, and it seems like no one knows much about him."

My annoyance began bubbling over into anger. "Why do you care? He has nothing to do with you."

"He's around *you*. That matters to me," Davis gritted out.

Oh, hell. This was the last thing I needed. Some sort of pissing contest between Davis—a man I wanted nothing to do with—and Anson, a man who wanted nothing to do with me.

I felt heat at my side and glanced to my left to see Thea moving in a bit closer. Her face had gone pale, and she'd fisted her hands at her sides. "Do you want me to find Duncan?"

Shit.

More of the pieces of the Thea puzzle fell into place, and I wanted to junk-punch Davis for triggering her.

"Excuse me," Davis bit out. "This is a private conversation."

I expected Thea to cower or retreat, but she surprised me. Her cheeks pinked, and she squared her shoulders. "Then maybe you shouldn't be having it in public, at Rho's place of *work*. Or maybe you shouldn't be having it at all because it sounds like none of this is your business."

Davis's jaw went slack as he stared at her for a moment. Then his gaze cut to me. "This is who you're choosing to spend time with? She clearly has boundary issues and is prone to inappropriate outbursts."

Thea's fists clenched at her sides again. "Looks to me like you're the one with *boundary* issues, buddy."

"How dare—?"

"Davis," I cut him off. "We aren't dating anymore. We were never serious or exclusive. I don't need you poking into my life or questioning who I spend time with. I think it's best for both of us if we keep our distance for a while. I hope you find the person who will make you happy."

"Spend time with?" he gritted out.

God, was that all he heard?

"You need to leave," I said. My voice was calm and firm, but a trickle of unease slid through me at Davis's persistence. It felt completely out of proportion given the time we'd spent together.

His eyes narrowed. "You'll be begging to make this up to me in a few weeks."

Thankfully, he turned on his heel and stomped off, just like a toddler throwing a tantrum.

I sighed, my shoulders slumping as I collapsed onto our soil display. "I'm so sorry. I swear I'm not usually a drama magnet."

Thea's gaze was still locked on Davis's retreating form. Finally, she forced her focus away from him and toward me. "You need to be careful."

"He's annoying but harmless," I assured her. "He's just used to women in our town falling at his feet."

She shook her head, her hair spilling over her shoulders. "You don't know that. Just promise me you'll be careful."

The panic in her eyes had me hurrying to agree. "I will. If he keeps bothering me, I'll talk to my brother."

Thea's brow furrowed. "The contractor?"

I chuckled. "No. But Shep would put the fear of God into him if I asked. I have three other brothers. The oldest, Trace, is the sheriff. He'd be more than happy to give Davis a little warning."

Thea's entire body stiffened at the word *sheriff*, but she turned to grab another bag of soil, fighting through her reaction. "That's a lot of siblings."

I could tell she didn't want to stay on the subject. Something about it had stirred up demons for her, and I knew how that was. I pushed off our pile and grabbed another bag. "Four brothers and two sisters. Since I was thirteen, anyway."

Thea stilled, a bag halfway to our pile. Her eyes asked countless questions, but she didn't voice them.

I appreciated that she didn't want to push. I didn't especially like dwelling on that time in my life. But maybe if I opened up to Thea, she'd eventually feel comfortable enough to tell me what she was running from. "My family passed away in a fire when I was thirteen. I didn't really have any remaining relatives—not any that wanted me anyway. My best friend's family took me in. They were already fostering others."

Empathy washed over Thea's expression as she dropped the bag of soil onto our pile. "I'm so sorry, Rho. I can't imagine how hard that must've been."

"It was. But I am incredibly lucky that I landed with the Colsons. They gave me a family when I needed it the most, and that has never stopped. A lot of foster kids aren't nearly as lucky."

Her lips rolled over her teeth as she nodded. "I'm glad you had that."

Thea jerked, her eyes going wide as someone grabbed me from behind, pinching my side.

I shrieked, whirling to find Shep's lopsided grin peeking out from below his ballcap. "You were in another world," he said with a chuckle.

I smacked his chest. "It's rude to sneak up on people."

"Just keeping you on your toes." Shep's gaze moved from me to Thea, who had taken a few steps back. His eyes roamed over her face, stilling on her mouth for a beat longer than necessary. "Hi. I'm Shep."

Thea swallowed hard, her throat working with the action. "Hi."

There was no warmth or welcome in her tone. Her voice might as well have been a stone wall.

Shep frowned in confusion. "I'm Rho's brother."

Thea nodded, turning back to her work without another word, completely ignoring him.

Awkward.

I had to fight a chuckle. Shep was so used to the women of Sparrow Falls clamoring for his attention. Or at the very least, being receptive to his golden retriever personality. Not the case this time.

"Thea's our newest hire, and I'm thanking my lucky stars Dunc brought her on."

Shep didn't look away from her as I spoke. "That's great. Where'd you move from?"

There was the slightest hitch in Thea's movements at the question. "The Midwest," she mumbled.

Shep's frown only deepened. He opened his mouth to ask another question, but I grabbed his arm, distracting him.

"What are you here for?" I asked, trying to rescue Thea.

He finally looked my way. "Decided to fill in more of the backyard up on Hillhurst."

"The back fence line?"

He nodded. "You were right, we need more shrubs and grasses."

I laughed. "Hold on, let me get my phone. I want to record that you're-right part."

"Shut up," Shep grumbled, giving me a little shove. "Duncan's having everything pulled right now, but I thought I'd come say hi."

I threw my arms around him and squeezed hard. "I'm glad you did."

He ruffled my hair. "Have to make sure you're not getting into too much trouble."

I ducked out of his grasp. "Good luck with that."

He chuckled. "I'd better go move the truck around. I'll be at the Victorian later."

"Sounds good."

Shep glanced in Thea's direction. "It was nice to meet you."

She made a humming noise and gave him a brief nod but didn't say a word.

Shep's frown was back, and I had to bite the inside of my cheek to keep from laughing. Someone was throwing his whole world off-kilter.

Chapter Fifteen

Anson

SOUNDS FROM OUTSIDE THE VICTORIAN HAD ME GLANCING out the window and scanning the makeshift parking area. It was just two of our guys shooting the shit on their break. Still no Shep.

"Dude." A voice broke into my thoughts. "What's your deal today?" Silas asked.

I sprayed the mix of chemicals on the framing that would help counteract the scent the smoke had left behind, even after all these years. "Just need to talk to Shep about something."

Silas's brows pulled together as he stopped his work. "Everything okay?"

I nodded with a grunt. But everything was far from okay. I'd found a string of five fires around the time of the one here at the Victorian that had me on edge. It was too many for a small town like Sparrow Falls.

"He probably just wants to crawl up Shep's ass a little more," Owen grumbled from the other side of the room.

He said it loud enough that he knew I'd be sure to hear it, which took some doing when we were all wearing N95 masks. My eyes narrowed on Owen. He'd made it clear he wasn't happy with my being in charge or his assignment of pulling drywall. But it was getting old, fast.

"Stop acting like a two-year-old who had his binky taken away," I snapped. "You don't want to do your job? Quit. It would probably make this restoration go quicker."

Owen straightened, the red on his cheeks peeking out from around his mask. "I can't have an opinion now? You're wasting our fucking time working on areas that don't need work."

My back teeth ground together. It was the same argument we'd been having all day. "Next piece of drywall you pull, take off your mask and smell the damn framing. Then tell me if you still think it doesn't need to be treated."

"Whatever," Owen mumbled, turning back to his work.

Carlos shook his head as he pulled a sheet of drywall. Lowering his voice, he said, "This restoration stuff isn't his gig. He's more into building from the ground up."

"Then he should walk," I snapped.

God, I was a prick. Everything about my discoveries from last night had set me on edge. I was probably the one who needed to walk away from the site today.

The sound of tires on gravel had me looking up. Shep's silver truck headed down the driveway. *Finally.*

"I'll be back," I told Silas and Carlos.

Silas gave me a chin lift in answer and turned back to his work.

I picked my way through the house, making sure to be careful where I stepped. Much of my path was pulled-up flooring that revealed the framework below. We'd placed boards that we could walk across, but you still needed to be cautious.

When I made it outside, I yanked off my mask and sucked in the fresh mountain air. A slight hint of smoke clung to it, likely stirred up by all our work. As Shep climbed out of his truck, I strode across the parking lot toward him.

"How's it going?" he asked as I approached.

"It's going. It'd be a hell of a lot quicker if Owen wasn't moaning and complaining the whole time."

Shep winced. "Sometimes, he's a great worker. Others, he's a liability. I don't get it."

"Control issues," I muttered.

Shep raised a brow in question.

Sometimes, I hated that I couldn't turn off the profiler part of me. The piece that analyzed everything and everyone. "He does well when he has tasks he feels in control of. When he has autonomy. But he just doesn't know enough to get those assignments on a restoration. So, he's throwing a fit."

Shep frowned as he stared at the house, almost like he could see Owen through the walls. "I could move him to another project. We've got plenty."

"Might be a mistake. He's gotta learn to do the things he doesn't want to do."

"True enough," Shep mumbled and then looked at me. "Something else?"

He always knew when I had something on my mind. I didn't typically hover and didn't seek out conversation. I liked to do my work in silence. It was almost meditative. I could pound out the demons while working this job.

"Did Rhodes play a spring sport in middle school? Before the fire, I mean."

Shep blinked a few times, confusion clear on his face. "Uh, yeah. She and Fallon played lacrosse in the seventh grade. They were both awful."

I wanted to smile at that. I could so clearly see her all smiles and trying with everything she had but being an absolute disaster on the field. But the fact that she would've frequented that locker room around the time of the fire swallowed all my humor in a single second.

"Did she spend a lot of time downtown around then, too?" I pushed.

Shep stiffened. "What's this about?"

"Just answer," I pressed. I didn't want to put any ideas in Shep's head before he answered me.

He scowled in my direction. "I don't know. All of us hung out downtown when we were growing up. Nine times out of ten, it was there or at the river. It's not like there's a lot to do around here." Then something shifted in his expression as if he were trying to grab hold of a memory.

"What?" I clipped.

"She and Fallon. They had this volunteer gig. All middle schoolers have to complete a certain number of hours. They helped the town landscaping crew that spring, replanting the beds by each crosswalk."

I wanted to let a million different curses fly. I'd seen those beds at each intersection. I'd seen crews revitalizing them just a few weeks ago in preparation for spring.

"Why are you asking?" Shep ground out.

"There were other fires around the time of this one," I said, gesturing to the house.

Shep frowned. "What are you talking about?"

"The one in the middle school girls' locker room."

"Sure," he said with a nod. "The firework prank. The principal was pissed."

I didn't argue with him. Not yet. "There was that series of dumpster fires downtown that weren't solved."

"Okay," Shep agreed.

"And then the fire in the bathroom at the river trailhead."

Shep's jaw worked back and forth as everything came together in his mind. "All places Rho frequented."

"Exactly."

"But other people did, too. Fallon and probably half a dozen others," he argued.

"They didn't have their house burned to the ground and their family killed."

Shep stared at me long and hard. "That's a stretch. Fires happen, and this one was an accident."

"Maybe," I muttered. "But I still want to see the fire reports."

My friend blinked at me. "And you want me to get them. How the hell am I supposed to do that? Unless I tell Trace you're ex-FBI with a sick hunch."

Just the idea of that piece of my history coming to light had pressure settling on my chest, making it hard to take a full breath. "You'll think of something. Get creative."

"Trace isn't exactly going to believe that I'm suddenly some sort of criminal version of *A Beautiful Mind*."

"Tell him something isn't sitting right about the fire here. That you did some digging. That's believable."

The urge to run fast and far was strong. I wanted to get the hell away from anything that had to do with fucked-up minds and evil of any sort. If someone had been setting fires at places Rho touched, they were definitely both of those things.

Shep cursed. "I'll do my best, but this means he'll start sticking his nose into this, too. He'll be around more."

I swallowed the aversion to having law enforcement anywhere in my vicinity—too many bad memories. Because if someone had been targeting Rho, that was exactly what she needed.

꩜

As I stepped outside into the early evening breeze, I ripped off my mask for the final time. God, I hated those things.

The rest of the crew did the same, heading for their various vehicles. But Owen hovered, not moving toward his beat-up pickup.

I finally glanced in his direction.

He crushed his mask in his grip, his gaze dropping to the gravel. "You were right."

I didn't speak, just let him get out whatever he needed to.

"About the fucking framing. It smelled like smoke," Owen grumbled.

I didn't get the urge to chuckle often these days, but I wanted to right now.

Finally, Owen's focus lifted. "Sorry I was a dick. I hate this meticulous stuff. It's why I'm crap at finish work, too."

"I get it," I said, letting him off the hook. "It's a hell of a lot more fun to see big strides every day."

"Yeah." He glanced back at the house. "I just get twitchy staying in the same spot for too long."

My brow furrowed as I thought about some other signs I'd seen from Owen. He might have ADHD. It would make working on a single task for long periods more than challenging. "I'll switch you up every couple of hours tomorrow. They may not be jobs you're excited about, but at least you won't be stuck in one for too long."

Owen looked back at me. "That'd be chill. Thanks."

"No problem."

"Me and Carlos are heading to the bar. You wanna join?"

I shook my head. "I'm good. But thanks."

Owen grinned, all teeth. "Why am I not surprised? You're real committed to that loner vibe, boss."

I scowled at him, which only made Owen laugh.

"See ya tomorrow," he called with a wave as he headed for his truck.

I didn't bother answering. I wasn't sure what was worse: the childish Owen or the friendly one.

The sound of laughter pulled me around the side of the house until the guest cottage came into view. But the moment it did, I stopped dead.

Rho had set up a sprinkler on the patchy, sort-of grass, likely to help the seed take root to even things out, but Biscuit clearly had other plans. The disproportioned dog barked in happy glee as he attacked the jets of water.

"Biscuit!" Rhodes yelled, no animosity in her voice. "Come!"

The dog ran toward her but then darted away. She dove at him, trying to catch his collar, but she missed and landed directly in the sprinkler's path.

She shrieked as the surely cold water blasted her, then dissolved into more laughter. "This was exactly what you wanted, wasn't it?"

Biscuit barked in answer.

Rho leapt over the sprinkler to chase him. The two slipped into some sort of game of tag where only they knew the rules. Rho's wild brown hair was slicked down, and her tank and shorts were plastered to her body. But she looked...happy.

A foreign feeling shifted through my chest, one I didn't particularly welcome. But I couldn't help but be drawn closer—toward that light and chaos.

Biscuit barked as he caught sight of me, then ran in my direction. He stopped just shy of me and shook. I wouldn't have thought it possible for a dog that wasn't all that large to have that much water in his fur, but I was soaked in a matter of seconds.

Rho's hand flew to her mouth, her gasp quickly turning into giggles as she took me in.

"Are you laughing at me?" I gritted out.

She smiled wide. "I'd never."

I scowled at her, my eyes narrowing. "If you trained your dog to obey your commands, this would've never happened."

"Oh, really?"

"Yes," I clipped.

In a move so swift I didn't have a prayer of escaping, Rho bent, grabbed the sprinkler, and pointed it directly at me. "What about this? Could I have trained this away from happening?"

Biscuit barked and leapt in the air, loving the new game.

The freezing water streamed over me, and I found myself running before I could think about it.

Rho shrieked as I dove for her, grabbing her around the waist and forcing her into the sprinkler jets. "It's freezing!"

"You think?" I yelled.

"Uncle! Uncle!" she screamed.

I hauled her out of the water but kept my grip firm.

Rho shoved her wet hair from her face, her hazel eyes locking with mine. Her breath hitched, and her gaze dropped to my lips.

Her breasts rose and fell with each inhale and exhale, pressing against my chest—so much heat despite the fact that we'd both been doused with ice water.

I needed to let her go. Step back. But I couldn't. All I could do was stare into those witch eyes. "You don't know what kind of game you're playing, Reckless."

It was one that could leave us both in ruins.

Chapter Sixteen

Rhodes

ANSON'S VOICE WAS PURE GRIT AND WARNING, BUT THE FEEL of it sent delicious shivers skating over my skin. I didn't look away from his icy stare. "Seems like a fun game to me."

His gaze dropped to my mouth. He was so close I could taste him in the air between us.

A bark sounded, and Biscuit launched himself against us, wanting in on the fun.

With an oof, Anson stumbled back a step. I instantly felt the loss of his heat, the air turning cold around me.

"He's got some surprising strength," Anson muttered.

Biscuit was probably forty-five pounds, but it was a muscly forty-five.

"Sorry about that," I said, my cheeks heating. God, had I been about to kiss him? Somehow, I didn't think that would have gone over especially well.

I motioned toward the cottage. "Come on. Shep left some

workout gear here in case he wanted to go for a run. You can borrow something of his."

"I don't need—"

I pinned Anson with a stare. "You really want to climb into your truck soaking wet and ruin the leather?"

He glanced over his shoulder at his vehicle as the few remaining others headed down the drive. "No," he muttered.

I nearly laughed. *Boys and their toys.* "You'd think I asked you to walk the plank. I don't think you'll die if you step inside my house."

Anson didn't say a word, just scowled as he headed for the door. He walked inside without asking but slipped his boots off on the porch. I followed behind him, doing the same with my flip-flops and holding the door for Biscuit, who'd shaken off most of the water.

Anson made his way down the hallway, coming up short in my living room that opened into the small kitchen. He gaped at the fireplace. "Is that a dick?"

He sounded so appalled that I couldn't help but burst out laughing. "It's my dick flower, if you must know."

His head whipped around in my direction. "Why?"

A genuine smile spread across my lips. "Lolli made it for me."

The appalled look morphed into one of understanding. "I like her."

"Well, the feeling is mutual, but watch yourself. She wants your mouth busy doing things other than talking."

An expression of true fear swept over Anson's face, and I couldn't help laughing again. He shuddered. "She's also terrifying."

"A healthy fear of Lolli is smart."

Anson merely grunted in agreement.

"Give me a sec. I'll get you those clothes." I headed for the hallway linen closet where Shep had stored a few pairs of shorts and tees. Grabbing one of each, I headed back to the living room and kitchen.

Anson studied everything around him, taking in every detail, and spoke without looking up. "It's not you."

My brows pulled together. "What do you mean?"

He slowly turned to face me. "The space. No explosions of color. No plants. No...*you*."

I swallowed hard. If I'd thought Trace was good at seeing the details, he had nothing on Anson. "I'm still getting settled."

He stared hard at me as I handed him the clothes. His gaze called *bullshit*, and I fought the blush wanting to rise to my cheeks.

I cleared my throat. "There's a bathroom in the hall. I'm going to get changed in my room."

I spun around, hurrying ahead of him so I didn't have to look at those blue-gray eyes that asked so many questions. Biscuit followed closely behind me. Shutting the door, I hurried to pull off my soaked clothes and went in search of fresh ones.

But as I did, I couldn't help but study my bedroom. It was the same setup I'd had for the past five years. Pale green duvet cover, a throw over the end of the bed. Nightstands I'd gotten on sale at a local furniture store that matched the dresser I pulled sweats and a tank out of.

Anson was right. None of this was especially me. Not even the print on the wall. It was pretty, a black-and-white photo of a lily. But it had no soul. Why would it when it was something I'd grabbed off a wall at Target, where it hung with countless others?

When I thought about changing it up, about making it mine, my heart started beating faster, and my breaths came quicker. My palms dampened as my stomach twisted. I closed my eyes.

In. Two. Three.

Out. Two. Three.

I repeated the process over and over until it felt like I had my body more under control.

What the hell was that?

The beginnings of a panic attack. Overthinking decorating a space in a way that fit me? That was ridiculous.

I hurried to pull on the soft sweats and simple tank, then tugged on my favorite fuzzy socks. I gave Biscuit a little scratch before heading down the hall. Part of me expected Anson to be long gone; instead, he was hovering in my kitchen.

"You're nosy, you know that, right?" I said.

He glanced in my direction, arching a brow.

"First, you analyze my living room, and now you're poking around my kitchen."

Anson shrugged, the action pulling the T-shirt taut across his broad chest. His feet were bare, and something about that was sexier than it should've been. *Did I have a foot fetish now?*

He lifted a copy of *The Little Princess*. "Reader?"

"One of my favorites."

Anson nodded slowly, fingering the bookmark made of pressed flowers. "You're almost done."

I moved deeper into the kitchen and toward the Crock-Pot I'd set to cooking before I went outside. "Finished this morning before work."

He frowned. "There are still three chapters left."

Heat hit my cheeks. "I don't like to read the endings."

Anson gaped at me, his jaw going slack. "You don't finish books? Ever?"

That twitchiness skated over me again. "I don't like the finality. Even if it is happy. I like thinking the story could go on forever."

He studied me for a long time, his fingers still toying with the bookmark. "Seems like a waste to go on that whole journey and not get the final payoff."

"But isn't it better to just enjoy the journey? Really take each moment in for what it is?"

Anson made a humming noise in the back of his throat as he stared at me. Something about his gaze told me he'd put together too many of my pieces. It only made the twitchiness worse. So, I focused on the Crock-Pot instead.

"It smells good," he said, taking pity on me. "What is it?"

The timer said five minutes to go. "Chicken tacos."

Anson gave another of those grunts.

"Want some?" I asked before I could stop myself.

He stiffened, just realizing that he'd backed himself into a corner. "I'm good—"

"It's just tacos, not torture or a marriage proposal. Plus, you'll get to eat in the ambiance of Lolli's dick flower. Unless you have something against tacos and dick flowers?" I challenged.

Anson's lips twitched the tiniest bit. It was so slight I would've missed it if I hadn't been focused on his face. He glanced at the Crock-Pot. "I like tacos."

"Good to know you're not a monster," I said. "Grab some plates. They're in the cupboard up—"

But Anson had already opened the exact right cabinet.

"You really were snooping, weren't you?" I accused.

He shook his head, placing two plates on the counter. "This was the most likely spot for them. Between the oven and the fridge. This counter space is obviously your workstation when you cook, so…"

I stared at him as I reached for the fridge handle. "Are you some sort of house psychic?"

Anson barked out a laugh—or something that resembled one. It was gritty and sounded rusty. "A house psychic?"

Opening the fridge, I peeked inside to find the things I needed. Salsa, sharp cheddar, lettuce. "You just seem to know all these things about my house without me telling you. Maybe it's because you build them for a living."

"Maybe," he agreed, but his voice had lost the edge of humor.

I handed him the cheese and a grater. "Think you can handle this?"

Anson scowled at me. "You and your brother never think I can feed myself."

I snorted. "Shep thinks it's his job to take care of everyone in his orbit. I, on the other hand, just want to make sure you're not going to maim yourself on my cheese grater. Not sure my homeowner's insurance covers that."

He let out a huff of air and set to work shredding some cheese for us.

I washed the lettuce and began chopping. It was nice having someone else in my space, even if he was quiet. The energy of another human being was comforting.

"This enough?" Anson asked.

I peeked over and nodded. "You can put it in a bowl. You probably know where those are, too."

Anson got the cabinet right on the first try.

"Freaky," I muttered.

He brought down two bowls, putting the cheese in one and setting the other next to my cutting board. His arm brushed mine—the hazards of a tiny kitchen. Just that faint touch of skin against skin sent a pleasant shiver skating over me.

Anson lifted the jar of salsa, frowning. "What brand is this?"

I stilled. "Brand?"

He nodded. "I've never seen it before."

I set the knife down on my cutting board and turned to face him, an appalled look on my face. "Anson Bartholomew Cattigan."

That lip twitch was back, a little stronger this time. "You know that's not my name, right?"

"Well, I don't know your full name, and I needed three names for emphasis."

"It's Anson Sutter Hunt."

It was my turn to scowl at him. "God, that's a good name. But that's not the point. We do *not* eat store-bought salsa in this house."

He smirked at me. *Smirked.* It wasn't a smile, but it was somehow better, the slight curve of those lips beneath his thick scruff. I wondered how that scruff would feel when he kissed you, how it would feel if he—*nope, nope, nope.* I was not going there.

I took the salsa jar from Anson's hand and opened it. "This was made with tomatoes, peppers, and onions from Nora's garden. And a blend of spices that Lolli has been perfecting for years."

Anson reached out and dipped his finger into the jar.

My jaw went slack. "You didn't."

He popped that finger into his mouth, and I shut right up. His brows lifted. "Damn, Reckless. That's good."

I swallowed hard, averting my gaze from that mouth. "Told you."

The timer dinged, saving me from making an utter fool of myself. I got to work pulling the tortillas out of the warmer and plating them so we could assemble our tacos. "You want a beer?"

"Don't drink."

I glanced at Anson as I handed him his plate. "Oh. I've got Coke, too. Water, milk, OJ."

"Coke's good," he muttered as he took the plate.

I grabbed a soda for him and a Corona for me, then paused. But before I could change my plan, Anson cut me off.

"You can have one. Not gonna send me on a bender or anything."

I bit my bottom lip but grabbed the beer. "I didn't want to be rude or unkind."

Anson lifted the lid on the Crock-Pot. "Went through a rough patch. Leaned a little too heavily on the bottle, so I just cut it out. Then it's not a risk." He motioned for me to go before him.

I grabbed the serving fork and quickly shredded the chicken, placing some on my two tortillas. "That takes some serious strength."

Anson merely shrugged as he served himself. "Don't miss it most of the time. The moments I do are exactly why I cut it out. Do ginger beer instead."

I studied Anson as I slid onto a stool at the island. There was so much I wanted to know yet couldn't bring myself to ask. "It's easy to try to numb yourself when you're going through something painful."

He took the stool next to mine, cracking his Coke. "You sound like you're speaking from experience."

I loaded my tacos with cheese, lettuce, and salsa, using that as an excuse to avoid meeting his eyes. "Not substances or anything. But I had to turn everything off after my family died. I couldn't look at pictures or see mementos. I had to pretend like they never existed at all."

It was the first time I'd actually said that out loud, admitted that I'd erased my family in my mind for so many years.

Anson was quiet. The silence swirled around us like a living, breathing thing.

Finally, I forced myself to look at him. I expected disgust or maybe judgment; instead, I found understanding in those blue-gray eyes.

"Sometimes, the only way to stay alive and breathing is to

pretend it never happened. Over time, you can let it in, piece by piece, but if you do it all at once, you could drown in the grief."

It was on the tip of my tongue to ask what he'd lost. Who. But I didn't want to ruin the gift Anson was giving me right now. Understanding. The feeling of not being alone.

I'd spent the last fourteen years surrounded by people. The Colsons' home was never quiet. People were always everywhere. But a small part of me still felt alone. As if no one really understood what I'd been through.

But the pain swirling in Anson's eyes told me he understood. The fact that I could spill the thing I was most ashamed of, and he got it? That was one of the greatest gifts I'd ever received.

I took a sip of beer, trying to clear the lump in my throat. "I still feel pretty guilty about it." That and the fact that the last few moments I'd shared with Emilia had been spent fighting about a stupid shirt.

Anson studied me for a long moment. "Is that what the house is? Atonement?"

I took a minute to really think about his question. To be honest with myself, even if I didn't like the answer. Finally, I shook my head. "It's my search for peace."

That was the real truth. Restoring the Victorian was me trying to finally put my family to rest, but at the same time, carry them with me. It was trying to truly have a home.

Anson nodded slowly. "There's no greater gift than peace."

His words were simple, but they carried weight. Because they were spoken by a man who clearly hadn't found it yet—not for any length of time anyway.

I picked at my tortilla, trying to get up the courage to ask my next question. "Do you get that peace anywhere?"

Anson stilled, his taco halfway to his mouth, his eyes cutting to me. "Sometimes. Working on a house, losing myself in the physicality of it all. Or for a few minutes in the quiet at the cabin. There's something about Sparrow Falls. It helps."

Every word he spoke felt like a treasure. Because I knew he didn't give this sort of thing to just anyone. Probably not even Shep.

"That's good. Hold on to those things," I whispered.

Anson grunted in what I thought was agreement and set to eating his dinner. I took that as a sign that chatting time was over. We ate in silence, but the comfort was still there. Both in having Anson here and knowing it was good for him to have the company, too. I couldn't imagine how lonely it was to live your life so cut off from others. And getting these true glimpses of him…it killed that he lived his life that way.

When we finished eating, Anson immediately set to cleaning up.

"You don't have to do that," I said.

He cut me off with a shake of his head. "You cooked. I clean."

His tone was so gruff I had to bite my lip to keep from laughing. "It was a team effort, so why don't we clean together?"

Anson arched a brow at me. "I grated cheese."

"It still counts," I argued.

A soft whine sounded from the threshold of the kitchen. Biscuit looked up at me with pleading eyes.

"Oh, all right." I plucked a piece of leftover chicken from my plate. "Sit," I commanded.

Biscuit plunked his butt on the floor, and I tossed him the chicken. He caught it on the fly and dashed to his bed.

When I turned around, Anson was shaking his head. "You're gonna spoil that dog."

"He deserves a little spoiling," I defended.

Anson muttered something under his breath that I couldn't quite make out.

"Just hand me those plates," I groused.

We fell into an easy rhythm. Anson rinsed the dishes and then handed them to me to put into the dishwasher. There was something about watching his hands in the suds as he scrubbed. Long, strong fingers bending and flexing, his forearm muscles pulling taut as he moved.

I forced my gaze away as I took the last plate, placing it in the dishwasher. As I straightened, I nearly smacked into Anson, not realizing he was still standing at the sink. "Sorry, I—"

My words cut off as my breath hitched. He was so close. I could smell the hint of sweat still clinging to his skin from the day's work, the tinges of sawdust and sage.

His eyes swirled, the blue disappearing completely into the stormy gray. "Thanks for dinner."

My gaze dropped from Anson's eyes to his mouth, the lips surrounded by scruff. The ache to know what they would feel like pressed to mine flared hot and bright. The need to know what he tasted like surged.

"Reckless," he growled.

My focus shot back to his eyes. They flashed, blue streaking through the gray.

"Don't."

"I—"

He cut me off with a single look. "This isn't that. I don't do relationships."

Pain flared somewhere deep, the agony of rejection making me start to pull away. But Anson grabbed my arm. His grip managed to be both gentle and firm. But his fingers burned, the contact searing into me.

"It's not you," he gritted out. "I don't do relationships with *anyone*. Not friendship, not more. Wouldn't want to saddle a single soul with the fucked-up shit that's me. But you keep looking at me with those kiss-me eyes, all green and sparking gold, and it's killing me. Doesn't matter how much I want to drown in your taste. How much I want to know what it would be like to sink into that sweet heat. I can't. I *won't*."

And then he was gone. Striding out of the kitchen before I could say a word.

The slamming of the door jolted me out of my haze.

My skin buzzed with the phantom energy Anson had left in his wake. I could still feel his fingers wrapped around my arm. Could hear his words echoing in my head.

I was too hot, my skin felt too tight for my body. I squeezed my thighs together on instinct, trying to relieve a little of the ache—one Anson had put there and refused to do a damned thing about.

I was so screwed. And not in a good way.

∽℘

My feet pounded against the floorboards of the Victorian as I raced down the hallway, screaming for my parents, for Emilia. My throat was raw as smoke choked me, but I only screamed louder. No sound came out.

I was almost to my parents' room. So close. They would be in there. They would keep me safe.

But just as I took the next step, the floorboards gave way with a horrific crack. Suddenly, I was falling, the flames swirling around me and swallowing me whole.

I jerked upright with a cough and sputter, breathing heavily. Biscuit whined next to me, his front paws up on the mattress.

"It's okay. I'm okay," I soothed as I patted his head. Or maybe I was reassuring myself.

I tried to even my breaths and slow the inhales and exhales, but something tickled my nose as I did. Fear slid through my veins, freezing me to the spot as my gaze jerked to the open window.

Smoke.

I leapt from the bed, grabbing my phone and rushing from my bedroom, Biscuit right by my side. No smoke alarms were going off in the guest cottage, and I'd replaced all the batteries when I moved in. It had to be from outside. A forest fire?

Quickly hooking Biscuit's leash to his collar, I stepped outside.

A gasp slipped from my lips, and my hand flew to my mouth. The house. *My* house. It was engulfed in flames.

Chapter Seventeen

Anson

FLIPPED OVER ONTO MY BACK, STARING AT THE CEILING. No position seemed comfortable tonight. Sleep wasn't typically a friend, but it wasn't usually this bad either.

Letting out a growl of frustration, I punched my pillow. Rho's face played in my mind on repeat. It was like a slideshow of torture. The first image was those gorgeous hazel eyes full of hurt. But the second was far worse. Want made the gold in them spark and swirl as need parted her lips.

"Fuck."

I never should've said yes to dinner. I should've blown her off and shut that door fast and hard. But I hadn't. And she'd somehow managed to slip past the defenses I'd so expertly built over the past two years.

My phone rang from the nightstand. The first tone had my blood turning to ice. The device rarely rang, and sure as hell not at three in the morning.

I grabbed it, jerking the charger cord free. Seeing Shep's name on the screen only drove my panic higher as I struggled to hit *accept*.

"What happened?" I demanded.

"Need you at Rho's." I heard the strain in my friend's voice. He was trying to hold back whatever emotion was trying to break free.

"Talk to me," I ordered but was already moving, pulling on joggers and a tee.

"There was a fire at the Victorian."

"Tell me she's okay," I growled.

"She's fine," Shep assured me. "It didn't get close to the cottage. The fire department has it out now. It was pretty contained to the part of the house that was burned before, so it didn't spread."

My footsteps faltered as I reached for my keys. It was hard to get something that had been burned before to burn again. It didn't make any sense. And that had my gut churning. "Be there in ten."

I hung up before Shep had a chance to answer. Slipping on my sneakers, I jogged out to my truck.

I made the typically fifteen-minute drive to Rho's in eight. Fire trucks were everywhere, along with sheriff's department vehicles and Shep's familiar silver pickup. I parked next to him, jumped out, and slammed the truck door behind me.

Striding across the gravel drive, I ignored every firefighter and cop, searching for one person only. The moment my gaze locked on her, all the air punched right out of my lungs.

Rho had a blanket wrapped around her shoulders and Biscuit's leash looped around one hand. Her face had gone completely pale, devoid of any color at all as she stared at her surroundings. But she wasn't truly seeing. It was as if she was in a trance.

I crossed to her on instinct. Not a damned thing could've kept me away. I came to a stop in front of her, but Rho still didn't react. Lifting a hand, I squeezed her neck gently. "Look at me, Reckless."

She blinked a few times, her focus finally coming to me. "Anson?"

"There she is." I searched those hazel eyes, so much duller than I was used to. "You okay?"

Rho nodded. "We're fine. I just—what are you doing here?"

"I called him," Shep cut in.

My hand dropped instantly as I turned toward my friend.

Shep's eyes narrowed on me, but he quickly shifted his focus to Rho. "Thought it wouldn't be bad to have our fire-restoration expert on hand."

Rho's brow furrowed. "It's the middle of the night. You shouldn't have woken him up."

"Yes, he should've," I growled.

Her gaze cut to me, and a little fire returned to those eyes. "It's ridiculous. It's not like you can do anything about this tonight." Her shoulders slumped. "Maybe the house is cursed."

Shep moved in then, putting an arm around her shoulders and pulling her into his side. "It's not cursed. We're going to figure out what's going on and fix it."

My back teeth ground together as heat prickled my skin. But it wasn't from the fire that was out now. This felt a lot like jealousy. Because some part of me wanted to be the person with his arm around Rho. Even though I knew I couldn't be.

Just then, another truck pulled up, and Nora and Lolli were out in a flash, running up the porch steps. They surrounded Rho, pulling her into hugs and then guiding her and Biscuit inside the cottage.

The moment the door closed, Shep crossed to me. "Trace is waiting for word from the fire chief. Come on."

I didn't say anything as I followed him toward the hulking sheriff and the officers surrounding him. Something about Trace always set me on edge. He had the kind of perceptiveness the Behavioral Analysis Unit was constantly on the lookout for. That meant my guard always had to be up around him.

Trace's gaze cut to us as we approached, his eyes narrowing as they landed on me. "Anson," he greeted. But my name somehow managed to be a question at the same time.

"Wanted him to take a look once the fire crew is done," Shep said.

A muscle along Trace's jaw fluttered. "He may not be able to. We're not sure what we're dealing with yet."

That prickle at the base of my scalp was back. Our crew was

careful with cleanup, and I'd been the last person in the Victorian last night. I knew nothing had been left behind. And with the electricity to the home still turned off, there was only one likely answer. Arson.

"Come on," Shep clipped, annoyance lacing his tone.

"This isn't something to fuck around with," Trace gritted out. "We move through our official processes."

Shep opened his mouth to argue, but I held up a hand to stop him. "Let's just see what the fire chief says. No one's going near the house until they clear it anyway."

Shep finally jerked his head in a nod.

Trace looked back at me, his assessing stare asking all the questions I didn't want it to.

"Colson," a man who looked to be in his late fifties called as he strode toward our group.

Trace turned to face him. "What'd you find, Chief?"

The older man nodded at a younger guy in full turnout gear at his side. The younger man dipped his head. "No question. It's arson. The whole east side of the house reeks of gasoline. Trailers lead outside where someone set it."

Shep let loose a dozen or so curses, but Trace remained completely quiet. The only sign of what he was truly feeling was a spasm in his jaw. Trace's gaze flicked to the fire chief. "When can I get my team in there to work the scene?"

"As soon as you'd like. It looked worse than it was. It was confined to the room on the northeast corner. There wasn't a lot for the fire to burn, even with the accelerant," the chief answered.

Trace jerked his head in a nod, turning to one of his deputies. "I want the county crime scene techs here now."

The younger guy nodded quickly and pulled out his phone.

"Would you mind if I took a quick look?" I asked. I tried my best to keep my tone casual yet respectful.

The fire chief turned to me, his eyes narrowing. "Who the hell are you?"

Shep stepped in. "Greg Nelson, meet Anson Hunt, my fire-restoration specialist." He turned to me. "Nelson's our fire chief."

He knew I'd put together that much already but made the introductions, nonetheless.

"You won't be able to do a damned thing until Trace's boys are done processing the scene," Nelson clipped.

"And girls," a female deputy in the circle muttered.

Nelson flicked a look in her direction. "Relax, Beth. I know you've got bigger balls than all of them."

Beth snorted. "And don't you forget it."

Trace ignored the back-and-forth between the two, his focus centered on me. "What are you hoping to see?"

I didn't answer right away. I needed to tread carefully and choose just the right words. Instead, Shep spoke for me. "Anson knows fire. He's been studying it for years now. He might see something that's helpful."

Trace's gaze had stayed firmly locked on me while his brother spoke. "If you go in, you go with me, and you don't make a single move without my okay."

I jerked my head in a nod. "You got PPE gear?"

"In my SUV," Trace clipped.

I'd seen the guy be warm and funny, but it was clear he wasn't going to be my number-one fan. That was all right. Good, even. I didn't need the liability of a friend.

I followed Trace to his vehicle, Shep at my side. In a matter of seconds, we were all donning the Tyvek suits and N95 masks that made us look like we were entering a chemical spill. And in a lot of ways, we were. None of us needed to be breathing the gas fumes, and you never knew what toxins a fire could expose to the air.

Trace reached out a gloved hand to open one of the back doors to the kitchen. He paused at the threshold. "Stay behind me."

A couple of firefighters still roamed the home, triple-checking that they hadn't missed any embers.

Trace led us down the hall and toward the library. As we moved through the space, I frowned. Something was off. My sixth sense flared to life. But Trace kept right on moving.

He stopped at the entrance to what had once been an office. The temperature shifted, heat still brimming from the space, even though the fire was out. "No farther. Not until my guys process it."

I didn't say a word, simply stepped to the side to get a better view. The room was charred beyond recognition, as if someone had thrown already burned logs onto a fire and turned them to ash.

"We'll have to rebuild this whole wing," Shep said quietly.

It would've been a lot worse if we'd been farther along in the restoration process. But maybe someone didn't want us getting that far. The thought had me retracing my steps to the library.

The space had been partially burned in the last fire but hadn't caught in this one. I pulled my mask down for an inhale. Gas. Everywhere.

I slipped my mask back into place and surveyed the room, trying to figure out what had tripped my radar. I began moving around the space, searching. There were still some books on the shelves that were in relatively good shape. A few knickknacks, too. Even a painting on the wall that looked only slightly discolored from its exposure to smoke.

"What the hell is he doing?" Trace muttered.

Shep pushed his brother back a step. "Just give him a minute."

I slowed in front of the bookcase. It wasn't a built-in, but it was nice quality. Mahogany if my guess was correct, maybe even African koa. The bottom third was cabinets, and above was all shelving.

The last cabinet door was open. I crossed to it, my Spidey sense tingling the closer I got. I crouched down and peeked inside. It was too dark.

"Flashlight?" I called.

Footsteps sounded, and then Trace handed me one. "Here."

I took it and pointed the beam inside. There was a stack of what looked like papers, but they didn't show any signs of fire damage.

A familiar unease settled over me. "May I retrieve?"

"Yes," Trace clipped. "I've got an evidence bag."

I reached a gloved hand inside to remove the stack. Rising, I set the flashlight on a shelf that looked steady, facing the beam of light up so we could better see. What I saw was newspaper clipping after newspaper clipping, all with coverage of the fire. They weren't new either. The corners were yellowed with age.

A smear of red caught my eye. Ink. *Not blood*, I reminded myself. Someone had circled text on the article. *The Stirlings' thirteen-year-old daughter is still in critical condition. It is uncertain if she'll survive.*

The two sentences were circled twice over, but the word *survive* was underlined three times. The action made my jaw clench as I turned to the next article. A different sentence was circled this time. *A firefighter wishing to remain anonymous said it was a miracle the young girl survived the fall from her balcony.* Again, the word *survive* was underlined repeatedly.

I flipped through article after article, each with the same refrain. When I reached the last one, nausea rolled through me. The word *survived* was underlined yet again, but this article had a photo. Clearly Rhodes' minor identity was no longer being protected.

It was a family shot that had likely been taken for a Christmas card or something similar. The group was posed in the field behind the Victorian, the mountains framing them. Only there were countless red circles around Rho's face. Over and over until the newspaper had torn in places. And below it was one thing.

MAYBE YOU DIDN'T DESERVE TO SURVIVE.

Chapter Eighteen

Rhodes

"**D**RINK YOUR TEA," NORA URGED, PUSHING THE MUG CLOSER to me.

Fallon squeezed my knee under the table. "Want some whiskey in it? That might help take the edge off."

"Fallon Rosemary Colson. She does not need liquor right now," Nora chastised.

Lolli fumbled in her purse. "What about one of my gummies? I just upped the potency of the blend."

"*Mom!*" Nora snapped. "Do not try to get her high. There is law enforcement right outside, including your grandson."

Lolli just kept right on looking. "Pot's legal now, dear. And Rho has been of age for quite some time. In fact, she had one of my brownies at—"

Nora held up a hand. "I don't want to hear this."

A laugh slipped from my lips and, God, I needed it. The release of pressure, of all the pent-up emotion.

Arden turned from her spot at the window, eyeing me carefully.

As if she was worried I was cracking. And maybe I was. The fact that our sister, who barely left Cope's property, was here in the middle of the night told me I should be concerned.

Her hand dropped to Biscuit's head, and she stroked him softly. The animals always found their way to her. It was as if she spoke some language only they understood.

"You can stay at Cope's if you want," Arden said, her soft voice carrying a hint of a rasp. "With the season, he won't be back for at least a month or two. And even if he was, he wouldn't mind."

I didn't miss that she didn't offer up her place. Arden liked her solitude, but even suggesting our brother's place was a sacrifice on her part. The only way it worked for her to even live on Cope's property was because hockey meant he was rarely home. Holidays and a few weeks during the offseason, that was it.

I smiled at Arden, trying to reassure her. "I'll be okay. Thank you, though."

"Just text if you change your mind. There are always guest rooms ready."

"I will. Promise."

Nora's hand stroked my hair as she stood behind me. "I think you should come stay with me and Lolli. At least until they know what caused this. It's too dangerous."

I tried to fight the grimace that wanted to rise to my lips. I appreciated Nora more than I could say, but the last thing I wanted was to be hovered over.

Lolli sent me a wicked grin. "I'll make you some more of those brownies…"

"Lolli, I was hallucinating for hours. No, thank you." When she offered me one a few years ago, I'd had no idea what her *special recipe* entailed.

She frowned. "I might've made that batch a little too strong."

Fallon snorted. "You think? Rho said the flowers in the garden were talking to her."

The front door opened, and Biscuit let out a series of barks and growls as he charged toward the group of men.

"Oh, crap," I muttered, jumping to my feet. The last thing we needed was Biscuit biting someone.

But Anson quickly moved in front of Trace, dropping low. As he crouched, he held out a hand. Biscuit slid to a stop.

"Easy, B," Anson said. "No one's going to hurt you."

Biscuit let out a low growl as he eyed Shep and Trace.

"They're friends," Anson assured the dog. He inched closer to Biscuit and scratched under his chin, then behind his ear. Biscuit's back leg thumped wildly.

"You got a leash?" Anson asked.

I grabbed one from the hooks on the wall and fastened it to Biscuit's collar. "It's okay, buddy. Everyone here is nice."

Trace looked from the dog to Anson. "You've got a way with him."

Anson shrugged. "Won him over with treats."

Shep chuckled, but the humor didn't quite reach his eyes. "Food is always the way."

I looked at all three of the men standing in my entryway. "You found something."

Trace wore his careful mask, the one that didn't show too much of anything. "Why don't we sit down?"

My stomach twisted, but I tugged Biscuit back toward the living room.

"Here," Arden said. "I'll take him."

I handed off the leash, everything feeling a bit hazy. My gaze swept the room, looking for a place to sit. The space wasn't exactly large and there were so many people.

Arden kept her spot near the window, off to the side—whatever place she could watch the room from best, keeping an eye out for any shift or change. Just like always. Lolli and Fallon were at the dining table, but their gazes were locked on Trace. There was no mischievous grin for Lolli, and no soft smile for Fallon. Nora stood, wringing her hands as if sitting was too much.

I lowered myself to the couch. There was a chair and an ottoman where someone could sit, but that was it. As if reading my anxiety,

Shep crossed to the couch and took the seat next to me. He patted my knee. "We're going to get it fixed. Don't worry about that."

I couldn't look at him. My eyes had locked on Anson's steely blues, and I couldn't look away. I tried to read something in his expression, but I couldn't pin anything down.

Trace cleared his throat and took a seat on the ottoman across from me. "There's evidence of arson."

I sucked in a breath. The inhale was so fast it hurt, my muscles seizing on instinct. "Someone tried to burn the house down?"

My voice didn't sound like mine. It was as if some other being had taken over my vocal cords.

Trace hid any reaction from his expression. But that was his gift—a terrifying one. He could turn off his emotions in any situation and just go totally and completely blank. "They did."

Nora was on the move then, crossing behind the couch. Her hands landed on my shoulders as if she needed to assure herself I was okay. "But who would do something like that?"

Trace's focus lifted to her for a moment. "We've got crime scene techs in there now. We're hoping we'll find prints or something that will lead us to the perp."

I felt Anson's stare before I saw it, the probing heat of a single-minded focus. I lifted my gaze to lock with those blue-gray eyes again. They were almost all gray now. That was my only hint that there was more.

"We found something else," Trace went on, but I didn't look away from Anson.

"What?" Nora demanded.

"Some clippings, writing. Things that tell us this person is fixated on Rho."

I tore my gaze from Anson and looked at Trace. "What were they?"

Trace shook his head. "You don't need to know the details."

"She does." It was Anson who spoke, his voice low and steady.

Trace's head snapped in his direction. "You don't know what my sister needs."

Anson didn't show any signs of reacting. He simply stared at Trace. "She needs to know the seriousness. Needs to know so she's careful. And she needs to know because it's her damned life."

The last sentence had a bit of a growl to the words, an edge that challenged.

That muscle in Trace's jaw ticked wildly. "She doesn't need this shit messing with her head."

"Trace," I said quietly. He turned slowly back to me. "It's my life." I echoed Anson's words. "I deserve to know everything you do."

Trace's jaw worked back and forth. "There were clippings of the coverage from the first fire." He took a deep breath. "One had a photo of you with your parents and sister. Your face was circled, and below it—"

His words cut off, and I struggled to swallow. "Below it, what?" I whispered.

A muscle fluttered right in the spot where Trace's jawbone connected to his cheekbone. "Below it, someone wrote, *MAYBE YOU DIDN'T DESERVE TO SURVIVE.*"

A series of gasps and curses rose around me, but I could barely take them in. My ears began to ring as my breaths came faster. My tongue stuck to the roof of my mouth as I struggled to speak, but I couldn't get words out—not that I had any idea what to say.

A million what-ifs circled my brain. And most of all, I tried to think of someone who hated me enough to wish me dead. I couldn't come up with a single person. Obviously, my radar was off because someone clearly did. "Do you have any idea...who...I mean, are there suspects?"

"We're not sure. Not yet," Trace said. "But we will find out. I promise."

Anson took a step toward me. "But until you get one hell of a security system in here, you're not staying alone."

Chapter Nineteen

Rhodes

"**T**HIS IS RIDICULOUS." I COULDN'T HELP THE EXASPERATION as sleeping bags were strewn across my living room floor.

Fallon wrapped an arm around my waist and squeezed hard. "It's this, or Mom moves you in with her and Lolli."

That had me snapping my mouth shut. Thankfully, I'd talked Nora, Lolli, and Arden into going home, but only after Trace and Shep promised they'd stay.

"Deal with it, Rho," Trace said, pinning me with a stare.

"What about Keely?" I pressed. "I'm sure her sitter doesn't want to stay all night."

He shook his head. "She's at a sleepover."

My shoulders slumped. "That floor is going to be ridiculously uncomfortable."

"Then go see what's taking Shep so long with the air mattresses," Trace grumbled.

I huffed out a breath, extricating myself from Fallon's hold and heading for my front door. The fire crew was gone, but the crime scene techs were still working. By the time Shep had gone to get camping gear and everyone else had left, it was almost five a.m. Sleep would be futile.

Tugging open the front door, I came up short as I took in Shep and Anson speaking in hushed but clipped tones. Anson's head jerked up at my flicker of movement. I swallowed hard. "Everything okay?" I thought Anson had taken off an hour ago.

Shep scrubbed a hand over his face. "Just making a plan for tomorrow. Need to move the crew to a different job for the day."

Shit. This was screwing up more than my life. I had to remember that. "Sorry, Shep."

He crossed to me then, two camping mattresses under one arm. He used the other to pull me into a half-hug. "None of this is your fault."

I eased into his side. "I'd like to junk-punch whoever did this."

Shep chuckled, but the sound didn't ring true. "I think that's more than fair."

Anson watched us in the glow of the porch light. "Be careful. This isn't someone you should be taking on."

I swore there was worry in Anson's tone, giving away that he might care more than he wanted to. Or maybe that was just wishful thinking. "I'll be careful. And it's not like anyone's going to make it through my two bodyguards."

"Three bodyguards." A voice cut through the dark as Kye's motorcycle boots hit the walkway up to the guesthouse. Even in the low light, I could see that his face was paler than normal, worry creasing his brow. "I'm sorry. My phone was on silent. I just saw all the texts and calls. You okay?"

He didn't move to hug me. That wasn't Kye. But I could see the true concern in his eyes. Guilt gnawed at me. This second family I'd found all carried their own scars, and here I was, triggering the hell out of them with this close call.

I did my best to force a smile. "Well, Lolli tried to get me high in an attempt to help, so it's not all bad."

Kye's lips didn't even twitch. "Rho."

My shoulders slumped. "I'm all right. Really. But Fallon was worried when you didn't answer. You should tell her you're okay."

Kye muttered a curse. "Yeah."

He headed inside without saying a word to Anson. It wasn't that he was trying to be rude. His head was just elsewhere.

Anson cleared his throat. "I'm going to head out." He glanced at Shep. "I'll touch base in the morning."

Shep gave him a chin lift in response. "Thanks, man. I really appreciate your help."

There was something about Shep's tone. There was a gravity to it that didn't quite make sense. But then again, I wasn't sure why Shep had called Anson in the first place. There wasn't anything he could do to help tonight.

Anson simply nodded, and then his gaze swept to me. I froze. Something about that look held me in place as it glided over me. It was as if he was checking for injuries, making sure that I really was okay.

"Be safe, Reckless," he gritted out.

It was my turn to nod because my vocal cords didn't seem to want to work. But Anson didn't wait for my response, he just took off for his truck.

Shep gave my shoulder another squeeze and then released me. "What's the deal with you two lately? I can't tell if you still hate each other or if you have some sort of weird friendship happening."

I grimaced. I wasn't sure Shep would appreciate the knowledge Anson had imparted on me earlier tonight. So, I kept it to myself. "I think we understand each other in a way."

Shep stilled, his gaze landing on my face. "What do you mean?"

I shifted from foot to foot. "He hasn't told me what happened to him or anything, but I know he's experienced loss. He gets what I went through. Some of the things that are hard to say. It doesn't make him less of an ass, but he's an ass I understand."

Wariness spread across Shep's expression. "Just be careful." He worried the inside of his cheek. "The shit Anson's dealt with…it's dark. Darker than anything we've seen. I don't want it to pull you down, too."

My stomach twisted viciously. Given what all my siblings and I had been through, we'd seen some of the worst of the worst. At least, I thought we had. What was darker than that?

∽ల

"No, we need Nutella and berries." A voice cut through my groggy mind.

"Lolli," Nora hissed. "I think the whipped cream is enough."

"The girl's house nearly got burned down, and she's got a creepy stalker. I think she's earned some chocolate," Lolli shot back.

A groan sounded beside me, and then Fallon's elbow landed firmly in my gut.

I let out an oof as I rolled to my back. "I'm too old for this."

"Sorry," she muttered, struggling to sit up. "You need a bigger bed."

"I didn't plan on having sleepovers at age twenty-seven," I grumbled.

Fallon arched a brow at me. "I think you need to be having some sleepovers of the grown-up variety."

I glared at her. "You're one to talk. When's the last time you went on a date?"

She snapped her mouth closed.

"That's what I thought." I scrubbed at my face. My eyes burned as if they'd been stewing in acid all night. Only I hadn't been asleep nearly that long. I glanced at the clock. Eight-fifteen.

Pots and pans clattered from the kitchen.

"Quiet," Nora hissed.

"Too late. Everyone's up within a three-mile radius," Kye called back.

Lolli giggled. "Sorry. But we've got waffles."

I couldn't help it, I smiled. God, my family was amazing.

Tossing off the covers, I sat up and slid my feet into slippers. I didn't bother changing out of my PJs, just made a quick stop in the bathroom to brush my teeth. By the time I made it to the living room, Keely was running down the hallway.

She hit me full force, looking up at me with accusing eyes. "You had a sleepover without me?"

"It wasn't planned. I swear."

Keely kept right on staring as though deciding if I was telling the truth or not. "Well, you better have another one when I can come."

I chuckled. "Fair enough. How about I make it up to you with waffles?"

"With Nutella," Lolli called from the kitchen.

"Yes!" Keely cheered and ran in that direction.

"Shoot," Lolli muttered. "I forgot the sprinkles in my car."

"We don't need sprinkles," Nora insisted.

"Of course, we do! They're unicorns," Lolli argued as she bustled by me and then Trace.

Kye stretched as he stood from the couch, intricate ink peeking out from his tee. "You need a better couch, Rho. It's lumpy as shit."

"Language," Nora called.

"I think I'll keep my lumpy couch to deter sleepover guests," I shot back.

Kye just grinned at me. "Good thing I've slept on way worse."

"I bet," Fallon grumbled.

To say Kye had a bit of a rebellious streak in high school was an understatement. Nora said he'd given her more gray hair than all her other kids combined.

Kye glanced at Fallon, frowning. "What's wrong?"

She bit her bottom lip. "You didn't answer your phone. You always answer. I was worried."

He always answered for *her*, was what Fallon meant. Because they had a bond that none of the rest of us had ever managed with Kye. He cared in his own way, but a way that enabled him to keep us at arm's length. But that wasn't the case with Fallon. He always let her in.

Kye winced. "Sorry. I forgot I had it on silent."

She stared at him for a long moment, something that looked

a lot like hurt passing over her face before she turned back to help Nora with the waffles.

A hand landed on my shoulder, and I glanced up into Trace's green eyes.

"You holding up okay?" he asked.

"Other than some internal bleeding courtesy of sharing a bed with Fallon, I'm good."

Trace chuckled, the faint lines around his eyes deepening. "She's tiny and quiet but secretly violent."

"Truer words have never been spoken." I studied him for a moment, trying to choose what I said next carefully. "Is there anything new?"

The amusement slid from his face. "Too soon. We need to run a bunch of tests, and that's not exactly a quick process. But I called in a favor at the lab, and I'm hoping they push you to the front of the line."

"You didn't have to do that—"

Trace squeezed my shoulder. "Rho. You matter. You mattered when you were just Fallon's annoying sidekick. But you're my sister in all the ways that count. I'd do anything for you."

My throat constricted, and I threw my arms around his waist in a hard hug. "If you make me cry before breakfast, I'm gonna be really mad."

Trace choked on a laugh. "God forbid we have a hangry situation on our hands."

"Someone feed her. Quick," Shep called as he handed a plate to Keely and then Arden. "I don't want to lose an eye."

"Shut up," I yelled.

"Look who I found," Lolli called from the doorway, mischief in her voice.

I peeked around Trace to find a deer-in-the-headlights Anson being dragged behind my eighty-three-year-old second grandma. His eyes were comically wide as he took in all the people.

Keely climbed up onto a stool at the counter to get a better look. "Are you my supergran's new boyfriend?"

Kye choked on a sip of orange juice as Nora let out a strangled sound. Fallon covered her mouth to try to hold in her laughter, but Shep just snorted as he glanced their way.

"What a catch, A," Shep called.

Color hit Anson's cheeks, but Lolli just cackled as she patted his chest. "I'm not sure I could keep up with this one." She winked at him. "But I'd sure like to try."

"Someone please bleach my brain," Trace begged.

Lolli smacked him upside the head as she passed. "I don't need any of that sass, young man."

We all filed into some sort of chaotic line to get breakfast. All my siblings teased Anson mercilessly but were soon distracted by the spread that Nora and Lolli had put together. There were waffles with all the trimmings. Blueberries, raspberries, and strawberries. Nutella, whipped cream, and sprinkles. Maple and marionberry syrup. And, of course, bacon and sausage.

We scattered across the living space, taking up every available surface to eat on. At least four different conversations had erupted, with all the distractions under the sun. Yet I kept seeking out one person.

Anson hovered near the outskirts, perching a plate on the end of the kitchen island. He watched the scene play out as if it were a movie. But as each moment went by, more and more shadows gathered in his eyes.

Shep's words echoed in my head. *The shit Anson's dealt with... it's dark. Darker than anything we've seen.*

Anson quietly slid his plate into the sink before slipping down the hallway. No one seemed to notice, as if he were practiced in moving like a ghost. But I saw him.

Pushing to my feet, I followed him down the hall. I quickly slipped on shoes and headed out into the sunshine.

Anson was already halfway across the lot, and I jogged to catch up. "Anson," I called.

His shoulders stiffened, but he slowed, turning around to face me.

I came to a stop just in front of him. I didn't say anything; simply searched his face, trying to uncover the secrets he'd buried so deep.

Anson's gruff voice cut through the early morning light, so in opposition to the sunshine. "You should get back to your family."

I frowned at him. "You're hurting."

He opened his mouth as though he were about to argue, then closed it again, his gaze drifting toward the mountains. "I'm always hurting. I'm used to it."

I reached out, my fingers curling around his. I felt the bumps and ridges of calluses, maybe a scar. Anson jerked, shocked at the simple touch. But I didn't let go. When was the last time someone had touched him with simple kindness? I didn't think I wanted to know the answer.

I looked up into those swirling, fathomless eyes. "You shouldn't be alone in it."

A muscle fluttered in Anson's cheek. "Alone is the only way it doesn't taint someone else."

Chapter Twenty

Anson

ER HAND BURNED. THE FEEL OF THOSE LONG, SLENDER fingers curved around mine seared me to the spot. It had been so long since I'd felt any sort of comfort like this—the feeling was completely foreign.

Rho looked up at me, those hazel eyes swirling. "Pain can't taint others. That's not how it works."

She was wrong. The ugliness I'd faced wasn't any sort of normal pain. And the events of last night had stirred it all up again.

Rho squeezed my hand, bringing me back to her. To the here and now. "But someone can help you carry the load. Whatever you've been through, I know it's heavy."

My throat constricted. Some part of me wanted to lay it all at Rhodes' feet. To tell her every fucked-up detail. But I couldn't stand the thought of seeing disgust in those gorgeous eyes.

"Anson!"

Shep's voice pulled me from my swirling thoughts, and I jerked my hand from Rho's hold. I didn't miss the flicker of hurt in her eyes. This was why I stayed away. Because I was already doing damage.

Shep jogged over to us. "You find everything we needed?"

I jerked my head in a nod. I'd been at the only electronics store in a hundred-mile radius that opened at eight. They'd had the kind of equipment that would at least tide us over until Shep could order more of the good stuff his tech-obsessed brain loved.

"They had the basics. You order the rest?" I asked.

"It'll be here the day after tomorrow. But this'll let us at least get the core system installed," he said.

Rho looked back and forth between us. "What are you guys talking about?"

Shep slowly turned toward his sister. "I know you're not crazy about alarm systems, but—"

"Shep," she growled. "You are not putting one of those ridiculous systems in my house. It's too much. I'll never remember the code. One of my foster critters or I will trip the sensors you love so much. And one of Trace's deputies will be out here every few hours. No."

He pinned her with a stare. "You need a system. It's this or you move in with one of us."

Defiance lit in Rho's eyes, making the gold dance. "Don't order me around, Shepard Colson."

He winced. "Rho. Someone set your house on fire last night. They left behind a very clear threat. You need protection, and you need it now."

All the air went out of her on a whoosh. "Trace is already assigning me to the drive-by route."

"Which means deputies will be out here every couple of hours. A lot can happen between those visits."

My gut soured at the thought, but I knew Shep was right. It only took seconds for your whole world to crumble.

Rho worried her bottom lip. "Alarm system, cameras *outside*, but no crazy sensors or anything."

"We have to install sensors on your doors and windows. That's how an alarm works. But I promise, no motion detectors," Shep vowed.

"Fine. But you'd better make the code numbers easy for me to remember," she grumbled.

"My birthday, then," Shep joked.

Rho stuck her tongue out at him. "You're getting socks for your next birthday and that's it. And I'm telling Lolli you want another shirtless elf diamond painting for your collection."

Shep's jaw went slack. "You wouldn't."

Rho just arched a brow in challenge. "That depends on if you keep your security system word. And that includes you not turning my house into some freaky robot home."

I choked on a half laugh, half cough, and Shep sent me a dirty look. His specialty was building homes with elaborate tech. Speakers built into every room for both stereo systems and intercoms. All appliances, lighting, and locks that you could control with your smartphone. He loved every nerdy detail, but it was clear that Rho did not.

"Some people would appreciate me bringing their homes into the twenty-first century," Shep groused.

"Then find those people. I do not want some possessed AI taking over my space and murdering me in my sleep."

Shep just shook his head at her. "You gotta stop going to those horror movies with Fallon."

Rho pinned him with a stare. "It could happen. You don't know what all that crud is capable of."

"It's capable of whatever I program it to do," he argued, looking at me for help.

I held up both hands. "I like the security, but I can leave the rest of that stuff. I like turning on the lights with a good old-fashioned switch."

"See?" Rho asked.

"You're hopeless. Both of you." Shep motioned me toward his truck. "Come on. Let's get started on the install."

I knew I needed to follow him, but I couldn't help stealing one more glance at Rho. To get another hit of that light. But she was already staring right back at me. Gone was the teasing expression she'd had for Shep. In its place was raw vulnerability.

"If you ever decide to let someone shoulder the load with you for a little while, I'm here." She didn't wait for me to answer; simply turned around and headed back to the guesthouse, taking her light with her as she left.

I watched her go for too long, as though I could see the particles she left in her wake. I wanted to grab each one and hold them close. But they were like fireflies. If you kept them captive, they'd die. All you could do was relish having them swirl around you in the moments they graced you with their presence.

As the door to the guest cottage closed, I forced myself to turn around. Shep waited at my truck, but his gaze was locked on me. His eyes weren't exactly hard, but they were wary.

A few colorful curses flew around in my brain, all of them directed squarely at myself. This wasn't me. Staring after some woman I barely knew and feeling like I was missing some fundamental part of myself when she walked away.

Except that wasn't exactly true. While I didn't know the ins and outs of Rho's day-to-day, her favorite color or food, we had shared my only real moments of truth since Greta's death. She was the only one I'd let see even a hint of my pain.

Because I hadn't felt like I deserved to let others in on my suffering. Not when the pain was my fault to begin with. But somehow, in those tiny stolen moments with her, Rho had shattered the walls I'd constructed around that pain. She'd made it okay to let some pieces free.

"Tell me what you're thinking," Shep said as I approached.

God, he did not want to know the honest answer there. That I couldn't stop thinking about his *sister*. A woman who was eight years my junior. Someone he was more than a little protective of.

"I think we need to get a system in place with a world of cameras," I muttered.

"Anson…"

There was so much there in just my name. A weight I wasn't sure I could shoulder.

"I need you, man. We need to know what we're dealing with. If you give Trace your credentials, he'll let you consult—"

"No." The word cracked like a whip. "No one knows."

It was a minor miracle that no one had figured it out yet. There'd been articles written about me. Primetime interviews. Not to mention the books I'd written on the intricacies of the criminal mind. Only the fact that I'd gone by my middle name as my last had saved me from simple Google searches.

It hadn't saved me from far darker forces.

"This is my sister," Shep ground out. "Some sick fuck burned her house and left a threat. We need to find out who did this."

That weight settled on my chest, the familiar tightness that made it hard to grab hold of even one solid breath. "I'm not sure you want me trying to figure it out."

Because I'd failed before—when it counted the most.

But even as the thoughts swirled, I knew I wouldn't be able to look away. Because Rho mattered. Even though I didn't want her to.

My brain was already trying to put together the pieces. It was searching for patterns and behaviors, triggers and responses. And I couldn't stop it.

Shep stared hard at me. "You're the best hope we have."

Fuck.

That was not what I wanted to hear. I didn't want to be anyone's hope. Not with my track record. But I still found myself saying, "Get me the fire crew's report. Have Trace pull any other fires in the year before or after that weren't wildfires. I know there are at least three. But *don't* tell him I asked."

"He's already getting me the report for the few you requested earlier, but I'll ask for any others."

My jaw worked back and forth. I knew it was a tell. I used to be better at hiding them, but emotion was riding me too damn hard. "What reason did you give?"

"Told him that some of what we were seeing in the rehab didn't match up with an electrical fire. Wanted to make sure we hadn't missed anything."

It was a good excuse. It also wasn't a lie. The fire didn't make sense. Not the fact that the smoke alarms didn't wake the family in time to escape, and not how quickly the blaze had spread.

Facts strung together in new connections, like a web of stars in the darkness of my mind.

"What?" Shep asked, instantly on edge.

I shook my head. "I don't know. Not yet."

But I couldn't help but wonder. What if someone had set that fire all those years ago? And what if they'd come back to finish what they started?

Chapter Twenty-One

Rhodes

AFTER MUCH PRODDING FROM ME, MOST OF OUR BREAKFAST crew took their leave. Trace had required my promise of texts every time I moved from one place to another, in addition to me enabling a danged app that let him track my location. But no matter how stifling, I knew it came from a place of love. Just as I knew Fallon's hovering did.

I leaned a hip against the counter. "You're going to work now, and so am I."

Duncan had texted early this morning, telling me to take the day off, but I'd assured him I'd be in, just a little later than usual.

Fallon's face screwed up. "I think you should rest today."

"If I lie around here all day, I'm just going to stew about everything that happened. I need to keep busy."

Her lips pursed as she seemed to mull over my words. "Then I'll come with you. Hang out with you and Biscuit."

The pup lifted his head at the sound of his name.

"Fallon, are you trying to play bodyguard?" I asked, a smile tipping my lips.

She let out a huff. "I can be intimidating if I want."

The laugh bubbled out of me before I could stop it.

Fallon scowled in my direction. "Well, that was just rude."

I held up both hands. "I have no doubt you could kick a man in the balls when he least expected it, but you don't exactly give off menacing vibes."

Fallon radiated the gentlest energy of anyone I knew. Because she was. An empath through and through, she took on the emotions of everyone around her. But that didn't mean she wasn't tough. If you hurt someone she cared about, watch out.

"Do I need to get Kye to give me a face tat?"

I choked on another laugh. "Maybe a dagger by your left eye?"

Her lips twitched. "How about *kill* in big letters across my neck?"

I pulled her into a hug. "I love you. You know that, right?"

Fallon hugged me back, hard. "I was so scared when Mom called me last night. It was just like all those years ago."

Shit. I hadn't thought about how this might be triggering for Fallon, too. She'd almost lost me back then, and this would have brought it all back. I squeezed her tighter. "I'm okay. Promise. Trace'll figure this out, and everything will go back to normal."

I said the words as much for myself as for Fallon, needing to believe it, too.

"You're right. He won't stop until he finds this asshole. And I'm going to bust his balls when Trace brings him in."

I released Fallon, my brows raising. "Vicious little thing, aren't you?"

She grinned. "See? Intimidating."

I chuckled. "Come on. I'll walk you out."

I wasn't giving Fallon any other options because she needed to go to work. She had a ridiculous caseload with Child Protective Services, and even one day out would mean her working triple-time the next day.

"But—"

"Nope." I wrapped an arm around her shoulders, guiding her toward the door. "You are going to work. I'm going to work. No one will worry because Trace has me basically implanted with a GPS tracker."

Fallon grumbled something indiscernible under her breath but let me push her along. As we made our way outside, I came up short.

I'd thought Arden was long gone, but there she stood at the base of my porch steps, a tiny ball of fur in her hands. Silas stood next to her, holding a box and looking at her with a gentleness I didn't think I'd ever seen on his face before.

Oh, shit. The last thing we needed was the town playboy setting his sights on Arden. She wouldn't have the first idea what to do about that. Her life had been too guarded. Not by her choice, but out of necessity.

I cleared my throat, and Silas's focus jerked from Arden to me.

"Hey. I was just coming to find you," he said.

I arched a brow. "Were you, now?"

His face heated. "Yeah. Uh, someone dumped some kittens at the other jobsite. I thought maybe your rescue thingy could take 'em. I don't want to take them to the shelter."

I crossed to him and Arden. The kitten she held was cuddled beneath her chin as she stroked its patchwork fur. Peering over the side of the box, I frowned. They were so tiny. My best guess put them at just over three weeks. They'd need to be bottle-fed every four to six hours, but they'd be able to go to the bathroom on their own.

"You'll take them, won't you?" Arden asked. I didn't miss the worry in her voice. Any creature that received an especially difficult set of circumstances always tugged on her heartstrings. "I'd take them, but I don't know how Brutus would do with them."

As sweet as Arden's massive dog could be, mixing him with three-week-old kittens probably wasn't a good idea.

"Let me call Nancy. If Biscuit isn't good with them, she'll probably be able to keep them."

The tension bled out of Arden. "Good. They should have a safe place to call home."

Silas glanced at her, his brow furrowing before he forced his gaze back to me. "Thanks, Rho. All these critters are lucky to have you."

I took the box from him, staring down at the sleeping pile of fur. "Well, I get paid in cuddles."

Fallon grinned at me. "The best kind of payment."

It really was.

∽

I carried the new box with fresh blankets and a hot water bottle toward Duncan's open office door, hoping my boss was in a magnanimous mood. He was leaning over his laptop, frowning at the screen. Lines of strain creased the area around his eyes as he frowned.

"Crunching numbers again?" I asked.

Duncan jerked upright. "Jesus, Rho. Make a little noise when you walk, would ya?"

I chuckled. "Sorry. I wasn't trying to be quiet. You were just in super focus mode. Mathing again?"

He shook his head, quickly shutting the laptop. "It never makes my head hurt any less." His gaze roamed over me, taking stock of every detail. "You okay? You didn't have to come in."

"I'll be better if I keep busy. And I'm all right."

A frown pulled at Duncan's mouth. "Trace called this morning. Wanted me to keep an eye out for anything suspicious while you're working."

I fought the urge to curse. It wasn't that I'd planned on *lying* to Duncan, but I certainly hadn't intended to give him every detail of the truth. "He's just being extra careful."

"Exactly as he should be," Duncan clipped. "This is serious, Rho. He said someone left a threat behind."

I bit the inside of my cheek, worrying the tender spot. "I know, I know. But we're being careful. Trace has a tracker thing on my phone, he has his deputies doing drive-bys, and, as we speak, Shep is installing some security system that would be better suited to NASA."

I expected at least a lip twitch at that last part, but there were no signs of amusement on Duncan's face.

"Worried about you," he said finally. "Are you sure you don't want to stay at my place? There's plenty of room."

I shook my head. "I'm good, really. I can stay with Nora and Lolli if I get spooked."

Duncan's mouth pressed into a hard line. "I'm not trying to be some sexist pig but staying with two women of retirement age doesn't really make me feel any better."

"Don't let Lolli hear you say that. She'll whoop your butt."

"I'm serious, Rho."

I sighed. "Fine. If I get spooked, I'll stay with Shep or Trace."

"That's a little better," Duncan grumbled. "Now, you gonna tell me what critter you have in that box that you want to keep in my office while you're working?"

I pasted on my brightest smile, but before I could utter a word, a mewl sounded from the box.

Duncan groaned. "Kitten season?"

I winced. "Kitten season. They're super sweet. But I can't leave them home alone just yet."

"First the dog, then the cats. Before long, this will turn into an animal shelter."

"We have gotten some cuties adopted out of here. That has to count toward your angel points," I said, giving him my best hopeful look.

Duncan pinched the bridge of his nose and groaned. "Fine. Tell me what you need."

After I got the kittens all set up in Dunc's office and gave them each a bottle, I headed out to find Thea so I could help with the watering. I waved at Heather behind the counter as I passed. "Thanks for watching Biscuit!"

"He's the best male company I've had in months," she called back, bending to give his head a rub.

I chuckled as I headed out the door and into the sunshine. I couldn't help but sweep my surroundings, looking for anything out of place. I hated that this was my instinct. And what did I think I would see? Some ominous figure holding a lighter? Someone in a hoodie making a throat-slitting motion across their neck?

Letting out a sound of frustration, I headed toward the far greenhouse. I forced myself to take in the good things. The scent of ponderosa pine in the air. The way the light caught on the blooms all around me. The feel of lavender between my fingers as I passed.

There was so much beauty. So much to be grateful for. I just had to pause to let it all in.

My phone dinged just as I reached the greenhouse. Pulling it out of my back pocket, I glanced down at the screen, and my good mood fled.

> **Davis:** *I told you messing around with that old house was a mistake.*

My stomach twisted like the grasses to my left spiraling in the wind. The moment I'd told Davis about my plan to rehab my old home, he'd been against it. Having grown up here, too, I'd thought he would be supportive, but he was dead set against it from the beginning.

All he had was a laundry list of reasons why it was a horrible idea. He'd wanted me to sell instead, to invest the money in stocks and buy something new. Something he'd hinted at us living in together. He'd never understood why I wanted to do this as part of my healing.

And when I'd used the Victorian as another reason for why I didn't have time for dating, he'd hated it even more. But did he hate it enough to try to scare me this way? And if he did, what else was he capable of?

Chapter Twenty-Two

Anson

I STARED AT THE GUEST COTTAGE'S FRONT DOOR LIKE IT WAS some sort of video game nemesis I had to defeat. And maybe it was. To pass or not to pass.

Shep had taken off hours ago, called to another jobsite when someone hit a pipe that wasn't where it should've been. So, he'd left me here to wrap up the install. He'd handled the actual security system, but I'd finished up the cameras. That piece of things wasn't difficult; it was just the sheer number of devices Shep had wanted put in.

The door to Rho's house mocked me. I should've taken the burst pipe, even though I knew next to nothing about plumbing. I flipped my cell phone between two fingers, swinging it in circles.

The door opened, and Rho filled the entryway. I spat out a curse. Her brown hair was tamed into pigtail braids, but a few wisps flew free, needing to remind the rest of her hair of its wildness. She wore a tank top that hugged her curves in a way that told me she had no bra underneath. And those damned shorts. They looked like ones she maybe slept in—soft, worn, and way too fucking short for someone battling temptation like me.

Rho arched a brow. "You gonna come in, or you just gonna stand there glaring at my door all night?"

My lips twisted into a scowl. She burst out laughing.

God, that sound. There was so much pleasure in it, the tone hurt to take in. Sheer amusement at my surliness.

That was the thing I was starting to realize about Rho. She wasn't afraid to show the world how she felt. Happy, sad, anything in between. She just let those emotions fly.

There was bravery in that freedom. And I admired the hell out of it.

"Come on, you broody ass. I've got baked chicken, potato-leek casserole, and a salad just about done. You can scowl while you're being fed."

That scowl only deepened. "What the hell is potato-leek casserole?"

Rho held the door open for me. "Only the best thing you'll taste this side of heaven."

"Bold claim," I challenged.

She shrugged. "I'll let you be the judge."

As we walked into the open-plan living room and kitchen, Biscuit scrambled up. He charged over to me, but there was no bark or growl; instead, there was just a wag of his tail. "Hey," I greeted, giving his head a rub.

A chorus of meows sounded from a box near Biscuit's bed. He let out a whine in answer.

Rho moved quickly, grabbing a tiny bottle from the counter. "Don't worry, buddy, I hear 'em." She glanced at me with a smile. "He's taken it on himself to mother them."

I slowly moved closer, watching as Rho helped the tip of a bottle into a tiny kitten's mouth. Its meowing stopped instantly. It sucked ferociously, and Rho gave it her fingers to knead. It all looked effortless, but I knew there was no way it was. "How often do you have to feed them?"

She stroked the kitten's head with one finger. "Every four to six hours. Makes for some rough nights for a while. It would be more like every two to three hours if they were any younger."

I winced. "Most people wouldn't sign up for that sort of thing."

Rho shrugged as the kitten finished its bottle, and she set it down. "I know what it's like to need a safe place to land."

Of course, she did. She knew better than anyone what it was like to be in the worst state imaginable and to feel like she had no one.

As Rho stood to get another bottle, my gaze slid to the scars peeking out from her shorts. I hated the pain they were evidence of. Hated that she carried that kind of reminder with her.

I watched as she fed kitten number two, marveling at how she'd dealt with it all. I hadn't paid nearly the price Rho had, yet she seemed to handle it all so much better than me.

"Gonna tell me what you're thinking about so hard over there?" The question was easy, casual. There was no pressure behind it. I knew if I said no, she'd leave it be. But I found myself wanting to answer.

"You," I finally said.

Her gaze flicked to me for the briefest moment. That swirl of green and gold mesmerized. Tonight, the gold looked like sunflowers in a field of grass. "Putting all the pieces of the puzzle together?"

It was a little too close to the truth of how my mind worked. "You take the bad and turn it into good."

Rho switched kittens again, feeding the third, a little black-and-white one with an especially potent wail. Once the bottle was in its mouth, she turned to me, those eyes searching. "I'm not one of those people who thinks everything happens for a reason."

All I could do was grunt in response. If everything happened for a reason, we were all walking around rocking some seriously horrendous karma. But I was surprised that Rho felt that way. She seemed like the kind of person who put meaning behind everything.

"Sometimes, absolutely horrible things happen. Things where no silver lining can justify the pain."

An invisible fist locked around my chest at her words, a reminder of the kind of agony she spoke of.

Rho's eyes locked with mine. "But good can come, even out of those darkest depths. It doesn't mean we're glad we went through it. It just means we won't let it change us for the worse."

She didn't look away as she kept going. "I've realized lately that because I lost them, I never take one second with the Colsons for granted. Because my mom can't see her garden bloom each summer, I take extra time breathing mine in every year. Because my dad won't ever get to read the new John Grisham, I'll read it for him and appreciate the twists that much more. And because Emilia won't ever get to grow old, I'm going to embrace every wrinkle and age spot."

Rho took a deep breath as she set the black-and-white kitten down. "It doesn't mean I'm glad they're gone. It doesn't mean I miss them any less. But I'm going to let that loss teach me, not harden me."

Every inhale felt like breathing fire. Flames scalded my throat and lungs. It was torture just to stay alive. That's what it had become.

"I don't think I'm as strong as you," I rasped.

Rho stared hard at me, not looking away in the face of my weakness. "Everyone has their own path to get there. Yours doesn't have to look like mine. You just can't stop walking it."

Blood roared in my ears. I hadn't let myself remember Greta. Because I was scared shitless that if I let myself remember the pain of losing her, of being responsible for her death, it would swallow me whole. I only let myself have tiny glimpses of her. It was all I could handle.

"You're not alone, Anson. Plenty of people would keep you company on the path if you asked. Me included."

Hell. She slayed me. That simple, bold kindness. So unafraid.

I opened my mouth, unsure what would come out of it, and then the kitchen timer went off.

This time, it was Rho who cursed, a creative one that somehow managed to be both sunshiny and bold, just like she was.

She climbed to her feet and crossed to the oven. Grabbing two mitts, she pulled out something that looked like a heart attack in a baking dish and smelled even better.

"Holy hell," I muttered.

Rho grinned. "No sense in wasting a meal on bad food. Make it count."

I was starting to realize that Rho lived every part of her life that way—not wasting a single moment.

I pushed to my feet. "What can I do?"

"Plates and drinks, please."

I circled the island and crossed to the cabinet that housed the plates. Rho bent, pulling out what looked like baked chicken, but I barely noticed the food. My eyes slid to her ass like it had its own gravitational pull. Her hips swayed from side to side as if moving to her own internal beat.

Images flashed in my mind that I had no right to. Fingers biting into her hips as I took her from behind. Her head tipped back, lips parted, begging for more.

"Anson?"

I jerked out of my lust-fueled stroke. "Sorry. Spaced." I quickly handed her the plates.

Rho frowned at me, then bit her lip. I wanted to nip it with my teeth. Know what it was like to taste her on my tongue, all sunshine and recklessness.

Opening the fridge, I stilled. There, on the top shelf, were six ginger beers. I didn't say a word; simply took one and let the kindness and knowing burrow into me. "Soda or beer?" I croaked.

"Coke, please," she called back.

I tried to get it together as I straightened, but dinner was an exercise in temptation. Every sound Rho made as she ate, every flick of her tongue to catch an invisible crumb, the way her lips closed around her goddamn fork. By the time I helped her clean up, I had a case of blue balls that would take me weeks to recover from.

Rho wrung her hands as she followed me to the door, an invisible energy almost making her vibrate. I slowed, taking her in. Rho always had vitality running through her, but this was something different. I let that other piece of my brain slide into place.

Breaths shallow and quick. Gaze darting in quick movements. Pulse thrumming. Worrying the inside of her cheek.

Damn it all to blue-balled hell.

She was nervous. Not some fighting attraction nerves, but *fear* nerves. Of course, she was. Someone had set fire to her house and all but threatened to burn her with it.

One call to Shep, and he'd be over. I'd just have to explain why the hell I was having dinner with his sister. But as I studied the woman opposite me, I knew she'd just send him away. Not because she was embarrassed to be scared but because she didn't want her family to worry.

I cleared my throat. "Why don't I stay on your couch tonight?"

Rho's gaze jerked to me. "What?"

"Give it a night to make sure the new security system's working like it should. Just to be on the safe side."

Her phone had gone off no fewer than half a dozen times during dinner, all with different siblings checking in. Her brother, Cope, had offered to send a full security detail to patrol the premises. I knew she wouldn't truly be alone, but she was clearly feeling that way. That was all that mattered. Because, for some damn reason, the idea of Rho in any sort of discomfort was more than I could bear.

"You won't get a good night's sleep on my couch," she mumbled.

Just the fact that she didn't blow me off outright told me she didn't want to be alone. That was enough for me.

"Your couch is just as comfortable as my lumpy-ass mattress back at the cabin."

Those teeth tugged on her bottom lip. "I could go stay with Shep or Trace."

"Or you can give me a blanket, and I can crash on your couch. I'll be out before your head hits the pillow."

Hazel eyes tangled with mine, those witch eyes pulling me in and putting me under their spell. "Might be nice to have someone here for one more night."

I didn't look away, couldn't have even if I tried. "Then here's where I'll be."

ↄe9

I lay on my back, staring at the ceiling as the early morning sun peeked through the curtains. I'd strung together maybe three hours. Every sound had me kicking off the blanket to walk the tiny house, rechecking locks and latches.

Except when I heard Rho. Her mattress creaked every time she tossed and turned. She hummed as she cared for the kittens in the middle of the night. And I swore she whispered as she dreamed.

Images of her tangled in sheets just feet from this damn couch haunted my every waking thought and taunted the little sleep I'd managed to get. Dreams of Rho. All curves and glowing skin, damp with sweat as I—

The sound of a door opening jerked me out of my thoughts. I sat up, pushing to my feet as I heard the shower turn on. She haunted me even now with images of water running down her neck as she washed her face, of that tangle of hair I wanted so desperately to get my hands on.

I stalked down the hallway, pissed as all hell. At her. At me. At the fact that my fucked-up brokenness meant that Rho was someone I should never touch with my tainted fingers.

She slipped out of the bathroom and came up short, lips parting. "You're awake."

I didn't answer. Simply stared.

Rho's hair was in a tangle she hadn't tried to tame yet. That tank top still taunted me, her nipples pressing against the fabric, beckoning me closer.

My back teeth ground together so hard I'd probably need a root canal. "Go back to your room," I gritted out.

A little furrow appeared on her brow. "Why—?"

"Because I'm holding on to my last shred of humanity, and if you stand here in those goddamn shorts for another ten seconds, it's going to snap."

Rho's breaths came quicker, her chest rising and falling with each one. Every inhale brought those curves closer—to my hands, my tongue. "What happens if you snap?" she whispered.

"I fuck you so hard you'll feel me for weeks. I'll ruin you, Reckless. You think I can't taint you with my pain and the darkness that lives inside me, but you're wrong."

Defiance swept into those witch eyes. "One." She licked her lips. "Two."

"What the hell are you doing?" I snarled.

"Counting down to the snap," Rho challenged. "Three."

Everything about her set my blood on fire, from her strength to her beauty to her fearlessness.

"Four…" she goaded, slipping one strap of her tank top down. "Five." The other fell free.

"Fuck it."

I was on her in two long strides. One hand sank into her hair, hauling her mouth to mine. The other dropped to her ass, pulling her flush against me.

Rho gasped into my mouth as my dick pressed against her. I swallowed that gasp, taking it all, every ounce of shock and need. My mouth tore from hers, tracing her jaw until I reached her ear.

"Is this what you wanted? To know that you've been torturing me in those fucking shorts?" I squeezed her ass, and Rho's thighs clenched in response. "In that damned tank top that shows me these pretty little nipples standing at attention?"

My hand moved from her ass, trailing up her waist to the most perfect breast. Palming it, I traced the peak with my thumb, and Rho shuddered.

My dick pressed against the zipper of my jeans so hard the metal would probably leave a mark. I didn't give a damn. I welcomed the bite of pain.

I tugged down the cotton of her tank and dipped my head. My mouth latched onto the bud, pulling it deep. Rho moaned, arching into me. Her fingers dug into my shoulders, nails clawing, everything drawing me closer.

I felt her need seeping into me, and I wanted it all. Every ounce she had to give me.

My hand dipped between her legs, stroking her through the soft cotton of her shorts, the fabric damp with need already. I released her nipple, and Rho let out a whimper as her nails dug deeper into my shoulders.

"Need something, Reckless?"

Her eyes flashed that molten gold. God, I wanted to see it spark and swirl as she came. Wanted to watch every flicker of movement in her face as she shattered. I needed that more than another breath.

"Anson," she gritted out.

I couldn't help it, I smiled. The feeling was so foreign my muscles barely recognized it.

Rho's thighs tightened around my hand, trying desperately for release.

That heat. It was the kind of flame you never recovered from.

My fingers teased her through the cotton. "Aching?"

She let out a little growl of frustration.

"Ask. Ask me to make you come. Beg."

Another flash of gold—that defiance I loved so much. "Or I could go back to my bedroom, get the toy from my nightstand, and finish the job myself if you're not up to the task."

A million images flashed in my mind, and my own growl left my lips. I cupped her between her legs, pulling her closer. "Wanna watch that, Reckless. Watch how you make yourself come. How you tease and toy. The way your breaths trip and tumble. Do you tweak your nipples, too?"

I twisted the peak with my free hand, and Rho arched into me, those perfect breasts pressing against my chest.

I couldn't wait. I needed to feel her, that wetness, the heat. My hand slipped into her shorts, gliding down to the apex of her thighs.

"Fuck," I groaned.

Like stroking silk. And that heat...

I slid two fingers inside, and Rho's head dropped to my shoulder.

I stroked, curling my fingers. She bit down on my shoulder to keep from crying out.

"Gonna brand me, Reckless?"

Rho's head pulled back, her hazel eyes swirling. "More."

I loved that she wasn't afraid to ask. No, not ask. Demand. To tell me what she wanted. What she needed.

I slid a third finger inside her heat, and Rho's legs began to tremble. I thrust, in and out, curling each time.

Rho grabbed my arms, holding on like I was her life raft on a stormy sea. "Anson."

My name on her tongue. Heaven and hell all at once.

I circled her clit with my thumb, and Rho's eyes closed as her mouth fell open.

I tweaked her nipple. "Eyes on me."

Those hazel beauties flew open, locking with mine.

"Want to see everything when you shatter. Don't want to miss a fucking thing."

My fingers thrust deeper, finding that spot that would bring Rho to her knees. She clamped down around my fingers as her lips parted on a quiet gasp. My thumb pressed down on that bundle of nerves as I stroked each wave that hit her. Again and again.

I watched the gold dance in her eyes as she struggled to keep them open. To keep them on me. The green all but disappeared, and Rho was only gold. Pure fire.

As the last wave hit her, her legs gave out. I caught her around the waist with my free arm, holding her to me, not wanting to let go. I didn't want to leave the warmth and life that was Rho.

A horn honked outside, and she jolted.

I cursed, pulling my fingers free.

Rho's eyes widened as she hurried to pull up her tank top. "Shep."

Oh, hell.

Chapter Twenty-Three

Rhodes

A WAVE OF SHEER PANIC HIT ME LIKE A FREIGHT TRAIN. "I forgot. Shep said he was coming early to show me how to work everything with the new system. Um, I'll just, uh—"

"Get dressed, Reckless." Then Anson licked clean the fingers that had just been inside me.

I gaped at him. "You didn't."

"Get dressed," he growled.

I startled, bobbing my head in a rapid nod before glancing down at Anson's crotch. "But, uh, you. Um."

"Fuck. Don't look at it. Makes it worse. I need to think about dirty gym socks or something."

I choked on a laugh. "I'm sorry. I really did forget he was coming over early. I just need to turn off the shower. I think we've let the water run too long already."

Anson scrubbed a hand over his face. "Please, for the love of God, get dressed. I'll deal with the shower and your brother."

I bit my lip.

"Don't do that either," he snapped, pinching the bridge of his nose. "Clothes. Please. Preferably a parka."

"I'm going." I hurried into my bedroom, finally letting my laugh free.

"My blue balls aren't funny," Anson called through the door.

"Maybe just a little bit," I yelled back.

I heard a muffled curse.

Biscuit lifted his head as if to ask what all the ruckus was about.

I covered my mouth with both hands. *What the hell had I done?*

My skin buzzed, and my muscles all but vibrated. I'd had a handful of relationships, even a couple of one-night stands in college, but I had never, not once, felt anything like what I'd just experienced in the freaking hallway.

We hadn't even had sex. But, God, I wanted to. I wanted to know what it would be like to have Anson moving inside me, to—nope, nope, nope.

"Get it together, Rho."

Biscuit cocked his head to one side.

I shook off my lust-induced haze and hurried to get changed. I put on khaki shorts and my usual work shirt with *Bloom & Berry* arched across the chest.

A soft mewl came from the box on the floor, and Biscuit was instantly on alert, heading over to nose at the kittens.

"Don't worry. I'll get them fed." Lifting the box, I headed toward the sound of muffled voices. "Anson, can you grab Biscuit? He needs to go out."

Anson let out a whistle, deterring the pup from snarling at Shep, and set to work taking him out on the leash. Back to communicating without words, I guessed.

Shep's gaze cut to me the moment I stepped into the living space, and my brother did *not* look happy. I winced. This would not be good.

"Morning," I greeted, trying to keep my voice as nonchalant as possible. I crossed to the kitchen, setting down the kittens and getting to work on their bottles.

Shep followed me, standing on the other side of the small island and staring me down.

Double crap.

"Want to help feed them?" I asked as if I had no idea he was giving me the death glare.

"Why didn't you call me?" Shep demanded.

I flicked my gaze to him as I mixed the kitten milk replacer with water. I always kept the stuff on hand because I usually ended up with babies this time of year, and if they were dehydrated, you had to move quickly. "About what?"

"If you were scared to stay alone, you should've called me."

The hint of hurt in Shep's tone had me stilling and guilt settling in. The last thing I wanted to do was cause anyone in my family pain. "Is that what Anson said?"

A muscle in Shep's cheek popped. "No. He said that he wanted to make sure the system was up and running properly before you stayed alone. But I would've stayed here. You know that."

I did. God, did I ever. I looked up at Shep, making sure he *really* saw me. "Not everything is your responsibility."

Shadows flickered in his amber eyes. "You're my sister in every way that matters. I just want to make sure you're safe."

But it was more than that. Shep carried the weight of the world, and I was starting to really worry about him taking on that sort of pressure. "It means everything that you care so much about me, but I can take care of myself. Sometimes, that means asking a friend to stay because I realized I wasn't quite ready to be on my own."

I wasn't sure what Anson and I shared could be classified as *friendship*. It was more. But something undefinable. The kind of bond that made you feel truly seen for the first time.

The fluttering in Shep's cheek intensified. "A friend?"

I let out a huff. "You asked me to cut him some slack. I did." I sent Shep a pointed stare. "He needs people. And I like his grumpy ass."

Shep scoffed. "Grumpy is an understatement."

My lips twitched as I lifted the first kitten out of the box to feed her. "True. But I find it kind of funny now."

Shep studied me for a long moment before finally lifting the black-and-white baby to give him another bottle. "You're right. He does need people."

"We all do. It's just harder for some to let them in."

Shep went quiet as he fed the kitten. "Your new coworker that way?"

My gaze flicked to him. "Thea?"

He nodded. "I've seen her at the bakery a few times. She's pretty abrupt. I feel like maybe I did something to piss her off, but I'm not sure what."

I bit the inside of my cheek to keep from smiling. Shep was wonderful in so many ways, but he was also used to women in this town falling at his feet. Between his golden-boy reputation, the successful business he'd built, and the Colson family name, he was a catch. But he might've gotten a little too used to the status.

I set the patchwork kitten back in the box and picked up the orange tiger stripe. "I get the sense she hasn't had it easy. She's guarded with me, too, but we've gotten friendlier as time has passed. Just don't push it."

Shep tensed. "What do you mean she hasn't had it easy?"

I sent up a mental curse. I never should've put it that way. That sort of thing set off Shep's white-knight complex. "As far as I know, she's good now. I can just tell she's been through some things." I glanced up at him. "You know how it is. We've got a radar for people with scars."

There was no way we couldn't when our siblings had been through so much. You developed a sort of alert system for people who had been through trauma. And I wasn't sorry about it. It had given us all empathy that most people didn't have.

Shep scowled down at the counter. "She shouldn't be dealing with whatever it is alone."

I smiled at him. "You've got the best heart, you know that, right?"

Redness crept into his cheeks. "I just meant she needs some friends."

"I know. But I love that you think that way."

The front door slammed shut, and Biscuit pulled Anson down the hallway, panting happily. As Anson came into view, my eyes widened. He had dirt streaked across his cheek and down one side of his jeans.

"What happened?"

Anson glared at Biscuit and then me. "He saw a bunny and thought it would be fun to chase it. He dragged me a good six feet through the dirt."

I rolled my lips over my teeth to keep from laughing.

"Do *not* laugh," Anson growled.

"I'm not," I said, barely holding it in.

"I see it in your eyes," he accused. He scowled at Biscuit. "No more treats until you get some proper training."

Biscuit just looked up at him with adoring eyes.

"Damn it," Anson muttered.

Shep chuckled as he set the black-and-white kitten back with its siblings. "You'll last an hour, tops, before giving that dog a treat. Even if you do look like you took a dirt bath."

Anson turned his glare on Shep. "I'm going to work."

He dropped the leash and headed for the door.

Shep and I shared a look, and then both burst out laughing.

"I heard that!"

∽ల

I pulled into a parking spot outside The Mix Up. A few cars were nearby, but it was still early enough that the big breakfast crowd hadn't descended, and thankfully, the mornings were still cool enough that I could leave the critters in my SUV while I ran in.

My phone buzzed in the cupholder, and I swiped it up.

> **Trace:** *Had a word with Davis. He's got an alibi for the night of the fire, but it's thin. Still waiting on prints to come back from the crime scene, but we have his from a drunk and disorderly during college. We'll be able to compare.*

I let out a long breath as I stared at the screen. Davis was the only person I could think of who had real anger when it came to me. I also couldn't imagine him wanting me dead. It seemed like a big leap. But I didn't have any better ideas.

> **Me:** *Thanks. I'm running to The Mix Up and then work. You need a caffeine and sugar hit?*

> **Trace:** *I'm good. Text me when you get to work.*

I sent him a salute emoji in response, then gripped the wheel and closed my eyes for a second. I forced myself to think about the good stuff. The things that weren't fire or threats or hatred. I thought about cute kitten mews. Biscuit dragging Anson through the mud. Anson's hand between my—nope.

My eyes flew open. That was a dangerous game. Better to think about whatever bakery treats I was about to indulge in. *Much* safer to everything except my cholesterol. Cracking the window, I turned off my engine and hopped out in front of the newly painted sign for *The Mix Up.*

The new owner had taken over less than a month ago but had already turned the place upside down in the best way. The previous owner had done a decent job with the baked goods, but the décor hadn't been anything special. Sutton had taken everything to the next level.

There were homemade breads, pastries, and treats on top of breakfast and lunch offerings. But her specialty was cupcakes. The creations she concocted were unlike anything I'd ever seen before. Everything from unicorns to monsters in every imaginable color.

But I wasn't looking for a sugar coma, just a pick-me-up to get me through the first few hours of work. The bell over the door tinkled as I stepped inside, the incredible smells wrapping around me. The space had white walls with dark, exposed beams overhead. Shabby-chic chandeliers hung, giving the place a feminine feel. And the accents of teal in the banquette seating and counter gave it a vibrant energy.

A woman with piercing, almost turquoise eyes smiled widely at me. "Morning, Rho."

"Morning. It smells amazing in here," I greeted as I made my way toward the counter. There were only two other patrons, both of whom were enjoying breakfast and their papers, so you could hear the soft strains of country music coming through the speakers.

"Always love hearing that," Sutton said, her eyes lighting. "What are you thinking this morning?"

I glanced up at the chalkboard behind the counter. The antique frame and curlicue writing only added to the charm of it all. My gaze landed on a new addition. An egg sandwich with caramelized onions and fresh greens. "Oooooh, I want the special to go."

"Perfect choice."

"I'm a sucker for anything with caramelized onions."

"It's the whole salty-sweet thing. What about to drink?" Sutton asked.

"I'll do a hazelnut latte."

"You've got it," Sutton said, turning toward the kitchen. "One special."

"Coming right up," an older voice called.

Sutton set to work on my coffee as I tapped my credit card against the reader. Then I moved down to the bakery case to admire some of her work. I just shook my head as I took it all in. There were cupcakes that looked like adorable buckets of popcorn, ones with strawberries cut to look like flowers, a few penguins, and her signature rainbow unicorns.

"I can't believe you can make all this," I muttered.

Sutton chuckled. "It's kind of an addiction. I love coming up with new ideas."

"Well, I'd say you have a gift."

"Moooom," a little boy called as he charged out of the kitchen.

Sutton gaped at him as he skidded to a stop in front of her. "Did you eat some of the frosting I was working on?"

The little boy's eyes shifted to the side. It would've been a dead giveaway of guilt if blue stains weren't already all over his face.

"Luca."

He grinned up at her. His teeth were blue, too. "The blue's the best kind."

Sutton shook her head. "Go wash your face in the bathroom. We need to head to school, and I can't take you looking like you're about to audition for The Blue Man Group."

His face scrunched. "What's blue man group?"

She ruffled his hair. "Musicians who dunk themselves in blue paint before every performance."

Luca looked thoughtful for a moment. "I'd try out if they dunked me in blue *frosting* before every performance."

I couldn't help but laugh. "Me, too. Blue is the best."

He grinned at me. "Mom's working on the cookie monster cupcakes right now. She'll give you one if you ask real nice."

"Thanks for the tip." I winked at him, and he charged for the bathroom. "How did you make such a cute kid?"

Sutton laughed. "His cuteness makes up for all the mischief he gets into. I swear, I need ten of me to keep up with him."

Her words had me taking stock of the strain on Sutton's face. She covered it well. Concealer hid the worst of the dark smudges beneath her eyes, and a wide smile disguised the lines of tension around her mouth. But I could only imagine what it took to run a bakery and be the solo parent to a six-year-old son.

"I bet. He looks like he has triple the energy I do."

"More like quadruple," Sutton said with a shake of her head.

"Order up," a man with white hair and a lined face said as he exited the kitchen. He grinned at me. "Thought it was you, Rho. How's Lolli?"

"Gettin' up to all sorts of trouble, per usual."

"You ask her when she's gonna marry me, will ya?"

I chuckled. "You know she's impossible to pin down, Walter."

He placed a hand over his heart as he handed me the to-go box. "It's the chase that makes it so fun."

"I'll see if she has any plans to let you catch her."

"You do that."

I gave Sutton a wave. "Thank you. And good luck with your own little cookie monster."

"I'll take it," she called. "Thanks for coming in."

I headed out into the early morning sunlight but came up short as a figure stalked toward me. Davis's lip curled as he glared at me. "You sicced your *foster* brother on me?"

Oh, shit.

I'd shared with Trace the text that Davis had sent yesterday because, as much as I didn't love all the brotherly interference in my life, I wasn't an idiot. That text was cruel at best, threatening at worst. And the fact that Davis was stressing the word *foster* only pissed me off more.

He'd never seen my family as true siblings. Never understood our bond. Once, when I was heading to Nora and Lolli's for dinner, he'd asked why I spent so much time with people who weren't actually my family when I could be spending time with him. That had been the end of things for me.

I rolled my shoulders back, reminding myself that people were just inside the bakery. "I didn't sic anyone on you. But I did share the text you sent with my *brother*, also known as the sheriff. Because he's trying to find out who set that fire you were oh so concerned about."

Davis's jaw went hard as granite. "Are you insinuating something, Rhodes?"

"No. I'm just sharing the facts. And you can lose my number. If you don't, I'll make sure to let Kye know just how intent you are on getting in touch."

Davis's face paled.

Guilt flooded me. Not that I'd scared Davis, but that I'd used Kye's reputation to do it. People saw the tattoos, knew his past, and put him in that *dangerous* category when he was anything but. But they didn't see how gentle he could be: with Fallon, with his niece, with every animal I took in.

"I don't know why the hell I ever thought you were worth it. You're nothing but a glorified gardener with a nice ass. I'll find better in two seconds," he snarled, charging down the street.

"Thanks for saying I have a nice ass," I called after him.

But a chill skated down my spine because I'd seen real hatred in Davis's eyes.

Chapter Twenty-Four

Anson

MY TRUCK HIT ANOTHER POTHOLE, AND I CURSED—THE potholes for still being there, even though Shep had put in numerous calls to our guy who typically handled grading our drives; my truck for not handling them better despite only being a year old; and most of all, myself.

Because here I was, driving back to Rho's house despite working on another site all day. Despite the fact that it was the *last* place I should go. Because I was weak when it came to her. Maybe Rho's reckless spirit was catching.

As I approached the guest cottage, it was to find Rho outside, damned shorts in full display and wearing fucking cowboy boots with colorful flowers all over them. She was bent over, perfect ass in the air, trying to pick up Biscuit.

I pulled up next to her SUV and climbed out.

"Thank God!" Rho huffed. "Can you please help me?"

"What exactly is going on?" I asked, my lips twitching.

"Don't laugh at me!" Rho grunted as she tried to haul Biscuit up. "I've been trying to get him into the car for thirty minutes. We're going to be late for his vet appointment."

I watched as Biscuit simply went limp as she tried to lift him. "I've seen you get him into your SUV at least a dozen times. He just jumps in."

Rho sent a scathing look my way. "It's like he *knows*. I didn't even say the V-word, but the moment we got outside, he wouldn't get closer than ten feet to the SUV."

The laugh tore free from my throat, the sound rusty like the action. But, God, it felt good.

Rho straightened, her expression softening. "Laughter looks good on you, Hunt."

The sound faded, but the heat it sparked stayed as I stared at Rho.

She motioned me forward. "If you get his back end, and I take his front, we should be able to get him into the back seat. He's heavier than he looks."

I crossed to the dog, who still lay on the ground, sending me an over-your-dead-body stare. "How are you going to get him *out* of the SUV once you're at the vet?"

Rho clasped her hands beneath her chin and sent me a pleading look. "If you help me take him to his appointment, I'll make you dinner."

I groaned but knew I wouldn't be able to say no. "Come on."

I bent, hauling Biscuit into my arms. "What the hell have you been eating?" I grumbled.

The dog let out a grunt as he tried to spring out of my hold.

"Told you," Rho said.

"No more treats for you, pal," I said as I held on to the squirming dog. I managed to awkwardly get him into the SUV and shut the door. I leaned against it, breathing heavily.

Rho scowled. "It's annoying how easy that was for you. I carry heavy things all day."

I chuckled. "Pretty sure it's a muscle mass issue, plus the fact that I've got almost a foot on you."

"I'm still annoyed," she grumbled as she moved toward the driver's door.

We both climbed into the SUV, and she backed out of the makeshift parking spot. Biscuit let out a mournful howl.

I glanced over my shoulder. "Dude, have some pride."

"Let him express his feelings," Rho chided.

Of course, she would want her dog to embrace the same freedom she had, letting everything fly. Biscuit howled again in answer, and I just shook my head.

Rho slowed as she reached the end of her gravel drive, putting on her blinker. Biscuit didn't miss the opportunity. He launched himself over the divider and landed hard in my lap.

Pain flared, hot and bright. I let out a strangled sound that didn't resemble anything human.

"Biscuit!" Rho scolded. She winced as she took in my face. "Are you okay?"

"I'll never have children, but other than that, dandy," I rasped.

She sent me a strained smile. "I can try to get him in the back again."

"Just leave him here. If he does that again, you'll be taking me to the hospital instead."

Rho rolled her lips over her teeth to keep from laughing. "I sincerely apologize to your balls."

"Don't say that word. They've had enough abuse from you today."

A pink blush stained her cheeks. "About that—"

"Nope," I said, cutting her off. "If we talk about that, I'm gonna get hard. I get hard right now, and I'll rupture something. Talk about something else. *Anything* else."

Rho bit her lip. "How about them Yankees?"

I sent her a sidelong look. "Are you a closet baseball fan or something?"

"I thought you all talked about sports when you were fighting off chubbies."

"Good God," I muttered.

"I'm *trying*," she snapped.

"You're good at a lot of things, Reckless, but not turning me on isn't one of them. Try being a little less fucking cute and not talking about my dick."

This time, Rho let the laugh free. It swam around us, creating a sea of sound that was better than any song I'd ever heard. Biscuit must've thought the same because he tipped his head back and howled.

He kept it up for the next ten minutes until Rho pulled to a stop in front of the vet.

"Stay there," she instructed. "I'll come around."

Rho rounded the SUV and opened my door. Biscuit made no sign of movement.

"Come on, buddy. It's just an exam and one little shot," she encouraged.

As if he knew what the word *shot* meant, Biscuit climbed me like a damn tree.

Cursing, I unfastened my seat belt and wrapped my arms around the dog. "This is embarrassing for both of us."

I maneuvered my way out of the vehicle, half-blind as Biscuit held on to me for dear life.

"I'll get the door," Rho called, running ahead.

I did my best not to trip over anything as I carried the way-heavier-than-he-looked dog into the vet's office. The moment the receptionist caught sight of us, her eyes widened comically. "Oh, dear. Why don't you just come straight back? We've got a room ready."

"Thanks, Ruby," Rho said. "We appreciate it."

"Dr. Lutz. We've got a nervous patient for you," Ruby said as a red-haired woman stepped into the hallway.

"I can see that," the middle-aged woman said, humor lacing her tone. "Why don't I see him next? Right this way."

I followed the vet into an exam room, Rho on our heels.

"Just set him right here," Dr. Lutz instructed.

I tried putting Biscuit down, but he just jumped right back into my arms.

"Looks like he's bonded to you," she remarked.

"I think he'd bond to anyone who might get him the hell out of here," I muttered but stroked the dog's fur. "It's okay."

"Rho, why don't you take this sweet boy's front half? Your friend here can stand behind him so he doesn't fall off the table."

Rho moved in, taking Biscuit's front legs. Together, we maneuvered him onto the table. Rhodes cooed and reassured, stroking his ears. He shoved his face into her neck as I held his back hips to keep him steady.

Dr. Lutz moved as quickly as possible during the exam. "He's actually in pretty good shape, all things considered. I wouldn't mind him putting on a little more weight."

"More?" I barked.

She smiled as she felt his abdomen. "His short legs are deceiving. I think he's got some mastiff in him. Needs a few more pounds."

I shook my head. "Gonna need a full crew to get him back here."

Dr. Lutz stepped back to retrieve a syringe from the counter. "Keep a hold of him. He might feel a little pinch, but that's it."

As she moved in to grab the scruff of Biscuit's neck, her eyes widened. "Oh, no. He's pooping."

And then, I felt it.

Chapter Twenty-Five

Anson

"STOP LAUGHING," I SAID THROUGH GRITTED TEETH AS I climbed out of Rho's SUV.

She rolled her lips over her teeth, doing her best to hide her amusement. But her eyes said it all. "Come on, he didn't mean it."

I just glared at Rho as she moved to open the back door for Biscuit. "That shirt will have to be burned. *Look* at what I'm wearing."

Rho couldn't hold in her laughter this time, not as the absolute absurdity of my T-shirt came into view. It was bright pink with an airbrushed kitten and rainbow on it. Not to mention the fucking *sparkles*.

Her laughter came harder as Biscuit jumped out of the SUV. Tears streamed down her face. "It was like projectile pooping. I've never seen anything like it."

"You won't be laughing when you get his back end next time," I mumbled.

Rho patted Biscuit on the head. "We'll get you a diaper next time. Didn't know you were a nervous pooper."

A diaper. Jesus.

"Come on," Rho said. "You can borrow Shep's running stuff again."

"I've got something in my truck." I didn't want to look too closely at the fact that I'd stopped at my place to fill a bag just in case Rho wanted me here.

"Well, you can use my shower while I feed the kittens and make dinner."

Her shower. Images of Rho joining me in said shower filled my mind. *Hell.* I needed to rein it in. One taste of her, and she was all I wanted. All I could see.

A million different alarms went off in my head. All the reasons why everything about this was a horrible idea. But I followed her inside anyway.

Heading for the bathroom, I turned on the water as cold as it would go. I'd freeze that need right out of my system. I ripped off the goddamn sparkly kitten shirt, tossing it to the floor. That thing needed to be burned, too.

I shucked the rest of my clothes and stepped under the spray. The curses I let loose would've made a sailor blush, but I didn't move out of the way. I let the ice-cold water hit me over and over again.

I made quick work of cleaning up before stepping out and toweling off. I changed into joggers and a fresh tee, scowling as I picked up the pink atrocity from the floor. I stuffed my belongings back into my duffel and headed toward the sound of humming.

As I reached the edge of the kitchen, the humming shifted to soft singing as Rho echoed the strains of a song I didn't recognize. It was beautiful, raw, and real, with a hint of imperfection that just made it more captivating.

"You've got a voice, Reckless."

She glanced up, a smile teasing her lips. "If you think I do, you should hear Arden." She whistled. "She's incredible."

I leaned a hip against the kitchen island. "Sounded pretty damn good from where I was standing."

"Well, thank you. I'll reward your compliment with this." She set some sort of bowl on a placemat on the island.

"What is it? Smells amazing."

"Mexican grain bowl. Got some leftover chicken, corn, black beans, sauteed red pepper, and onions. You can add salsa and guac if you want—homemade, of course."

I chuckled as I crossed into the kitchen. "Of course." I glanced around the space. "Trash can under the sink?"

"Yup," Rho answered, then frowned. "Why?"

I held up the pink T-shirt. "I'm getting rid of this atrocity."

She snatched it from my hand. "You are not."

I arched a brow at her in question.

Rho hugged it to her chest. "It's a memory."

"Of me being shat on," I grumbled.

She giggled. "Yes, but also of you helping me when I needed it. We're not throwing it away."

"All right. Do whatever you want with it."

"I'll wash it and use it as a nightshirt."

Oh, hell. I didn't need that image in my head.

I did my best to shove it down. I hadn't let myself dwell on the consequences of this morning's encounter. Wouldn't let myself go down the road of what it could mean. But I couldn't stop remembering the feel of Rhodes strangling my fingers, the breathy moans, the mark she'd left on my shoulder. And her taste. That taste would haunt me for the rest of time.

Get ahold of yourself.

I tried switching my focus to helping Rho with dinner. Tried not to look at any one part of her for too long while we ate. Because, somehow, any part of her was dangerous. From the tips of her toes to the ends of her hair.

Despite my obsession with Rho's goddamn toes, dinner felt normal. All a little too routine. As if we'd been doing this for years.

Even the cleanup. We worked in tandem, rinsing dishes and placing them into the dishwasher. It was a silent dance we'd somehow already memorized the steps to.

"You get any updates from Trace?" I asked as I wiped down the kitchen counters.

There was a slight hitch in Rho's movements as she put the detergent into the dishwasher. "Nothing, really. He's interviewing people. Still waiting on results from the lab."

I'd heard pretty much the same from Shep, but we still hadn't gotten the fire reports. Something told me Trace was holding back on handing them over because he knew they'd end up in my grasp, and he didn't quite trust me.

"You notice anyone hanging around who shouldn't have been the past couple of days?" I couldn't seem to stop myself from asking all the questions I would've asked in my former life. Couldn't keep from trying to help, even if I'd failed spectacularly at it before.

Rho's eyes stayed focused on the dishwasher, but she didn't answer right away.

I stiffened, my hand stilling on the counter. "Reckless."

She straightened. "My ex is being a douche canoe, that's all. Trace talked to him because of our history, and Davis didn't handle it all that well."

My hand tightened on the paper towel. "What. Did. He. Do?"

"Anson."

"Tell me, Reckless." Just knowing he'd been in her space, causing her grief after everything she'd been through in the past couple of days, made me want to rip out his jugular.

Rho worried the corner of her lip. "I ran into him outside the bakery, and he made it known he wasn't pleased that I'd *sicced* my foster brother on him."

A muscle along my jaw jumped. "You mean your brother."

She let out a huff. "He always tried to lessen my connection to them."

Sounded like an abuser in the making, trying to isolate Rho from her loved ones. "If he approaches you again, call Trace and then me. You might want to consider an order of protection, too."

Her brows lifted. "That's cop-speak."

Shit. I needed to watch it. "I've watched my share of *Law & Order*. Just promise me you'll tell us if he approaches you again."

Rho's shoulders slumped. "I don't want it to be him."

My chest constricted. No one wanted to think that someone close to them could do horrendous things. I moved into Rho's space, unable to resist the pull of her pain. I wrapped my arms around her. "Might not be. But you should keep your distance either way."

She nodded into my chest.

We stood there for longer than was safe, and if I stayed a moment longer, I'd end up doing something really stupid. So, I forced myself to release Rho. But I didn't make a move to head for my truck. I simply got the blanket out of the hall closet and headed for the couch.

It seemed ridiculous after the moment we'd shared in the hallway this morning, but I couldn't risk getting any closer to Rho than I already was.

Rho hovered in the hall, worrying her bottom lip. "You don't have to stay."

"I know, I don't." I was anyway. Couldn't get myself to leave her alone here with everything that'd happened. Even if I knew sleeping mere feet from her would be torture.

A little of the tension bled out of her shoulders. "Thank you."

"G'night, Reckless."

"Goodnight, Anson."

Her lips around my name had everything in me winding tight again, but I shoved it all down. Counted to one hundred as she carried the box of kittens down the hall. Biscuit followed her toward the bedroom, and the lights went out. I stared up at the ceiling, listening to every tiny sound from down the hall.

The opening and closing of drawers, the rustling of bedding, the switch of the light. I lay in the dark, listening for anything else. Rhodes tossed and turned a few times, and then there was nothing.

I relaxed a fraction at the lack of sound. She was asleep. It eased something in me, knowing she was at peace. And I didn't want to look too closely at that.

I thought sleep would be elusive, but it pulled me under, thanks to the lack of it the night before. Dreams swirled in my mind. Some good. Some bad. But all of them had one common thread…Rho.

She haunted me in my waking hours *and* in my sleep. I couldn't escape her. And maybe I didn't want to.

I didn't know how long I'd been out when a whine sounded by my ear. I shot up to sitting, my heart pounding against my ribs.

Biscuit let out another whine.

"What's wrong?" But I was already moving, heading straight for Rho's room.

The sound of whimpering reached my ears before I'd even rounded the corner. When I hit her doorway, I saw Rho thrashing in the sheets. She was running for her life somewhere deep in her subconscious.

I made it to the bed in three long strides. "Rho," I whispered, hands going to her shoulders. "Wake up. You're okay."

She jolted, her eyes flying open. The moment she took stock of me, those hazel orbs filled with tears, and she threw herself against me.

I caught her with an oomph, arms encircling her. "Easy, now. You're okay."

"It was so real. I was trying to get out, but I couldn't. And Emilia was screaming for help. I couldn't find her."

Agony ripped through me at the fear and grief in Rho's voice, at how desperately she clung to me. I held her tighter against me. "You're safe. I promise."

But I knew that was a promise I couldn't keep. Because I'd failed before, and it was always the people closest to me who paid the price.

Chapter Twenty-Six

Rhodes

THE MIXTURE OF MEMORY AND IMAGINATION WAS SO POTENT, so brutal, I couldn't catch my breath. The only thing I knew was that Anson was here. The feel of him against me was the one thing I knew I could count on. The steady beat of his heart against me. His strong arms engulfing me.

"Breathe, Rho. You're going to slip into a panic attack." Anson's hands squeezed my shoulders. "Follow me. In for four."

He waited as I attempted to follow.

"Hold for seven."

Trying to lock my breaths down felt like swallowing fire, but I battled to do it anyway.

"Now, out for eight."

He walked me through it four more times, squeezing my shoulders with each count. Slowly, I came back to myself, bit by bit. I pulled back, taking in Anson's worried face.

He brushed some hair out of my face, his fingers lingering in the strands. "How do you feel?"

"Okay," I rasped. "Where'd you learn how to do that?"

Even in the dark, I saw the shadow of something pass over Anson's eyes.

"I've known people who suffer from anxiety attacks. Sometimes, that breathing technique helps."

I studied him for a long moment. There was so much more to Anson than I knew. Because the man I'd seen didn't let anyone in. So, who had he known well enough to help them with panic attacks?

"Well, it clearly works," I said, pulling my knees up to my chest.

Anson's fingers stroked up and down my arm. "You wanna talk about it?"

I dropped my chin to my knees as I gripped my legs tighter. "It was the fire again. But different. Usually, I'm a kid, but I was an adult this time. Emilia was screaming. So scared. And I was trying to get to her, but there were flames everywhere. Burning me."

Anson leaned into me then, his face going to the crook of my neck as if he, too, needed reassurance that I was all right. I leaned into him, soaking in his strength and the fact that I wasn't alone. His fingers trailed up and down my spine through the thin cotton of my nightgown. "The fire stirred everything up."

I nodded against him. "It always does. Even if it's just a wildfire in the summer, I always have a hard time sleeping after. The scents, the sirens, it brings it all back."

"You're so fucking strong," Anson whispered against my skin.

"I don't feel that way," I admitted. "I feel weak. Like the guilt could eat me alive. Why didn't I hear the fire alarm earlier? Why didn't I try harder to get to them?"

"Rho," Anson croaked, pulling back. "Do you think they would've been okay losing you for a chance to get out?"

Tears brimmed in my eyes, spilling over and tracking down my cheeks. "No. But sometimes, I wish they hadn't left me behind."

Anson pulled back, his hands cupping my face and raising it off my knees. His roughened thumbs swept across my cheeks, clearing away the tears. "Sometimes, being the one who's left behind is the heaviest weight. But it doesn't mean you stop fighting."

I stared into those blue-gray eyes. There was pain there. Not just because I was hurting but because he truly understood. And I knew then that he'd been there. "Anson," I croaked.

Agony streaked across those beautiful eyes. "I lost my little sister. My fault. Might not have dealt the death blow, but it was on me just the same. Worst pain imaginable. Would give *anything* to take her place."

Oh, God.

We were so different. Vibrant color and shades of gray. Bursting blooms and the darkest night.

But we were also the same. Older sibling to someone we'd lost, someone we always wanted to protect. We carried the scars of that. And we were both doing our best to make it through.

"I'm so sorry," I whispered into the dark. The words weren't enough, not even close, but they were all I had to give to him. Those and one more thing. "She wouldn't want you to trade places with her."

Blue flashed in Anson's irises. "You didn't even know her."

"But I know *you*. You're worth the life flowing through you. And I know she would think the same."

His jaw clenched and flexed as if each word were a physical blow.

I placed a hand over his heart. "You matter, Anson. You're a good man."

"Reckless." The word was more rasp than syllables.

"A *good* man. No matter how much you try to hide it."

His Adam's apple bobbed as he swallowed. "You need to go back to sleep."

I would've smiled if I weren't hurting so badly for him. Anson would do anything to avoid praise. But he deserved it. He was the kind of man who stayed, even when it risked the walls he'd built. The kind of man who helped, even when it was inconvenient. The kind of man who didn't look away in the face of pain. And that was the greatest gift of all.

I stared into those swirling eyes. "Stay with me?"

His stubbled jaw flexed again. "Okay."

I shifted, scooting over to give Anson room. He didn't move fast or slow, but methodically. And as soon as he was beneath the covers, he pulled me to him, my back to his front.

"Sleep, Reckless. I'll keep the demons away."

And he did.

Chapter Twenty-Seven

Rhodes

HEAT SWIRLED AROUND ME. BUT THIS WASN'T A WARMTH THAT brought fear. This was a heat that was pure comfort. The kind I wanted to swim around in and never leave.

I burrowed deeper into the sea of warmth, settling in to stay a while.

An arm tightened around my waist.

I froze.

An arm. Around *my* waist. One that wasn't mine.

My eyes flew open as memories came flooding back. The nightmare. Anson.

He'd stayed. Of course, he had. Because that was who he was.

Anson nuzzled my neck and mumbled something in his sleep.

A smile teased my mouth at the adorable innocence of it. But then he shifted, pressing something very *not* innocent against my backside.

A little moan slipped from my lips as my thighs clenched.

Anson's arm tightened around me. "Morning."

His voice was pure sandpaper and grit, and, God, it did something to me. I might need some sort of brain scan. Maybe I had a tumor. Because a man's voice shouldn't have wetness gathering between my thighs.

Anson's fingers traced circles on my belly through the delicate fabric of my nightgown. "You sleep okay?"

"Better than I have in years," I said honestly. There was a touch of rasp to my tone, as well. I hoped I could pass it off as sleepiness and not the turned-the-hell-on truth.

His hand slid lower, the circles turning to nonsensical designs.

I shifted, my thighs rubbing together as nerve endings sparked to life. But it didn't help. An ache had rooted itself inside me, and there was a desperate edge to it.

"You keep moving like that, and we're gonna have a problem."

I stilled, swallowing hard. "What if I want a problem?"

Anson's fingers halted their absent swirling. "Such a temptress." His hips rolled, pressing into me from behind, his dick nestling between my ass cheeks. "Fuck."

My breaths came quicker, one after the other in a tempo like sending some sort of Morse code message.

His fingers slipped lower, beneath the fabric of my nightgown, trailing up my thigh. He traced the mottled skin of my scars. Most guys I'd dated had avoided them, not knowing what to say or do, but not Anson. His fingers moved over the raised flesh as if he were memorizing it.

"So fucking strong. Beautiful. Brave."

His words hit like tiny, beautiful barbs, embedding themselves in my skin. But they were also dangerous, making me want to reach for more with a man I wasn't sure could give it.

Anson's fingers skimmed higher, and my lips parted. "Been dreaming of your taste for the last twenty-four hours. Want to drown in it. To burn it into me so it's all I have on my tongue."

This time, I whimpered. I was too wrapped up in need to care that it gave me away.

"Gonna give me that taste, Reckless?" His fingers hovered just shy of where I wanted him the most.

"Yes," I breathed.

Anson closed the distance, but his fingers stilled at the apex of my thighs. "No fuckin' panties?"

The smallest giggle slipped free. "I don't wear underwear to bed."

Anson moved in a flash, his hands going to my hips. He hauled me up and over him until my legs straddled his shoulders. "Grab the headboard."

"Anson," I squeaked.

"My reckless girl," he growled. "Been dying for this. Now, grab the headboard and ride my face."

My heart skittered and skipped, each beat tumbling over into the next as I gripped the white, wrought iron headboard.

Anson gripped my hips, slowly lowering me to him. Each millimeter twisted every fiber inside me tighter, a rope being spun in circles until it was twisted so tight it might fray in an explosion of need.

His tongue flicked out, barely teasing my flesh, but the groan Anson let loose sent vibrations sweeping through me. That rope twisted tighter, desperate for more, for relief, for *him*.

"Killing me, Reckless." Anson's fingers dug into my hips, pulling me down more.

His tongue teased and toyed, circling the places I needed him the most. My hands gripped the headboard tighter, the metal details biting into my palms. The tip of his tongue grazed my clit, and I couldn't help the whimper that left my lips.

Anson's fingers on my hips tightened to the point where I thought they might leave bruises. But something about that had more heat flushing through me—the thought of Anson leaving his mark on me.

"Need more?" Anson growled.

"Yes." The word tumbled out without restraint.

There was no pretense or warning. Anson's tongue drove into me, and I cried out. God, it was heaven. Yet hell, too. Because I wanted *more*. Wanted to know what it would feel like to have all of him.

Anson filling me, stretching me. Taking me over and over.

His tongue curled, and my mouth fell open on a gasp.

He swirled it inside me, and my thighs started to tremble. Each swipe and circle drove me into mountaintop highs and valley lows. My hips moved with him, riding each high and low as if I could read his mind.

Anson's tongue disappeared, replaced by his hand. But his mouth wasn't gone for long. That dangerous tongue circled my clit as his fingers pumped in and out of me. But it wasn't enough. It was a torturous game of almost.

"Please," I begged.

Anson chuckled against my flesh, his fingers still moving, teasing, thrusting. "Now you know what it's like, watching you move around in those fucking shorts. Making me dream of having you but knowing I can't, shouldn't."

I let out a growl of frustration. "Looks like you've got me now."

His fingers curled. "You make me break all the rules."

Anson's lips closed around that bundle of nerves, sucking deeply as the tip of his tongue worked my clit.

There was no prayer of holding back. As his fingers pressed that spot somewhere deep inside, I shattered. The little pieces of tape and glue I'd used to hold myself together fractured in a heartbeat.

The only thing that existed was feeling. Wave after wave of sensation. I lost myself in it, finally letting go completely.

Just as I thought I was coming down, Anson built me back up. But it was only to let me crash again in a cascade of light and color.

Finally, his ministrations eased, his tongue retreated, and he lifted me from above him. My chest heaved, but it was more. Something had shifted inside me. Something fundamental. As if I'd realized I was still holding back from life in certain ways. But Anson made me want to smash those walls.

He stared at me, his eyes still hazy with lust and need. "One hell of a breakfast."

I gaped at him, then grinned. I reached for the waistband of his joggers, but then my doorbell rang. I froze.

Anson groaned. "You've got to be kidding me."

A laugh bubbled out of me as I scrambled off the bed, grabbing my robe. Biscuit was already barking his head off from the living room.

"Rho," a voice called.

"That's Owen," Anson grumbled as he got out of bed. "Cockblock."

I glanced down at Anson's obvious hard-on. "You might want to stay back here, buddy. You could put someone's eye out with that thing."

Anson only scowled. "I'm gonna kill him."

I patted Anson's chest. "Let's try to save murder for after seven a.m., okay?"

He didn't say anything, but I headed for the door. Biscuit was instantly at my side as I pulled my robe on. I scratched his head. "It's okay. Just a friend."

Biscuit let out what sounded like a grumble.

I held his collar with one hand and opened the door with the other.

Owen frowned down at Biscuit, his gaze roaming over my robe-covered frame. "Sorry. Did I wake you? You're usually up and going by this time."

I did my best not to flush. "Little bit of a later start."

"Have you seen Anson? His truck's here, but I can't find him anywhere."

I cleared my throat. "He crashed on my couch last night. He's just grabbing a shower."

Owen's expression went blank as he took me in with new eyes. And I knew what he likely saw: the hair a mess, flushed cheeks. *Hell.* I hoped he didn't say anything to Shep.

A muscle fluttered in Owen's jaw. "Right. Well, tell him the rest of the crew is arriving. We're supposed to start at seven-thirty."

He turned on his heel and stalked off toward the Victorian.

Biscuit let out a low growl at my side. I tugged him back inside, groaning. Sometimes, knowing just about everyone in your small town was the worst. Shep's whole crew saw me as a little sister they thought they needed to protect.

I released Biscuit and headed back down the hall to find Anson had, in fact, taken a shower. He was dressed again, a tee pulling tightly across his broad chest—an expanse my fingers itched to roam over. His hair appeared darker in its wet state, and the glower on his face had him looking every inch the avenging angel.

I bit my bottom lip. "How was the shower?"

The scowl deepened. "Cold."

I couldn't help it, I laughed. "You could've waited for me. I would've helped you with your...situation."

"For the love of God, Rho. Please, don't talk about my dick before I have to go work with about a dozen guys who are going to wonder why the hell I have a hard-on."

I only laughed harder. "I'm sorry."

That scowl shifted to an accusing glare. "You're not sorry at all."

I grinned at him. "No. I'm really not."

Anson moved in a flash, pinning me to the wall and pressing his hips into me. "You're gonna pay for this, Reckless. I'm going to tease you until you're begging, pleading. And then maybe, if you're really good, I'll fuck you senseless."

Then, he was gone.

And I was left just as desperate as he was.

Chapter Twenty-Eight

Anson

THE DAY WAS NEVER-ENDING. PART OF IT WAS THE FACT THAT we had to start over in more than a few areas of the house after the fire. Redoing work we'd already completed felt like Sisyphus and that damn rock.

Another piece was that Owen was in a mood. Back to his petty shit and testing my authority. The rest of the crew was giving him as wide a berth as possible.

And Shep kept looking at me. Not staring, exactly, but every so often he'd glance my way with a furrowed brow. It made me twitchy and feel more than a little guilty.

What the hell was I doing?

Rho was the last person I should've been getting involved with in *any* capacity. I gripped the crowbar tighter as I moved to the next section of drywall. I should tell her it was a mistake, that it couldn't keep happening.

The thought had me wanting to heave the crowbar into the wall and destroy everything around me. Because the moments I was with

Rho, when I heard her laugh, drowned in the feel of her, they were the only times since Greta died when I felt true peace.

I couldn't give that up. Even if I should. I guessed that made me a greedy bastard. But what else was new?

I moved to the next section of wall but was so distracted I nearly knocked into Silas. Cursing, I moved out of his way. "Sorry," I muttered.

Concern seeped into his expression as he took me in. "Everything all right?"

He pitched his voice low so no one else on the crew could hear. I should've appreciated that and the worry, but I was too pissed at myself to let it land. "Fine," I clipped.

Silas held up his hands. "Just asking before one of us takes a crowbar to the back of the head or Owen suffocates one of us behind the drywall."

I sighed. I was an ass. "Sorry. Not the best week."

Silas nodded, then cracked his neck. "I feel you. Must be something in the atmosphere."

I studied him closer and saw the shadows rimming his eyes. "You need anything?"

Who the hell was I? Offering help wasn't exactly my M.O. But spending time with Rho was changing that.

Silas shook his head. "I'm good. Just been helping a friend with a project and not getting enough sleep."

But as I really took him in, I wondered if it was more. I remembered Shep saying he hadn't had the best homelife growing up. That kind of thing could have long-term effects, and not all kids were lucky enough to land with the Colsons. Some just had to endure their nightmares the best they could.

"Lunch," Shep called, breaking into my thoughts. "Got subs delivered."

There were a few cheers from the crew as everyone stopped what they were doing and made their way toward the front of the house. I let them go first, taking a moment to get my head right.

Finally, I headed outside. The moment I stepped into the

sunshine, I ripped off my mask. The pine air rushed through me in a welcome, cleansing breath.

But the relief was short-lived as Shep stepped into my line of vision. He frowned at me. "What's with you today?"

My jaw worked back and forth. *Hell.*

"You're edgy or something. Everything okay?"

I was edgy because I wanted another hit of Rho. I'd gotten a taste and was dying for more, only I had to hide that because I worked with her *brother.*

"The princess probably didn't sleep well since he crashed on Rho's *couch,*" Owen bit out.

The look I sent him should've made Owen shit himself, but he apparently hadn't grown out of his stupid phase.

Shep's gaze jerked back to me. "She was still freaked?"

I shifted uncomfortably. I didn't know how to explain that it was impossible for me to leave her alone in that guest cottage. That wondering if she was okay would've been torture and something I couldn't deal with. "She's not quite one hundred percent steady."

It wasn't a lie. Rho's easy acquiescence meant she wasn't ready to stay alone. But I was still throwing her under the bus.

Shep muttered a curse. "Thanks for staying with her. I don't know why, but it's easier for her to ask you than one of us. Probably because we've been hovering."

"She doesn't want you guys worrying about her," I told him. I knew that was the truth. Rho didn't want to put her fears on anyone else's shoulders.

Shep lowered his voice. "Is she okay?"

I nodded. "The fire stirred up a lot for her, but she's dealing." I wasn't going to tell him about the dream. It was too personal. If Rho wanted to share that, she could.

Shep slapped me on the shoulder. "Appreciate you looking out for her."

Guilt niggled again. I was a crap friend.

"You've gotta be shitting me," Owen groused. "You read us all the riot act about leaving your sisters alone, and then you're just cool with him sleeping there?"

Shep turned to Owen, his expression taking on a hardness I knew meant he was at the end of his rope. "I told you to treat my sisters with respect. Which Anson is doing."

I winced. I wasn't sure if this morning could be classified as *respect*, but then again, worshiping Rho's body had some reverence to it for sure.

"This is a bunch of bullshit," Owen clipped. "You treat that prick like he's the Second Coming. Then he's a grade A dick, bossing us around. Wasting time when we could be making real progress."

Shep's jaw worked like he'd taken a chaw of tobacco. "That's enough."

"What, we can't speak our minds now?" Owen snapped.

"You could if you were being respectful. But you never are, Owen. You act like a three-year-old throwing a tantrum when you don't get your way. And I'm done with it."

Owen stiffened. "You firin' me?"

Shep stared him down. "I'm giving you one last shot. You get your shit together, don't cause problems or drama, and do the tasks you've been assigned...*well*. That, or you ship out."

Owen glared at Shep before finally throwing up his hands. "Fuck this. I can get a job with a crew who knows what the hell they're doing."

"Good luck with that," Silas muttered.

Owen made a dive for him, but Shep caught him by the shirt. "Keep moving to your truck," Shep said, giving him a shove.

"Get off me," Owen barked. "I'm going."

He stalked toward his beat-up pickup, climbing inside and slamming the door behind him. The fact that it took three tries to get the vehicle going diminished a little of the effect. But he gunned the engine to make up for it.

As gravel spat, Carlos shook his head. "Tiny dick disease."

Shep barked out a laugh, and the rest of the crew joined him. "Let's get some grub and then get back to work."

The crew headed for the boxes and coolers of food in the back of Shep's truck, but I waited for him. "Sorry about the drama."

He shook his head. "It's not on you."

"The guy never liked me." And I wasn't sure why. I'd been pretty inobtrusive in terms of additions to the team. And crew members were always coming and going. That was the nature of the work.

But as I watched Owen's truck fishtail onto the two-lane highway, I knew this was more than simple dislike. Owen was pissed as hell that I'd come out of Rho's house this morning. And that set me on edge.

Shep sighed. "Should've fired him a long time ago. He's always been a loose cannon. I just hoped he'd get his shit together."

Shep wanted to help everyone, give them chance after chance—even if they didn't deserve it. Especially if he had a tie to them. But that sixth sense of mine was starting to prickle. "He grew up here, right?"

Shep nodded. "Went to school with Fallon and Rho."

Hell. My brain flashed back to the fire at the middle school. Then the ones downtown and the river trailhead. "He spend a lot of time with them?"

Shep's eyes narrowed on me. "What are you thinking?"

"I'm taking a look at everyone who's been in Rho's orbit." It was the truth. I hadn't been able to stop myself, even if I knew it was a dangerous road for me to go down. Rho's douche of an ex was first on my list, but I was adding Owen.

I should've taken a second look sooner. Owen had a number of narcissistic traits, including believing that everything was someone else's fault, never his. But he wasn't the only one. That was the problem with looking at everyone as a profile. You realized more people than not were capable of doing very bad things.

"You think I should float his name to Trace? Have him take a look?" Shep asked, concern bleeding into his tone.

My jaw worked back and forth as I tried to get the muscles to loosen. "Wouldn't be a bad idea. Just tell him he's been combative lately. He knows the layout of the Victorian well. He'd be able to move through the space quickly if he set the fire."

Shep cracked his knuckles. "Half the town knows the layout of this place, being here for cookouts and holiday parties back in the day."

My back teeth ground together. You'd think Sparrow Falls being a small town would mean a smaller pool of suspects. But it was the opposite. Everyone seemed to open their homes to the entirety of the town's population, and everyone was connected. It made pulling a single thread nearly impossible.

"Just have Trace run his alibi. It's a start."

Shep jerked his head in a nod. "I'll text him." His gaze bored into mine. "Thank you. I know this isn't easy for you—"

"It's nothing," I cut him off. I didn't want to dwell on the realities of the road I was going down, and I couldn't handle Shep's gratitude.

He shook his head, reading the no-go zone. Instead of pressing, he slapped me on the shoulder. "Come on. Let's get some food before those mongrels eat it all."

I chuckled, moving to follow him, but my phone buzzed in my back pocket. Frowning, I tugged it out and stared at the screen.

The number flashing there had my blood turning to ice. It was one I hadn't seen in way over a year.

I swallowed the bile trying to make its way up my throat. "Be right there."

Shep kept moving, and I turned to face the mountains as I hit *accept* on the call. "Hunt."

"Anson, it's Helena."

The familiarity of her voice washed over me—that smoker's rasp she could never kick, just like she'd never been able to kick the cancer sticks themselves. Our job had held too much stress to give her a prayer of breaking free.

"What happened?" My voice didn't sound like my own. Too detached. Too empty. But I knew she wouldn't be calling for anything good.

In true Helena fashion, she didn't beat around the bush. "He's back."

The ice spread, moving from my veins to my muscles and then to my organs. Everything froze to the point of agonizing pain.

"Got a note addressed to you. Opened it. Same fuckin' clues."

A million images flashed in my mind. The word games he loved to play with me. Box lettering that disguised his handwriting. But no fingerprints. No DNA. The guy was a ghost.

"It's a copycat. It has to be." There was no reason The Hangman would be back. Not now. Not when I'd stayed gone. Lived completely under the radar.

"It's *him*," Helena pushed. "There are too many details we never gave the press."

My gut churned, sickness taking hold. I'd played by his rules. I'd stopped hunting him. I'd hidden away. But now he was back anyway, as if he had some sort of radar that told him I'd found a flicker of happiness. Something that gave me peace. And he couldn't have that.

"We need you, Anson. You gotta come back," Helena said, transforming her voice into that gentle tone she used with victims.

"No." It was the only thing I could say. Nothing in this world could drag me back into the hell that returning to the FBI would be.

"Anson—"

"No," I clipped.

"He'll keep killing."

I knew he would. Now that he'd started again, nothing would stop The Hangman until death found him. And that would just be another scarred mark on my soul. Another thing I'd blame myself for. But what was one more? I was already drowning in guilt anyway.

Chapter Twenty-Nine

Rhodes

I STARED DOWN AT MY PHONE. THE UNANSWERED TEXT MESSAGE glared up at me, taunting.

> **Me:** *How about dinner in exchange for you helping me wrangle Biscuit into a bath? Steak and roasted potatoes… Maybe something else for dessert? ;-)*

"What'd that phone do to you?"

Thea's voice broke into my staredown. I quickly locked my screen and shoved the phone into my back pocket. "Boys are stupid."

She arched a brow at that as she lifted another shrub from the back of a Gator and placed it in our display. "You say that like it's a new discovery."

I snorted. "You've got a point there."

Thea paused as she reached for another plant, really taking me in. "Is that guy bothering you again?"

My brows pulled together. "Which guy?"

"Fancy-pants. Nice shoes, expensive watch."

"Oh, Davis? No." I hadn't seen him since that scene outside The

Mix Up. "Different troublemaker, and a whole different kind of trouble, actually."

One corner of Thea's mouth kicked up as she lifted another shrub. "Sounds like you might *like* that kind of trouble."

I grunted as I reached for another pot. "I like it a little too much, I think."

I wasn't sure I'd ever been this *invested*. And it made me twitchy.

A hint of worry swept away the amusement on Thea's face. "Is he playing games?"

I shook my head. "He's not a game player." Anson wasn't the type. But the fact that he hadn't texted back had a niggle of worry working its way into the back of my brain. Did something happen? Had he changed his mind? Or was he just busy working and didn't have his phone on him? It *was* the middle of the day.

Setting down the shrub, I shoved it into position. "I'm not used to caring this much."

Thea placed her pot next to mine. "You're used to keeping it casual?"

"Not exactly." I'd dated before, had a handful of relationships. But this felt different. I realized something as I thought back to the guys I'd been with in any capacity. "I think I've always picked men I knew didn't have the potential of forever."

Thea moved back to the Gator but glanced my way. "That's a hell of a thing to realize."

I chuckled. "I'm more of a mess than I thought."

She stilled. "We're all a mess, Rho. We all have our baggage. It's how we deal with it that counts."

I forced myself to keep moving, to keep lifting and sorting as if that would help the realizations not hurt quite so much. "I think I'm scared of forever. Of anyone who could mean that much to me."

Maybe I avoided reaching for forever the same way I avoided reading the ends of books. Because I knew that, sometimes, forever got ripped right out from under you.

"Duncan told me about the fire," Thea said softly.

I fought off a twinge of annoyance at that. I hated people talking about what had happened to me behind my back—or in front of my face, for that matter. But I knew it wasn't malicious. Duncan was likely trying to look out for me by giving Thea the information.

"That kind of loss and trauma messes with your head," I admitted.

Thea was quiet for a minute. "Sometimes, it feels safer to just keep everyone out. Removes the potential to be hurt again."

My movements slowed as I looked Thea's way. Shadows swirled in her deep brown eyes. "Sometimes, it does," I agreed.

She swallowed hard. "But it can be lonely."

"Look a little happier, would you?" Duncan called, striding toward us, his camera raised.

Thea jolted, her spine snapping straight. "What are you doing?"

He frowned. "We're updating the website. Needed a few shots of the grounds and the staff working."

The blood drained from Thea's face, turning her olive skin unnaturally pale. "Did you take any of me?"

"Sure. You and Rho unloading the shrubs. But you guys looked about as happy as a kid who didn't get any ice cream."

"Delete them," she snapped. "You have to delete them right now."

Confusion swept over Duncan's face. "You look fine—"

"Please," she begged. "You can't put me on the website or social media or anywhere else. Please."

The panic in Thea's voice had true worry settling deep. She was terrified.

I grabbed the camera from Duncan. "I'll delete them. He's not going to put your picture anywhere. Right, Dunc?"

"No," he said, dropping his voice low. "We'll make sure of it."

Thea set the shrub she was holding down, and I didn't miss the way her hands shook. "Thank you. I-I'm just going to grab some water."

"Sure," Duncan agreed quickly. "Why don't you take your break? You're due."

Thea nodded but didn't say a word as she hurried off.

I quickly deleted any photos of Thea, but there were only a couple. There were more of me.

Duncan muttered a curse. "She's running from something."

I handed his camera back. "Yeah."

"She tell you anything?"

I shook my head. "Only hinted at it." My gaze followed Thea until she disappeared into one of the greenhouses. "I think we just have to give her a safe place. Maybe she'll open up eventually."

Duncan sighed. "You're right. But I feel like an ass for freaking her out."

I reached out and patted his shoulder. "You didn't know that taking a picture would spook her."

"Hey," a new voice called.

I looked up to see Felix striding toward us, a bright smile on his face. I tried to answer it with one of my own but worry for Thea hung in the back of my mind. "Back again so soon?"

He chuckled. "My mom is on a tear this year. She said she needs more dahlias."

The look of confusion on his face had a flicker of a smile finally reaching my lips. "Lucky for you, we've got plenty."

"Thank God. Because if she keeps talking my dad's ear off about it, I think they might be headed for divorce."

"Come on, I'll show you." I glanced at Duncan. "I'll finish these in a few. That okay?"

He nodded absently, waving me on. "Sure. I'll be in the office if you need me. Want me to feed the kittens?"

"That'd be great. You're the best, Dunc."

His expression softened. "No problem."

I turned back to Felix. "Let's go save your parents from divorce."

He chuckled. "You're doing the plant gods' work."

"I need that on a T-shirt."

Felix was quiet for a moment as we walked, but I could feel his eyes on me. "You hanging in there? I heard about the fire."

I twisted my work gloves, my fingers needing a task. "I'm fine. Didn't touch the guesthouse."

"Silas and Carlos said the cops think it was arson."

I would have to ream those two for being gossips. "They're still trying to put the pieces together."

Felix drummed his fingers against the side of his thigh as we walked. "You need to be careful, just in case. Keep your circle small. Your most trusted people only."

I bit the inside of my cheek to keep from snapping at him. I didn't need another protective male in my life. "I'm good. Swear. Now, let's go get those dahlias."

~

As I reached my SUV, I arched back and then bent over to touch my toes. The muscles around my spine protested. I'd overdone it just a tad today.

Tonight called for a bath with a heavy dose of Epsom salts. As I straightened, I pulled out my phone. It looked like that bath would be decidedly lonely.

I tried not to let the lack of response from Anson sting. But it did. Too damn much.

Beeping the locks on my SUV, I opened the back passenger door for Biscuit. "There you go."

He jumped up but looked a little mopey.

I scratched behind his ears. "I know you miss your kittens, but Thea wanted them tonight."

It was more than that. I thought she *needed* them. I could tell she was on edge for the rest of the day, the photo incident sticking with her. Maybe cuddling a few kittens for the evening would help.

Closing Biscuit in, I moved to the driver's door and opened it. I hopped in and dumped my phone into the cupholder. I couldn't help but scowl at the device. Maybe Thea had it right with the no-technology thing. There'd be fewer disappointments.

My phone buzzed, and I fumbled to grab it. A wave of disappointment hit me when I saw my brother's name on the screen. Fast on disappointment's heels came guilt.

> **Cope:** *How about a trip to Seattle? I've got an extra playoff ticket.*

I sighed, my fingers flying across the screen.

Me: *Thanks, but I've got work and stuff with the house. But I'll be watching from here.*

Cope: *Come on Rho-Rho. Come hang with your favorite brother for a week.*

Me: *You mean my favorite doofus? Sorry, can't. But I know what you're trying to do, and I appreciate it.*

Cope: *Worried about you.*

Another wave of guilt hit me, but I couldn't stay stashed away just because my family was worried.

Me: *I'm being cautious. Promise. Love you, doofus.*

Cope: *Love you, too, dorkus.*

I dropped my phone back into the cupholder and pressed the button to start the engine. Carefully, I backed out of my parking spot. The nursery was already empty, but you never knew what random detritus could be in your path.

In a matter of seconds, I'd navigated to the property's exit and flipped on my blinker. One of the things that I loved about working out here was the commute. I wasn't sure if you could classify fifteen minutes on winding country roads a commute, but I claimed it as one.

Every season brought a new landscape. Fall had crisp skies and forests occasionally dotted with orange and red. Winter produced stark, snowy landscapes and breathtaking ice-capped mountains. Spring ushered in the endless beauty of wildflowers. And summer gifted the land with the ripple of golden fields against the majestic Castle Rock.

The wildflowers were just beginning to pop up now—my very favorite season. Before long, the meadows I drove by would be dotted with color.

I was so distracted by searching for those hints of blooms that I didn't notice the SUV behind me until it was right on my tail. Black and oversized with a massive grille, the driver gunned its engine.

I scowled into my rearview mirror and tapped my brakes in

warning. *Freaking tourists.* They were always in a hurry to get somewhere. Usually, the mountains or Castle Rock. Or maybe Crystal Lake, a couple of hours north.

The SUV didn't heed my warning, only inched closer.

My heart rate sped up, those quick, tiny beats like a hummingbird's wings. "Idiot." He was going to get someone killed. Not that I could see through the sun's glare on the windshield to tell if it was a male. But the vehicle screamed *I have a small penis and must overcompensate.*

I put my foot on the brake, slowing so he could—and hopefully would—go around me. But instead, the person behind the wheel gunned it and slammed into the back of my SUV. My head snapped forward, hitting the wheel with a force that had me seeing stars.

Biscuit let out a yelp from the back seat, but thankfully, the fabric divider kept him from doing a header into the front.

I pressed harder on the brake as my SUV slid to the side of the road, hitting gravel. I did my best to course correct, not wanting to slide down the steep embankment on my right. It wasn't horribly deep, but it wasn't shallow either, and I didn't want to find out what damage it could do.

Behind me, an engine revved again, and I cursed.

My gaze flew to the rearview mirror to see the SUV backing up and then jolting into drive. Panic seared me, and blood roared in my ears. I pressed down on the accelerator, trying to find a route that would get me out of the black SUV's path. But there was nowhere to go. Two lanes and a ravine on either side.

The world slowed. Everything happened in snapshots. The beat of my heart, the click of the shutter.

The SUV slammed into me, and then we were spinning. Round and round, so fast the world blurred. And then, I was going over.

Chapter Thirty

Anson

I HEAVED THE DAMAGED DRYWALL INTO THE DUMPSTER WITH A grunt. My arms and back burned with the effort, but I welcomed the bite of pain. I bent and picked up another panel, tossing that into the dumpster, too.

Shep did the same, grabbing another sheet from the pile. "Would've thought you'd be in a better mood with Owen gone."

I just grunted in response, tossing more drywall. We'd made good progress today. Partly because I was determined to drown out everything around me. I'd done Owen's work and mine. Probably another chunk, too.

Shep kept on working and talking. "Gotta admit, I don't miss his moaning and complaining."

If I'd been able to take anything in this afternoon, I probably would've noticed the change in the air with Owen's absence. But I hadn't. The only thing I could do was lose myself in the work. The same way I had when I'd first come to work for Shep. The physical strain, the repetition, it all helped to fight back the demons.

The only problem was that Helena had set them free today. Every jerk of my crowbar, every heave of damaged material had all been some futile attempt to battle them back into their cage.

I let out a growl of frustration as I threw one more drywall panel into the dumpster. I turned to reach for another, but there was nothing there. We'd finished a pile that should've taken us well into tomorrow morning's work hours.

That was when I glanced around for the first time. The sun had dipped low in the sky. The only two vehicles in the lot were Shep's silver truck and my black one. Everyone else was long gone.

I looked down at my watch. Five-forty-five. *Hell.*

"You should've left by now," I muttered.

Shep just stared at me. "You think I'm going to leave your ass when something has you this tweaked?"

My back molars ground together. "I'm fine."

"You've been a broody asshole of epic proportions this afternoon."

I kicked at a rock with my boot. "I'm not a ten-year-old girl. I don't chitchat and gossip. I'm here to work."

Shep arched a brow at me from beneath his ballcap. "Well, you were tearing that house apart like a man possessed. Pretty sure the crew's planning an exorcism for tomorrow."

"We needed to make up for Owen," I defended.

Shep took a step toward me, making sure to meet my eyes. "Anson, it's me. Don't bullshit. Who was on the other end of that call? Your mom?"

I recoiled as if I'd been slapped. "No. You know I'm the last number she'd ever dial."

"Then who the hell was it? I haven't seen you this bad since you first got here."

My throat worked as I struggled to swallow. "Someone from my old team. They think The Hangman's back."

Shep went stock-still. "Anson."

"They got another note. Could be a copycat." But even as the words left my mouth, I knew it was a lie. Helena wasn't one to jump to conclusions. If she thought it was The Hangman, then it was.

Shep blew out a long breath. "No wonder you're a mess."

I scrubbed my hand through my hair. A mess was an understatement. Memories clawed at the walls I'd created to keep them out. Each one reminded me of why I couldn't have a normal life. Why I didn't deserve the tendrils of happiness that had woven themselves around me with Rho.

"What are they doing to find him?" Shep asked.

It was a simple question, but he didn't know how loaded it was. "They have to find the body first."

Each time a note had been delivered to us, we'd known what it meant. Someone, somewhere, had lost their life. But I hadn't let that truly register. Not really. I'd been too caught up in the unsub and trying to put together all the clues.

I'd always had a thing for word games, so my boss had set me loose on each and every note. I could untangle the web the quickest. Each hint gave us a letter of the location, and every clue was branded in my brain. But it was all a game to him. A fucked-up version of hangman.

But I'd gotten a charge out of being the one to figure out the riddles the fastest. I felt a surge of pride in leading the team toward the next piece of the puzzle. I'd been so determined to be the one to stop his reign of terror that I hadn't realized he was weaving me into his web.

"Do they have any idea where?" Shep asked, breaking into my memories.

I shook my head. "I didn't ask."

I didn't want to know. I knew too much already. Someone, somewhere, had lost the person who meant the most to them. A daughter, wife, mother, sister. And they would be tormented by that loss compounded by notes from the bastard who'd taken her.

Just thinking the word *sister* had agony shredding my chest. God, I missed Greta. The way she'd give me shit on our weekly phone calls. *"How's the nerd squad doing this week?"* Always laughing at her big brother. But she'd also been proud of my work and the life I was building.

It was just that neither of us knew how empty that life could be. Not until it was too late.

Shep studied me carefully. "Does your team think you're at risk?"

"Not sure. They were asking me to come back." Just saying the words aloud was like spitting acid.

Shep's brows just about hit his hairline. "You thinking about it?"

"No." The answer was instant. Final. "I don't want that life anymore. Wouldn't be able to handle it even if I did."

Empathy swept over Shep's face, making me want to look anywhere but at him. "It wasn't your fault, Anson."

"Don't," I clipped.

Something in my tone had Shep backing off. "Okay. Why don't we get some takeout? Bring it back to my place."

I was about to open my mouth to decline, but the ringing of Shep's phone cut me off.

He pulled it out of his back pocket and swiped his finger over the screen. "Yep?"

Everything slowed as I watched the color drain from Shep's face.

"Where?" he barked.

There was a brief pause.

"On the way."

Shep was already moving, but I was at his side, some part of me taking on his panic. "What?"

He glanced over at me. "It's Rho. She was in an accident."

Chapter Thirty-One

Rhodes

I WINCED AS THE EMT SWIPED SOMETHING THAT FELT VERY MUCH like an alcohol pad over the gash on my forehead. Biscuit growled from his place on the gurney. He'd refused to leave my side since they'd pulled us from the now-trashed SUV.

"Sorry," the young EMT said, her face sympathetic. "Gotta make sure it's clean."

"It's okay, Susie," I assured her. The other EMT, Shawn, hadn't been able to get close, thanks to Biscuit's defensiveness.

"You need to go to the hospital," Trace gritted out.

Biscuit let out another low growl at my brother's tone.

I shook my head quickly. Hospitals were not my thing. Not since I'd spent so much time in one all those years ago. "No."

That muscle along Trace's jaw fluttered wildly. "You have a concussion."

"A small one," I argued. "And Susie can put some of that fancy glue on my forehead to get me all stitched up. Right, Susie?"

She looked back and forth between Trace and me as if scared to speak.

"She's not supposed to," Shawn muttered. He was older, in his late forties, with some salt and pepper in his hair and beard.

Susie, on the other hand, was younger than me and in PA school. Which meant she knew all about this sort of stuff. I would totally be her practice dummy if it got me out of going to the hospital.

A blacked-out truck skidded to a stop outside the fray. Its sleek lines and faint design detailed in black on black were familiar.

Fallon jumped out of the passenger seat, running toward me as Kye followed quickly behind. "Are you okay? What happened? Someone forced you off the road? What the heck, Rho?"

Kye's hands dropped to her shoulders, squeezing gently. "Breathe, Fal."

She closed her eyes for a moment, inhaled deeply, then opened them again. "Are you okay?"

I nodded, instantly regretting the action as it pulled on my wound and made my head ache. "I'm fine, promise."

Fallon scowled at me. "You're bleeding from the head. That's not fine. And let me guess, she's refusing to go to the hospital?"

Trace jerked his head in assent. "Stubborn as hell."

Fallon huffed out a breath. "I knew you would, so I picked up Dr. Avery on the way."

I glowered at her. "You kidnapped a doctor?"

Kye's lips twitched, but I still saw a hint of concern and maybe even fear swirling in his eyes. "She's slightly terrifying when riled."

"I'll agree with that," Dr. Avery, a man in his early sixties, said. He'd been my doctor since we moved here when I was a kid, just like he was for most of the rest of town. He moved purposefully through the crowd of emergency services. "Rhodes, I don't like meeting like this."

My mouth curved. "You and me both."

Biscuit let out a low growl as Dr. Avery got closer.

The doctor eyed my protector. "We might need to have him moved first."

"Good luck," Trace muttered. "He's like her bodyguard now."

"Think he'll come with me?" Fallon asked.

"We can try," I said, scratching behind Biscuit's ears. "You gotta go with Fallon for a minute, okay? I'll be right here." God, I was glad he was all right. It could've been so much worse, but we both seemed to have escaped without any major injuries.

Fallon took Biscuit's leash and lifted him to the ground with a grunt. "I gotcha. Gonna give you all the cuddles while your mom's getting fixed up."

The moment Biscuit was out of his path, Dr. Avery got to work. He did the little penlight test and examined my wound. "This would be a lot easier at my office," he mumbled.

"Better to just get it done," I said quietly. Even being in his office was hard for me. Checkups were one thing, but something like this? Just seeing some of the instruments he pulled out of his travel bag had my breaths coming faster.

Dr. Avery frowned down at me. "I can close this with medical glue, but you'll need to keep it dry for at least four days."

"I can do that."

Dr. Avery glanced at Susie. "Would you like to assist?"

She nodded enthusiastically.

They worked in tandem as I tried to let myself float away and not feel the pain of Susie holding my wound together or the glue being placed across my flesh. I hummed to myself, keeping my eyes closed.

The screech of tires had my eyes flying open. I quickly spotted Shep's truck, but it wasn't him my gaze landed on. It was Anson. He stalked across the pavement, his eyes wild. His dark gray T-shirt was pulled taut across his chest as it heaved with his ragged breaths. Everything about him was swirling darkness, as if shadows clung to him somehow.

The sea of emergency services personnel parted for him as if sensing the darkness. He prowled toward me, something in his movements more animal than human. His blue-gray gaze swept over me, assessing anything that was out of place in a matter of moments.

He slowed just as he approached the gurney, and I opened my

mouth to tell him I was okay, but I didn't get a chance. He pulled me into his arms, the move heartbreakingly gentle and forceful all at once.

I felt each heave of Anson's chest against mine. Each inhale and exhale felt jagged as if they caught on tattered pieces of his heart. "Reckless," he choked out.

My arms went around him, and I held on tight. "I'm okay."

"You're not," he growled. "There's a goddamn gash on your forehead, and someone drove you off the fucking road." Anson's arms shook around me, vibrating with fury, and maybe even fear.

I gripped him tighter, trying to assure him with my body as much as my mind that I was okay. "The doctor already fixed my head. I'm okay, Biscuit's okay. I just need to go home and have a long soak in a bath."

Anson kept holding on. "Someone tried to hurt you."

The words were barely audible, more sound than syllables. Tortured and coated in barbed wire.

The reminder had *my* body trembling. It hadn't been an accident. Whoever it was had wanted to harm me. I wished I could believe that it was a random tourist experiencing a blast of road rage, but I knew that wasn't true.

Someone had tried to burn my house down a couple of nights ago, leaving behind what might as well have been a death threat. And I hadn't wanted to deal with the reality of that. But now, I had no choice.

Someone out there hated me. Hated me so badly they wanted to hurt me in the worst ways possible.

Anson pressed his face to my neck. "Nothing can happen to you."

I wanted to reassure him that nothing would, but I wasn't so sure I could.

"What the hell is going on with you two?" Trace's deep voice broke into the bubble surrounding Anson and me.

As I tried to pull back, I remembered that we had an audience, and every pair of eyes was now glued to us.

Oh, shit.

Chapter Thirty-Two

Anson

FELT EYES ON ME. COULD SENSE THE HEAT OF THEM BORING INTO my back. But I couldn't look at anyone but Rho. While the damage to her forehead had been dealt with, I could still see the angry gash—something violent, something that had torn at her flesh.

The thought had nausea sweeping through me, fury fast on its heels. Because someone had tried to hurt Rho. Someone had tried to snuff out the only tiny pinpricks of light I had in my life.

Shep had shared what little he knew on the ride over. Someone had forced Rho off the road and down the side of a ravine. God, it could've been so much worse. It could've meant the sort of damage that was permanent.

Rho worried the corner of her lip, but my fingers flashed out, gently pulling it free. I couldn't stand the thought of her being in any more pain, even the slight kind brought on by a nervous habit.

"What the hell is going on?" Trace barked.

That had me whirling on him. "Don't speak to her in that tone."

The menace lacing my words had Trace's eyes widening. If I

wasn't mistaken, a hint of respect entered his expression. His face quickly resumed its careful mask.

"Let's just dial it back a notch, everyone," Rho said. Her voice was a balm to my overheated skin. She laid a hand on my back, the feel of her palm branding me, even through the cotton of my T-shirt. "Anson and I are…friends."

"Friends," Trace huffed.

"This isn't important," I snarled. "What's important is finding out who the hell did this to Rho."

Trace straightened, reading the accusation in my tone. "We've got an APB out, and I've got officers scouring the area. An SUV matching the description Rho gave was reported stolen from a trailhead."

"Where?" I clipped.

"About ten minutes south of here. Within walking distance of downtown."

My mind swirled, trying to put the pieces together. The fire, in the past and now, the photo left on her porch, the newspaper clippings, and now this. Everything was reactive. A balance of gifts and punishments.

Shep moved into my line of sight. "What are you thinking?"

He knew I wouldn't be able to stop myself from analyzing the circumstances, even if I didn't want to. "Whoever this is, they're impulsive. They don't think about long-term consequences. But the photo left on Rho's doorstep shows a level of manipulation."

Trace's eyes narrowed on me, but he didn't say a word. I could feel Rho stiffen at my back, even though I couldn't see her, as if the air shifted with her rigidity. But Shep kept pressing. "What does it mean?"

I pushed to my feet, clawing panic forcing me to move. I didn't want to put the pieces together. Didn't want what I was thinking to be true. "They're all signs of psychopathy."

Trace's jaw worked back and forth. "And how would you know what those signs are?"

My gaze flicked to Rho. Her expression was wary. I tried to tell myself that was good. She *should* be careful around me—around anyone who hid a part of themselves so well.

I forced my focus back to Trace. "I used to be FBI. Worked for the Behavioral Analysis Unit."

Surprise lit in Trace's eyes. "Profiler?"

I nodded.

"And now you work construction…" He was trying to put the pieces together.

My throat worked as I swallowed. "It wasn't for me anymore."

My gaze shifted to Rho, and everything in me tensed. Her face, usually so wide open, like a projector screen of all her emotions, was closed down. I couldn't read a damned thing other than the echoes of hurt in those hazel eyes.

Rho glanced at a middle-aged man standing near the gurney. "Can I go now? I'd like to get home."

The quiet whisper of her voice killed something in me, and guilt like a boa constrictor wrapped itself around my insides and squeezed.

The man nodded. "Someone needs to stay with you so they can wake you up every two hours and ask you simple questions. If you seem at all confused, they need to take you to the emergency room."

"I'll stay with you," Shep offered.

"No," Rho clipped. "Fallon will."

Fallon looked between them as if assessing a standoff. "Of course."

"Rho," I said softly as she slid off the gurney.

"No," she bit out.

Pain flared hot and bright, like what I imagined being gut shot felt like. I couldn't stop myself from moving toward her. She was still a beacon of light for me, even knowing I'd done something to dim it.

Rho let out a long breath. "You don't owe me your secrets. I know this isn't…that. I just—I need to go home."

But some part of me knew I did owe it to her. I'd been playing a game of deception, and she got burned. "I didn't want anyone to know," I said, my voice low.

That gold in her eyes dulled as her gaze flicked to her brother and then shifted back to me. "I bet Shep knew."

"Because I've known him since college," I explained. "He's always known. And when I needed a place to go where no one knew my past, he gave me that."

She nodded, understanding filling her expression. But it didn't drown out the hurt. "I get it. I really do. But it doesn't change that I told you *everything*, and you only gave me crumbs."

Each syllable was a slice to my skin, flaying me open and pouring acid in the wound. "I told you more than I've told *anyone*."

Rho just shook her head, but as she did, more pain flared in her eyes. "I can't do this right now." She turned to Fallon and the tattooed behemoth near her. "Can you take me home?"

Fallon was at her side in a second, gently wrapping an arm around her shoulders as she held Biscuit's leash in her other hand. "Of course. Come on."

I didn't move. Not as Rho walked away. Not as she climbed into the darkened SUV. Not as the vehicle pulled out and left. I just kept staring. Watching as the one thing that had made me happy for even the briefest moment disappeared right out of my life.

Chapter Thirty-Three

Rhodes

I PULLED THE THICK, FUZZY BLANKET OVER ME AS I LOOKED UP at the starry sky from the chaise lounge on my back deck. My head thrummed in a steady beat, but the dose of Tylenol had helped cut back the pain. It hadn't done a damned thing for the ache in my heart, however.

"More ice cream?" Fallon asked hopefully.

She wanted to fix it and make everything better. But since I'd remained tight-lipped on the ride home and for the past hour or so, ice cream was the best she could offer.

"If I have another bite of double chocolate fudge brownie, I'll explode."

"We need to work on your ice cream-eating skills," Fallon mumbled as she set her bowl on the table between us.

I chuckled, and it felt good to let the sound free. But it didn't take root the way my laughter usually did.

We were both quiet for a moment before Fallon spoke again. "Are you okay?"

I leaned my head back to look up at the sky. Thanks to my concussion, the stars were a little blurrier than normal, but I knew that wasn't what Fallon meant. I teased the corner of the blanket, my fingers looking for any signs of a loose thread I could pick at.

"I knew he had secrets."

Fallon made a humming noise in the back of her throat. "Mister king of the brood? Of course, he did. Those eyes scream secrets."

I turned on my side to face her. "So, why did it kill so much to find out what one of them was? It's not like I have a right to know everything about the man."

She studied me for a minute. "What's going on with you two? The way he stormed through people to get to you today...that's not just *friends*."

I let out a huff of air. It wasn't cold enough to see the expulsion around me, but I could feel it hanging there. "I don't know how to explain it. We understand each other in a way I've never had with anyone else. He gets what I went through."

I didn't miss the tiniest flicker of hurt in Fallon's eyes. She'd experienced her own loss. Her dad and brother. But it was different. While I knew she was always there for me, I hadn't been able to show her the parts of myself that I was most ashamed of. The pieces I'd set out so easily for Anson.

Fallon pulled back the hurt, shoving it away so she could be there for me. "I'm glad you have that. That he gave you that."

I licked my lips. "And there's a pretty potent attraction."

One corner of her mouth kicked up. "Is there, now?"

Heat rose to my cheeks. I was sure Fallon could see it, even in the dark. "He's made me come harder than I ever have in my life."

Fallon let out a hoot that made Biscuit howl in response from inside. "Why is this bad? Emotional connection. Physical connection. Sounds like a relationship to me."

"It's not. He's not—" I didn't know how to explain it.

"He's not a relationship kind of guy?" Fallon asked.

"He said he doesn't do them. And I'm not talking a he's-sleeping-with-everything-that-moves-and-doesn't-want-to-settle-down type of thing. He doesn't want to care about *anyone*. He even holds back from Shep, and that's his best friend."

She was quiet for a long moment. "He might not *want* to care about anyone, but he does. He cares about *you*. You were there tonight. Anson was out of his mind seeing you hurt. It scared the hell out of him."

"I hate that," I whispered. "I don't want to be a source of pain for him." Even hurting as much as I was right now, I never wanted to inflict that sort of agony.

Fallon stared at me through the darkness. "You can't truly live without some sort of hurt. If you're so focused on avoiding discomfort, you end up living a half-life. You might get to skip the lowest lows, but you don't get the highest highs either."

God, she was right. And I'd been doing that. Even though I tried to appreciate each moment as the gift it was, all the things in my life that I was grateful for, I'd held myself back from letting *new* good into my life. Nothing that was permanent anyway.

Rental houses and foster pets. Even the flowers I favored tended to have finite timelines, ones that bloomed once instead of every year. And all of that was especially true when it came to relationships. I dated guys there was no chance of a future with, and kept the ones there might be something with at arm's length. I was doing the same thing Anson was, just in a less obvious way.

"I've been scared," I finally admitted to Fallon.

She sat up, crossing her legs beneath the blanket and taking me in. "I know."

Tears burned the backs of my eyes. "Of course, you do."

Fallon chuckled. "I love you, Rho. You've always been the sister of my heart. But that doesn't mean it hurts any less that you lost Emilia. Or your parents. You lost your family in one of the most horrific ways imaginable. It's completely understandable that you'd be a little gun-shy about starting a family of your own."

My heart picked up speed, my ribs tightening around my lungs. "I have you, Nora, Lolli…our whole brood."

She sent me a sad smile. "You didn't have any choice with us.

And I think you still hold back a piece of you, even from us. Keeping that somehow makes you feel safe."

The tears came then, spilling down my cheeks. "I'm so scared of losing one of you. I don't think I could take it."

"Rho," Fallon whispered hoarsely, then kicked off the blanket and crossed to my chaise, wrapping me in a hug. "I know. It's terrifying. But don't let it stop you from loving fully while we're all here."

I hugged her as tightly as I could, my arms aching with the action. As though if I just held on tight enough, I wouldn't lose her, too. "I love you, Fallon."

"I love you, too. More than you could possibly know. And I'm here for you, for the good and the bad, however messy the feelings."

I laughed through my tears. "I'm glad, because I'm pretty sure I fell in love with a guy I don't even really know."

Fallon released me so she could take in my face. Easing back onto the edge of her chaise, she grinned at me. "On the upside, it sounds like he was a pretty badass FBI agent."

I couldn't return her smile. "It's that he had this whole other side of himself that he didn't share with me. And I showed him the things I don't give anyone else."

The grin slipped from Fallon's mouth. "I know that had to hurt like hell, but I think you need to talk to him. Give him a chance to tell you why he kept it from you. Because it would be a shame to lose someone who makes you feel seen."

It was more than that. Anson saw the dark, twisted parts of me and understood them. They didn't scare him away or make him see me differently. And just maybe, he even cherished those parts because they were part of who I was.

"I don't know if he'll be back." I spoke the fear I hadn't realized was floating around in my brain. Now that everyone knew this piece of Anson that he'd been so desperate to hide, he might bail. Find a new town to disappear into, where no one knew the scars he carried.

A small smile pulled at Fallon's lips. "I wouldn't be so sure about that."

A floodlight switched on at the side of the house, and I jerked up. Anson was illuminated in silhouette. He'd obviously showered and changed at some point, but deep ravines were carved into his hair as if he'd run his fingers through it countless times.

Fallon stood, sending me a grin. "I'm going to let you guys talk. I'll get a ride home with Kye."

My gaze flicked quickly to her. "Thanks, Fallon. For everything."

"You know I always have your back."

"Love you," I whispered as she headed for the front of the house.

"Love you, too," she called through the darkness.

My eyes were already locked back on Anson, taking in every inch of his ravaged expression.

"Can't handle being away from you," he croaked. "Especially not when you're hurting." He swallowed hard. "I didn't want to care about *anyone*. But you shot that all to hell."

My heart hammered against my ribs, butterfly wings dying to break free.

A muscle fluttered in Anson's cheek. "You didn't sneak past my defenses, you bulldozed them. Reckless to the bone. And maybe you made me brave enough to be reckless, too."

I threw off the blanket, moving before I even realized I'd commanded my legs to do so. I ran across the deck, jumping the two feet down, and hit him full force. He hauled me into his arms. I didn't care that my muscles ached or that my head thrummed. Because Anson had me in his arms. And he was letting me *in*.

Chapter Thirty-Four

Anson

I T TOOK EVERYTHING IN ME TO KEEP MY HOLD ON RHO GENTLE. Today had been countless torturous lifetimes of her slipping through my fingers, from others' vicious actions and my own stupidity. But having her in my arms again, feeling the beat of her heart against my chest, melted the worst of that away.

"You shouldn't be running," I rasped. "Or jumping."

"Shut up," Rho mumbled, shoving her face into my neck and breathing me in.

Keeping Rho in my arms, I climbed the two steps up to the deck and crossed to the back door. Opening it, I stepped inside. I kicked the door shut with my boot and flipped the lock. Darkness swirled around us as I strode down the hall and into the living room. Lowering to the couch, I cradled her against me, not bothering to turn on the light. She burrowed into me, and I trailed my fingers up and down her back, relishing the feel of each vertebra in her spine, the rhythm of it, the vibration.

"Thanks for coming back," Rho whispered.

My fingers stilled. "Told you. Can't stay away. You clawed your-self inside. Walking away would be like tearing out a part of myself—even if it would be the smart move."

She shifted then, moving so she could straddle me. It wasn't sexual; it was pure dominance as her eyes narrowed on me. "Why?"

I knew I'd have to tell her. Knew that coming back here meant only one thing. Telling Rho *everything*.

That oppressive weight resettled on my chest, the icy dread seeping in. But then Rho slid her fingers through mine, grounding me in the here and now. Her touch was better than any damn breathing exercise or anti-anxiety med. "You can tell me anything. I promise."

My eyes burned as I stared at Rho through the dark. Even in the shadows, her beauty stopped me dead. The wildness of it, the freedom. I didn't want to lose the way she looked at me. And I knew telling her the truth might do just that. But there was no other choice, no place left to go.

"After college, I went straight into an accelerated doctoral program in psychology."

"So, you're a shrink?"

"Technically. But I never went into practice." This was the easy part, the clinical piece, but even it seemed to stick in the back of my throat. "One of my professors had ties to the bureau and suggested I apply to their Behavioral Analysis Unit."

Rho studied me, not letting go of my hands. "And what does that unit do, exactly? Trace said profiler, but I don't think I've ever heard the term outside movies and TV."

My thumbs traced designs on the backs of her hands, and I used the feel of her skin to keep me steady. "We're the law enforcement nerds, honestly."

She gave me a droll look. "You're hardly a nerd."

"Don't be so sure. I've got an IQ of one-forty-four."

Rho's brow lifted. "Interesting. So, I'm shacked up with a genius."

"I prefer nerd."

"Okay, I can go with nerd. Do you have any black-framed glasses to complete the effect? I think I could be into that."

I shot up, kissing her. My tongue swept in, stroking and teasing but not taking it any further. Not until she knew the truth. I pulled back to find those hazel eyes slightly unfocused. "I'll bring my reading glasses next time."

Rho stared down at me, waiting.

I sighed. "Profilers are sort of like analysts. We take all the facts from a series of crimes and build the image of a suspect. Age, sex, race, personality traits."

"How do you get your cases?"

"We have to be invited by local law enforcement, or another arm of the FBI could ask for our help when crimes cross state lines."

"That's a lot of moving around with no real roots," Rho mused.

"We were on the go a lot. Living out of hotels."

She looked down at me, adding shades of color to the image she had of me in her mind. "How long did you work there?"

"Almost five years."

Rho gripped my hands tighter. "You probably saw a lot of awful things."

My mouth went dry, but I forced the words out anyway. "I did. But I didn't see enough."

She frowned, curiosity brimming in those soulful eyes.

"I didn't let it in. I should've. But I turned off that part of myself. I saw crimes as data and not the human beings behind it."

"That makes complete sense. How could you? If you let yourself truly see that day in and day out, you'd drown in grief. It was a self-protection mechanism."

That was Rho. Always seeing the best in everyone, in me. But she gave me too much leeway, too much grace. "I'm sure that was part of it. But there's an ugly piece, too."

Rho kept a grip on my hands and didn't look away.

It took everything to hold her gaze as I continued. "I thought I was hot shit. It was like my mind was made for profiling. I saw connections no one else did. Things that led to more case closures than people with a decade or more on the job."

I gripped her hands harder, needing to feel the contact with the

here and now. "I got cocky. Wrote a few books. Got some press attention. Kept working cases."

"Anson," Rho said quietly. "There's nothing wrong with being
good at your job."

"Maybe not. But I was a dick. Thought I knew everything."

"And something happened," she whispered.

I moved my head up and down in the barest nod. "We started
working a case of serial murders that crossed state lines. Everywhere
from the Southwest up the coast to the Pacific Northwest. All women.
Restrained. Ligature marks on their ankles, wrists, and necks. But the
cause of death was always the severing of their carotid."

There was the tiniest jerk of Rho's hands. A jolt of shock. "He
slit their throats."

"Yes. But every time he did, he mailed a letter to local law enforcement. A clue. A *game*."

Rho's expression was everything I should've felt about the case
but didn't. "That's awful."

"He gets a thrill out of it. It's almost sexual for him, that cat-
and-mouse back-and-forth. Each note had a word game. Clues that
gave a letter, and the letters gave a location. They started calling him
The Hangman."

"And that location was where the body would be," Rho finished
for me.

"Yes." I traced more circles on the backs of her hands, a swirl of
my callused fingertips against the smooth silk of her skin. "I was good
at his game. Too good. We gave one press conference, and something
I said during it tipped him off that I was the one solving his riddles."

Rho gripped my hands so hard I'd likely have bruises tomorrow.
"He fixated on you."

My throat worked as I swallowed. "The clues started being sent
to the BAU and addressed to me. I should've known he'd dig. He
sent letters to the victims' families afterward, notes that told us he'd
watched them. Interviews, social media posts. He tracked them because he got off on their pain. The emotional torture of the loved ones
was as much of a high as the physical."

She shuddered against me. "Anson…"

"I was stupid thinking I wouldn't end up as a target, that I was out of his reach. I'd used my middle name as my last when I published my book and never went public with my last name at press conferences. I thought that would be enough."

Fear swirled in Rho's eyes, dulling the gold to a deep amber. "What did he do?"

"Found my family. My sister. Grabbed her outside the hospital she worked at in Portland. Kept her for twenty-four hours. Then he sliced her throat and sent me the clue to find her. We didn't even know she was missing. She always worked crazy shifts as an ER nurse. I didn't know that he was terrorizing her for a full day, *slicing* her throat, because I was too caught up in my own bullshit."

"Anson," she rasped. "Tell me they got him. That they put him away for the rest of his life."

I shook my head, the agony digging deeper at yet another failure. "No idea where he is. Cases are still open, but he went quiet when I quit the bureau." I swallowed hard, trying to choke back the pain. "I'd already gotten my sister killed, and when my father had a heart attack three months later, I knew I killed him, too. My mom thinks so. Said as much at Dad's funeral."

Rho only held my hands tighter, not wavering. But tears brimmed in her eyes. "*You* didn't do this, Anson."

"I might not've held the blade or stopped the heart, but I may as well have," I bit out.

She shook my hands this time, nails digging into my skin. "You were trying to stop him."

I had tried. Before Greta died and I realized it was all pointless, I'd given it everything. Nights of barely any sleep so I could keep digging when the bureau moved us on to other cases. Endless phone calls and flying back to crime scenes on my own dime. But was it obsession more than anything? I didn't know. Maybe it was that ego-driven need to defeat him more than dedication to the greater good.

Rho released one of my hands and brushed the hair away from my face, her fingers lingering there. "None of us is just one thing.

We're not all good or all bad. We're a blend of shadow and light. And those sparks only shine because of the darkness."

My throat constricted, air barely getting through.

"I *hate* that this happened to you. That you lost people you loved. That a *monster* ripped away so much from you. But you are a beautiful person, Anson. A *good* person. And you are that way because of what you've been through."

Rho's eyes bored into me. "You are the kind of person who takes time with a terrified dog to show him that all men aren't bad. The kind of person who sleeps on a lumpy couch because you knew I was too proud to say I was scared. And you're the kind of person who made it safe for me to say some of the things I was most scared to give voice to."

Her fingers trailed down my neck to my shoulder. They dug in there, squeezing as if to ask if I was *really* paying attention. "You made me feel seen, Anson. Understood when I always felt like a bit of a freak. Do you get what a gift that is?"

"Rho." Her name was more plea than anything else.

"So, you had a big head. Maybe you were a cocky prick. So what? You think that means you deserved to have your life shredded? To have your sister killed?"

My jaw clamped shut, teeth grinding.

"Guess what? It wasn't about you. It was about some sick asshole and *his* obsession. You didn't do it. *He* did."

Something about what Rho said, the ferocity with which she said it, penetrated. For possibly the first time. *It wasn't about you.*

She was right. If I hadn't been at the bureau then, the unsub would've fixated on someone else. It could've been anyone, for any reason. It just happened to be me.

"Sometimes, it feels like the guilt is going to swallow me whole," I admitted.

A few tears spilled over Rho's lids, dropping to my chest. Her hand slid down, covering the spot where they'd fallen. "I know. I'd give anything to take it away for you. *Anything.* But I can't. All I can say is that *I know.*"

And she did. Rho knew, unlike anyone else ever could. The circumstances were completely different, but the weight was somehow the same. The price we paid for still breathing amidst the loss.

"The only thing we can do is let them teach us how to live," Rho whispered.

I stared up at her, those wild brown locks swirling around me, blocking out the rest of the world.

"We know there are no guarantees. So, we live life to the fullest. We don't miss a second. And we appreciate all the things they loved so much."

A lump formed in my throat, a boulder I had to clear before I could speak. "Greta loved flowers."

Rho's fingers clamped down on mine.

My mouth curved the slightest bit. "But she was awful at taking care of them. We talked every week, and she would moan about killing another one. She would've *loved* your back deck."

Even in the dark, I could see all the color out the back doors—more pots than I could count. Red, yellow, pink, purple. So much life.

I looked back at Rho, the same swirl of color, of life, in her eyes. "I wanted to climb into the grave with her."

"I know," Rho whispered. "But she wouldn't want that."

"No," I croaked. "She wouldn't."

Rho bent, lowering herself slowly until her lips were just a breath away from mine. "So, live."

And for the first time in two years, she made me want to.

Chapter Thirty-Five

Rhodes

THE STORM CLOUDS ROLLED THROUGH ANSON'S EYES AS I waited, blue and gray battling for dominance. He needed both, the shadow and the light, just like I'd said. But right now, I prayed the blue won and those flickers of life took hold.

"You make me want to reach for things I thought were dead and buried. You make me *feel* again," Anson said, his hand gliding up my thigh to my waist. "Even if it's pissing me the hell off."

A laugh bubbled out of me. "Sometimes, we need a little anger to remind us there are still things we care about."

Anson's fingers slipped under my T-shirt, sliding across the bare skin of my belly. "I care about you, Rho. I didn't want to, but I didn't have a choice."

I scowled down at him, and Anson burst out laughing. God, the sound was beautiful. Rich and deep with a rasp that had goose bumps rising on my skin in a way that told me all my nerve endings were paying attention.

"You know," I began, my fingers tracing a figure eight over

Anson's heart, "some people might take exception to you saying that you didn't *want* to care about them."

He grinned, his teeth a flash of white in the low light as his hand skimmed higher, playing over my rib cage. "Or you could take it as a compliment. Not just anyone could smash through those walls."

Warmth spread through me at that, a buzzy heat intensified by Anson's exploring fingers. "But you have to want me there now," I said softly, fear edging into my words. I wouldn't force this on him. He had to want me to stay.

Anson's eyes sparked. "Here is the only place I want you. And the only place I want to be."

His hand skated higher, palming my breast. He groaned. "What is it with you and no underwear?"

I started to laugh, but it died in my throat as Anson found my nipple, his roughened thumb circling. My lips parted on a quick in-hale. "Why would I wear the torture device that is a bra when I'm in my own home?"

"Fair point," Anson said, his voice deepening.

It seemed he wasn't in any rush, content to just revel in the feel of me. I arched deeper into his hand, needing more pressure, more contact.

"Even your skin's responsive," he murmured, transfixed. He skated a fingertip over the swell of my breast. "The way it pebbles when you like something." His thumb swiped around my nipple again. "The way it tightens, trying to get closer."

My breaths came quicker—short, staccato pants.

"I could watch your body react for hours on end just to figure out the pattern."

I stared down at him. "Profiling me?"

Anson chuckled, low and throaty. "Maybe. I could get behind this sort of breakdown." He stared at his hand working beneath my tee. "Do you like this?"

He kneaded my breast, not too hard, but not too soft. The kind of pressure that made you sit up and pay attention.

"Or this?"

His thumb and forefinger twisted my nipple.

A gasp left my lips as I rocked my hips against his on instinct.

"She likes a little pain with her pleasure," Anson growled.

I licked my lips, which suddenly felt as dry as a desert. "It's always that delicate balance, isn't it? The pain drives the pleasure higher."

Anson's hand slipped from mine, and he grabbed the hem of my T-shirt, pulling it up and over my head and sending it floating to the floor. "Wouldn't mind exploring that with you."

The cool night air sweeping in through an open window only made my body feel hotter, the juxtaposition acute.

Anson simply stared at me, taking in every detail. His fingertips traced over my breast and down my sternum. He took a detour to my side, tracing the scars the fire had left behind. "Your beauty scalds, Reckless. Anyone who's ever had the pleasure of looking at you will never be the same."

Breath caught in my throat. "Anson."

"Everything about you is made to burn into a man's brain. And I'll never get tired of staring." He rose, coming closer. "Or tasting."

Anson closed the distance, taking my nipple into his mouth and sucking it deep. I ground into him, feeling him hardening beneath me. It was a surge of power, knowing that my touch and taste made him react this way.

Anson's teeth grazed the bud, and I let out a whimper. He smiled against my flesh as he released me. "Wonder if I could make you come just like this. Just teasing these pretty nipples over and over, bringing you to the brink."

I rocked my hips against him as wetness gathered between my thighs.

He let out a growl, his hands dropping to my hips. "Reckless..."

A devilish smile rose to my lips. "You play, I get to play."

Anson's breaths sped up as I rocked, my eyes fluttering closed and then open as I moved. He appeared in my vision in beautiful snapshots. Such adoration there. Reverence, even. And my traitorous heart hoped for more, even if I wasn't sure he could give it.

"Rho," he groaned.

I reached down, grabbed his T-shirt, and tugged it off. The moment I tossed it behind me, my hands were on him. I hadn't gotten the chance to explore before. Not really. My fingers ghosted over tanned skin.

His chest rose and fell in rapid pants as I traced his nipple and ventured lower. The ridges of his abdominals should be illegal. But the fact that they came from hard work instead of hours in the gym only made me want to worship them more.

"You keep touching me like that, and I'm gonna come in my pants like a thirteen-year-old," Anson growled.

There'd be a certain power in that, but it wasn't what I wanted. Not what I needed.

I stood then, letting the cool air hit me. My fingers dropped to the waistband of my sweatpants, and I slowly slid them down. There wasn't even a flicker of unease or uncertainty. Because Anson made me comfortable showing him everything.

I slid one leg out and then the other. Then I simply stood there, letting him look his fill.

Anson stroked a hand over himself through the thin cotton of his joggers, just watching. "Dreamed of getting all of you. Never dreamed it would be this good."

I took one step and then another.

Anson moved in a flash, shucking his joggers and then reaching out for me. He lifted me as if I weighed nothing until he was lying back on the couch, and I was hovering over him. Then he cursed. "Condom."

I grabbed his arms. "I'm on the pill. And I've been checked."

His Adam's apple bobbed as he swallowed. "There hasn't been anyone in a long time. And, fuck, I want to feel all of you. Everything."

God, I wanted that, too.

So, I moved, hovering over him, so close I ached.

Anson's fingers tightened on my hips, guiding me down.

The first hint of him had everything in me tightening, yearning for everything to come, for all of *him*. And then there was more. My eyes watered as I sank down, the stretch a delicate balance of pleasure and pain.

And I only wanted more.

Anson's hand slid up my body to my neck and finally tangled in my hair. His grip was gentle and forceful all at the same time. And I wanted more. More of both. More of him. The darkness and the light.

As I sank fully onto him, a gasp left my lips. So full. So *everything*.

"Heaven and hell," Anson gritted out. "Never felt anything better."

My hips began to rock, and he groaned.

"Killing me."

Anson gave me control, letting me find my rhythm in my time, to adjust to all of him and find my way back to us.

My hands moved to his chest, using it for purchase to slide up and down. I took him deeper with each pass, my back arching.

He met me then, in the gray that was us, the mixture of light and dark.

Anson's restraint snapped, and he gripped my hips so hard I'd carry marks tomorrow. Marks I *craved*. I met him thrust for thrust, taking him deeper than I thought possible.

My thighs burned, and my muscles quaked as I reached for more. Anson groaned as he arched into me, hitting the spot that had light dancing across my vision. My inner walls tightened, beckoning him.

"Rhodes." His hold on me seized. "Eyes on me. I need it."

So, I gave it to him. Forcing my eyes open, I locked them on Anson. I watched everything play across his face as my hips shifted. I didn't lose him as everything in me shattered. As I spasmed around him, taking all he had to give.

Anson came on a shout, pounding into me as I met him in every moment, every shadow. And as I collapsed onto his chest, I knew that all I would ever want was the murky gray in this twilight of us, where the sparks of feeling shone brighter than the sun on a summer day.

Chapter Thirty-Six

Anson

THE FAINT BEEPING OF AN ALARM SOUNDED. FAINT BECAUSE I was pinned to the mattress by a tiny yet surprisingly strong starfish.

Rho groaned. "Make it stop."

I chuckled as she burrowed her face deeper into my neck. "What's your name?"

"'*I'm gonna kick your ass if you ask me one more time*' is my name."

I grinned into her hair. It smelled sweet, something floral, which shouldn't have surprised me, given Rho's love of plants. I'd also learned that she loved her sleep. She'd been like a snarling kitten every time I woke her during the night for her concussion protocol.

Struggling to extricate my arm from beneath her, I reached for my phone and shut off the alarm.

"Better," she grumbled.

I stroked my hand up and down her spine. "How do you feel?"

Rho made a humming noise against my neck. "Good."

Her voice was like liquid heat spilling over me.

"Reckless..."

"My head hurts a little." She levered up so she could look into my eyes. "But the rest of me feels great."

Rho shifted so she was straddling me, my body coming awake beneath her. My hands ran up her thighs beneath the oversized T-shirt she wore—that damn airbrushed kitten shirt from the vet's office. But even the ridiculous top couldn't dull my need for Rho. I was insatiable.

The need clawed at me from the inside out, and I knew it would never stop. The flicker of an alarm bell lit in my brain, but I shoved it back. As my fingers slid higher, Rho's back arched. But as it did, she caught sight of something and froze.

"It's seven a.m.?" she shrieked. And then she was off me in a flash. "I'm going to be late."

My dick throbbed in an angry beat. "You can't work today."

"Of course, I can." Rho was already grabbing clothes from drawers as Biscuit lifted his head from his bed. She slid on a pair of pink panties with daisies on them, giving me a shot of her delectable ass that only made my dick angrier.

"You have a concussion. You need to rest," I argued, sitting up.

"A *mild* concussion. I won't do any lifting. I'll just sit behind the counter. But I'm supposed to open in thirty minutes."

I pushed to my feet, grabbing the clothes I'd discarded last night. "Call your boss. I'm sure he'll cover for you."

Rho pulled on some sort of bra thing with a million straps crisscrossing her tanned back. The view had me imagining different kinds of straps tying her down while I—*shit*. I needed to get a hold of myself.

"I don't like missing work," Rho muttered as she stepped into shorts.

I moved into her space as I pulled on my T-shirt. "Rho."

She looked up as she tugged a tank top over her head. "I'm fine."

I wrapped my arms around her, the move so easy, as if there'd never been a time when I *hadn't* done this. She fit in my hold, my body molding to hers. "You were in a car accident last night."

Rho shivered against me, and I hated myself for even bringing it up. But she needed to remember to take it easy. She rested her chin on my sternum and looked up at me. "I know. And if I lie around here all day, all I'll do is think about it. If I go into work, I'll at least have distractions."

Just the thought of her being out of my sight had anxiety and fear clawing at my insides. Someone had forced her off the road yesterday. Hurt her. Was maybe even trying for worse.

Her thumb stroked back and forth over my spine. "I'll be with people all day," she assured me as if reading my thoughts. "You can drive me, and I'll have someone give me a lift home."

"I'll drive you home," I argued.

Rho huffed out a breath. "Fine. But we need to go, or I'm going to be late."

"All right," I grumbled.

She stretched up onto her tiptoes, kissing the underside of my jaw. "I gotta brush my teeth."

We both went through an abbreviated morning routine, and Rho grinned as I used her toothbrush. I rinsed my mouth as she took the brush and put it back in the holder.

I shook my head. "Not like my mouth hasn't been plenty of other places."

Rho stuck her tongue out at me. "I know. But I like you using my toothbrush. Makes this feel real." She stilled then. "It is, isn't it? This wasn't some one-time freak-out because I could've died, and now you're going to get all weird on me sort of thing, right?"

An ache wrapped around my chest. I'd injected that doubt into Rho with all my back-and-forth bullshit. I pulled her gently into my arms and brushed my lips across hers. "This is real. I'm probably going to fuck it up a million times over, but I won't stop trying."

Rho melted against me. "I'd rather have you and your fuckups than anyone else."

I chuckled, kissing her forehead. "Lucky me."

"Come on," she said, heading for the door and whistling for Biscuit. "If Sonny's already at the café, I'll con him into making us breakfast."

My stomach rumbled at that. I followed Rho as she hooked

Biscuit's leash to his collar and opened the door. As we stepped outside, her steps faltered. The crew was milling around the Victorian, ready to get started on the day.

"They're all seeing you come out of my house," Rho whispered.

They already knew I'd spent the night before, so it wasn't exactly new information. I could pass it off as me looking after a friend when they'd been through something horrible, but I didn't want to lie. Didn't want to deny what Rho was to me.

I wrapped an arm around her and pulled her into me, my lips close to hers as I stared into those green and gold eyes. "No more hiding."

Those eyes flared. "No more hiding," she whispered.

I dipped my head, my mouth taking hers. My tongue stroked in, her taste exploding in my mouth. God, I could drink her in for an eternity. But I forced myself to pull back.

Rho's focus was a little hazy as I did, making me grin. But when I stole a look at the crew, they were all frozen, staring. A few had slack jaws. Then one of them whistled. A few others hooted or shouted something I didn't want to hear. Shep just stared hard at me.

Shit.

I owed him a conversation. But right now, I needed to get Rho to work. "Come on," I said, guiding her gently toward my truck.

She paused to let Biscuit do his business, and then I lifted him into the cab before helping Rho into the passenger seat. I turned to meet Shep's angry gaze after closing her door.

Apparently, the conversation couldn't wait. "Shep—"

"Tell me you're not messing with her."

My jaw hardened as I struggled to keep my temper in check. "You know me better than that. If I needed to blow off steam, I sure as hell wouldn't do it with your sister."

He kicked at a piece of gravel. "Hell."

"I *care* about her." That word seemed so lacking, but it was the best I had right now.

Shep's shoulders slumped. "You've both been through so much. I don't want either of you to get hurt."

I saw it then. His genuine care for us both. His worry. Shep carrying the world on his shoulders yet again. "The fact that we've been through so much is what bonded us. I told her. Everything."

And, God, such a weight had been lifted by doing that. Giving Rho my greatest shame and knowing that she accepted me anyway.... That she *understood* me.

Shep's eyes widened. "You told her about Greta?"

I nodded. Hearing Greta's name aloud wasn't as painful this time. It was almost...*good*. I needed to pull her out of the dark and bring her back into my life. Remember her. Not just the guilt that surrounded her death but also the amazing life she'd lived.

Shep's gaze flicked to the truck and then back to me. "Then I'm glad for you. You needed to let someone in."

He extended a hand, and I took it in a shake. "Thanks, Shep. For everything."

"I'll always have your back." His grip on my hand tightened, and he jerked me forward. "But if you hurt her, I'll bury your body under one of my construction sites, and no one will ever know."

"Shit," I muttered, trying to extricate my hand from his grasp.

The passenger door opened. "If you two are done having a pissing contest over my virtue or whatever this is, can we go? I'm going to be late for work."

Shep released my hand. "Be careful today. And take it easy. Trace said he'll have deputies hanging around the nursery." Shep glanced at me. "He wants to talk to you at some point, too."

That familiar weight settled in. Of course, he did. I was sure Trace wanted to know why I'd hidden my past, and if I had any insights on what was happening. I wouldn't have any choice in the matter because I'd do whatever it took to keep Rho safe.

"Yeah," I muttered. "I'll talk to him."

Shep slapped me on the back. "Then get your ass back here because we've got work."

Rho watched me as I rounded the truck and climbed inside. She didn't say anything as I backed out and headed toward town. It was only when I was pulling into the nursery that she finally spoke. "You don't have to help Trace."

I turned off the engine and looked over at her. "I'm not helping Trace. I'm helping *you*."

Rho shook her head, her hair swishing around her shoulders. "I don't want you to cause yourself pain to do it."

I reached over, sliding a hand across her jaw. "I'd go to hell and back for you." I already was. Because diving back into the world that had destroyed me before would be like walking through fire. But I'd always do that for Rho.

"I don't want you to have to," she mumbled.

My thumb stroked her cheek. "We're going to find who's doing this. Whatever it takes."

Rho leaned forward, resting her forehead against mine. "Promise you'll let me be there for you while you do this. I don't want you to be alone in it."

"I'm not. Not anymore." Rho had given me that. It had been so long that the feeling was foreign. But, damn, it was good, too.

She quickly pressed her lips to mine. "Good."

And with that, she hopped out of my truck.

I followed behind, helping Biscuit out and handing Rho his leash. The nursery was quiet; no one else seemed to be around yet. "When does everyone else get here?" I asked.

"It'll explode in about fifteen minutes," Rho said, pulling keys out of her pocket. "We get lots of early morning traffic."

I'd stick around until then.

As we approached the main greenhouse, Rho's steps slowed. "That's weird. We don't carry cut flowers here."

I followed her line of sight, my body instantly on alert. There, in front of the door, was a massive bouquet of flowers. Rho bent to pick them up, but I quickly grabbed her shirt, tugging her back. "Don't," I clipped.

She looked at me, frowning. But I was already scanning the area. There wasn't any sign of anyone.

"Don't move," I commanded. "Don't touch anything."

I jogged back to my truck, rustling through the contents in the bed until I found a box of gloves. Pulling out a pair, I quickly donned them.

Rho's face went pale as she took me in. "You think it's him?"

"I don't know, but we need to be careful either way."

I leaned over and plucked up the note that rested on the flowers. Scrawled across the envelope in jagged block letters was *RHO*. Just seeing her name had nausea rolling through me.

I opened the envelope and tugged the card free. Written in the same jagged handwriting was a single word.

SORRY.

Chapter Thirty-Seven

Rhodes

"R HO, HAND TO GOD, THIS IS BETTER THAN ANYTHING I have ever tasted," Carlos said as he shoved a mouthful of the balsamic chicken pasta into his mouth.

Silas nodded. "I gotta be honest, I wasn't sure when we pulled up. It looked like fancy food. But, damn, it's good."

I couldn't help laughing at that. Apparently, pasta containing spinach and goat cheese was suspect to a construction crew. But I'd won them over.

"I'd never steer you wrong," I said with a grin.

"Thanks, Rho. You're spoiling us rotten," Shep said, getting another helping from the massive aluminum baking dish I'd used.

"I like having the project," I said, leaning back in the folding chair.

Busy. I'd needed to stay busy. Because after the flowers, I hadn't been allowed to go anywhere alone. At first, Trace had stationed a deputy at the nursery. But it was really more of a bodyguard. They followed me everywhere I went, and it scared customers.

I'd finally asked Duncan if it would be easier if I took some vacation time. He'd hemmed and hawed but eventually admitted it might be a good idea. It killed, stepping away from my job, even temporarily, but it was the right thing to do.

So, I'd worked on my garden at the guest cottage. After a week, the whole thing was brimming with so much color and foliage I didn't have room for a single new plant. Then, I'd moved on to cooking. Every day, Anson dutifully drove me to the grocery store, and I loaded up on ingredients. The crew acted as my test dummies. I'd made elaborate meals for the past week and change, getting more and more intricate as I went.

But it wasn't enough. I was still twitchy. There'd been no more notes, threats, fires, or collisions. Instead, it felt like a creepy waiting game.

A hand slid over my thigh, squeezing gently in silent reassurance. I looked over at Anson. He still wore a mostly blank expression around the crew. But around me, he smiled more. Even laughed. And I soaked up all of it.

He leaned over and brushed his lips across my temple. "Best one yet."

His touch eased the worst of my fraying nerves, but the frenetic energy still pulsed through me. The need to get up and *do* something. Maybe I needed to train for a marathon. That would tire me out.

An image of half a dozen deputies running with me filled my mind. Because that was what Trace would require if I started jogging. My shoulders slumped.

Silas sent me a hopeful look. "You make dessert tonight?"

Carlos cuffed him on the back of the head. "Don't be greedy."

Shep chuckled. "When it comes to food, he's always going to be a greedy bastard."

Silas patted his stomach. "Takes a lot of energy to look this good."

I just shook my head but stood and pushed my chair back. Dashing into the kitchen, I grabbed the baking dish sitting on the counter and headed back outside.

Lifting the baking dish into the air, I grinned. "Chocolate peanut butter poke cake."

Silas groaned. "Chocolate, peanut butter, *and* cake? All of my favorite things in one."

Carlos just started clapping.

At least I had my community amid all the upheaval in my life. People who made me smile and laugh, who were there in good times and bad. And when I really thought about it, that's what you needed in life: people who helped you make the best out of any circumstances.

We demolished the cake. The guys told stories of ridiculous things that had happened on past jobs. I laughed to the point of tears. And then they all helped me clean up.

One by one, they left for the day, until only Shep and Anson remained. "Hey," I said, glancing at Shep. "What happened to Owen?"

It wasn't unusual for him to disappear for a few days. He'd take off on his bike and ride, probably end up shacked up in a roadside motel with whatever woman he could talk into bed. But I hadn't seen him in weeks.

Shep winced. "I had to fire him."

My eyes widened. "Seriously?" It wasn't that I didn't think Owen had earned that with his behavior over the years, but I never thought Shep would actually pull the trigger.

"It was time. I wanted to give him a chance to grow up, to change, but it just never happened."

I wrapped my arms around Shep in a hug. "You're a good one."

Shep hugged me back and then ruffled my hair. "So are you. Thanks for the incredible food."

"Anytime. I'm thinking Mediterranean bowls tomorrow."

Shep chuckled. "Can't wait to see what they think of that." He gave Anson a chin lift. "See you tomorrow."

"Tomorrow," Anson echoed.

Shep headed out the back door, and Anson locked it behind him. I hit the start button on the dishwasher and closed it, peeking over the island to make sure Biscuit was still sleeping in his bed. Since the dinners had started, he'd come around the crew. They played fetch with him and gave him scratches now. It wouldn't be long before he was ready for adoption.

Anson's hands landed on my shoulders, kneading the muscles there. I let out a moan. "I'll give you forever to stop doing that."

He chuckled. "Gonna tell me what's going on in that beautiful brain of yours?"

I turned to face him, leaning into his body. "What do you mean?"

"You've been off. Going a million miles a minute, hardly sitting down for more than a handful of seconds, never calming."

I scowled at him. "You know, there are downsides to dating a profiler. You see too much."

Anson grinned and brushed his lips over my temple. "Not a profiler. Just a guy who works construction."

"Fine," I huffed. "There are downsides to dating a handyman with a genius brain."

He nipped my earlobe. "Talk to me, Rho."

I sighed. "I feel like I'm crawling out of my skin. I like being productive. Having a purpose. I'm just spinning my wheels with too much energy to burn. I've been half-tempted to ask Shep to give me a job."

Anson slid his hand up my spine, his fingers curling around the back of my neck and squeezing. "I think you'd look pretty damn hot rocking a tool belt."

I grinned up at him. "The one time I tried to help with something, I broke my thumb with a hammer."

Anson winced. "Maybe we keep you away from the tools, then."

"Unfortunately, that's probably a good idea."

His fingers slid into my hair. "I can think of a few other things that might burn away a little of that energy."

All the minuscule nerve endings in my body woke up at Anson's words. "Can you now?"

A sly smile spread across his face. "You wanna play, Reckless?"

My skin began humming with the promise of what was to come, already knowing the pleasure Anson could bring. "Yes."

He moved then, taking my hand and tugging me toward the bedroom. The moment we were inside, he shut the door behind us. It closed with a quiet snick, but the noise sounded more like a cannon in the silent room.

"You sure you want to *play*?" Anson asked, grit and need coating his voice.

I swallowed hard. "Yes."

"Strip." The single word was a command. The force behind it had a shiver skating over my skin, but there was nothing unpleasant about it.

I kicked off one flip-flop and then the other, stepping onto the lush carpet in my bedroom. My gaze dipped as I moved for the hem of my tank top, but Anson wasn't having that.

"Eyes on me," he ordered.

My focus shot to him. The blue in his eyes sparked and swirled, need blooming there. I didn't look away, and my fingers hooked in the cotton. Tugging it up and over my head, I lost sight of Anson for the briefest moment. And then he was there again, eyes blazing.

I reached behind my back, fingers unfastening the clasp of my bra.

"Slowly," Anson gritted out.

My pace eased, and I felt everything. The way my breathing quickened. The sensation of the lace skating across my skin. And maybe that was what Anson was after. For me to be in the here and now.

As my bra fell to the floor, Anson's hand lifted. His thumb grazed his bottom lip as he stared at me, the sun streaming in. "Could look at you for years and still see something new every time."

My pulse thrummed in my neck as he took one step toward me and then another.

"Like this little freckle." He bent, his lips grazing the mark resting just below my collarbone.

My breath hitched.

Anson straightened, everything in his body tight, restrained. "Climb on the bed."

I licked my lips. "I thought I was supposed to strip." I was still wearing my shorts.

"Such sass," Anson muttered. But then he moved. So fast I gasped. He grabbed hold of my shorts and underwear, yanking them down. He stared up at me as the movements slowed, lifting one leg out and then the other. "Now, you don't have to."

I certainly didn't.

Anson's gaze didn't waver. "Climb onto the bed."

My heart hammered as I took one step back and then another. When I hit the edge of the mattress, I turned, climbing on just as he'd instructed.

An audible breath sounded behind me. I glanced over my shoulder and locked eyes with Anson. He stroked himself over his jeans. "That ass. Gonna kill me."

Heat rose to my cheeks—not embarrassment, but pleasure.

"Lay on your back. Arms above your head," Anson gritted out.

A flicker of nervousness shot through me, but I obeyed. Nestling into the pillows, I lifted my arms.

"Grab the headboard." Anson's voice was more growl than anything else, the sound sending a fresh wave of shivers coursing through me. My fingers curled around the wrought iron bars.

Anson took a step forward, unbuckling his belt. He tore the leather from the loops on his jeans in one fluid movement, and my jaw went slack. He kicked off one boot and then the other, then climbed onto the bed.

There was something about being completely naked while Anson hovered over me, still fully clothed. It heightened everything in my body. The feel of the breeze through the open window. The way the soft cotton of his shirt brushed my nipples.

Anson reached above me, weaving his belt through the bars and around my wrists. My pulse kicked into overdrive as he fastened the leather and gave it a testing tug. His face was close to mine but not touching in any way. "Too tight?"

I gave my head a tiny shake. "No."

"Good."

Then he was off me and the bed. He moved to my nightstand, opening the top drawer and pawing through the contents.

"Hey," I protested. "What're you doing?"

Anson shot me a wicked grin. "That first day in the hallway, the time you left me with the worst case of blue balls known to man?" I just gaped at him in response. "You threatened me with a toy. And I think it's time for a little retribution."

"You're not," I said through gritted teeth.

He opened the second drawer, and his eyes lit up. "Bingo."

Anson pulled out a black velvet drawstring bag. Opening it, he retrieved a compact, gold bullet vibrator.

My face flamed. "Anson," I growled.

He rolled it between his fingers, testing the weight and then turning it on and testing the speeds. "Perfect."

He moved to the end of the bed. "Spread your legs. Time for me to give you a little of the torture you've given me."

Oh, hell.

Heat and wetness pooled in my core. But I wanted to obey. Wanted to be at this man's mercy.

Slowly, I parted my legs.

"Such a beautiful sight," Anson murmured, his gaze fixed on the apex of my thighs.

He lifted one knee onto the bed and then the other, settling between my legs.

"Already glistening for me."

My hips rocked against the mattress, needing some sort of contact, anything.

"My greedy girl," Anson cooed.

He trailed a single finger up my thigh to my center. That finger circled my opening, teasing, toying. I whimpered, trying to shift my hips to get more of him.

Anson's other hand whipped out, sending a stinging slap across my thigh. "Still."

The sting of one hand crashed against the pleasure of the other in a delicious stew of sensation. All I wanted to do was move. Get more. But I stilled. My hands tightened on the headboard's metal bars.

"Good girl," Anson murmured and slid two fingers inside me.

I let out another whimper, my legs and hips dying to move.

"Let's see how still you can stay." Anson's fingers slid in and out of me, over and over. It was a torturously slow pace, completely unhurried.

My mouth opened and closed, trying to back my demands for more.

"So perfect," he crooned, and then his fingers curled in a come-hither motion.

I moaned. It was loud and desperate, but I didn't even care. Anson hadn't said a damn thing about being quiet.

"I love the noises you make. The whimpers and moans. The way you suck me in, desperate for more."

I bit the inside of my cheek so hard that the metallic taste of blood filled my mouth.

"How about now?" Anson twisted the vibrator until a buzz filled the air. "Think you can stay still now?"

The cool metal of the bullet almost made me jump as he touched it to my skin. Then the vibration lit through my muscles.

"Anson..."

"So beautiful when you beg," he growled, circling my clit with the bullet as his fingers thrust in and out of me.

"I can't," I whimpered. "I have to move."

"You can. Hold it, Reckless."

I gripped the metal bars harder, the belt biting into my wrists. The tiny flicker of pain helped, but it also drove me higher.

Anson slid a third finger inside me as he circled the vibrator closer to that bundle of nerves. "Such a good girl."

Tears filled my eyes. Ones of a desperate need to let go—of all these sensations, but also everything I'd been holding in. The stress, the fear, the anger.

"Anson," I pleaded.

"Almost. You're almost there. A little more."

My thighs shook from the effort it took to keep from moving them. My wrists ached from pulling against my bonds. Everything inside me trembled as black dots danced across my vision. Peaks and valleys swept through me as I tried to hold back the full force of them.

"Now," Anson commanded.

My hips arched into him as he pressed the bullet to my clit, his fingers driving in and pressing down on my G-spot. Everything hit me all at once: the hint of pain and the tsunami of pleasure.

I cried out as I shattered. Wave after wave engulfed me. Anson coaxed and corralled each crest and break, playing my body like a master musician. Just when I thought he was done, he'd wring another out of me, over and over until I collapsed onto the mattress, unable to move.

Anson shifted, shutting off the vibrator and moving to lay next to me, his fingers tracing a million different designs on my bare skin. "What's in that beautiful brain now?"

"Nothing," I muttered, barely coherent. "Absolutely nothing." And it was glorious.

"Good." Anson unfastened the belt, rubbing each wrist as he freed it. "Never seen a more beautiful sight than watching you shatter."

I curled into him and the beautiful, heady haze he'd given me. Three little words played on my tongue, but I held them back. "Thank you," I whispered.

"I'll always give you what you need, Reckless."

And Anson had. Because now I was floating in that afterglow bliss where everything was just a bit fuzzy in the very best way.

But then his phone rang and ruined everything.

Chapter Thirty-Eight

Anson

I MUTTERED A CURSE AS I SHIFTED TO PULL MY PHONE FROM MY
back pocket. The name on the screen had my blood turning to ice,
but not answering wasn't an option. Because the what-if would be
even worse.

Hitting an icon on the screen, I pressed the cell to my ear. "Hunt."

"We've got two more," Helena said, not wasting any time.

The wave of nausea hit me hard and fast.

"And he's getting closer to you."

That had me sitting up, then standing, needing to move.
"Where?"

"First vic was in Montana. A waitress at a roadside diner. Next
two were in Idaho, only an hour's drive apart."

The ice was back, the kind of cold that was so frigid it hurt.
"He's escalating."

"Something's pissing him off," Helena agreed. "I gotta ask,
Anson…has anything in your life changed?"

I stilled as Rho came into view. She'd gotten dressed in sweats and a tee, lines of concern etched into her beautiful face. Fear slammed into me. No, it was more than fear. It was terror. "I'm seeing someone."

Helena cursed. "He's still got eyes on you."

Those eyes were just virtual. We'd been able to piece together that he watched our victims' families and loved ones after killing the women. His notes to them made that much obvious. And we knew he must have hacked into my computer to get information about Greta. But he'd never left any traces that our tech team could find. He was too good.

But I was more careful now. The security on my laptop was top-notch. I locked down my digital footprint. But there were crumbs. Texts between Rho and me. A few photos of her on my phone.

Had he gotten access to those?

"Anson," Helena clipped.

"I know," I said. God, I sounded defeated. Because no matter what I did, this monster found ways to steal the best things in my life. But I wasn't about to let him steal Rho.

I heard Helena moving through what I guessed was a police station. The din and occasional snippets of conversations were familiar. Finally, the noise lessened as a door closed. "My guess is that he's making his way to you."

"Know that, too." The urge to bolt was strong. But I knew there was nowhere I could go that he wouldn't find me. Nowhere he wouldn't rip my world apart, piece by piece.

"We want to take you into protective custody. You can assist with the case if you want, or you can pretend none of this is happening."

"No." My answer was instant. The only thing protective custody would do was delay the inevitable.

"Don't be an idiot, Anson. He's never killed two people this close together before. He's unraveling, and you know what that means."

It meant that his patterns could change. His M.O., too. He could come for me as easily as he did his typical female victims. "I'm tired of running, Helena."

"I know. We're gonna get him. I feel it in my bones. But I'd still like you to be breathing when we do."

I went quiet.

She sighed. "Promise me you'll at least think about it."

"Okay," I agreed, knowing it was the best way to get her off my back right now.

"Do you want updates?"

I mulled that over for a moment. "Yeah." I was in it now whether I wanted to be or not.

"Okay. Be safe."

"You, too," I answered.

She hung up without a goodbye. Maybe that's where I'd gotten the trait. Goodbyes were too final for people like us.

I lowered the phone, gripping it tightly. Rho stared at me, so much worry in those beautiful eyes. "Who was it?"

"One of my old team members. The Hangman killed two more women." There was no point in holding back. Rho deserved to know what she was mixed up in, what I'd put her in the path of. Because it wasn't enough that she already had one twisted person after her. I'd added the potential of a second.

She reached for my hand, weaving her fingers through mine. "You're not alone."

"I should be."

Rho's fingers spasmed around mine. "Don't."

"It's the truth. I knew this bastard had ways of getting information on me, ways of finding out who was important. But I still let myself get mixed up with you."

She gripped my hand tighter. "Anson."

I swallowed hard as my back molars ground together. "No one's more important to me than you, Rho. You're everything. And he probably knows that. Which means there's no one he'd rather hurt than *you*."

Every word burned on the way out of my throat, scarring the flesh as they entered the air.

Rho yanked my arm so hard the force had me stumbling forward. "You are not bailing on me."

"Rho," I croaked.

"You try and bolt, and I'll hunt your ass down."

My lips tried to twitch, but they couldn't quite get there. "I worked for the FBI. I think I could evade you."

Rho arched a brow. "You don't know my skills. I found out my college roommate's boyfriend was cheating on her five states away with nothing more than a first name and the color of his car."

This time, my mouth succeeded at curving.

"So, I'd find you. And then I'd kick your ass for trying that BS. So, don't. Or if you do, take me with you. I'll run wherever you want. We'll make *here* wherever you need it to be."

My throat burned; so much emotion was building there. Maybe I should say yes to protective custody, take Rho with me, and stay until Helena got The Hangman, and Trace caught whoever had Rho in their sights.

I pulled Rho into my arms, dropping my forehead to hers. "You're with me. If I leave, if I stay, wherever the hell the path leads, you're with me."

Rho's hands fisted in my tee. "Always. Whatever comes our way."

But I knew how dark and twisted *whatever* could be. And you never knew when it might strike.

Chapter Thirty-Nine

Rhodes

I STRETCHED, MY ARMS REACHING TOWARD THE SUN AND loosening the muscles that wove around my spine. The new flower bed was officially turned over for planting. Because that was what you did when you ran out of space but were desperate for a project.

A horn gave two short honks, and I turned to see the familiar truck with *Bloom & Berry* on the side. Duncan navigated over the pothole-riddled gravel drive until he reached the side of the guest cottage. Biscuit lifted his head from his spot on the deck where I'd placed his bed in the sun, but he didn't growl. Progress.

Duncan slid out of the truck as I made my way toward him. The moment I was within arm's reach, he pulled me into a hug. "I've missed you."

I hugged him back hard. "Me, too. I'm hoping I can come back soon."

Duncan released me, his gaze sweeping over me in assessment. "Looks like that gash is healing."

It was just an angry red line instead of a scabby wound now. But I was sure I'd have a scar. Just one more to add to the bunch.

"It's totally fine."

"Good." He shifted his weight from foot to foot. "Trace have any leads?"

I sighed. "Not yet. They found the stolen SUV that ran me off the road, but it was wiped clean of prints."

Duncan's jaw tightened. "You'd think they'd have found *something* by now."

"Maybe it's over, and whoever it was moved on." But as soon as the words left my lips, I knew they were a naïve dream. Whoever had been toying with me was likely just biding their time. Because these days, nobody left me alone for even a moment.

Between what had happened to me and The Hangman, no one in my life was taking any chances. Anson stayed every night, with Trace ordering drive-bys every couple of hours. During the day, the crew was here, but I also had frequent visitors. Nora came by to help clean an already spotless house. Lolli brought over a kit so I could make my very own diamond art dick flower. I'd gotten countless texts from Cope, checking in between games and practices. Fallon brought buckets of ice cream, and Arden even made a few stops to check in.

The only one who hadn't been by was Kye. But I understood. He didn't handle people he cared about being at risk well.

Duncan toed a piece of gravel with his boot. "Maybe they have." He looked around my outdoor space. "You've certainly put your time off to good use."

I grinned, following his line of sight. The entire garden was brimming with color. My mom would've absolutely loved it. To her, a garden should always be rainbow chaos. "It's been fun to have some time to really bring it to life."

"I've got everything else you asked for and a few hours to help you get it plugged in."

I glanced at Duncan in surprise. "You never take off in the middle of a workday." In fact, I would've thought he'd send someone else to make the delivery.

Duncan bumped my shoulder with his. "Told you. I missed you."

Warmth spread through me at that. I had an incredible community around me. And that was more than enough to be grateful for.

"Let's get started," I said with a grin.

We set to work unloading the truck and then positioning the plants where I wanted them. It took a few rearranging attempts and talking things through, but we finally got things laid out in a way we were both happy with. I'd forgotten what great instincts Duncan had when it came to garden planning.

Before long, we had everything plugged in and were carefully watering the new additions. They were beautiful and melded into the gorgeous views beyond of the mountains and rock faces.

Duncan shut off his hose. "Do you mind if I take some photos for the website? It'd be great to have people see some end results."

"Of course, not." It was a great idea for a selling tool.

I kept watering the new plant babies until I heard a click and looked up.

Duncan grinned. "Action shot."

I stuck my tongue out at him. "Living my best model life."

He chuckled. "We could make you the Bloom mascot."

I snorted at that. "I think I'm good with my usual dirt-covered existence."

The sound of tires on gravel had me looking up to see a familiar BMW sedan making its way toward us. A trickle of unease slid through me. I hadn't seen any sign of Davis for almost a month now, but I should've known I couldn't escape him entirely.

Duncan frowned. "What's the douche doing here?"

"Your guess is as good as mine." But I braced. Trace said he'd been keeping a close eye on him. So far, nothing linked him to the things that had happened to me.

Davis climbed out of his sedan in his now-typical preppy look, and I couldn't really picture him getting his hands dirty to set a fire. He frowned as he walked toward us, taking in my current state. "You're covered in dirt."

"Good to see you, too," I muttered, turning off the hose.

"I'm sure you could hire someone to do this for you."

I sighed. This was why he and I never would have worked. "I don't want to hire someone else. I like doing this. Actually, I *love* it."

Davis's frown only deepened, but he shot a look in Duncan's direction. "Would you please give us a moment?"

Duncan looked at me in question.

I nodded. "It's okay."

Davis bristled at that but controlled the slight flare of temper as Duncan walked toward his truck. "Rhodes."

It was my turn to bristle. "Rho. Everyone calls me Rho. It's what I prefer."

He opened his mouth to argue and then snapped it closed. "Rho." I tried to ease my posture at his acquiescence but couldn't quite get there. "I wanted to apologize."

My eyes flared. I wasn't sure Davis had *ever* apologized to me for anything. Even for being a dick of epic proportions.

"I was upset after Trace paid me that visit. My reputation is very important to me. But I shouldn't have taken it out on you. I'm sorry."

I knew how much it likely took for Davis to actually admit to overreacting. "Thank you. I appreciate it. Water under the bridge."

It eased something in me to have us on better terms. Because in a town this small, Davis and I would always run into each other.

He smiled then, a flash of white against his perfect complexion. "Good. I've been worried about you. I heard about the accident."

"I'm okay, really. My SUV is toast, but a replacement's being delivered tomorrow morning." Thankfully, the insurance was covering the lion's share of that.

Davis's mouth thinned as his gaze skated over my forehead. "That's going to scar."

I shrugged. "Not the end of the world."

"Why don't you come stay with me for a while? It'd be safer than you staying here all alone."

Well, crap.

It didn't surprise me that word hadn't gotten around about Anson and me because we weren't actually spending time together in public places—not with everything going on. I didn't want to give Davis false hope, but I didn't want to hurt him either.

"I actually haven't been staying alone. My boyfriend's been staying with me." Calling Anson my boyfriend felt ridiculous, but I wasn't sure what other term to use.

Davis stilled, a flush creeping up his neck. "*Boyfriend?*"

I swallowed hard. "Yeah. We've been seeing each other for a few weeks now."

"Who?" Davis demanded.

I did my best not to wince, but a flicker of the movement slipped free. "Anson. You met him the last time you were here."

"The interfering prick?" Davis snapped.

"Don't," I shot back. "He's a good guy, and we aren't doing anything wrong. You and I haven't been seeing each other for over a month now."

Davis's chest rose and fell in quick, angry pants. "We were in a relationship, and you jump into bed with the first moron behemoth to crook his finger at you? I should've known you were nothing but a cheap slut."

I reeled back as if he'd struck me.

"What. Did. You. Just. Call. Her?" Anson growled.

Davis whirled on him, his face paling. "I called her what she clearly is."

Anson prowled toward him, his panther-like grace in full effect. "I warned you to stay clear of her. And now you show back up and insult her at her own home? I don't think you're learning, *Davy.*"

"M-my name is Davis."

"No. Davis is a man's name. But you aren't a man, are you?" Anson challenged.

Davis straightened his shoulders. "You don't know me."

Anson grinned, but it had a slightly terrifying bent. "But I do, Davy. I know you didn't leave your job in Silicon Valley because you were swimming in cash. You got fired."

My eyes widened. Davis had told me and everyone else who

would listen that his stock options had meant he could take a ridiculously early retirement.

"Fired because you were harassing a woman at your company," Anson pressed.

Davis's face had gone fire-engine red. "She was a liar. She was just mad that I rejected her."

Anson chuckled, low and menacingly. "Hardly. But you couldn't handle the rejection, so you came back here and played the part of rich tech king. Only you aren't rich, are you, Davy?"

Davis's teeth ground together, his fists clenching at his sides.

"You're *drowning* in debt. In fact, that BMW is two weeks away from repossession, and that house of yours is about to go into foreclosure. So, no wonder you were so determined to move in with Rho. It was her or back in with your parents."

I gaped at Davis, remembering how hard he'd pushed me to sell the house and move into a modern build together. It had been way too early, but he wouldn't stop bringing it up.

"I could sue you for slander," Davis snarled.

Anson shrugged. "It's only slander if it's a lie, Davy. And I have all the proof I need to back this up." His eyes narrowed on my ex. "And I can keep digging. I have resources you can only dream of. And you and I both know there's more dirt to uncover."

A muscle in Davis's cheek fluttered wildly, telling me that was true.

"So, leave," Anson ordered. "And don't come back. If you see Rho in town, you'll keep right on walking. She does not exist for you. Crawl back into your pathetic hole, and don't come out. Because if you do, I will rip apart your life, piece by piece."

Vitriol shot from Davis's eyes. "You two deserve each other."

Anson simply grinned at that. "Thanks, Davy. So nice of you to say."

Davis just glared before turning on his heel and stalking back to his car.

Duncan lifted both hands from where he leaned against his truck and started to clap.

I burst out laughing.

Anson stalked toward me, pulling me into his arms and kissing me deeply. His tongue stroked mine, demanding better access as if he were desperate to sear my taste into his memory.

When he finally pulled back, I struggled to catch my breath. I searched his stormy gaze. "You okay?"

"I hate that prick."

I brushed a strand of hair away from his forehead. "You didn't say anything about looking into him."

Anson's mouth thinned. "Because I'm looking into everyone in your orbit." I shivered at that, and he pulled me tighter against him. "I'm not taking any chances. You mean too much to me."

I wanted to mean something to Anson. Relished that. But I hated the price he had to pay for it. Because I knew going down this road meant he had to face every demon that lurked there. And the price might be too high for him to pay.

Chapter Forty

Anson

STOOD AT THE BACK DOORS, LOOKING AT THE BEAUTIFUL garden Rho had created and taking in the landscape beyond it. The sharp mountain peaks, the intricate rock faces. It was beyond stunning. But it was more. Somewhere along the line, it had started to feel like home.

Arms wrapped around my waist from behind as Rho pressed her cheek to my back. "Hi."

My mouth curved as I covered her hands with mine. "Hi."

We stood like that for a long time, neither of us needing to say a word. The comfort was in the easy silence.

Finally, I twisted in Rho's hold, wrapping my arms around her, as well, and dropping a kiss on her forehead. Then I really took her in. God, she was gorgeous. Her mahogany hair fell in waves over her shoulders, but she'd taken pieces on either side of her head and braided them into a delicate crown.

She wore a hint of makeup. Rosy cheeks. Something that made

the green in her eyes pop. And a gloss on her lips that had me wanting to nip the bottom one.

"You're beautiful."

Rho's expression softened, a tender smile pulling at her mouth. "It's rare for me to get cleaned up these days."

"Maybe we need to find a few more excuses to do that." Hell, I hadn't even taken Rho on a proper date.

She worried her bottom lip between her teeth, and I reached up to gently tug it free. "Don't." I toyed with a strand of her hair. "What's got you worried?"

"Is this going to be too much?" Rho asked softly. "I don't want to push. Too much. Too quickly."

I pulled her tighter against me. "It's not too much. I want to get to know your family better."

She winced. "We're a lot on a good day. Maybe you should do one or two at a time instead of all at once."

I chuckled. "You sound like I'm going to be fighting to the death, not attending a family dinner."

"You never know. Battles have occurred over mashed potatoes before."

I skated a thumb up and down her back. "I want to go. I may not be good at it, but I want to try."

Socializing was a rusty skill that I wasn't sure I'd ever be able to sharpen, but I didn't want Rho to feel like she had to compartmentalize her life either.

She stretched up onto her tiptoes, brushing her lips across mine. "I like you just the way you are. Broodiness and all."

I grinned against her mouth. "Even if I never wear color?"

"One day, you're going to rock the hell out of a pink shirt."

I grunted. *Not likely.*

My phone buzzed in my back pocket, and I tried not to stiffen. Releasing Rho, I tugged it free. Helena's name flashed across the screen, but I couldn't quite make myself hit *accept.*

There'd been no news from her for the past week, so we'd lived waiting for the other shoe to drop. Maybe it had.

"Answer," Rho whispered. "I'm right here." She slid her fingers into my front pocket as if to link us somehow.

I tapped the screen and pressed the phone to my ear. "Hunt."

"We've got another one," Helena said. "Just over the border into California."

I frowned. That didn't make any sense. Montana, then two in Idaho. Washington or Oregon should've been next. He should've been closing in on me. "You're sure?"

"It's him. Note's a match. Woman found at a campground just off I-5 southbound."

"So, he…what? Drove right past where I am and kept on going? That doesn't seem likely."

A door shut on Helena's end of the line. "I think there are two possibilities. One is that he feels us closing in. We know his usual hunting grounds—near freeways and highways. Always snatches young women alone. We have more manpower looking for him now. Maybe he got spooked. Moved along."

"The other?" I asked.

"He doesn't know where you are. Doesn't have access to your tech. Maybe there was another stressor in his life that got him killing again. You know these guys don't just stop."

That much was true. Unsubs with the psychological makeup of The Hangman couldn't turn it off. Killing was a compulsion. He might be able to shut it down for a while or change his M.O., but he'd never be able to stay away forever. Just like he couldn't stop playing the game.

"So, what's the plan?" I asked.

"Sit tight. We're running everything now, but the ME's best guess is that she was killed yesterday. He's likely still close by. Maybe we can get him."

I wasn't holding my breath, but I also wasn't about to shoot down Helena's hope. You needed it in that kind of work. "Thanks, Helena. Stay safe."

"You, too. If anything tweaks you, call."

"I will." I hit *end* and shoved my phone back into my pocket.

Rho looked up at me with expectant eyes. "So?"

"He killed someone in California."

"Poor woman," she whispered.

I pulled Rho into my arms again. "Helena thinks he may not know where I am. That another stressor got him killing again."

Her brow furrowed as she stared up at me. "What do *you* think?"

"It's possible. I think it would be really hard for someone like him to keep his distance if he knew where I was. The temptation would be too great."

Rho's muscles eased beneath my hands. "I'm glad. Maybe that makes me awful because he's obviously going to keep killing until someone stops him, but I don't want him to know where you are."

I brushed my lips across her temple. "That doesn't make you awful. It makes you human."

Rho burrowed into me. "I can call Nora and tell her we can't make it. She'll understand. I could use a quiet night in to finish my book anyway."

I arched a brow at her. "You mean read until the second to last chapter?" Rhodes had read countless books in the past few weeks, but I hadn't seen her *finish* a single one.

She stuck her tongue out at me. "It's my process."

I wrapped an arm around her, pulling her into me. "I know, but we can save the non-finishing for another night. Family dinner is exactly where we should go." Just saying the word *family* was a struggle. I hadn't been a part of one in years, and the idea of letting those sorts of relationships grab hold had a familiar weight settling in.

Rho looked up at me. "Should we have a code word in case you want to leave?"

My lips twitched. "Code word?"

"You know, like…fuzzy pink bunny. Or the eagle lands at noon."

I barked out a laugh. "How am I supposed to work that into casual conversation?"

"I don't know. You could get creative."

"How about I just squeeze your hand four times if I need out?"

Rho laid a hand over my heart. "I guess that works, too."

"Come on, let's go. I've been eating lukewarm Nora meals for a year and a half. I'm dying to have one hot out of the oven."

We took Biscuit out one more time before leaving him with a bone to gnaw on, then climbed into my truck and headed for Nora and Lolli's. I could feel Rho's nerves. It was also evident in the tap of her fingers against my thigh, and the slightly increased rate of her breathing.

I laid a hand over hers as we pulled up to the massive ranch house. "I'm going to be fine."

Rho looked over at me. "Are you sure?"

I nodded. "Know how I know?"

"How?"

I weaved my fingers through hers. "Because you're with me."

Rho's eyes glittered in the low light of the evening. "I worked very hard on this makeup, and if you make me cry right now, I'm going to be really mad at you."

I chuckled. "Never." I kissed her quickly as I released her hand. "Let's go."

Sliding out of the truck, I rounded the hood to open Rho's door.

"Such a gentleman."

"Sometimes," I said, taking her hand.

She sent me a mischievous smile. "Oh, trust me. I know how wicked you can be."

My dick twitched at the husky promise in her words. "If I have a hard-on walking into dinner with your family, I'm going to spank your ass."

Rho only smiled wider. "Promises, promises."

"Hell," I muttered.

She tugged me toward the farmhouse, a skip in her step that came from knowing she was torturing me. The little witch.

I tried to focus on the house itself. It was huge with white siding in immaculate condition. A porch wrapped around the entire building with countless rockers and two porch swings. It looked like the house out of that old show *The Waltons*. Picture-perfect with sprawling pastures surrounding it and a barn.

Just as we reached the top step, the door opened to reveal Lolli. She wore a billowy dress with an accompanying shawl made of so many colors I couldn't identify them all. Necklace after necklace looped around her neck, and I was pretty sure one of the chains had a pot leaf dangling from it.

Her blue eyes sparkled as she took in our joined hands. "Finally, someone is testing out the brooding god's goods!"

"*Mom!*" Nora shouted from inside.

"Oh, hush, child. Don't ruin my fun," Lolli called back. She turned to me. "I knew you wouldn't be able to resist my Rho for long. Now, I hear you were a Fed. Please tell me you aren't one of those anti-marijuana sticks-in-the-mud who thinks missionary position is the only way anyone should ever have sex."

"Lolli!" Her name was shouted by at least three people at once, including Rho.

Fallon appeared then, wrapping an arm around the older woman. "I'm so sorry, Anson. You'll have to excuse Lolli. She's going a little senile." Fallon gave her a stern look as if to punctuate the point.

Lolli just made a *pfft* noise and waved her off. "I'm not going to let my granddaughter be stuck in missionary position for the rest of her life."

"Do *not* talk about Rho and sex in the same sentence. *Please,*" Trace said with a shiver. "It's just wrong."

Lolli rolled her eyes as we followed her and Fallon into the house. "How did I get stuck with such a prudish family? Sex is a natural thing."

Kye shot her a grin from his spot on an overstuffed chair. "Not all prudes, Lolls, don't you worry."

"At least I raised one of you right," she harrumphed.

Rho burrowed into my arm, trying to stifle her laughter. "If she only knew what you can do with a bullet vibrator and a determined tongue."

Fire swept through me. "I'm going to make you pay for putting that image in my head right now."

Her laughter came free and easy. "Well, welcome to Colson chaos. I always knew it would be a hell of an introduction."

One of the doors at the back of the massive living space swung open, and Keely raced inside, Arden following behind her. "We rode for a full hour! We even galloped!" she cried.

Trace sent Arden a warning look. "You said no galloping."

Arden winced. "It was more like a fast canter."

The little girl ran right past her dad and skidded to a halt in front of Rho and me. Her eyes went wide as she took me in. "You're not Supergran's boyfriend, but are you Auntie Rho's?"

Shep choked on a laugh. "Not sure you call someone a boyfriend when they're thirty-five, Warrior Princess."

Her brows pulled together as she frowned up at me. "Man friend? Grown-up friend?"

Kye started coughing from his spot in the corner. "That's what I'm going to start calling it now."

"How about you just call me Anson?" I asked the little girl.

"I gots to call you Mr. Anson because my dad says that's having manners. But you can call me Keely," she said easily.

Rho leaned into me, patting my chest. "I don't know, I'm kind of partial to grown-up friend."

I sent her a scowl and mouthed the word *spanking*.

The ringing of a phone cut through the air, and Trace stood, pulling his cell out of his pocket. He frowned down at the screen. "Sorry. Give me a second."

He disappeared down the hall, but my sixth sense was already tingling.

"Anson," Nora said, crossing to me. "I'm so happy you could make it." She didn't waste a moment, simply pulled me into a hug.

I patted her back awkwardly, not used to the easy affection. "Thanks for having me."

She smiled warmly as she released me. "You're welcome any Sunday and whatever other days we manage to get together."

"Thank you. I appreciate that."

"We'll just ignore the fact that you rejected *my* offers for the past year and a half," Shep goaded.

Rho stuck her tongue out at him. "Don't be jealous that I have the touch."

Shep shook his head. "Don't think Anson is interested in *my* touch."

"Jesus," I muttered. This family was sex obsessed.

"What does that mean?" Keely asked, full of innocence.

Nora gave Shep a glare. "Nothing, baby. Want to come help me finish dinner in the kitchen?"

She nodded easily, following her grandmother out of the fray.

Just as they disappeared, Trace strode back into the living room. I recognized his expression instantly. The hard set of his jaw, the tight grip on his phone. Whoever had been on the other end of the call, and whatever they'd said, it wasn't good.

Rho saw it, too. "What happened?"

Trace strode toward us, his face warring between pissed off and gentle. "That was the station. We got a call about a dead body."

Rho sucked in a sharp breath. "Who?"

"I'm sorry, Rho. It was Davis."

Chapter Forty-One

Rhodes

ANSON WRAPPED A BLANKET AROUND MY SHOULDERS, GENTLY tucking one end beneath the other, making sure I was as warm as possible. But I still shivered. It was the kind of cold that seeped into your bones and was nearly impossible to get out.

Davis. Dead.

The two words were so incongruent. They didn't fit. I'd seen him two days ago, being a total and complete douchebag. Even with the stunt he'd pulled, I never wanted anything like this.

Anson lowered himself to the spot next to me on the couch and pulled me to him. He didn't say everything would be okay or give me any other platitudes that felt incredibly false. He just held me.

We didn't have a lot of information. Davis's body had been found next to the dumpster behind the bar. The Sagebrush wasn't a place he typically frequented, but he could've been nursing his wounds after Anson's verbal assault.

"What the hell is happening?" I whispered as I stared out the windows into the darkness outside. "This is supposed to be a quiet town. Safe. Now the fire, getting run off the road, *murder*."

Anson gripped me tighter, practically pulling me on top of him. "When I was digging into Davis, I found some things."

I stiffened. I hadn't missed how Anson had pulled Trace aside before we left Nora's. How he'd spoken in hushed tones. I had to assume it was about this.

"He's got ties to a loan shark who works out of Portland. If Davis wasn't paying that guy back, there's always a chance this was done to set an example."

My stomach twisted. So, chances were Davis had gotten himself killed. And for what? Image? Prestige? "What a waste," I muttered.

Anson's lips ghosted over my temple. "I'm sorry you're hurting."

"He wasn't always like the person you met. He used to be funny, a little cocky, but kind deep down. I don't know what happened to him."

"It could've been a million different things. That's the thing about life. Events and circumstances have the power to mark you. Change you."

I burrowed deeper into Anson's hold. "I don't ever want to let those difficult things change me into a hard person."

He brushed the hair out of my face. "You won't."

I looked up into those blue-gray eyes. "You sound so sure."

Anson stared down at me. There was so much tenderness in his expression. "I am. You've faced more hardship than almost anyone I've known. But you've never let it *harden* you. That's a miracle, Rho. You let those things make you better instead of worse. There's no way you won't live the rest of your life that way."

My heart pounded against my ribs. Those three little words swirled around my mind and teased my tongue, but I swallowed them back. "Thanks for believing in me."

"There's no one on this planet I have more faith in."

It wasn't an *I love you*, but I would take it. I moved in to brush my lips across Anson's when Biscuit let out a low growl.

I straightened, twisting to find the pup. He'd crossed to the windows and was baring his teeth at something through the glass.

Anson instantly pushed up from the couch, moving to a bag he'd brought in from his truck—the same duffel he'd taken to carting back and forth with him as he came and went.

"Biscuit," I called. But the dog didn't respond; simply kept growling at the glass.

Anson pulled a metal box out of his bag, quickly pressing in some sort of code. The lid popped open, and he retrieved a metal object.

I gaped at him. "Is that a gun?"

He glanced at me quickly as he wrapped his fingers around the grip and moved to the windows. "Yes." He pulled one curtain and then the other as Biscuit kept growling.

"You brought a gun into my house?"

"Rho, I always have a gun within reach. It's a safety measure. I'm trained. I don't put them anywhere a child or someone untrained has access."

My stomach roiled. Anson always had a gun within reach because he never truly felt safe. The thought was enough to make me sick.

He moved quickly around the room, shutting every blind and curtain. "Hand me your phone."

I stood, handing it over. "It was probably an animal."

"You're probably right, but let's be safe." He took the device from me and punched in my code.

My jaw went slack. "How did you know my code?"

His lips twitched the barest amount. "I was a profiler, remember?"

Damn him.

I waited as he opened the security camera app, twisting my fingers in my sweatshirt as nerves took hold. Too much had happened lately for me to be anything more than jumpy.

Anson cursed.

I couldn't help but jolt as he shoved the phone back at me. "Call

Trace. Tell him someone's lurking around your place. Tell him I'm in pursuit and armed."

I fumbled the phone and then reached out, grabbing Anson's shirt. "You can't go out there."

His face was a mask of barely restrained fury. "We're ending this. Now. If we wait for the cops to come, he'll probably be long gone. Stay here, keep the windows covered."

"Anson…"

He tugged me toward him, kissing me fast and hard. "I'll be back."

My stomach dropped as he stalked silently toward the front door. He locked it behind him, leaving me alone except for Biscuit. I quickly tapped my phone screen, hitting Trace's contact. He answered on the second ring.

"You all right?"

I could hear voices in the background and wondered if he was still at the crime scene. "Anson saw someone on the cameras outside my house. He went after them. He said to call you and tell you he was in pursuit and has a gun."

Trace cursed. "Idiot. Should've waited for backup."

"He's out there, Trace," I croaked.

"I'm on my way. I'll inform dispatch," Trace said. "Rho, stay where you are."

"I will. I—"

A crack pierced the air. Like a clap of thunder but fainter. A gun. A bullet.

I was already running, promises be damned.

Chapter Forty-Two

Anson

I RACED THROUGH THE FIELD BEHIND RHO'S HOUSE, THE FIGURE in front of me nothing but a dark outline in his hoodie and jeans. "Stop!" I barked.

The figure didn't listen; he kept right on running. It was a damn good thing I'd been running out my demons on the trails near my cabin; otherwise, this guy would've easily left me in the dust.

That in and of itself gave me information. Young. Able-bodied. Likely an athlete or at least someone who stayed in shape.

A list of suspects began building in my mind. I hadn't wanted to ask Rho about any of the people on my short list because I hadn't wanted to put doubts in her mind about people she knew. Not when the unsub could've just as easily been someone she'd never even talked to.

People could fixate without any true relationship. They would build something out of nothing in their mind. And it could so easily be twisted.

The figure in front of me caught his foot on a log and cursed.

More information. Definitely male. Not that my half-completed profile suggested anything else.

I gained on him, my muscles burning as I pushed harder.

Something flew in my direction as I ran. I ducked just in time as a rock whizzed past me, grazing my cheek. I couldn't help the curse I spat.

How the hell had he managed to get his hands on a rock? When he tripped?

At least that told me he likely didn't have a weapon. But he was also desperate, so who knew what he'd do?

My mind moved through countless psychological equations. A million different possible outcomes based on the circumstances. There was no way I could know for sure how he'd react to any given stimuli. I just had to take my best guess.

We were fifty yards from the tree line, give or take. It was now or never because he'd soon have coverage.

I stopped dead in my tracks and lifted my weapon. I aimed at the tree ahead of the figure and squeezed the trigger. The release of the bullet sent a crack through the air.

The recoil was familiar, the bite into my muscles.

The man spat a slew of curses but didn't stop. He only ran faster. *Hell.*

I'd hoped it would spook him enough that he'd turn himself in. But my wager had been wrong.

I started after him again, refusing to lose sight of the figure. He didn't get to terrorize Rho. Hurt her. That familiar surge of fury gave me a dose of adrenaline, helping me gain on the man.

"Cops are en route. There's no way out of this," I yelled.

He only kept running, reaching the trees and disappearing into the thickest foliage.

"Damn it," I muttered, slowing.

I stopped for a brief second to listen.

The snap of twigs to my right told me where he was. I followed the sounds as quietly as possible. The task was nearly impossible, with the moon providing the only light. I picked my way through brush and trees, but then the noises stopped altogether.

I slowed, trying to see into the dark.

A fist crashed into the side of my face out of nowhere. The force of it had me stumbling back a step and seeing stars, but instinct had me blocking the next blow and returning the strike.

The man grunted as my left fist connected with his jaw. It was his turn to fall back. I couldn't make out a face, just shadows beneath the hood of a black sweatshirt.

I raised my gun. "Don't fucking move."

But the man wasn't in his right mind. "You're not going to hurt her!"

He charged.

I fired.

The shot clipped the man's shoulder just before he collided with me. He screamed out in pain but kept right on going.

We hit the ground with enough force to knock the wind out of me.

He pressed his forearm into my neck, cutting off my air supply. So, I did the only thing I could. I punched him right in the bullet wound.

He cried out in agony.

It distracted him enough that I was able to clock him with the butt of my gun. The man went down like a ton of bricks.

I shoved him off me, struggling to my feet just as someone crashed through the trees. I whirled, aiming my weapon.

Rho skidded to a stop in front of me, her eyes going wide. She stood there in tie-dyed sweats, her hair wild, and her feet fucking bare. Tears glimmered in her eyes. "You're okay?"

"Where are your shoes?" I barked.

She didn't say a word; simply threw herself at me. "You're okay."

Her arms ran up and down me as if checking for wounds. "You're okay," she said again.

"I'm good, Reckless."

She shuddered against me, her head bobbing up and down in a staccato nod. She let out another breath. "Where is—? Oh, God."

Rho jolted as she took in the figure out cold on the ground.

I pulled back, trying to take in her face. "You know him?"

Her eyes cut to me, and I saw so much hurt there. "Felix. The first boy I ever kissed."

Chapter Forty-Three

Rhodes

I COULDN'T SEEM TO MAKE MYSELF LET GO OF ANSON. I CLUNG to him like a barnacle, affixing and never letting go. Not when Trace interviewed us or the EMTs gave Anson a once-over. He'd likely have a shiner where Felix clocked him one, but the cut from the rock thankfully hadn't needed stitches.

Anson's hand trailed up and down my back, but the entirety of his arm kept me close as we sat on my porch steps. It was as if he needed the nearness as much as I did.

"How's your head?" I asked. I was sure the continual flashing lights from the various emergency services vehicles weren't helping.

"I'm good." He skated his free hand over my legs, which he'd positioned on his lap. "How are your feet?"

The moment the EMTs arrived, Anson demanded they look at my feet, despite the fact that he was the one with the head injury.

"They're fine," I said. He'd tried to get me inside once before, but I wasn't going without him. The truth was, my feet ached and stung. I'd scraped them up and gashed one on an especially sharp rock. But they'd heal. Probably in less time than it took for my heart to mend.

Felix.

The man I'd always thought of as a sweet boy. As if I'd frozen him back in the time of that first kiss. But that picture wasn't the truth. Maybe it never had been.

Trace stalked across my gravel drive. He wasn't trying to hold tight to his mask tonight. He was letting the whole world know how pissed off he was. He crossed to us and crouched so he was at eye level with me. "How are you feeling?"

"I'm fine. What do you know?"

Trace's jaw worked back and forth, taking a moment to speak. It was then that I realized he *was* holding back. The anger making itself known on his face was the fury that had slipped past the walls he typically guarded so well.

"Felix regained consciousness in the ambulance, but he's not saying a word other than *lawyer.*"

Anson grunted, making his opinion on that perfectly clear.

Trace pushed on. "We found his truck a ways down on the main road." Trace's jaw moved side to side again as if he were struggling to voice his next words.

"You found something," Anson said, sitting up. It wasn't a question. He was certain.

Trace jerked his head in a quick nod. "Storage box in the bed was a treasure trove. Gas and rags I'm guessing will be a match to the fire here."

I grabbed Anson's arm, needing to ground myself in the here and now.

"Newspaper articles covering the recent fire and the fires from fourteen years ago, including the one here. And photos. So many goddamn photos." Trace's voice took on a smoker's rasp as he spoke, knowing how much his words had to hurt.

"You think he started them all?" I croaked.

"It's still early," Trace said. "But one thing's clear. He's fixated on you. There are photos of you from afar. At work. In town. At home. It looks like they were taken with a telephoto lens."

My stomach roiled, and I suddenly felt dirty, like I needed to take a shower.

Anson's arm tightened around me. "You said he was your first kiss."

Bile swirled in my stomach, but I nodded. "The night of the fire."

He tensed and shared a look with Trace. "Escalated things. He didn't want anyone around who might come between him and Rho."

That muscle in Trace's jaw fluttered again. "But he just as easily could've killed Rho."

I felt Anson's struggle to keep his hold on me gentle—the re-adjusted grip, the deep inhales and exhales.

"He probably thought she'd have plenty of time to get out. Her room was on the opposite end of that hallway. A thirteen-year-old kid isn't going to be a fire wiz, no matter how much he's been play-ing with it. And an old house will catch quicker than a new build."

Trace nodded and then scrubbed a hand over his face. "I didn't see it. Not for a single second."

"Neither did I," I whispered, unshed tears burning the backs of my eyes. "Why start it all up again?"

Anson went rigid. "Because of me. You haven't ever been se-rious about anyone, but I'm sure word's gotten around that we're together. If he's been watching or talking to people on the crew, he knows I've been staying here."

Bile surged again. "It's not your fault."

"No, it's not. But I'm still fucking sorry," he gritted out.

I twisted, pressing my face into Anson's neck. "Don't let him get inside your head."

Anson stroked the side of my face. "You're right." Letting out a long breath, he turned to Trace. "Get this fucker."

Trace jerked his head in a nod. "I'll lock him down. You take care of my sister."

Asking Anson to step in was like a nod of approval from Trace. And Anson didn't miss it.

"I'd do anything for her."

Trace pushed to standing. "Good. Call if you need anything. I'm going to put a rush on the evidence we found."

And then he was gone.

But my world was left spinning.

Anson didn't wait. He lifted me into his arms and carried me inside. Biscuit rushed to meet us, letting free a little whine, but I was too dazed to even let it register.

Did this mean someone had killed my family? It wasn't an accident. It was pure hatred. And for what? Some sort of twisted obsession?

The tears came then—one sob and then another, ragged and brutal as they tore from my body.

"I got you," Anson whispered.

He lowered me to my bed as more sobs racked my body. He curved around me, cocooning me in his warmth. "Let it out. I'm right here."

So, I did. I released all the pain, anger, and grief, knowing Anson would be there to catch me.

～♋

The sun streamed down from high in the sky as I stood on my back deck, the rays catching the shimmery threads on my cowboy boots. I'd needed the bright spot, even if it was just in my footwear. Everything felt so eerily quiet compared to the chaos of last night. No lights. No sirens. No deputies traipsing all over my yard.

I frowned at a flower bed that had gotten the worst of the officers' carelessness. I'd have to run out to Bloom to get some replacement plants. I wouldn't be working. Duncan had told me, in no uncertain terms, that if I showed up at the shop, he'd fire me.

Instead, I was standing outside, twiddling my thumbs and

about ready to crawl out of my skin. I glanced down at my phone. Eleven-thirty.

I still needed to kill fifteen minutes before Fallon showed. She'd wanted to eat here, but I needed to get out of the house. Away from the ghost town.

I missed the noise of the crew, but they'd been told to halt work until further notice just in case the main house needed to be reexamined. So, they'd switched to a different jobsite. Anson had gone in hours late and practically kicking and screaming. And only after a deputy was stationed in his vehicle outside my house. He wasn't taking any chances with The Hangman still at large.

At least, this was some time away from Anson's watchful gaze. Time to try to process the fact that Felix had been the one to tear my life apart all those years ago. Who'd been determined to do it again.

My stomach dipped and rolled. The boy I'd kissed. The one I'd thought would change my life.

In the most twisted way, he had.

My eyes burned, pressure building behind them. I shoved the tears back. I couldn't cry. Not again. I'd sobbed until I passed out last night, and I didn't welcome the idea of going down that road again.

I took a slow, steadying breath as I walked farther into my garden. I let the scents of lilac and lupine fill my nose, calming me. I focused on the wind in the trees.

My phone buzzed, and I tugged it from my back pocket.

Fallon: *Be there in five.*

A little of the tension in my chest eased. If anyone could distract me from this nightmare, it was Fallon. I jogged up the back porch steps, locking the door behind me. I gave Biscuit some scratches and a bone to chew on, then grabbed my bag and headed for the front door. Stepping outside, I locked the door and headed toward the squad car standing sentry.

As I got closer, light and shadow played over the open window.

My steps faltered as my brain tried to compute the sight in front of me. A body was slumped against the wheel. And there was blood. So much blood. I turned to run, but it was too late.

"Hello, Rho."

The voice was familiar but deeper somehow, darker.

I turned to find the source of the tenor, to fight, but I didn't get a glimpse of more than a corner of a T-shirt before pain bloomed in my temple, bright and sharp. The world tunneled as I fell, but I could only think of one thing.

Anson.

Chapter Forty-Four

Anson

CURSED AS MY HAMMER MISSED THE NAIL, NARROWLY AVOIDING my thumb.

Shep straightened from his spot on the opposite side of the new deck we were putting in. "I'd tell you that you should be using the nail gun, but if you were, you probably would've put a nail through your hand by now."

I scowled at him as I stood, tossing my hammer onto the deck and cracking my neck. I'd been a mess all morning. And Shep was right, it was a miracle I hadn't seriously injured myself.

"What's going on?" he asked, moving in my direction. "Was there a new update on The Hangman?"

I shook my head. All was quiet on that front. But quiet made me twitchy. Like I was waiting for the other shoe to drop. "No. They're still working the last crime scene and canvassing the area."

Shep studied me for a long moment. "Still worried about Rho."

It wasn't a question, but I answered him anyway. "It's hard for me to turn it off."

Just because they had the person who'd been harassing Rho in lockup didn't mean I could erase the protective urge. Too much had happened to both Rho *and* in my past. It was the sort of thing I worried she wouldn't be able to handle in the long run. So, I'd shoved it all down and gone to work today, even though it was the last thing I wanted to do.

Shep clapped me on the shoulder. "Come on." He started toward his truck, expecting me to follow.

"Where?"

"Fallon is picking Rho up for lunch. We'll crash their day date."

I frowned at him. "We're already behind with not having access to the Victorian. I thought you said we needed to get this deck done today."

Shep beeped the locks on his truck. "The rest of the team is working double-time on the Evans' project. That'll help us make up some time. And you and I can knock this one out this afternoon."

I opened the passenger door and climbed inside. "Thanks." Taking the time now meant us working faster this afternoon and maybe even staying late. But Shep knew I needed to lay eyes on Rho. Needed to touch her and assure myself she was okay.

He pressed the button to start the ignition. "You've been through one of the worst things imaginable. It's understandable that you might need a little extra reassurance when it comes to the safety of the people you care about."

I stared out the window as Shep navigated the gravel road that led back to Rho's. I wasn't good at the feelings stuff. As much as I'd studied emotion and psychological makeup, expressing it when it came to me wasn't easy.

"Makes me feel weak," I admitted.

Shep's gaze flicked to me. "Because you care?"

"Because I can't stop obsessing. Thinking about the million things that could go wrong."

He adjusted his hold on the steering wheel as he made a left turn onto the two-lane highway. "I'd say that's normal. You've been through trauma twice over. Give your mind and body time to recover. And the last thing Rho will think is that you're weak."

I knew he was right. Rho would talk me through it and see the silver lining in it, the strength. "I'm an idiot."

The corner of Shep's mouth kicked up. "You said it, not me."

I chuckled. "What about you? You've usually mentioned a woman you're seeing by now."

Shep was the king of casual dating. I tried not to analyze the fact that he always seemed to come up with a reason to politely end things around week three or four. It was better than stringing someone along if he didn't see a future, but I also worried he might be looking for something that didn't exist.

Shep shifted in his seat, not looking in my direction.

I was instantly on alert. "What?"

He scowled at the windshield. "Nothing."

"It's obviously *something*."

He finally let out a breath. "I asked someone out, but she said no."

I was silent for a moment, and then I burst out laughing. "Is that the first time you've been rejected?"

Shep turned his glare from the road to me. "No. Abbie James dumped me for Robbie Allen in third grade."

I only laughed harder, to the point where tears filled my eyes. "Who is she? I think I want to buy her a drink."

"You're an asshole," Shep grumbled.

"I am. But you already knew that." I glanced over at my extremely annoyed friend. "Seriously, who is she?"

He didn't answer right away but then finally gave in. "Thea. She works with Rho at the nursery. I get the sense she's been through some stuff. A little gun-shy. I asked her to coffee, and she shot me down with zero explanation."

I studied him for a long moment. "You sure this isn't just your white-knight complex coming into play?"

"I don't have a white-knight complex."

"You do. You have a compulsion when it comes to fixing people's problems. It's good in small doses, but you need to look at why you have the urge." If he didn't, he'd never actually find happiness in a relationship.

Shep glowered as he turned onto Rho's drive. "Stop shrinking me." Then, he sighed. "There's something about her. She sees things others miss. She's got this hard exterior, but when she thinks no one's watching, she's got a gentleness about her."

Oh, damn. This sounded like a little more than a crush.

"Then give it time," I encouraged. "If Thea's been through something hard, it'll take time for her to feel comfortable opening up to anyone."

"You're probably right," Shep said as he rounded the Victorian to the guesthouse.

Fallon's car was parked next to Rho's new one, but that wasn't what caught my attention. It was Fallon herself, bent over on the gravel, heaving.

Shep slowed. "What the—?"

I didn't wait. I threw open the door and ran toward Fallon. "What is it?"

Fallon choked as she heaved one more time but pointed at the cruiser. I ran toward it, skidding to a halt as bile surged up my throat. The man who'd greeted Rho with a quick joke this morning was slumped against the wheel, his throat slit.

I whirled, panic setting in. "Rho. Where's Rho?"

Tears streaked down Fallon's face. "I-I don't know."

Nausea swept through me, fast and fierce. My ears rang as I stalked toward the front door. I had a set of keys Rho had given me, but they were supposed to be used if I got home before her, not because a deputy was dead outside, and we had no idea where she was.

"Gloves," Shep yelled at me, his arm around Fallon and his face pale.

I didn't want to waste time on fucking gloves, but I turned back, ran to his truck, and grabbed a box out of the bed. If something had happened to Rho, if someone had her, we'd need all the evidence we could get. All the clues to find her.

I turned it off—everything inside me that made me human again. Everything Rho had brought back to life. I didn't have any other choice.

I tested the front door. Unlocked. *Fuck.* The moment it swung open, Biscuit ran at me, barking his head off. I grabbed his collar, quickly hooking a leash to it. "Easy, boy. Easy."

But I didn't feel the words. Nothing about me was easy, and Biscuit knew it. He went unnaturally quiet at my side.

Everything about the place was silent. Too still. There was no music or humming, no sounds of laughter or chatter. It didn't feel like Rho's place.

I found no sign of her in the bedroom or bathroom, but nothing was out of place either. I headed back down the hall. I stilled when Biscuit and I reached the living room and kitchen. Nothing was out of place, not exactly, but something was *off*. Something that had triggered my sixth sense.

I walked deeper into the living space, coming up short as I reached one of the bookcases. The entire world dropped away.

A note was held to the shelf by a photo of Rho and her family. Scrawled across the paper was blocky lettering, familiar in a way that had dread sinking deep.

YOU WERE SUPPOSED TO SUFFER. HOW QUICKLY YOU FORGET. YOUR SISTER MUST'VE MEANT NOTHING TO YOU AT ALL. BUT RHO DOES. AND I'LL MAKE SURE YOUR TORTURE AND HERS LASTS FOREVER THIS TIME. SHE WAS ALWAYS SUPPOSED TO BE MINE ANYWAY.

LET THE GAMES BEGIN.

-THE HANGMAN

Chapter Forty-Five

Rhodes

IT WASN'T A SOUND THAT WOKE ME, IT WAS A FEELING. A thumping inside my skull like my pulse lived there and only there.

I tried to open my eyes but couldn't quite get them to obey. It was as if they were glued in place. Confusion swept through me. That shouldn't be possible.

Trying harder, I finally got them to flutter. I was blinking so fast, the images filling my vision looked like they were bathed in strobe lights.

Nausea swept through me, whether from my weird vision or the fact that I had some sort of migraine; I wasn't sure.

I tried to slow my breathing, inhaling through my nose and out through my mouth. I tried opening my eyes again, slower this time. As my surroundings came into clearer view, I stopped breathing altogether.

I was lying on charred flooring surrounded by the remnants of what looked like some sort of burned-out cabin. The only thing left of it were pieces of framing. Everything else had been burned away.

Even pieces of the floor revealed a drop-off into nothing but the darkness of a basement below.

None of it was familiar. Not the structure itself or the forests beyond it. That simple fact had my heart rate speeding up as I struggled to sit.

The moment I pushed up, a wave of dizziness swept over me, bringing nausea flaring back to life. I lifted my fingers to my head and winced as I connected with a lump. Pulling my hand back, I saw flecks of dried blood there.

Crap. What the hell happened?

I searched my memory. Flashes of the day came back to me. Forcing Anson out the door to go to work. Getting ready for lunch with Fallon. Walking out to meet her—

My spine jerked straight as I remembered. Deputy Rolston. All the blood. My stomach pitched as I swallowed back bile. But the memories kept coming. That voice, something about it so achingly familiar but not exact. Then the pain. The falling.

I clambered to my feet, the world swaying around me.

Shit, shit, shit.

I reached out, grabbing for something to hold, anything. My palm hit rough wood, and I gripped it hard. Splinters pierced my palm, but I didn't give a damn. I needed to stay upright. There was no way I could sustain another hit to the head without passing out.

Slowly, the dizziness faded, and the world came back into focus around me. But I had to blink to make sure that what I was seeing was real. It shouldn't have been. It was a photo of me that looked to be from high school or college given the haircut. I was working at the nursery but caught in a moment of laughter, my head tipped back and hair tumbling around me.

I swallowed hard and began scanning the space with new eyes. It wasn't the only photo. There were countless images. My stomach hollowed out.

This wasn't happening. Maybe if I believed that deeply enough, I could alter my reality and transport myself to early this morning so I could redo everything.

I picked my way through the rubble of the house to the next photo, careful to avoid the places where the floor had fallen away. This shot was more recent. I was working in the garden at the guest cottage, my hands deep in the dirt. I could tell from the grainy quality that all of them had been taken with some sort of zoom lens—one that enabled whoever it was to invade my privacy with the press of a button.

But it couldn't have been Felix. Not if I was here now.

That thought had my gaze whipping around. No one was with me. Not a single soul. But I also didn't know where the hell I was. The trees were too thick for me to get a good sense of direction, but being lost in the woods would be better than being at the mercy of some creepy psycho.

I hurried toward what looked like it had once been an entrance to the home, but as I reached the threshold, I came up short. The photo there was from many years ago.

It was me in shorts and a tank top at the river. I was among friends, and Emilia was with us. I remembered that day. She'd begged me to come, and Fallon and I had finally given in. She'd had the time of her life.

My eyes burned as I reached out to touch the image. To touch her.

"It's always been you." A voice cut through the quiet from behind me. I stiffened, my muscles turning to cement. "Even back then. You saw me when no one else did."

I turned so slowly, like I was moving through quicksand. Because it couldn't be. His dark, shaggy hair was swept across his eyes as he looked at me with what could only be called reverence. "Silas?" I croaked.

Chapter Forty-Six

Anson

THE ROOM BUZZED AROUND ME. VOICES, CELL PHONE ALERTS, the crackle of radios. But I couldn't differentiate one from the other. It was just a din of chaotic noise. All I could do was stare at the piece of paper in the evidence bag.

LET THE GAMES BEGIN.

My stomach roiled. I knew his games. They were ones full of pain and twisted torture. And inflicting those things on Rho was the best way to do the most damage to *me*. The Hangman wouldn't be able to resist.

My mind swirled, all the puzzle pieces mixing together in an ugly stew as I stared at another line of the note.

SHE WAS ALWAYS SUPPOSED TO BE MINE ANYWAY.

It shouldn't have been possible. Rho's stalker and my tormentor were one and the same. We'd always thought The Hangman had made his home somewhere on the West Coast. It was what made the most sense, given where his victims had been found.

So, Oregon was on the list of possibilities. I'd known that when

I moved to Sparrow Falls. But I'd also thought that the chances of him finding me here, in a tiny town far away from any of the major highways that were his hunting grounds, were slim to none. I'd been so fucking wrong.

He'd already been here.

And it must've given him one hell of a thrill to have me walking back into his net without him lifting a finger. It made sense now why he'd stopped killing for so long. Because he'd gotten a front-row seat to my suffering. It was a different sort of pain and torture, but a kind that was just as alluring to him.

He'd likely been watching Rho the same way. He'd seen her life ripped apart by the fire, the physical and emotional agony she'd been in during the aftermath, and he'd gotten off on it.

"Anson."

Helena's voice cut through the haze of my spiraling thoughts. I looked up, blinking a few times and trying to clear my vision. I just stared at her. I had nothing to say sitting here in this damn sheriff's station conference room. All I had was pain.

Helena was good at guarding her emotions, hiding them under layers of practiced indifference. Being a woman coming up in the bureau, she'd had to be. But I could see her pain now. For me. "Sheriff Colson brought me up to speed."

My gaze shifted to Trace then. He stood to her left, just behind my right shoulder, and he looked *ravaged*. I knew he was doing his best to hold it together, but he'd had to cede control of the investigation to his second-in-command, thanks to his close ties to Rho and the severity of the case.

Helena getting the information from him instead of Deputy Hansen was a kindness she offered Trace. But then again, she had her hands full organizing the search.

"Tell me what you're thinking," Helena prodded.

"Nothing," I said, sandpaper coating the word. I couldn't think a damn thing other than, *This is all my fault.* If I'd never touched Rho, maybe The Hangman would've been content to watch us suffer—our pain giving him just enough of the drug he craved.

Helena's jaw hardened. "Bullshit. You know this case better than anyone."

I stood, shoving my chair back and almost sending it tumbling to the floor. "Obviously, I don't. Because this fucker has been under my nose for a year and a half, and I didn't see a damned thing," I spat. And the cameras outside Rho's house hadn't either. They'd gone mysteriously blank thirty minutes before we arrived.

She sucked in a ragged breath and let it out slowly. "You know better. We've always known The Hangman is a psychopath. And they blend. They can be charming. They have long-term relationships, even marriages and families."

I knew she was right, but I'd always thought I'd just...*know* if I ever saw The Hangman.

A hand clamped down on my shoulder, and I turned to find Trace. He met my gaze and didn't look away. "This isn't on you. You think I don't feel responsible? I've been in charge of Sparrow Falls for a hell of a lot longer than you've been here. I missed him, too. Right under my nose for *years*. How do you think that makes me feel?"

A muscle fluttered in my cheek. "None of the murders were in your jurisdiction."

"Sure. But he *lived* here. I've probably talked to him more times than I can count. That's gonna mess with my head for the rest of my days."

"Psychopaths are good at deceiving everyone around them."

"Yeah," Trace agreed. "So, listen to what you're saying. You couldn't do anything to prevent this from happening. But you *can* help us now—if you stop feeling so goddamn sorry for yourself and do the work only you can do."

From Trace, that might as well have been a hug and a back pat. But it *was* what I needed. "Starting fires is an early sign of psychopathy," I finally said. That and harm to animals were usually the things we saw the most. "At some point, that wasn't enough, and he escalated."

Trace nodded. "I've already got all those case files pulled. Deputies are combing through every single fire we've had here in the past two decades."

"I'm guessing our unsub is a contemporary of Rho's. A few years younger or older. Someone she likely went to school with."

Helena shook her head. "Could also be a teacher, coach, or family friend."

"No," I said, certainty curling my voice. "If it was someone older, they either would've stuck with arson or would've escalated earlier. Setting those fires was a kid's tantrum at not getting his way."

"A seriously fucked-up tantrum," Trace muttered.

"You're not wrong there. Whoever this is, they have contact with Rho," I said.

Trace gritted his teeth. "That could be anyone. You know her. Everyone she meets is her new best friend. She's never known a stranger."

I did know her. And more than that, I *loved* her. My throat constricted, a burn alighting there. I should've told her. As if not saying the words would somehow protect me if I lost her.

I struggled to keep my breathing even and stay in the here and now. "Let's use the small town to our advantage. Text your siblings, Rho's boss, and anyone else who sees her on a regular basis. Ask if anyone's disappeared this afternoon when they shouldn't have."

Trace jerked his head in a nod. "Will do."

"You got anyone who should have eyes on Owen Mead?" I asked. He'd alibied out for Rho's car accident, but a friend had supplied the alibi. I wasn't about to take any chances.

Trace's gaze cut to me. "He got a job with another construction crew in town. They don't do work as good as Shep, but it's still steady. You still think this could be him?"

"I just want to cross all our Ts. He's got a few things that ping the psychopathy checklist, and he's in Rho's orbit."

Trace was already pressing the phone to his ear. "Hey, Bob. Owen working for you today?" A moment of silence. "No, don't need to talk to him. Anyone on your crew miss work today?" Another beat. "Okay, thanks."

Trace hung up, his jaw working. "Bob said he was watching Owen do crappy tile work right then."

I didn't know whether to be relieved or pissed. Either way, we needed to move on.

A ring cut through the air, and Trace looked down, tapping his phone's screen. "What do you have, Shep?" There was a brief pause where Trace's expression completely shut down. "You're sure? You go by the clinic?" Another pause. "Fuck. Okay. Don't do anything stupid."

Trace hung up and turned to me and Helena. "Silas Arnett begged off work mid-morning. Said he wasn't feeling well. Shep went to his apartment, and he wasn't there. Drove by Dr. Avery's office, and he wasn't there either."

Everything in me locked. A million different encounters with Silas swirled in my mind. It was like looking at those memories through a kaleidoscope. Each switch of the dial made me see the image a little differently.

Charming. A womanizer. But no *deep* ties. It all fit. But we could be wrong, too. It could all be smoke when the fire was somewhere else entirely.

"Get me absolutely everything you have on him. If he has a friend, I want them here. We need Shep. He's worked with Silas the longest." I looked between Helena and Trace. "We have a few hours at best."

We all knew what would happen if those hours ran out. And I wouldn't survive it this time.

Chapter Forty-Seven

Rhodes

I BLINKED SO QUICKLY THAT THE IMAGE IN FRONT OF ME BLURRED. The smudged version was better because this one couldn't be right.

Silas.

The boy who'd always been funny. A little crass but in a harmless sort of way—or so I'd thought. He'd been a year older but blended into the larger group of friends I'd been a part of since moving to Sparrow Falls. But like with everyone other than Fallon, I'd drifted away from him after the fire.

The fire.

A fire that had killed my family. Almost killed me. A fire that Anson and Trace now thought had been set intentionally. We thought it had been Felix, but it wasn't Felix standing before me now. It wasn't Felix who had taken me. Who killed Deputy Rolston.

Bile surged up my throat at the memory of Rolston slumped against the wheel. All the blood. And Silas had killed him. The same Silas who had brought me kittens to take care of. Who had sat at my picnic table and complimented me on my food. Who had been on the outskirts of my life for as long as I'd lived in Sparrow Falls.

I swallowed hard, trying to force down the sickness. "What's happening, Silas?"

The corners of his mouth kicked up into a smile. "Don't play dumb, Rho. It's beneath you."

My heart rate kicked up, the organ feeling like a Ping-Pong ball in one of those lotto wheels. "Okay. *Where* are we?"

"That's better." He began walking around the demolished house. He moved without looking where he was going, seeming to have memorized every crumbling floorboard and unsteady wall. "This is where I grew up."

I frowned. I knew Silas had a mother and sister—a mom who had struggled to make ends meet working at one of our gas stations. They'd moved to Florida when he was in his early twenties, but I didn't remember hearing anything about the house burning down. "When was the fire?"

Silas raised and lowered a shoulder casually. "I don't know. Years ago. Time really is fluid."

I took one step backward, trying to feel for the edge of the entryway. I would have to make a run for it and hope for the best. But there was a significant drop-off from the entry to the ground. And running for it would be easier if I didn't break my neck first. "I just don't remember hearing anything about it."

He picked up one of the photos that had been plastered around what remained of the house. It was one of me at a dance in middle school. My hair was piled on the top of my head in ridiculous curlicue ringlets, and I wore a dress that shimmered beneath a mirror ball. "Why would you? No one cares if a falling-apart cabin burns."

My toe caught the edge of the drop-off, and I halted, trying to feel if anything was below it, like crumbling steps. "I'm sure the fire department would've."

Silas scoffed. "People would've thought it was simply a large trash burn if they saw the smoke in the distance. And this town didn't care about me or my family. We were invisible to them." His gaze snapped to me. "But I wasn't invisible to you, was I?"

Something about the question had ice sliding through my veins. I had a feeling how I answered it would dictate important next steps. "Of course, you weren't. We were friends. We—"

"We were a hell of a lot more than friends, Rhodes. You saw me." Silas's expression softened. But something about the gentleness terrified me way more than his anger. "Without you, I would've failed Spanish. Maybe would've had to drop out. But you studied with me every day in the library."

I thought back to that seventh-grade year. He'd been a year older but had been held back in Spanish. I'd known he was struggling and easily frustrated. I remembered helping him during our free periods, bent over books in the library.

It had seemed like nothing. Spanish had always come easily to me. And spending some time helping someone who needed it was… nothing.

"You shared your lunch with me," Silas said, his voice taking on a dreamy quality. "You took care of me."

That came flooding back, too. The memory of seeing that Silas only ate chips and candy bars from the vending machine. I'd asked my mom to pack him a lunch, too.

"So kind. So gentle. We shared a bond. Even if people kept interfering in our relationship, trying to keep us apart."

My stomach roiled at the transformation. Gone was the gentleness. In its place was fury and more than a little instability. I struggled to keep my breathing even and my expression neutral, but I had no idea what to say that wouldn't infuriate him. "Who tried to keep us apart?"

Silas's hands clenched and flexed over and over again, almost as if he were sending some sort of silent message with the long and short punctuated movements. "You know."

I shook my head, the action making pain flare in my skull. "I don't. Everyone I know liked you."

"Felix fucking didn't," he spat, tearing the dance photo from a half-demolished wall. He shook the paper at me. "He was drooling over you this night. Told his friends he was going to ask you out the next day. Should've gutted him then. Tried to set him up, get him riled up that you were in danger and sent him poking around your house. Thought maybe the profiler would kill him the other night. But he can't do anything right, can he?"

My pulse thrummed—in my neck, my head, traveling down my arm. He said *profiler* with such familiarity. "How did you know Anson was a profiler?"

Silas sent me a smarmy smile. "Come on, Rho. Small towns are gossip mills. I've had at least half a dozen people ask me if I knew. So sad that boy couldn't cut it."

I bit the inside of my cheek.

He made a tsking sound. "Now, now. Your temper's giving you away. Don't pretend you *care* about him." Anger flared in Silas's eyes. "You were trying to make me jealous, weren't you?"

Nausea swept through me again, but this time, my head injury had nothing to do with it. I couldn't tell Silas the truth. It would only mean rage and possibly violence. What I had to do was buy myself some more time. Find a moment when he was distracted and run.

I swallowed down the bile surging into my throat and lied. "Yes," I said, my voice barely audible. "I'm sorry."

Silas's eyes narrowed on me. "You should be. The kindness is always a lie. I keep trying to find a woman who isn't a dirty liar, but they all are. They pretend to like you, pretend to be *nice*. But it's all fake. A deception until they have you in their clutches and break you."

His jaw clenched. "Arden has it, too. I almost fell for it, was *this* close. That fake kindness. She pretended to care about those kittens, but she just wanted to trap me. Maybe I'll visit her after this. Show her what happens to liars."

Panic sliced through me as my breaths tripped over each other. Arden. My sister. I'd seen the way he looked at her. I thought he'd had a crush, but it was so much more. A twisted narrative taking over his mind.

"I didn't lie," I whispered.

Silas surged forward. "You did! You made me think you loved me. But you didn't. You were using me to feel good about yourself. Playing games," he spat. "Making me burn things to keep us together."

My mind swirled. It didn't make sense. *Burn things to keep us together?* "I-I don't understand."

He scoffed. "You kept spending time with them. Paying them attention when it should've been me. I had to warn them to stay away."

"Oh, God," I whispered.

A smile spread across Silas's face. "You missed it all, didn't you? Right in front of your face, but you were too selfish to realize. Felix's family's restaurant after he started walking you to lunch. Outside Fallon's locker when you went with her family to the coast instead of to the lake with the rest of us. The trailhead when you ignored me to hang out with your sister at the river."

Tears filled my eyes, acid tracking down my cheeks. "My house. My family."

Silas stormed toward me, moving so fast I didn't have a prayer. His hand wrapped around my neck, squeezing. "Don't you cry for them! They didn't love you. Your parents let you go to that party where Felix felt you up in the closet. They let you be a dirty whore."

The tears only came faster; I didn't have a prayer of stopping them. Mom. Dad. Emilia. They were dead because some sicko had been obsessed with me. Dead because of *me*.

"And you needed to *pay*. To be *punished*," he snarled. "I thought the flames would get you, too. Take you down so I could finally be free of your lies. But you made it out."

Silas pulled something from his waistband, and then cold metal traced my tears. "My little phoenix, rising from the ashes. I knew then that you were meant to live. It was so much better. I got to see you *suffer*."

His face pushed close to mine, and I shuddered. "I watched you in the hospital. So much pain. Watched from the doorway as the nurses changed your bandages. Saw the way you cried." The tip of the blade traced my tears again. "So pretty when she cries."

I tried to stop the tears, but I couldn't stanch the flow.

"I realized then. Watching the living in the aftermath was so much better. The way you sobbed at the memorial. How you couldn't stand to go back to the house. The way you never found love again. My phoenix was too scared."

Silas's hand on my throat tightened, his jaw clenching. "But something changed."

I'd gotten brave enough to go back to my home. I'd met Anson. Through it all, I'd taken the final steps to my healing, and Silas had seen me happy.

He shook me, making dark spots dance in front of my vision. "You needed to remember. To go back to the pain. The photo I left on your porch sent you there for a minute. Shep said you were upset, had a panic attack. But then you were happy again."

Silas spat the words like a vicious accusation. "So, I brought back the fire." He grinned against my cheek. "That was good. I saw the shadows in your eyes. Too scared to stay alone. I bet you remembered that night. I bet it took you back to the fire and the pain."

It had. I'd remembered just how terrified I'd been. Remembered losing my family as if it was yesterday.

"But then you betrayed me all over again," Silas snarled, jerking back. "You let *him* touch you. I saw it. It was all I could do not to kill you both. Driving you off the road was rash, too much too fast." He took a deep, shuddering breath. "But sometimes I can't control myself. And you make me so mad."

A tremble took root in my muscles. Every single thing had been him all along.

"I try to beat it back, but sometimes I can't. Like that fucking pissant Davis. He hurt you."

My eyes jerked to Silas's face, confusion filling my expression, but dread came fast on its heels.

His thumb stroked my neck as his grip on my throat loosened for a moment. "I'm the only one who gets to hurt you, Little Phoenix. Your pain is mine alone."

With his words came a fresh flood of fury. So much better than the fear. "Anson's going to find you," I growled. "He's smarter than you'll ever be."

Silas laughed then, but it was a sickening sound. "Oh, Rho. I've already beaten him more times than I can count. Every woman that reminded me of you. Every bitch who lied with her kind eyes. I made them scream before I slit their throats. The sweetest sound."

"Every woman that reminded me of you." The words echoed in my head as they landed over and over again. My stomach roiled as true terror set in. What had Anson said about The Hangman? He cut their carotid arteries. My mind spun as a million pieces tried to come together.

"But poor ol' Anson could never get there quite quick enough. He was close with his sister, but I dallied. I liked her screams a little too much."

Blood roared in my ears as a fresh wave of bile surged. "No."

He only grinned wider, his mouth twisting with the movement. "Yes. What are the chances that everything would come back to where it all started? Poetic, don't you think? The perfect piece of art. The final clue in a master game."

Silas's tongue swept across his bottom lip. "I've been making him suffer for years. His pain was the best. So deep, so feral." Silas's expression went hard as his hand tightened around my throat again. "But you tried to steal that, too. You won't succeed."

"Y-you're The Hangman." Nothing in the words sounded like my voice. It was completely foreign.

He leaned in close. "Nice to meet you, Rho." Then he licked the tears from my cheek.

My knee came up on instinct, catching him in the balls. But it wasn't enough. Silas's hand tightened on my throat, completely cutting off my air supply. "Listen here, you little bitch. I've had enough of your games. I'm the chess master, and it's time I took control of the board."

He breathed ragged pants through his nose as he struggled for control. "It's just too bad you have to die for my perfect end game."

Chapter Forty-Eight

Anson

"I HAD A DEPUTY DOUBLE-CHECK PROPERTY RECORDS," TRACE said, striding back into the room. "There's nothing. He's got the apartment in town, and that's it."

Hell. I wanted Trace to find something, anything that would lead us to Rho. Just thinking her name had pain stabbing deep. Images flashed in my mind, horrific what-ifs rooted in other realities. It made the imaginary slideshow that much more devastating. Each image was a possibility, even a probability.

I bit down hard on the inside of my cheek until the metallic taste of blood filled my mouth. I needed that flare of pain to keep me grounded. "What about any LLCs or corporations registered in his name?" I asked. "It's possible to hide ownership that way."

Trace flipped open a laptop on the conference table and began typing. "Running a search in the State of Oregon's database."

I fought the urge to stand, to pace. But movement wouldn't alleviate the agony coursing through me.

"Nothing. Not a damn thing," Trace growled.

I glanced at Shep, who sat across from me at the conference table. His expression was completely blank. He'd locked down everything he was feeling so tightly that no emotion had a prayer of breaking free.

"What about places Silas frequents?" I asked Shep. He wouldn't take Rho to a new place. He'd go somewhere he knew, someplace he was comfortable.

Shep squeezed the back of his neck. "I don't know. He's into fishing. He always used his vacation days to take trips for that sort of thing." Shep's expression finally changed, but it looked as if he might be sick. "There wasn't any fucking fishing, was there? He was using those trips to go on his twisted murder sprees, wasn't he?"

A weight settled in my gut, not for me this time but for my friend. Helena and I had worked the timeline. The best we could figure, all the recent victims had been killed on weekends. And all incidents had occurred within a nine-and-a-half-hour-drive radius of Sparrow Falls. Close enough that Silas could make the journey and be back for work on Mondays.

"We don't know. Not yet." But my gut screamed it was him. "If you have a list of those dates, the BAU team can work on matching them to the murders."

Shep nodded slowly, but there was such defeat in the movement. "Yeah, I've got software I track all that in. I can give them the login."

"That'd be good. But now, I need you to think. There must be places around here that Silas went to often. Comfort spots," I prodded.

"I doubt he took her to the fucking bar. And that's the only place I know of," Shep snapped.

I struggled to control my temper. Shep was hurting, and worse, he felt responsible. "Tell me about Silas growing up." If there wasn't a spot linked to Silas today, maybe it was somewhere from his past.

"I don't fucking know," Shep growled, shoving his chair back and running a hand roughly through his hair.

"I do."

The voice was quiet, barely audible, but it still made everything stop.

Fallon hovered in the doorway to the conference room, her face pale and hands gripped tightly together.

"Fallon, what are you doing here?" Trace asked.

She swallowed hard. "Shep said you were looking for Silas."

Trace sent Shep a scathing look.

"We needed as many eyes on the lookout as possible," Shep shot back.

I stood, crossing to Fallon. "Did you know him growing up?"

She nodded slowly. "He was a year above us but in our bigger group of friends. You know, not the ones you're super tight with but the kind you do things with."

"Sure," I assured her. "What do you know about his homelife?"

Fallon twisted her fingers like she was wringing out a towel. "I remember his dad left when we were young, maybe third or fourth grade. I think his mom had a hard time with that and making enough money to keep them afloat."

"What makes you say that?"

"His clothes were always a bit worn, and sometimes they were a size too small," Fallon said softly.

"How did he get along with his family? Do you know?"

Fallon licked her lips nervously as she thought. "He had an older sister who he said was hard on him. I got the sense his mom annoyed him. But that's true for most kids."

She was right there, but that sort of disdain could be a clue to something.

"Where are his mom and sister? Can you bring them in?" I asked Trace.

He shook his head. "They moved to Florida about six years ago."

That prickle along my scalp lit. "You have confirmation of that?"

Trace frowned. "What do you mean?"

"Has anyone talked to the mom and sister since they moved?"

"I don't know. They didn't have real deep ties. Carina, the sister, had a best friend, but she moved to Idaho last year," Trace said.

I glanced at Helena, who'd been typing away on a laptop but had stopped to listen to these latest developments. "Have someone run them. I want to know if there's any evidence of them actually moving."

Helena jerked her head in a nod. "On it."

"What are you thinking?" Trace pressed.

"Six years ago, Silas would've been twenty-two or twenty-three. That's right around the point where we see escalation in psychopaths. It would not surprise me if his mom and sister didn't move at all."

Trace gnashed his teeth together. "You think he killed them."

Fallon sucked in a sharp breath, her face paling further. "Oh, God."

Shep crossed to her, wrapping an arm around her shoulders. "Come on, Fallon. Why don't I get you home? You shouldn't be here for this."

She jerked out of his hold. "You sound like Kye," she snapped. "I'm not weak. Stop treating me like I am."

Shep reared back as if she'd slapped him. "I don't think you're weak."

"You wouldn't know that by how you all treat me." Fallon turned to me. "What else do you need to know?"

I did my best to ignore the family drama playing out and focus on what was important. Each sliver of information was another puzzle piece on the board. "Where did his mom and sister live?" If they owned property, it was likely sold, and that would require a paper trail.

"They stayed in the house Silas grew up in. From what I heard, it was a pretty rundown place up in the mountains. A ways out of town."

I turned to Trace, whose fingers were already flying across the keyboard. He frowned at the screen. "It's still in Lucinda Arnett's name, but the property taxes haven't been paid in"—his head jerked up—"six years."

Hell. I was right. He'd killed them both. They were likely his first hands-on kills. Up close, more than setting a fire that took people out in its path. Something must have set him off and made him snap. "Where?"

The prickly sensation across my scalp intensified. The house was the place. I knew it in my gut. It was where he'd brought Rho.

"I've got an address," Trace said. "Let me call in SWAT and get blueprints sent to our phones."

I shook my head. "There isn't time for SWAT. We've got Feds and county deputies. We go now."

Helena stood, shoving her chair back. "You aren't on the job anymore, Anson. And this is a conflict of interest anyway."

I struggled to hold back the choice words I wanted to spit at her. "I'll go on my own if I have to. You know better than anyone that every second matters. And you know that I'll never forgive myself if I'm not there."

Helena cursed. "You stay back. You do not engage. But you can be there when we bring her out."

I didn't argue, simply moved. Officers spat orders, and radios crackled, but I was already heading toward the rented Suburban I knew would be Helena's. I climbed into the front seat while Trace took the back. I knew he was trying to sneak in under the radar, but he'd also come prepared.

"Take it," he said, handing me a set of body armor. "Just in case."

I pulled the vest on over my head and secured it while Trace did the same.

Helena scowled at us both as she climbed into the SUV and started the engine. "You both stay back, or I'll put you in cuffs myself."

We grunted in response.

"Men," she huffed.

The parade of law enforcement vehicles raced down the two-lane highway, but none used a siren. The only sound was the discussion of our approach to the property. The plan was to park a ways back and make the assault on foot, hoping for an element of surprise. But no one knew exactly what we'd be walking in on.

Trace and I studied the blueprints that arrived. It was a two-story cabin plus a basement and attic. Lots of little hidey-holes. And that was never good.

Helena made a right onto a winding gravel road. Each hairpin turn made my gut twist tighter, and Rho's face played on repeat in my mind. The way her eyes lit when she laughed. Her wild waves falling across her face as she sank her hands into the dirt. The way her lips parted as I sank into *her*.

Pain ground into my chest, followed quickly by a dose of fury— at myself for failing Rho and not telling her what she meant to me. At Silas for everything he'd done and what he was doing now.

Helena jerked the SUV into park as other vehicles filed in. Hushed orders were whispered, and everyone went radio silent.

Trace and I both checked our weapons as we followed behind Helena and her new partner. The climb to the property was steep, and my thighs started burning a few minutes in. I relished the sensation. It was a reminder that I was alive and had me believing with everything I had that Rho was, too.

Helena held up a hand as we reached the edge of a tree line, and I froze. There was no house in front of us. Just a burned-out shell of what had once been an old cabin. But there was more.

There was Rho.

And Silas had a knife pressed against her throat.

Chapter Forty-Nine

Rhodes

THE BLADE OF THE KNIFE PRESSED AGAINST MY NECK, PIERCING the skin as white-hot pain bloomed. It was so similar to the feeling of a burn. Too similar.

"I tried to come up with another way, Rho. I really did. But nothing will hurt him more than losing you. But it has to be right in front of his eyes this time. It's the only way to end it," Silas said, desperation in his tone.

As his words took root in my brain, realization bloomed. He didn't expect to get away with this. The only thing he wanted was to hurt Anson the most.

"You don't have to do this," I pleaded.

He laughed then, the sound having a shrill quality to it. "But I do." His fingers released my neck, and he moved his hand to stroke my face. "We'll find each other in the afterlife. We'll finally be together like it was always supposed to be. Just you and me. No more lies between us. No one else there to take you away."

A fresh wave of nausea rolled through me. "Please."

A twig snapped, and Silas moved so fast that everything was a blur. He shifted so he was behind me, the blade still at my neck, and his other hand gripping my hair so tightly my eyes watered. "Come out, come out wherever you are," Silas singsonged.

Nothing moved or made a sound.

Silas let out an exaggerated sigh. "Come on now. We're all better than this. You know I'm here. I know you're there. If I had to guess, you've got officers surrounding me right now."

"This is the Mercer County Sheriff's Department. Release Rho and drop your weapon. Hands on your head."

I couldn't see Beth, but I recognized her voice—that authoritative tone she used when she was in deputy mode.

Silas made a tsking noise. "I don't want to talk to you, Bethy. Where's the profiler?"

"He's not here," Beth called back. "You're going to have to deal with me."

Silas sighed again but then yanked my hair so hard I couldn't help but cry out. "Don't. Lie. To. Me. I know that bastard is here. There's no way he wouldn't be."

A second later, there was movement.

Panic seared me. "No! Anson, he wants to hurt you."

Silas pressed the blade harder against my neck, digging in, and I couldn't help the sound I made as blood trickled down my throat. "You'll pay for your betrayal," he snarled. "I could've made this quick and painless, but now you're going to suffer."

I knew Silas wouldn't have sent me off pain-free. There was no way. He liked the reaction to his torture too much.

"I'm here," Anson growled.

Tears pooled in my eyes. "Don't," I whispered. The word couldn't have actually reached his ears, but as I took him in, I knew Anson had read it on my lips.

Agony swirled in those blue-gray eyes—something I never wanted to see there. There were a million things I wanted to say to him. But they were things I knew would escalate the situation, so I only said them in my mind. A silent whisper between me and the wind.

"Profiler," Silas almost cooed. "Finally, we *really* meet."

Anson hid his emotions well, but because I knew him as I did, I saw his struggle to keep them contained. "I don't think you've ever truly met someone, Silas. Because you can't be honest with who you really are."

Silas's hand tightened in my hair. "I know *exactly* who I am, and I'm not afraid of it. I'm a killer. I love the feeling of life bleeding out of them and into me. It makes me more powerful than you'll ever be."

Anson arched a brow in challenge. "You sure about that? Because you've only ever picked victims who were weaker than you. I don't think that makes you powerful. It makes you a sniveling coward."

Silas's breaths came quicker in my ear. "You're the coward," he shot back. "You could never do what needed to be done to find me. Could never face what lived inside you enough to see the truth. That you're the weak one."

Anson's eyes flashed, and Silas grinned. "I wish I would've recorded your sister's screams so you could hear how beautiful they were. But I'll just have to settle for you listening to Rho's. Watching the blood drain from her body. Maybe this is always how it was meant to be. The three of us together. You'll relive the pain, over and over again. You'll never escape it."

"It's me you want to end, Silas. Let me trade places with her," Anson said, panic bleeding into his voice.

Silas made that tsking noise again. "You know it can't be that way, Profiler. You have to live with the pain. That's the best torture of all."

Silas pulled me harder against him as he moved backward, one step, then two. I tried to reach behind me and punch at his ribs, but Silas jerked my hair, pressing his face to mine. "Don't make me end this early, Rhodes."

Tears filled my eyes as my gaze collided with Anson's. His hand curled around his weapon, but he didn't lift it. He didn't have a shot. No one did. Every angle risked taking me out along with Silas.

At least I knew this was the end for him, no matter what. Silas wouldn't hurt any other women. Because he wouldn't make it out of this. He'd just take me with him when he went.

Tears tracked down my cheeks as Anson's face blurred. "I love you," I croaked.

"Shut up," Silas barked, tugging my hair in a vicious shake.

The tears fell faster as pain surged in my head, but I didn't stop. "I don't regret loving you for a single second. Scared the hell out of me, but it brought me back to life."

"Reckless," Anson choked out.

"I'll always love you."

"Stop it!" Silas screamed, tugging me backward.

There was a crack so loud and long it sounded like a vicious clap of thunder. At first, I thought it was a gunshot and braced for pain. But it wasn't. The floor beneath our feet gave way, the boards snapping.

Everything slowed. It was as if I could see each millisecond in a snapshot. Anson screaming my name. Law enforcement charging out from the trees.

Then we were falling, descending into darkness. I couldn't see where we were going. One second, shadows engulfed us. Then there was pain. Finally, only blissful nothingness.

Chapter Fifty

Anson

MY FIRST THOUGHT AT THE CRACKING SOUND WAS *BULLET*. That some wet-behind-the-ears deputy had decided to take their shot. But as Silas stumbled back a step, I realized I was wrong.

The entire house had been burned beyond recognition, so it was no wonder the floor was unstable and had given way.

The world dropped away as I saw them start to fall. Silas's grip on Rho's hair was so strong she didn't have a prayer of breaking free. I yelled her name as if that would do something, as if I could change the course of what was about to happen.

I knew from the blueprints that the house had a basement below the ground floor. But I had no clue how deep it was. Was it a mere eight feet, or was it something deeper? How would they fall? What would they land on?

My mind worked out every twisted scenario as the horror played out in front of me. But my body was already moving, rushing forward, trying to do something, *anything*.

I leapt onto the cabin's frame in what looked like it had once been an entryway. I charged forward toward the gaping hole in the floor. But a hand caught my vest and tugged me back hard.

"Don't," Trace barked. "You'll go over with them."

He was right. But I didn't care. Wherever Rho was, that's where I wanted to be. The cost didn't matter. Because she was my sanctuary. I'd just never realized how fragile it all was.

The house made a series of noises that sounded like they'd come from a horror movie. A plume of dust and soot rose from the hole in an ominous cloud. Dread churned in my gut. "I've gotta get to her."

"I know," Trace said, gripping my vest tighter. Pain dug grooves into his face as he looked over my shoulder into the depths below. "But we need to be smart about it. Get gear."

"I've got some, boss," a young deputy called. "Our search and rescue stuff."

I whirled around. "Toss me a harness."

Trace eyed me. "You've had training?"

"The basics," I said as the officer tossed me what looked like a rock-climbing harness. "We're often searching for victims."

"Boss," the guy said, lifting another harness.

Trace held out a hand for it.

In a matter of seconds, we'd geared up, done a quick check for each other, and hooked into a belay system with two other officers.

"EMTs are five minutes out," Deputy Hansen called.

I just hoped like hell they got here in time. "Anyone got a headlamp?"

"Yeah," the same young deputy said.

A fuckin' Boy Scout. But I was grateful. He tossed it to me from his gear bag, and I put it over my head as Trace fixed a first-aid bag around his body.

"Belay on," I called to the deputy behind me.

"On belay," he answered.

Then, I was moving toward the opening. The charred floor groaned beneath me as I walked, and I knew it could give way at any second. I needed to move quickly but carefully.

My ribs squeezed around my lungs as I approached the edge. The beam of light from the headlamp and the sun overhead revealed a horrific tableau. Burned wreckage. So much soot that it made it hard to make out what was what.

Then I saw him. Silas had fallen awkwardly. His legs were sprawled in a way I knew meant broken bones, and his neck rested at an unnatural angle. His eyes were open wide but completely unseeing. Gone. The Hangman, the demon who'd haunted me, the one who had stolen my sister's life, was no more. But I felt no relief, had no time to take that in and let it land.

My gaze was instantly searching again. It was the glimpse of one pink-and-teal flower that had me stopping. The toe of one of those damn boots. My heart stopped altogether as I took in the entirety of Rho.

She wasn't moving. Not even the slightest bit. I couldn't see from here if she was breathing. But her eyes were closed.

"Fuck." The word clogged in my throat, tangled with tears and the sob trying to break free. "Going over," I shouted. "Slack."

The deputy gave it to me, and I went over the edge. The way down was a painstaking volley of words with my belay. Trying to get to Rho and scared out of my mind she wouldn't be there when I arrived.

Finally, my feet hit the cement floor, cluttered with debris. "I'm down," I shouted.

I instantly felt the slack in my tether as Trace landed next to me. But I was already moving, running to Rho, tripping over beams and God knew what else. I fell to my knees as I reached her, not giving a damn about the jarring pain.

Soot covered her beautiful face. I reached out, my hand stopping just shy of her neck. Blood pooled around the wound there, her life force spilling out.

"Do it," Trace choked out.

I placed my fingers on her neck, closed my eyes, and prayed. The moment they pressed into her flesh, Rho let out a soft moan.

Relief and fear coursed through me in equal measure. "Rho, can you hear me?"

Her eyelids fluttered until they finally opened. "Hurts," she croaked, trying to shift.

"Don't move," I ordered, panic surging. We had no idea what sort of injuries Rho might have, and I wasn't about to risk her spine.

"Anson." Her voice was weak, and her eyelids drooped.

I took her hand, squeezing. "Don't close your eyes. Stay with me. Help's almost here."

Rho's eyelids fluttered again, and I saw her struggle. Felt it.

"Don't, Reckless. Don't leave me." I squeezed her hand harder. A tear slipped free, landing on Rho's cheek and turning the ash pure black. "I love you."

But Rho didn't answer. She didn't speak at all.

Chapter Fifty-One

Rhodes

THE FAINT BEEPING GRATED AGAINST MY EARDRUMS LIKE A loud, annoying bee. I tried to swat at it but couldn't seem to move my arm.

"Easy, Reckless," a deep voice crooned. "You're okay. I've got you."

Something about the voice soothed, but I wanted to see the owner of the deep timbre. Needed to be closer to it as if I could wrap myself in the comforting tone like a blanket.

Fingers trailed over my arm in gentle strokes. The sensation was so lovely I almost didn't notice the pounding in my head. But not quite. The steady drumbeat in my skull made it feel like my head was about to explode.

"You gonna wake up and give the hospital hell that there isn't a speck of color in this room?" the voice asked.

Another layer of awareness slid over me. I knew the owner of that voice.

Anson.

My eyelids fluttered on instinct, my eyes desperate to see him. It took a few tries to get them open, but I finally succeeded. Anson stared down at me, his blue-gray eyes swirling. His thick scruff was even longer, and he had smudges of darkness under his eyes. But there was such tenderness in his expression. "There she is."

"Hi," I croaked.

Anson moved but didn't let go of my hand. He grabbed a cup of water with a straw and held it to my lips. I took a few tentative sips, then a deeper drink, trying to put the pieces together.

I finally registered that I was in a hospital. I frowned as Anson pulled the cup away. "What—?"

It all came flooding back. Silas. The attack. The knife. The standoff.

"We fell through the floor…"

Anson reached up, gently brushing the hair away from my face. "Took ten years off my life." He leaned down, his forehead resting against mine. "But you're okay."

It sounded like he was saying it as much for himself as for me. I tried to lift my hand to his face but couldn't make it work. I frowned as Anson pulled back, and I saw why. My entire arm was in a bulky cast.

"You broke your arm in a couple of places," Anson said. "Needed some of that medical glue on your neck, bruised your ribs, and you have a nasty concussion. But the doctors said you'll likely be able to go home the day after tomorrow."

I wanted that. Home. With Anson. "Biscuit?" I asked.

"Arden's been taking care of him. He's just fine. And Thea said she can keep the kittens."

Good. That was good. I looked up into Anson's eyes and asked what I'd been too scared to voice until this very moment. "Silas?"

A muscle in his jaw tensed. "He's dead. He broke his neck in the fall."

Everything inside me twisted in an ugly stew. Relief. Sadness. Even an echo of fear. "Are you okay?"

Anson's thumb ghosted across the swell of my cheek. "She's lying in a hospital bed and asking if *I'm* okay."

"Because I love you, and you just went through hell all over again." I wasn't sure which would be worse, being the person taken or watching the person who meant everything to you at the hands of a madman—a psychopath who'd already stolen your sister.

Anson's throat worked as he swallowed. "I'm not a good man. I'm glad the bastard's dead. He was a monster. The world is a better place without him in it."

I managed to raise my uncasted hand to Anson's face, careful not to pull at my IV. I stroked his thick stubble. "You're the best man I've ever known."

That muscle along Anson's jaw began fluttering wildly. "He hurt *you*," Anson growled, shoving to his feet, my hand falling away. "He almost *killed* you." He began pacing the small, drab room. "And all because I didn't see what was right in front of my face."

"Shut up," I snapped.

Anson jerked to a surprised halt. "What did you just say?"

"I said *shut up*. You're a genius. You should be smarter than blaming yourself for not seeing someone who was clearly a master manipulator." My heart cracked, splintering, grooves driving into it. But I knew Anson wouldn't respond to gentleness and empathy right now. He needed to be snapped out of his self-flagellation.

Anson's jaw worked back and forth. "I'm trained to see through manipulation."

"You didn't have all the information you needed. So, how could you have?" I pressed. Everything ached at the thought of Anson taking all this on his shoulders. The blame that had clearly been piling on while I'd been unconscious.

"I didn't want to see," he said finally. "For the past year and a half, I've been trying desperately to turn off the part of me that analyzes people."

"And there's nothing wrong with that."

"If I hadn't, maybe I would've seen the signs."

"*No one* saw the signs, Anson. Not Shep or the rest of the crew. Not Trace. Not me. No one. And it's not any of our faults."

Tears glimmered in Anson's eyes. "I almost lost you."

My throat constricted as I struggled to get words out. "Come here."

Anson didn't move.

"Come. Here."

He took one step and then another, and then he was at my side.

I lifted my free hand and tugged him down to the bed, then pressed my palm to his cheek. "I'm okay. I'm here. Because you found me."

Anson reached out, his hand ghosting over my face, then down the side of my neck before simply resting there. "I didn't want to let you in. Didn't want to care about anyone. It felt like such a risk."

My heart hammered against my ribs as blood roared in my ears. Was this it? The time he told me he couldn't do this? Couldn't handle the pain a relationship could bring?

"But you stormed in anyway. You tore down every wall I put up. I didn't want to love you. But I fucking do. With every part of me. It's not a sappy love. It burns. Scars. It changed me. All in the best ways. I love you, Rho. And it killed that I was too scared to give you those words until now."

Tears pooled in my eyes, spilling over and tracking down my cheeks. "I love you, too. I don't want sappy love. I want the real kind. And that's what we have."

Anson leaned down, his lips ghosting over mine. "Even though I'm a broody asshole?"

I grinned against his mouth. "Yes."

He kissed me again. "Even though I hate color?"

I chuckled. "I still think I'm going to get you into a pink shirt one of these days."

Anson's forehead rested against mine. "You know, I'd do anything for you. Even wear a damn pink shirt." He cupped my cheek. "I love you."

"With every part of me."

Chapter Fifty-Two

Rhodes

TRACE, KYE, AND FALLON ALL RUSHED FORWARD AS I STOOD from the hospital bed, all talking at once.

"Don't move so fast," Trace chided.

"Watch your arm," Kye shouted.

"Let me help you," Fallon said.

I gave them all an exasperated look. "Guys, I'm okay. Chill."

With Anson finally being forced to leave the hospital for his interview with Deputy Hansen and the FBI, I'd thought I would get a break from the intense overprotectiveness. But that was not the case. My siblings had filled that role without missing a step.

The only one who hadn't rushed forward was Shep. He stood in the spot he'd favored over the past twenty-four hours, in the corner, against the wall, his arms crossed. He'd barely said two words to me other than, "I'm so sorry."

I was starting to worry that what had happened might've scarred Shep more than anyone. I understood it in a way. He'd hired Silas right out of high school, worked with him every day for almost a decade, and hadn't seen Silas's darkness.

No matter what I said, it didn't seem like Shep could let it go. Hopefully, that would change as he saw me doing fine. Or I'd eventually be able to get through to him.

"Give the girl a little breathing room, would you? She's gonna suffocate."

My head jerked in the direction of the voice. The move was too quick, and a wave of dizziness hit me, but I did my best to hide it. "Cope?" I choked. "What are you doing here? I thought you had a game."

He strode across the room, all six feet five inches of pure muscle. He wrapped me in the gentlest of hugs. "My sister gets kidnapped, and you think I'm not going to come see if she's all right?"

"I told you I was fine," I said, hugging him with my good arm.

Cope pulled back, shadows swirling in his eyes. "I needed to see for myself."

"I'm not going to complain about having you home." It was such a rarity these days. Ever since he'd been drafted into the NHL right out of college, really. Even his few months of offseason weren't really free. There were press obligations and charity work. We were lucky if he got two weeks here.

"That mean I get to drive you home?" he asked hopefully.

I arched a brow at him. "Did you bring that ridiculously expensive SUV?"

Cope chuckled. "It's not that bad."

"It's a freaking Bentley," I argued.

He just shrugged. "Handles like a dream."

"You can only drive her if you promise to drive carefully," Fallon said, moving toward us.

Cope turned, sending her a mischievous grin. "I *always* drive carefully."

Fallon just scoffed.

"I will ticket you," Trace growled. "Don't think I won't."

"Geez," Cope muttered. "I'm going to drive like a grandma, promise."

"Enough," I said. "Can I please go home? The beige in this place is starting to give me a headache."

"Let's go," Cope said, wrapping an arm around me. "Your wheelchair chariot awaits."

~

Cope kept looking over at me as we made the almost-hour drive from the hospital to home. As if he were checking to make sure I *truly* was all right. But it wasn't until we were within town limits that he asked anything.

His hands adjusted on the steering wheel as he cleared his throat. "How are you really? More than physically."

I appreciated that Cope simply asked straight-out. No beating around the bush. And it was a fair question. "I'm okay. Not great. But not awful. I'll get there."

I'd had a couple of nightmares last night, but Anson was there and finally just got into the hospital bed with me.

"You will," Cope said with certainty.

I worried the corner of my lip. "I feel bad for Felix."

Once Silas's true nature had been revealed, Felix had started talking. Apparently, Silas had befriended him along the way. From what Anson could put together, given what I'd shared and what the FBI had found out about Silas, he liked the emotional torture just as much or more as the physical. He loved listening to Felix talk about how I was the one that got away. How the fire had stolen everything from us both.

When Anson and I started getting closer, Silas began planting seeds in his conversations with Felix. Silas told him he'd seen Anson berating me and bruises on my arm. Silas wove his web of lies and convinced Felix that Anson was abusing me. He'd come to the house that night to get proof to take to Trace, and everything had gotten completely out of hand.

Felix having feelings for me all these years broke my heart. Because we were never meant to be. And the fact that Silas had manipulated it all to his advantage made me sick to my stomach. Anson had dropped any charges against Felix, and the district attorney had finally agreed not to prosecute the trespassing and assault.

Cope blew out a breath. "You know what happened to Felix isn't on you."

I did. But it didn't change the fact that I was still dealing with a heavy dose of guilt. Even more when Trace shared this morning that his team had found evidence linking Silas to Davis's murder. But that had only been the tip of the iceberg.

A search of Silas's apartment revealed that he had hacked into my phone and computer and had been monitoring them since high school. They'd found trophies from dozens of murders, beginning with Silas's mom and sister. Cadaver dogs were currently searching his family's property, hoping to find the bodies so they could finally be put to rest.

Cope reached over and squeezed my hand. "It's going to take time, but you will heal. I promise."

I knew he was right. And even more, I appreciated the reassurance. I squeezed his hand in return. "Lucky to have you."

He grinned at me as he turned onto my gravel drive. "Don't you forget it, Rho-Rho."

I snorted. "That nickname can die a thousand deaths."

"Never," he shot back.

As Cope pulled up to the guest cottage, Anson stepped out the front door, Biscuit on a leash at his side.

"That your new guy?" Cope asked.

"Don't even think about pulling your intimidation tactics," I warned.

"What? I can't ask a simple question?"

"I know how you work, Copeland Colson."

"Shit, full-naming me? You must like him," Cope grumbled.

"I love him," I said honestly.

Cope jerked in his seat, turning toward me. "You *love* him?"

I nodded.

"You've never gotten serious about anyone." A hint of concern laced Cope's words.

I shrugged. "He gets me. Sees the part of me I always thought I needed to hide and loves me anyway."

Something I couldn't quite discern passed over Cope's face. "I'm glad for you."

"Thanks."

My door opened, and Anson was there. His gaze roamed over my face. "You okay? The drive wasn't too much? How's your pain level?"

I pressed a palm to his chest. "I'm good. I swear."

Anson leaned in and kissed me, his tongue stroking in for the briefest of moments.

"Dude, that's my sister. I don't need to see that crap," Cope muttered.

Anson pulled back, humor dancing in his eyes. "Nice to meet you, Cope."

"I wish I could say the same, but your tongue was just down my sister's throat."

I smacked him with my good arm. "Shut up. Do you know how many girls I've had to see you make out with over the years? And let's not forget the time I walked in on you and Kate—"

Cope covered my mouth with his hand. "Don't go there. For the love of God, erase that moment from your memory."

I nipped his hand.

"Ow," he said, jerking back. "That hurt."

I rolled my eyes. "You get slammed into the boards by massive enforcers. I think you can take it."

"Come on, Reckless," Anson said. "Let's get you inside before you do real bodily harm."

He helped me out of the SUV, and I bent to give Biscuit love. He whined and danced around me but seemed to sense he needed to be gentle. I looked up at Anson. "I missed him."

He guided me toward the guesthouse. "You'll get all the cuddle time with him you need since you'll be resting for the next couple of weeks."

I didn't miss the warning tone in Anson's voice. "You're going to be my prison warden, aren't you?"

One corner of his mouth kicked up. "Already took leave with Shep."

I groaned. Anson wouldn't let me get away with anything.

My mind again flickered to Shep. Besides his worry about me, he had to be behind on his jobs with all the setbacks, losing Anson for a couple of weeks, and Owen permanently. Owen, who apparently hadn't learned his lesson and mouthed off so badly to his new boss that he'd been fired there, too.

"There's my baby girl," Lolli called from the porch, pulling me out of my worry spiral. "You need anything? Some of my special brew? My poppy tea will cure what ails you."

Trace slammed the door of his SUV. "You did not seriously say you are making opium tea in front of me."

Lolli just shrugged. "I'm not selling it. The seeds are legal, you know."

"Jesus." He pinched the bridge of his nose.

"Auntie Rho!" Keely called, darting around Lolli. "You're home! Are you okay? Does your arm hurt? Can I sign your cast? I'll draw a real pretty picture on it."

Trace hoisted her up into his arms. "Keels, baby. Let's give Rho a chance to get settled."

I grinned at her. "You can decorate my whole cast if you want."

Keely's eyes went wide. "Really? I got my markers here, too. I've been drawing with Supergran. But her flowers look funny."

Lolli beamed at me. "More dick flowers for you, my girl."

"Lolli," a chorus of voices shouted at once.

Nora sent her a scathing look as she wiped her hands on her apron and maneuvered toward me. "I've got soup on the stove and a few casseroles in the freezer. I stocked up some ginger ale in case the painkillers are rough on your stomach. I've got everything cleaned, including fresh sheets on your bed. I'll bring more food over tomorrow and—"

"Nora," I cut her off.

She halted just in front of me.

"Thanks for being the best second mom I could ever ask for," I whispered.

Nora's eyes filled as she wrapped me in the gentlest hug. "Best honor I could ever have, getting to be a part of raising you. Loving you."

"Love you so much," I choked out.

"More than all the stars in the sky." She finally released me and wiped at her eyes. "Let's get you settled."

And that's what she did. I let Nora mother me onto the couch she'd set up with blankets and pillows. My siblings created quiet chaos around me, eating and talking but keeping things light.

Anson settled on the couch next to me, Biscuit between us, already happily snoring. Anson scratched between his ears. "What would you think about keeping Biscuit?"

The question was about more than adopting a pet. It was asking if I was ready for real permanence in my life in a way I'd been too scared to reach for before. My fingers sifted through Biscuit's fur. "I actually texted Nancy from the hospital and asked if I could."

Anson's mouth curved. "You did?"

"I did."

His hand covered mine on Biscuit's back, and his gaze bored into mine as if trying to read every micro expression. "Do you still want to live here? Still want to fix up the house? Or do you want to start fresh?"

I thought about it for a long moment. There was so much pain here, but there was far more joy. That was life. The valleys only made you appreciate the mountaintops more. "He doesn't get to steal the magic of this place. I won't let him."

"That's my girl." Anson's fingers wove through mine. "How would you feel about my moving in here while we bring that magic back?"

My eyes burned. "You want to live with me?"

"Home is wherever you are," he whispered. "You're my sanctuary. Where I feel peace. Where I feel seen. Don't want anything more."

"Yes," I whispered. "I want you to move in." My eyes watered as my lips pulled into a smile. "You're going to have to deal with dick flowers and color, though."

Anson barked out a laugh, then leaned in, his lips hovering just above mine. "Small price to pay for a life with you."

Epilogue

Rhodes
SIX MONTHS LATER

I TURNED ONTO THE DRIVE LEADING TOWARD THE VICTORIAN, but my SUV didn't bump and bounce now. The road had been transformed, and Anson hadn't been willing to settle for simply regrading the gravel; he'd had the whole thing paved. Once I had decided to stay and keep rebuilding, he became dedicated to making everything...perfect.

Biscuit's head popped over the divider, resting on my shoulder as he took in the sights in front of us, just like I was. I'd expected to see an endless array of trucks. Shep had brought in every single one of his guys for the past two weeks in hopes of *finally* finishing the restoration.

They'd run into more issues than I could count but hadn't given up. And the past three weeks, no one would let me inside to see the final progress, wanting it to be a surprise. But now, there wasn't a single vehicle in the area other than Anson's.

Instead of heading for the guest cottage Anson and I had

made our home for the past six months, I guided my SUV toward the main house. I pulled to a stop in front of the flower beds that flanked the front door. While they lay mostly dormant as winter was about to set in, I knew what lay beneath the soil—the promise of a riot of color come spring.

Just knowing that had warmth spreading through me as I climbed out of the SUV. I moved around to the back to let Biscuit out. He no longer required a leash. Anson had worked some fancy training mojo I couldn't even begin to wrap my head around.

I glanced around, itching to peek in the windows, but then my gaze caught on a piece of paper taped to the front door.

Come in, Reckless. I know you're already snooping.

A laugh bubbled out of me. Damn that profiler for always knowing me so well.

My heart picked up speed as my hand rested on the door-knob. This was it. I was going to see my house for the first time in almost fifteen years. My *home*.

No, *our* home. Anson's and mine. Because he had been the one to help me bring it back. But more than that, he had helped me find the strength to see it through. He was there as I healed phys-ically and as I put the pieces back together emotionally. Just like I was there for him.

It could never be anything other than *ours*. Our safe place. Our sanctuary. Our home.

Biscuit leaned into my side as if urging me on.

"Okay, buddy."

I twisted the brass knob, and the door opened easily. As it did, I sucked in a breath. Everything about the space was stunning. Gleaming wood, a gorgeous chandelier, and...my gaze locked on the wallpaper.

My eyes burned as I took it in. The fairies with shimmery wings. The same pattern my mom had picked out so many years ago. "How?" I croaked. When we'd tried to find it, the manufac-turer had told us it was out of stock.

Anson's deep voice cut through the quiet space. "I got a list of stores that carried the brand from the manufacturer and started calling. A place in Ohio had it. Ordered everything they had left."

My gaze moved to him. He wasn't in dirty work clothes. He'd showered and wore a flannel shirt with...strands of pink in the patchwork of threads. "How many stores did you call?" I whispered.

"Three hundred and thirteen."

Of course, Anson knew the exact number. Of course, he hadn't stopped with that many nos.

"I love you," I breathed.

One corner of his mouth kicked up. "I know."

"Jerk," I muttered with a laugh.

"You want to see some more?" Anson asked, his grin widening.

"I don't know if I can handle more. I'm only in the entryway, and I'm already a puddle."

Anson shook his head. "My girl can handle it. Strongest person I know."

I moved then, crossing to him and wrapping my arms around him. "I'm getting dirt all over you, but I can't *not* hug you."

He brushed some hair out of my face. "Never mind your dirt." His lips brushed over mine. "Missed you."

Anson said those words every day when I got home from Bloom. Duncan had held my job for me, Thea picking up some of the slack by taking on extra hours. But when I was ready to come back, they welcomed me with open arms.

Just like Anson welcomed me home with those words. *Missed you.* And I felt them. In that spot somewhere in my chest that was only his. Because we didn't take a single day for granted. We lived each one to its fullest.

I breathed him in, relishing the feel of his strong arms around me, the way his hold made wherever we were home. "Thank you."

"You haven't seen everything yet. I could've botched something," Anson said, his lips ghosting over my temple.

"You didn't." I was more sure of that than anything.

"Why don't you at least peek in the library?"

My insides twisted as pressure built behind my eyes. Memories of all the time my dad and I had spent reading in there. Him with his thrillers or the books we were reading together, and me with whatever adventure he'd set for us.

"Okay," I breathed.

Anson released me then, moving to the sliding doors that opened to the library and office. They were dark wood punctuated with thick glass that allowed light through but distorted the image of what lay behind it. The design was absolutely stunning.

His fingers caught on the brass handles, and he slid the doors open effortlessly. As he stepped inside and out of my way, I gasped again. Biscuit was instantly at my side, checking to see if I was all right. My hand dropped to his head, but I couldn't say a word.

It was my dad's library but more. Anson had added one of those antique library ladders and chosen a deep teal for the walls that was more *me* than the reddish color that had been in here before. He'd also created something different on the far wall.

Instead of a single painting, he'd made a gallery wall. It was full of art pieces he'd managed to salvage from the fire wreckage and an endless sea of photos. He'd obviously gotten Nora's help on that. There were pictures of my mom, dad, Emilia, and me. Ones of Fallon and me. Of all our siblings. Of Nora and Lolli. Some of me and Anson. And, of course, Biscuit.

Tears brimmed in my eyes as I turned to the wall of books next. Anson had clearly paid attention to every detail I'd told him because there was a section of thrillers, including all my dad's favorites. Then a section with all the stories Dad and I had read together. And then, lastly, a series of shelves with new books Anson and I had been reading.

Finally, my gaze came to Anson. He stood there looking... nervous. For maybe the first time. "So?"

I didn't wait. I ran at him. Anson caught me with a muttered curse as I flung myself into him, legs going around his waist. "I love you," I murmured into his neck.

Anson chuckled, the sound sweeping through me in warm vibration. "I'm taking that as you like it."

I pulled back so I could see his beautiful face. "I love it. I've never seen anything more perfect."

Anson's expression went soft. "Wanted it to be you and him."

"And us," I added.

"And us," he echoed.

As Anson stared into my eyes, he walked toward the bookshelves, my legs still locked around his waist. Without looking, he pulled a book from the shelf and handed it to me.

A Wrinkle in Time.

It was the same worn copy I'd read with my dad.

"Flip to the end," Anson said softly.

My throat constricted, winding tight. But I was braver now. And I trusted this man with everything I had.

My hands trembled as I flipped through the yellowed pages until I reached that final chapter. I stilled as I got to the last page. A beautiful bookmark lay there, one with flowers pressed into the thick paper. And on it read, *The End is only a chance for another beginning.*

Tears spilled over as Anson pulled the bookmark free. At the end of it was what I first thought was a charm. But it wasn't. It was more.

I stopped breathing as I took in the ring. A bronzy gold with the most stunning pink stone I'd seen surrounded by tiny diamonds that made it look as if the ring itself were the most beautiful blossom.

"Anson." It was the only thing I could get out.

He gently unfastened the ring from the bookmark and took my hand. "You gave me air when I thought I'd never breathe again. You gave me color when my world had gone black. You see every part of me. I don't want to spend another moment without you. Marry me."

My heart thudded against my ribs. "Yes. Wherever you are is where I want to be."

Anson slid the ring onto my finger. "Had to be a pink diamond for my colorful, reckless girl. A flower for the queen of life." His lips hovered over mine. "I love you."

"I love you, too. Love this beginning." Because that was what Anson gave me over and over. The chance to begin again. And I knew that would never end.

Acknowledgments

Embarking on new series, especially after loving the one before it so deeply is *always* a challenge. Will I love this one just as much? Does it feel *too* different or just the right amount? Do you *feel* these characters as deeply? Ah, the existential crises of a writer. Thankfully I had lots of people who helped me on the journey of this story.

Sam and Rebecca, who read an early draft when I was freaking out and needed perspective. Thank you both for always being sounding boards and pep talk givers. I truly do not know what I'd do without you. Your friendship is the ultimate gift. Elsie, who sprinted with me day in and day out to make sure the words got done and always makes me laugh, even when the world goes wonky. No, especially then. Thank you for always cheering me on and having my back. Immunity necklaces forever! Melanie, who got a very panicked voice memo in my series plotting phase and gently talked me off that cliff, helping me find what this story and series needed to be. Paige B, who helped me discover some details in this book that just made things *click*. Jess, who listened to the kernel of this story idea and helped it take root. Laura and Willow, who keep me laughing amidst the chaos of this business with cute pet pics and hilarious stories, and who made sure the edits on this baby actually got finished with those final sprint sessions. It's the *Rocky* theme song that always does it...

To all my incredible friends who have cheered and supported through all the ups and downs of the past few months, you know who you are. Romance books have given me a lot of things but at the top of that list are incredible friends that I am so lucky to have in my life. Thank you for walking this path with me.

And to the most amazing hype squad ever, my STS soul sisters: Hollis, Jael, and Paige, thank you for the gift of true friendship and sisterhood. I always feel the most supported and celebrated thanks to you.

To my fearless beta readers: Crystal, Jess, Kelly, Kristie, and

Trisha, thank you for reading this book in its roughest form and helping me to make it the best it could possibly be!

The crew that helps bring my words to life and gets them out into the world is pretty darn epic. Thank you to Devyn, Margo, Chelle, Jaime, Julie, Hang, Stacey, Katie, and my team at Lyric, Kimberly, Joy, and my team at Brower Literary. Your hard work is so appreciated!

To all the reviewers and content creators who have taken a chance on my words...THANK YOU! Your championing of my stories means more than I can say. And to my launch team, thank you for your kindness, support, and sharing my books with the world. An extra special thank you to Crystal who sails that ship so I can focus on the words.

Ladies of Catherine Cowles Reader Group, you're my favorite place to hang out on the internet! Thank you for your support, encouragement, and willingness to always dish about your latest book boyfriends. You're the freaking best!

Lastly, thank YOU! Yes, YOU. I'm so grateful you're reading this book and making my author dreams come true. I love you for that. A whole lot!

For a full list of up-to-date Catherine Cowles titles,
please visit www.catherinecowles.com.

About

CATHERINE COWLES

Writer of words. Drinker of Diet Cokes. Lover of all things cute and furry. *USA Today* bestselling author, Catherine Cowles, has had her nose in a book since the time she could read and finally decided to write down some of her own stories. When she's not writing, she can be found exploring her home state of Oregon, listening to true crime podcasts, or searching for her next book boyfriend.

Stay Connected

You can find Catherine in all the usual bookish places…

Website
catherinecowles.com

Facebook
facebook.com/catherinecowlesauthor

Catherine Cowles Facebook Reader Group
www.facebook.com/groups/CatherineCowlesReaderGroup

Instagram
instagram.com/catherinecowlesauthor

Goodreads
goodreads.com/catherinecowlesauthor

BookBub
bookbub.com/profile/catherine-cowles

Amazon
www.amazon.com/author/catherinecowles

Twitter
twitter.com/catherinecowles

Pinterest
pinterest.com/catherinecowlesauthor

Made in the USA
Las Vegas, NV
23 May 2024

90266863R00215